AGE OF AZURIA BOOK FOUR

FOREST DEEP

BETH BALL

Forest Deep is a work of fiction. Names, characters, places, and incidents either are a product of the author's imagination or are used fictitiously. Any resemblance to actual persons, living or dead, events, or locales is entirely coincidental.

Copyright © 2025 *Forest Deep* by Beth Ball

All rights reserved.

No part of this work may be reproduced in any form or by any electronic or mechanical means, including information storage and retrieval systems, without written permission from the author, except for the use of brief quotations in a book review.

Published by Grove Guardian Press

Edited by The Blue Garret

Cover design by Mibl Art

Ebook ISBN 978-1-952609-31-2

Paperback ISBN 978-1-952609-32-9

Hardback ISBN 978-1-952609-33-6

groveguardianpress.com

To Carolina
my Vera, forever

Hammerfell
Old Bastion Highlands
The Elven Realms
Andel-ce Hevra
Tor'stre Vahn
Nortelon
Isla de Hossa
The Howling Wastes
The

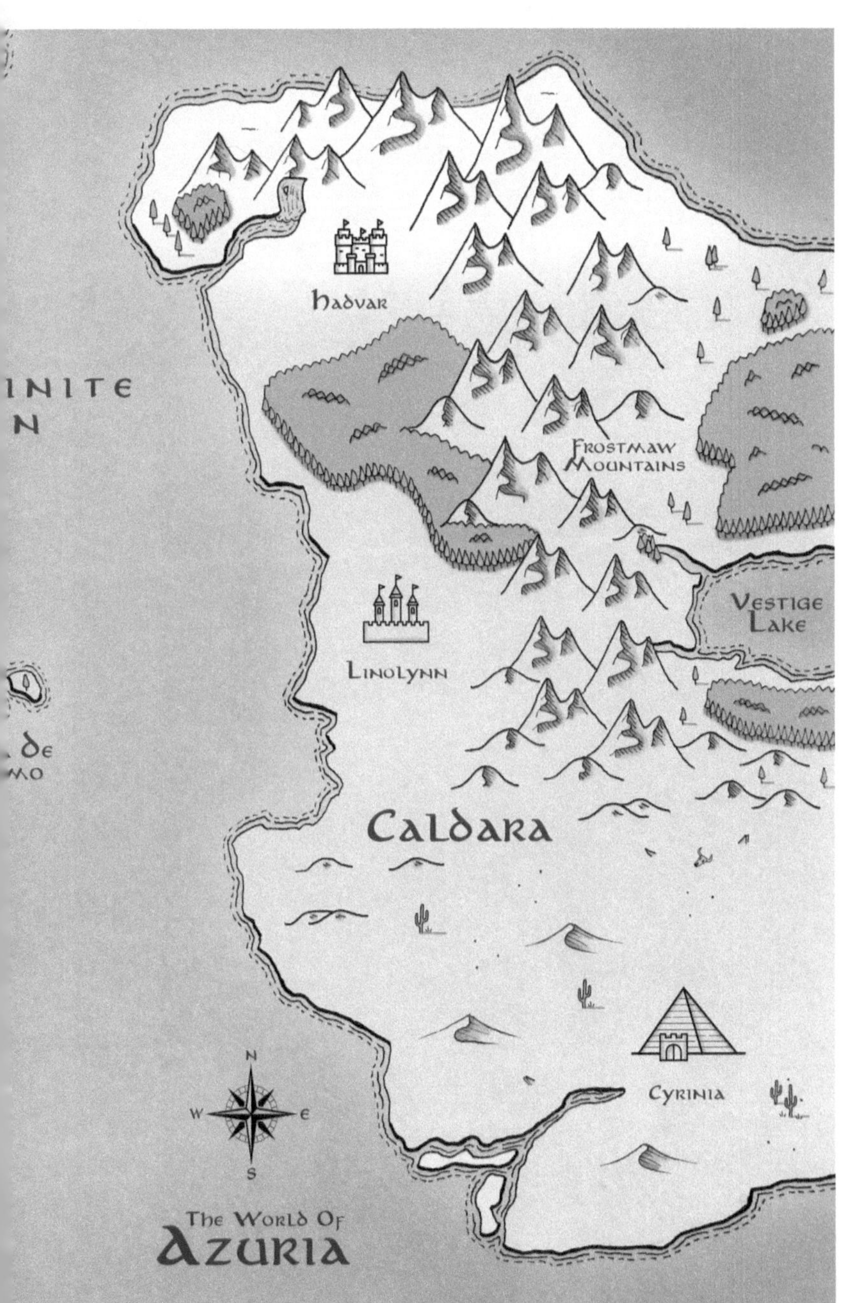

hadvar
Frostmaw Mountains
Linolynn
Vestige Lake
Caldara
Cyrinia
N
W E
S
The World Of
AZURIA

CHAPTER 1

PERSEPHONIE

Veins of thick blue vines twirled around one another and spun off into darkness for as far as mortal eyes could see as Boss Gilsen's muster traveled with Persephonie, Rennear, Jezebel, and Juliet upon the threads of fate. The threads were a forest of vines all around them, surrounded by nothing but swirling black space and clusters of stars. The vines gave off various shades of brilliant blue light, casting their glow upon the wagons and the travelers within them. The widest vines allowed three wagons to travel side-by-side, and the muster sent scouts ahead to avoid passageways too narrow for wagons to pass or too steep for the horses to climb.

Tradition held that only saudad and those blessed by Cassandra could make such journeys upon the threads, but Persephonie wasn't going to leave Rennear and Jezebel behind and under Dasia's power, especially not after the leader of the Awakened had sought to kill Rennear and only been prevented by the spirit of the shepherd, Rowan, who was the true denizen of the fortress hidden deeply within the heights of the Cienne Mountains.

As their journey began, Persephonie tried to ignore her sense of foreboding, lest a member of Gilsen's muster sense it and uncover her companions. That she was traveling to an unknown location with a muster of Malura worshippers didn't help her unease.

Cassandra sent me on this quest, she repeated to herself. Go to New Orison. Find the wheel, and stop whatever threatened it. Hopefully that part of her quest could wait until after she uncovered what exactly the wheel was. From what Rowan had told her, it was something like a portal that also influenced the threads the saudad traveled across.

Through the first hours of the journey, Persephonie hovered on the bench beside their hiding place in the wagon's floorboards. Most wagons were built with similar compartments—saudad were not always welcome wherever they traveled and sometimes had to make a strategic, hasty exit from inhospitable settlements. The compartments were meant to temporarily shield members of a muster who would be held by local officials and not designed to hold a fae warrior and an Andel-ce Hevran guard for hours or even days.

Normally Persephonie spent the first part of her journey upon the threads at the front of the wagon, telling stories or singing with her datha. But no one here knew her, so they wouldn't recognize a deviation from her normal behavior.

"How many days do you think we'll be traveling?" Persephonie asked the driver through the open window that looked out over the front of the wagon. Rennear and Jezebel didn't speak enough Saudad to understand her question. She would have to devise a way of communicating the answer to them through the clapboards.

"Three days at least, miss. Maybe more."

A stifled groan rose up from the back of the wagon, which Persephonie tried to disguise as her own, rubbing at her stomach. It had been Rennear, by the sound of it, a low, uncomfortable whimper-growl. He was still recovering after the ambush, when Dasia's scouts had killed his pack and almost killed Rennear. Without first Jezebel's intervention and then Rowan's, she would have lost him.

Juliet helpfully began yipping in the back of the wagon, sitting directly over the seam that would allow her friends out again, blocking out any additional groans that might echo out from below.

"Forget to feed yourself and the creature this morning, miss?"

"Erhm, yes," Persephonie answered quickly, glancing back at Juliet. Was the fox trying to tell her something was wrong? "Just nervous about going to a new place is all."

The driver shook his head. "The threads hold us—and only us—wherever we need to go."

The sensation of cold needles pricked down Persephonie's spine. She wetted her lips, searching for an appropriate reply that would disguise how near to the mark the driver had come to her true source of distress. There was a similar blessing, one that thanked Cassandra for watching over their travels across the threads, but what would a worshipper of Malura say in reply? "Especially when we're going home," she added, bunching her skirt in her hands and hoping her insincerity would go unnoticed.

He grunted his approval. "Gilsen said you were a strange one but that it was crucial you came along. Said you'd be an asset."

Beyond the driver, unfamiliar star patterns lit the inky sky, mingling with the pale, glowing blue of the thick thread they traveled across. The swirling blues and purples lent the vast network of the Weave the appearance of the Shadowlands forests, lit from below by bioluminescent ferns in the undergrowth.

"Where is New Orison?" Persephonie asked before she could stop herself.

"The Negative Planes."

Persephonie sucked in a breath. No wonder the stars were unfamiliar. "Are you certain?" It wasn't that travel to the Negative Planes was forbidden, but in all the stories, crossing into Pandora's realm required sacrifice.

The most dangerous place her datha had ever led the muster was the Shadowlands, and even then, they limited their travels to remain in proximity to their allies and portals that would return them to the threads of the Weave should they need to retreat. Varra Yvayne had warned them away from traveling too near to her mother's domain when Persephonie had asked about visiting her birthplace. "Your people's wealth of memory would be too great a temptation for her to resist," the fae had said simply. Datha had taken extra care after that.

What would he say about her traveling to the Negative Planes? Pandora's realm was the birthplace of the negata, who resettled across the three Planes of Life, but the Negative Planes were also said to hold secret strongholds belonging to Alessandra, domains even more frightening than the Howling Wastes. How could the followers of Malura believe that the saudad's new homeland was somewhere so unknown?

"We were alarmed too, when Gilsen first told us," the driver admitted. "He said it's a place held apart from the rest. A place we can finally be safe. Separate."

"Thank you," Persephonie murmured, slipping back

onto her bench seat. There were a few rumored portals that bridged between the Negative Planes and the Shadowlands, though locating them was exceedingly difficult and required skilled interplanar navigators who were even fewer in number than the saudad.

Persephonie closed her eyes and leaned her head back against the wall of the wagon, allowing the familiar sway of travel to lull her into a state of ease.

Just as she was beginning to relax, a sharp rap sounded against the rear wagon door.

Juliet scrabbled over the floorboards and crouched by the door, growling, her fur poofed out along her back and tail.

"Shh," Persephonie hissed. Juliet was just as likely to draw extra attention to Rennear and Jezebel as she was to protect them with her immediate paranoia.

A second, loud rap sounded through the wagon. "Gilsen?" a shrill voice rang out.

The hairs along the back of Persephonie's neck stood on end and flutters of purple sparks burst from her fingertips. Whoever this was, Juliet was right to be on edge. "He's not here," Persephonie called back, keeping her voice as innocent as possible.

Her stomach sank as the outer wooden latch slid free and the door creaked open.

Juliet yapped at the intruder who jolted back at finding a fox on the narrow floor of a wagon.

"What—Restrain your beast immediately," the woman ordered, glaring over at Persephonie. She wore a thick gray hood that hid her face. The pale blue light of the threads lit upon her silver-streaked black hair. Two dark, oblong shapes decorated the backs of her hands and a large, thirteen-pronged amulet hung from her neck.

The antlers were almost perfect imitations of those grown by antlered hares.

"She doesn't like strangers, and this is her first time upon the threads," Persephonie shot back. Her stomach rolled with the wagon as the wheels dipped, swaying both the woman and her necklace to the side.

A small, white skull hung beneath the tangle of antlers—precisely the size of an antlered hare.

"Is there something I can help you with?" Persephonie prodded as the glaring woman failed to state any further purpose. Her shadow seemed to grow within the wagon the longer she perched upon the back step.

"Just looking for some supplies Gilsen stashed for me."

Persephonie's heart hammered in her ears, louder than the wheels and clomp of hooves. "Which supplies?" Her voice wavered, and the woman leaned closer, sensing her weakness. "I can help you find them."

"No assistance needed," the woman cooed in a sing-song voice. Her tattooed hand—depicting a closed eye on the back, one of the more obscure symbols of Malura—shot out, reaching for the floorboards that hid Jezebel and Rennear.

Before Persephonie could react, Juliet sprang into action. She snarled and leapt forward, latching onto the woman's hand and scratching at her cloak.

The fox was a scarlet blur of fur, teeth, and claws. The woman screamed and fell back off the back of the wagon.

"Juliet!" Persephonie yelled, jumping out after the fox.

The cloaked woman and Juliet fell upon the center of the thread. Persephonie breathed out a prayer of thanks to Cassandra that the fox hadn't fallen.

Juliet's snarling grew louder as she refused to release the woman's hand. The moment the woman hit the ground, she emitted a piercing shriek and continued to screech from the ground.

The wagons around them slid to a halt.

"Juliet!" Persephonie called again. She darted forward and tried to grasp onto the fox's whirling form.

A burly man stomped forward, his glare upon Juliet. He brought his foot back.

"Stop!" Persephonie called. She held up her hands toward the man and let free a swarm of blue butterflies that splashed across his face, temporarily blinding him. He stumbled backward into several more men who caught him and righted his balance. The crowd pressed close.

Persephonie launched herself forward again and caught Juliet around her middle. The woman gasped in pain as she yanked Juliet away. Her hand was a shriveled mess of blood and bone.

"Strangers!" the woman screamed. "She brings strangers into our midst! She will doom us all!"

Persephonie froze.

The figure on the ground stared up at her, a twisted grin upon her face. "You thought your goddess was the only one who grants sight, little fool?" the woman sneered, her voice low so that only Persephonie and those nearest by could hear.

Juliet bounded out of Persephonie's arms and back toward the wagon. As she leapt onto the rear step, the floorboards burst up and Jezebel sprang out, wings unfurled and sword in hand.

"Ah ha!" the woman crowed. "The strangers reveal themselves! The fool of Cassandra need not even lie! Malura unveils all falsehood!"

Persephonie turned back to the fae, her eyes wide.

They couldn't be out here. Not now. Not when they were so far from New Orison.

Not when the mood of an entire muster was turning against them.

A few of those gathered pulled the woman to her feet. "Dispatch them!" she cried with a wave of her unbloodied hand.

"No!" More sparks sizzled from Persephonie's fingertips. Rennear pushed himself out of the back of the carriage, his face impossibly pale.

She couldn't risk a large spell upon the threads, the black glimmer of the void all around them. A slip upon the threads could leave one falling for years through the void. And there was no telling where—*or when*—the fallen one would land.

In a blur, Jezebel flew in front of Persephonie, interposing themself between her and the glowering mob. Rennear limped to Persephonie's side, his jaw set.

Persephonie's mind raced. The incensed mob might throw her and her companions over the side.

A trio of men drew crossbows and took aim.

Or they might dispatch us right here.

"Enough!" Gilsen shouted, raising his hands overhead as he shoved his way through the crowd. He was out of breath by the time he arrived. "Malura herself brought this one and her companions to us, a priestess chosen by flame was the signal we awaited before traveling to New Orison. Or do you not remember?" Gilsen stared into the gathered faces of his muster, his dark eyes glimmering with threat.

In front of Persephonie, Jezebel's chest rose and fell rapidly, their wings fully unfurled. Juliet crouched at Persephonie's feet, her fur on end and nose wrinkled in a snarl. Beside her, Rennear hunched in a half-readied stance, his hand slipping into the pouch at his side, searching for the sachet of silver needles so he could prick his finger and spark his werewolf transformation.

Her heart swelled remembering the moment he'd entrusted his needles to her. The werewolves sworn to serve Andel-ce Hevra were unique in that silver catalyzed their transformation rather than the waxing of the moon.

He'd taken the pouch back upon the mountainside when the Awakened attacked his pack. They'd agreed he would hold the needles until they were safe again.

"We remember, Gilsen." The woman who'd invaded the back of the wagon strode forward, her upper lip curled in disgust. The wound on her hand had disappeared.

She faced Persephonie rather than her muster boss. "And we will relent for now." At her word, the archers lowered their bows. Those with swords were slower to react but they, too, complied when the woman glared at them. She bore all the trappings of a priestess of Malura, with closed eyes tattooed onto the backs of her hands and a dangling pendant bearing thirteen prongs.

Persephonie shivered at the memory of the cursed village they'd passed through with the Untamed, when she'd been saved by the harpies who had warned her of the dangers ahead.

"Enough, Carnine," Gilsen urged.

"Enough." The woman cast one final glare back over her shoulder at Persephonie, a clear warning that made her companions bristle on her behalf, a growl prickling low in Juliet's throat, before she slipped away, disappearing into the clustered throng.

"A matter for another time," Gilsen muttered to Persephonie. As the daughter of a boss, she was well aware of the dangers a challenger to leadership could be. Upon the threads, no less, a muster could not afford to be divided amongst its members.

Gilsen puffed out his chest, watching over the dispersal of his muster back to their wagons so they could resume their path ahead. Wearily, he gestured for Persephonie and her companions to join him in the back of the central wagon.

Tensions remained high once they were all shut away from easy view. Persephonie murmured a spell under her breath and caused flowered vines and mosses to grow up around the windows, muting the sound while helping her order her thoughts.

Jezebel's hands clenched and released the hilt of their sword. Rennear leaned back, his expression taut with pain, eyes shut with beads of sweat pooling over his brow. The time hidden beneath the wagon's floorboards had chipped away at his recovery, as had the shock of their discovery.

Gilsen sighed and shook his head. "I should have thought through the plan more thoroughly."

Had it been her datha, Persephonie would have sought to reassure him. As it was, she was angry with herself for not taking better precautions. Rennear and Jezebel had been placed under threat because she hadn't devised a better plan herself.

Juliet twisted herself between Persephonie's feet, mewling. Persephonie scooped the fox unwillingly into her arms, wincing as Juliet's nails pricked through her layered skirts. Petting the fox's thick fur, her thoughts slowed, ordered themselves. "I thought you said your muster was without a priestess." Persephonie barely restrained the accusation from her voice.

Jezebel straightened beside her, reacting to the coldness of her tone.

Gilsen slowly met her gaze. "There are no priestesses that are officially recognized by myself or my muster."

She ran her tongue over her teeth, choosing her next move carefully. Gilsen was the closest they had to an ally at the moment, and his leadership teetered on a knife's edge. "None yet anyway."

He inclined his head. "If I can get them to New Orison, reason may yet hold sway." He mumbled the words as a prayer, a glimpse into the inner dialogue that had led him to swear allegiance to Dasia while also offering Persephonie and her companions aid.

"I'm sure you're right," Persephonie assented, making her voice as bright as possible and only just falling short of believability. The next few days would prove trial enough as tempers wore thin with the dangers of traveling upon the threads. It had been Gilsen who had summoned her in the middle of the night, encouraging her to bid a hasty goodbye to her mother before they set out.

They wouldn't have been safe under Dasia's rule. They weren't safe with Carnine's growing influence either.

That afternoon, Persephonie explained to her friends what she'd learned from the driver while Juliet napped upon her lap. Gilsen had departed to confer with a few elders. Jezebel's protest was stronger than Rennear's once they understood the proposed destination. "All you are going on is impressions," they argued. "Coincidences. You have no way of knowing for certain whether or not a sign of one of these wheels is located in New Orison. For all we know, we'll be trapped somewhere in the Negative Planes with no way out."

Persephonie crossed her arms and scowled at the fae. "I thought you said you trusted me?"

"I did—I do. It's just—"

"What do you imagine following Cassandra to be like beyond trusting an internal impression and following the signs she leaves?"

Jezebel leaned closer to her, nodding toward the driver and the rest of the muster waiting beyond the walls of the wagon. "*They* do not follow Cassandra," Jezebel reminded her. And they were right. Boss Gilsen and his muster openly paid homage to Cassandra's shadow, Malura, goddess of misfortune. The fae, whose own fate had been twisted by both Cassandra and the guardian Apollo, had greater cause to fear such a recurrence than Rennear, who had fallen asleep on a cushion between the benches, his leg elevated beside her.

"Perhaps that is all the more reason she has led us onto this particular path," Persephonie whispered back. Though she'd added what plant covering she could, she was hesitant to utter too great a condemnation of the muster's worship of Malura, especially seeing the curse they had left upon the mountain village. She had never witnessed its like.

The next few days of their travel upon the threads passed without incident which, opposite Persephonie's hopes, only served to increase Jezebel's sense of foreboding.

Rennear had been intrigued by the threads at first but by the end of the third day, the novelty had begun to wear off for him. "I only wish I could understand how you navigate such winding trails." He waved his hand, indicating the glowing threads all around them. "I cannot make sense of the constellations here to tease out our direction. How are you even certain this trail leads to New Orison and not somewhere altogether more troublesome?"

"Do not worry yourself with such matters, soldier-wolf," Boss Gilsen said, his voice loud and jovial as he waddled around the corner of the wagon.

Rennear glanced at her apologetically before pushing himself up with a soft groan and settling on her other side to allow the muster boss access to their seat at the rear of the wagon. Though Rennear's condition was much improved after Rowan's healing charms, he still moved stiffly, and his energy had yet to return to what it had been before the Awakened's attack. Persephonie couldn't tell whether the injury itself was what drained him or if it was the length of his recovery that was beginning to wear.

"We trust our horses," Boss Gilsen continued, "and Malura will guide us back to our true home."

Persephonie bit the inside of her lower lip. The way Gilsen spoke of New Orison, he and his muster had heard stories sent by ravens but had never traveled there themselves. The name of New Orison—a renewal of the original home of the saudad, the city of Orison that disappeared into the sea in Eldura, long before the War of the Champions—was symbolically clear, but how it had come to be and how Gilsen had originally learned of it were questions to which she still did not have answers. "How did you know it was time to make your way to New Orison?"

Boss Gilsen chuckled. "As I told Carnine's zealots, your arrival was the final sign we awaited. One marked by the phoenix signaling the time for our own rebirth." Silence stretched between the three of them.

"And what are you hoping to find once we arrive there?" Persephonie asked when it became clear that Gilsen was not going to volunteer anything further.

"A warm welcome for one, and a reunion with friends long-parted-from." He sat back, staring out at the sea of blue vines stretching all around them. "What I truly hope for is a home from which we might never be parted."

Persephonie glanced at Rennear who slid his hand into her lap and intertwined his fingers with hers. He did not seem as worried at the idea of being forever parted from Andel-ce Hevra as she would have been had someone told her she would never see her datha or her brothers again. Rennear was leaving behind his father in the city, but after what his father had done to him and after Rennear had sided with the Untamed, it might never be safe for him to return. He was without his pack now as well—they lay buried in the mountain snows after the attack by the Cult of the Awakened.

For Persephonie, the travel itself was home. Why Gilsen would deny his muster their birthright, why so many of them seemed to desire stasis, she still could not understand.

"I know our fate tends toward New Orison and that there we will find important clues about the wheels," she confided in Rennear after Gilsen had left them to consult with his navigators. There were storms up ahead—gathering clouds filled with darkness with crashing bursts of lightning bolting from one side of the storm to the other. The sort of storm musters became lost in and were never heard from again. "But I cannot help feeling trapped already, and we have not even arrived."

Gilsen's return interrupted her swirling fears. His face was grim. "Have you often traveled upon the threads of fate or did your datha leave you behind because of, well—" Boss Gilsen nodded at Persephonie as though his implication was perfectly obvious.

She ground her teeth together, understanding him well enough. He meant because of her mother, her mixed heritage. "We have never had troubles upon the threads of fate as I am no less saudad than anyone else in my muster. Do *you* fear to travel across them?" Persephonie narrowed her gaze and stared directly at the thirteen-pronged antler pendant that rested upon his chest. "Being so far from Cassandra's gaze and embracing her shadow instead, you might have reason to fear."

Gilsen glowered back. His demeanor had changed after his consultation with the navigators. "Our destination lies square in the center of the storm," Gilsen added. "That would be troubling enough, but our calculations indicate that it's heading this way and quickly. We won't be able to dart around it in time without losing our path entirely."

Something dark swirled behind Gilsen's gaze, a hidden intention or course of action already decided upon.

Persephonie's free hand slid toward the dagger hilt tucked into the back of her skirt. It was inadvisable to fight upon the threads of fate—too quickly, those in a tussle could lose their balance and plummet into the blackness, falling through space and time until another thread found them, but the two might never overlap again.

"My Seers believe Malura may be angry with us, carrying outsiders as we are toward the refuge she has been so benevolent as to provide for us. A refuge safe *from* outsiders."

Persephonie gripped the blade's hilt. "And so what do they suggest?" Seers of Malura could not be trusted. Cassandra's shadow was judgmental, fond of sacrifices and tricks. The muster followed her in fear rather than love and belief.

"Judging by your reaction, you know well enough already." Gilsen's gaze darted to Persephonie's arm tucked behind her hip, but such a reaction was too close to an act of aggression toward her for the untransformed werewolf at her side.

Rennear snarled, launching himself off the back seat of the wagon and latching his hands around the neck of the rotund muster boss. Gilsen cried out, struggling with Rennear, and lost his footing, bringing the injured werewolf down with him.

Persephonie shouted Rennear's name and leapt down off the wagon seat after him. He had gained the upper hand on Gilsen and perched over the man's gut, landing strike after strike upon his face.

Gilsen screamed, part pain, part fear, and the guards who answered his command came pouring out of their wagons in his defense.

"Stop!" Persephonie shouted, but the words came too late.

Rennear snarled over Gilsen and reached into the pouch at his side—searching again for the silver needles that he'd gifted to her. The needles were one of his father's great innovations, a fulfillment of his promise to the werewolf clans of Tor'stre Vahn. He had granted them control over their transformations, removed the curse of the moon and of silver. Rather than being vulnerable to silver, it enabled him to transform.

With the prick of the needle, his teeth began to lengthen. He raised his hand overhead—it was already covered in fur, claws as long and sharp as arrowheads emerged from the tips.

Rough hands grabbed her from behind—too many of them for her to fight off at once. She screamed as one of the men tugged at her hair. Another pulled her off her feet and dragged her toward the vine's edge.

"Let him go or we toss 'er over," one of her captors

shouted at the snarling Rennear, fully transformed into a werewolf and surrounded by two dozen guards.

"Do it and die," a low alto voice rumbled from overhead. Jezebel hovered aloft, their skeletal wings coated with bladed feathers, beating against the still air of the threads and casting a harsh wind into the faces of those who held Persephonie. The guards tightened their grasp on her but tiptoed back from the edge, their attention torn between the werewolf who held their boss pinned and the fae hovering overhead, shining sword in hand.

Persephonie's lips parted, staring up at the fae. Jezebel had never revealed the feathered version of their wings to her—she had thought them merely remnants of bone that served as a shield behind the fae.

The thunder from the storm rumbled low in the distance. Persephonie's hair stood on end all along her arms—the fate-storm was rolling nearer to them. And without a unified plan, they'd be hard-pressed to weather it without loss.

They needed to focus on the matter at hand, surviving the storm, not searching for the cause of their misfortune. At a later point, she would add this to a running list of reasons not to follow Malura. What could they possibly have expected?

What would Datha have done in this situation? Persephonie whirled back through the stories Datha had told her as a child on their winding routes across the threads of fate. She shut her eyes, hoping to drown out the shouting all around her—their tempers were stoked by the storm whether they could sense it or not. *There.* Persephonie seized an amethyst gem of a memory and examined it, her father's voice filling her mind. 'This is where fate joins the weave of magic, Sephie,' Datha had explained on the first trip she could remember through the Weave, though he had likely said as much to her when she was a babe in arms as well. 'Between the realms, fate and magic become one, and that is what we walk, from whence our magic comes.'

Lightning flashed across her closed eyelids just before the rumble of distant thunder shook her bones. Cassandra was trying to show her something—teach her something she would need for the days ahead. She thought of the fates as Jezebel raised their voice above the shouts of the saudad, booming their threats out to the brilliant blue threads all around them. Three fates, three wheels—their working must be like that of the weave, magic and fate intertwined, for how could it be otherwise?

Her eyes darted open at Rennear's growl and Gilsen's screech.

"Spiders!" came a cry from the edge of the muster. "Into the wagons," another voice yelled.

CHAPTER 2

YVAYNE

Yvayne's fingertips twitched against her legs. In her front hallway, the faeries' voices had faded to a soft, babbling murmur and fell further into an uneasy silence, like the sound of a creek bed being strangled by debris before drying out.

Across from Yvayne, Vaxis flipped through the pages of an ancient tome, alternately shaking her head and emitting frustrated hums of disapproval. The fae's research quest absorbed her attention, muting her awareness of the faeries' distress.

We won't find the answers we're looking for in the books, Yvayne wanted to say. The time for the lorekeepers' study had passed. Their age of action had arrived.

Amethyst, Vaxis's firefox familiar, curled up on one of the toadstools at the fae's feet. Her brilliant purple eyes shone against the forest hues of her fur as she stared toward the treehome's entrance, her perked ears flickering side to side in wait. Vaxis and the fox had relocated to Yvayne's treehome tucked away in the northern Caldaran wilderness due to disturbances in the Brightlands. After they'd had a chance to regroup, they would return and see what aid they could lend.

A whimper caught in the fox's throat, catching Vaxis's attention. "Yvayne, what is happening?"

She raised a finger to her lips in answer.

As one, three pairs of ears flicked toward the entry of Yvayne's treehome.

A solid knock resounded against the arched wooden door.

"What is he—"

"Shh," Yvayne urged. She hadn't wanted to alarm Vaxis, but she had been expecting a visit from Apollo ever since Persephonie slipped away from Caisteal Tulach with the muster of Malura worshippers. He would be angry and suspicious, blaming Yvayne for his ward's disappearance from the domain of his influence, especially given Rowan's proximity to the saudad. It wouldn't matter to the guardian that Persephonie was but one of a trio of druids under Yvayne's protection.

Yvayne lowered herself onto a stump in the center of her home, perched on the edge, her back straight. She released a controlled exhale and waved her hand toward the door.

The guardian strode in with solid, stomping footsteps, his wings dragging through the grass and leaves that lined the entryway.

She felt rather than heard the faeries' gasps of concern as Apollo trod past their tiny dwellings. They would usher their pet fireflies to holes in the bark, shielding their charges from the guardian.

"It has been some time since you have invited me into your home, Varra."

Yvayne unclenched her jaw. "Nearly as long as the last time you found it necessary to use my honorific."

Apollo scoffed at her retort as he came fully into view. His wings filled the doorway opening onto the central chamber of her treehome, the barbed talons at the top scraping the heartwood of the upper frame, his shoulders nearly brushing the sides.

Was he deliberately distorting his size or had she forgotten the truth of the guardian's bulk in the ages since they had last worked side by side? There had been periods during the War of the Champions where she had seen the guardian glamour his appearance and swell, both intentionally and inadvertently. Which instance was this?

"Are we not friends?" He gestured to the skittering lines of roots that had snaked out from beneath her stump, the energy of the earth responding to her nerves.

Amethyst darted from the toadstool onto Vaxis's lap, curling tightly against her mistress. The fae wrapped her arms around the firefox but kept her chin raised, gaze narrowed at the encroaching guardian.

Apollo spared her companion a glance but quickly returned his focus to Yvayne. "Were you not expecting my arrival, given the circumstances? Cassandra has explicitly placed any prospective chosen under my wings."

Yvayne rose. The nails of her right hand pricked her palm, bidding the roots to remain where they were rather than flock to Apollo's feet. She had no desire to repair and rearrange the sweeping rows of scrolls that decorated the inside of the tree. "Persephonie ventures beyond your grasp of her own accord, guardian. If Cassandra leads her to New Orison, who am I to interfere?" She saw no need to confess to Apollo that she feared for Persephonie's safety traveling upon the threads of fate just as much as he did.

Apollo stomped closer. Against her will, the roots slithered toward him.

She stretched out her fingers, freezing them in place. The guardian was still her ally, if in name only. He would not have been able to find her home if it were not so. Her wards remained in place.

The guardian's jaw flexed as he watched her struggle. He rolled his shoulders back. Restraint didn't come easily to either of them, humility even less so. "You are her protector," the guardian answered. "And need I remind you of the promises you made to me?"

Vaxis sprang to her feet. "What promise was that?" Her chin jutted higher in the air. Yvayne had kept secret even from Vaxis the promise of mutual aid she and Apollo had exchanged at Rowan's graveside. The fae had a natural suspicion of the guardians' fickle nature, a doubt shared by all long-lived beings who had survived the War of the Champions. "How many of Cassandra's chosen will you find yourself entitled to?" Vaxis demanded.

His golden eyes flashed. "However many it takes to break my curse," he growled. Apollo had failed to protect Cassandra's first chosen, Circe, and the goddess of fate had cursed him, binding him to her service until adequate recompense had been made. Furious at the limitations to his magic, he fixated upon assisting Cassandra's prospective chosen like Persephonie, believing that if he helped one to rise fully in the goddess's graces, Cassandra would remove his curse and unfetter his power. Energy radiated off of the guardian, causing flickers of orange light to flare from the shimmering sconces embedded throughout Yvayne's tower.

"As I said, she has moved beyond you." Yvayne interrupted their quarreling—trust a Brightlands fae and a wounded guardian to anger one another further and cause untold damage to her carefully maintained records, ages' worth of work of the lorekeepers. "That does not mean she has stepped into peril."

"How convenient," Apollo sneered, twisting back to regard Yvayne. "Is that what your lover told you as her spirit emerged?"

She could not help the spring of the roots that time. They lashed out toward Apollo. *Rowan is helping Persephonie*, she nearly growled. She had to be. Rowan's spirit had gravitated to Persephonie the moment she emerged. If Rowan had sent her to New Orison, there was a reason. *There had to be.*

The guardian answered with a clap of thunder, throwing his hands out toward her and Vaxis. Earth, roots, and stumps flew back from Apollo's explosive radius. Bark-bound tomes and ancient scrolls rained down as heavy drops of hail, the lorekeepers' records of the past warning the three of them of the ramifications of discord among their own ranks. They all knew that inter-ally fighting could bring about the end of worlds.

"Leave Rowan out of this," Yvayne warned. Tendrils of ice crackled in her voice and frost coated the ends of her fingers.

Apollo coolly surveyed the swaying books along the tower walls. Many trembled upon their perches. Ravens cawed their distress from high inside the tower, flapping to reestablish their perches after the thunderous disturbance. He turned back to Vaxis. "I can feel your concern as sharply as my own."

Her friend's gaze darted from the guardian to Yvayne

and back. "She knows my fear is for her wellbeing, not fueled by my own pride," Vaxis answered.

Yvayne's eyes widened, shocked that her friend had met the guardian's challenge so boldly. Amethyst peeked out from behind her mistress's legs, emboldened by the fae to stare up at Apollo. Yvayne knew Vaxis feared the effect Rowan's return would have on her, especially in moments like this one—Rowan's place in her heart left a gaping hole in her internal armor.

"I had thought it possible that you might change given enough time." Apollo crossed his arms over his chest, tapping talons against swollen biceps. "Rowan remains the same as ever, retreated to her castle on work of her own volition." He ran his tongue over the front of his teeth. "She remains your weakness even now."

His bravado could not hide his fear for Persephonie's safety in New Orison, the unknown machinations of their shared enemy—Lucien, in service to Alessandra. "Call it whatever you like, guardian," Yvayne replied. "Your disdain will not bring Persephonie back within your grasp."

"Nor will your desperation return Rowan to your arms." He delivered his parting barb as a curse, drums of thunder thrumming deep within his chest, but he kept the magic contained this time. Apollo spun on his heel to stomp out of her home, possibly for the last time.

"Wait!" Vaxis cried. She held one hand against her chest, the other extended toward Apollo.

The guardian paused, turning to look at the fae over his shoulder.

"Wait," Vaxis repeated, calm coating her voice. "I understand your lack of trust in one another," she continued, "truly I do. But I felt Rowan's spirit this time. The phoenix reawakened." The words trembled in Vaxis's throat and she blinked back tears.

The memory of the revolutionary Rowan had been, the hope she had inspired, shone forth from the fae. Having known Rowan so intimately, sometimes Yvayne forgot her role as a symbol of their resistance movement, the rebellion she'd galvanized, even after all seemed lost.

Apollo's shoulders fell from their combative position. "Rowan has succeeded in the past where others could not." He kept his back to Yvayne but twisted to face Vaxis, giving her his full attention.

"I think Rowan's spirit went to find something in her archives," Vaxis whispered. "Persephonie's mission might be connected to the Soul Shepherds. And she does not venture to New Orison alone. Both the werewolf guard, Rennear, and your fae guardian, Jezebel, went with Persephonie," she added. "What is left to us but to trust?"

Apollo dropped his head and cast a glance to Yvayne. A smirk tugged at the corner of his lip. "To trust and worry as ever we did before?"

Yvayne almost smiled at that, and a flash of memory caught her around the shoulders as Apollo once had, his strength forcing—allowing—her to fulfill her destiny when she had not the strength herself.

A chirruping chorus of faeries filled the silence between them and they swirled in a sparkling halo around one of the toadstools on the edge of the tower furthest from the shadow of Apollo and his wings.

Three piping mugs of tea appeared in their wake, and they burbled their encouragement to Yvayne.

She sighed, taking the faeries' cue, crossed the tome-littered earth of the tower, and lifted the tray the faeries had prepared.

Vaxis took the mug Yvayne offered her with a smile and turned to Apollo.

The guardian fixed golden eyes on Yvayne as she stopped before him. He waited for her to meet his gaze, searching for some confirmation in her face, some mote of trust or confession of vulnerability. Finding it, he seized a cup between his talons. What fit comfortably between Vaxis's two hands seemed diminutive in his.

Yvayne set down the tray and grasped her own mug of peace tea between her hands as well. The steaming liquid thawed the ice from her fingertips. It dripped to the floor and sank into the earth.

"To trust and worry," she proposed.

Her companions echoed her toast and the three of them drank deeply. Curls of steam trickled up to the top of the tower, sealing the renewal of their combined fate once more.

CHAPTER 3

IELLIETH

Iellieth pressed her fingertips into the soft island sand, allowing her gaze to trail over each member of the group circled within the shade of the rowan tree that had appeared after the lightning strike that had killed the revenant, Lorieannan. Marcon stared up at the tree, a furrow caught between his brow. Should she apologize to him for destroying Lorieannan? Or was that even the appropriate response? The vengeful revenant was no longer the woman he had loved so long ago. She didn't want to lie to him, and she wasn't sorry the revenant that haunted their steps was gone.

Quindythias lounged back upon a patchwork collection of towels to protect himself from the sand. He alternated between examining his fingernails and watching a butterfly, only partially listening to the debate swelling around them.

Genevieve sat stiffly on Quindythias's other side, her back straight, complexion still pale from her transformation during Lorieannan's attack. Her conclave's dagger—magically reformed by the lightning—rested upon her lap.

Teodric folded and refolded the letter from Syleste, his admiral, claiming to know his father's location.

Iellieth took a deep breath—she had to approach this conversation carefully. She, Marcon, and Quindythias had to get to the Realms as quickly as possible or risk losing the sixth seal piece forever. If it fell into Lucien's hands, he could make a seal of his own, endangering this world and the sealed-off elemental planes. But she knew Teodric would want to sail immediately in search of his father. "In your admiral's note, she said she knows where your father is. She didn't say he's in danger."

The tanned captain ran his tongue over his teeth, avoiding her gaze. From the bronze of his skin to the bands of light in his hair, the scowl about his eyes, the sea and this admiral were chiseling away the boy she had known. The boy she had once loved. Her Teodric was still there, wasn't he? Buried somewhere beneath.

"Wherever Syleste is, there is danger. Pain. Suffering." He leaned back, crossing his arms over his chest, still avoiding her gaze. Lean strips of muscle rippled beneath his skin, more prevalent than they had been before.

But they *had* been there. She remembered hugging her knees into her chest in his family's sitting room, listening by the warmth of the fire while Teodric practiced for one of his performances, tested new songs. His parents had sat together, holding hands. His mother with a cup of tea, his father with a small glass of brandy.

What devastation her stepfather the duke had wrought by sending Teodric's family into exile, and for what selfish purpose? Enriching the already overflowing Amastacia coffers? Removing any rival for the king's trust and favor, a position that had never been insecure in the first place?

A crisp sea breeze whistled through the island's trees,

calling her back to the task at hand. The Iellieth of the past would have been more forthcoming with her friend. Perhaps she needed to try something akin to that openness now.

Iellieth leaned her elbows onto her knees, staring at Teodric, willing him to meet her gaze. "I know you don't want to talk to me about Syleste."

His jaw muscle tensed, but he did not deny it.

"And I'm sorry for what she's put you through . . . for what you and your parents have endured over these last five years. Maybe . . ." She glanced at Marcon and Quindythias. Marcon was watching her intently, as always. She and Teodric might never recover what they had, but there were new possibilities on the horizon for her. And for Teodric too, if he was willing to see them. "Maybe I haven't been forthcoming enough with you either. It's all still so new to me, but perhaps if I explain . . ." *You'll understand. You'll see why it's so important to take me to the Realms.*

Iellieth's stomach twisted. She hated asking Teodric to choose her and her mission over his father. But if they didn't find the final seal piece before Alessandra—the price would be too high. More families than she could possibly imagine would suffer fates like that of the Adhemars or worse.

Marcon nodded to her. Genevieve, too, leaned closer, encouraging in her quiet, curious way.

"I told you of my mis-transmigration and finding Marcon. How we traveled together to find Quindythias beneath Io Keep. The gnome, Red, who has been helping us, he sent us to Hadvar to find one of the final two missing pieces of the planar seal. We succeeded"—she glanced at Genevieve—"with Yvayne's help."

A frown flickered across the druid's brow, but

Genevieve said nothing. The help she had received from Yvayne—Iellieth knew the circumstances were painful. It was a pain the three of them shared, which was part of what she needed Teodric to see.

"But only barely. There was a creature—winged, magical . . ." Iellieth shivered, recalling the way Lucien had slithered into her mind. How nearly they had come to him taking the piece for himself, returning it to his mistress. "He knew me, or knows me, in a way." Parts of her story, even she didn't fully understand. How could she expect others to?

"It's who he's working for that makes our journey to the Realms so important. An ancient goddess, Alessandra—she's trying to acquire the seal pieces herself. Lucien is helping, working for her. Back during the wars Marcon and Quindythias knew, the elemental titans sealed away their planes to protect themselves and their worlds from her. The seal keeps her out. But her power has grown beyond what we can resist. If Azuria—the whole of our world—is to survive, we need the help of the elemental titans once more. Together, we can stand against her."

The ekhidna, a snake-like embodiment of Alessandra formed into flesh she had encountered in that forest carried only a fraction of Alessandra's might. There, where the five seal pieces waited, she'd met the other versions of herself. Her soul? Those who had stood up to Alessandra through the ages. "Stopping her is a quest others have pursued before us. Marcon and Quindythias fought to protect our world from her."

"A fight we failed," Marcon added. "That cannot happen if you wish those you love to survive."

"That's precisely what you don't get, isn't it?" Teodric sprang up from their circle at the base of the tree, his hands clenched. He paced away from them, then a few long strides back before he spun to face Iellieth. "My family is already in danger. *Already* unlikely to survive."

Iellieth's lip trembled, but she pressed on nonetheless. "And how many other families are you willing to see suffer a similar fate to protect your father? If you save him, and we're too late—"

"It will all have been for naught," Genevieve said. "Iellieth is right. We have to trust that your father will be able to hold on for a few more weeks until we can reach him."

"We?" Teodric tilted his head, studying the druid-were-wolf. "Are you saying that you would come with me and abandon your own quest to aid the daimon and find this Yvayne?"

Genevieve's lips opened and closed. She dropped her gaze from Teodric's accusatory scowl. Behind the druid, a blonde sailor muffled a cry and darted away.

Only the day before, while they practiced a spell together, Beryl and a few of the stone people looking on, Genevieve had told her of her own hopes for going to the Realms. A daimon from the Brightlands, Sariel, had asked for Genevieve's help in working with the elves to expand the daimon's territory into the Elven Realms.

"And the pair of you?" Teodric jabbed his chin toward Marcon and Quindythias. "You know enough of this seal piece and the dangers of the Realms' forests to protect Iellieth and allow her to succeed?"

Marcon bristled, rolling his shoulders back at Teodric's insinuation. He glanced at her and softened. "I have sworn myself to your protection, lady. Not only because we are bound or because you awakened me, nor because you are allowing me the chance to succeed where I failed before." His smoky azure eyes burned with the reason he would not say, what remained unspoken between them.

He turned to Teodric instead, whose jaw had clenched yet again as he watched Marcon. "In short, yes. By my life, I will protect her."

"And I'm from the Realms," Quindythias added brightly, sitting up to rejoin the conversation as though the group was sharing jovial after-dinner drinks and not engaged in a heated debate about the futures of themselves and their world. "Or what was once very near to what is now the Realms. Regardless of the geography, I'm certain that I'm an ancient hero or some such, celebrated, known, and beloved by all." The copper in his gaze shone as he stared out at the sea.

To Quindythias, did the waves sound like an adoring crowd, shouting his name? *Quindy-thias*.

Iellieth smiled to herself, imagining her friend's polite wave from a parapet before one of the great cities he and Marcon had described, large beyond imagining. "That can only help us."

Finally, Teodric looked at her.

"I need you to tell me true." She held his gaze. "This admiral, will she harm your father in her impatience?" Iellieth swallowed hard, not wanting to ask what came next, but she had to. "Or will she wait? To cause more pain to you?" She blinked back the tears that rose to her eyes. She could never shed enough to wash away what had happened to Teodric. The scars upon his back that she could never un-see. Yet the scars upon his heart, she knew, were far more painful still.

Teodric sighed. "I do not think so. Of course she did not specify *where* he was, only that she knew. But it is likely that he is in one of her prisons, which are . . ." His gaze grew distant as he rubbed his hand through the back of his hair, shaved close now, with the top knot above. "Heh. They are best not described. But I believe you are right, as usual." A small smile, just for her. A tiny mote of her Teodric, returned. "She will wait and use my father to break me. More than she has done already." He nodded to himself, resolved. "Very well, we will sail for the Realms. I will see the preparations begun."

The captain turned away and strode off across the sand, his shoulders set back in the appearance of ease.

More than she has done already. Iellieth's stomach twisted again. "Wait!" She sprang up from her log and ran after Teodric before she lost her nerve.

He stopped short but did not turn back.

Iellieth slid to a halt by his side, taking his hand in hers. New calluses roughened his palms, from ropes and the wheel and she knew not what else. But the lutist's calluses were there too, scratchy against the calluses at the base of her own fingers, new as well, from her combat practices with Marcon. "I know all of this is . . . rather impossible." She waved her other hand. For some things, there were not proper words. "But I have to believe—I *choose* to believe that we're not in this alone. That there are reasons why we've been, well, chosen ourselves. Even if it doesn't seem like it right now."

His dark brown eyes met hers. So familiar and yet so strange. "I have not the slightest doubt that you were specially chosen, Iellieth Amastacia." He cupped her chin, angling her face toward his. "I have sensed as much from the moment we met, all those years ago. For myself, I am less sure, but before you protest—"

She responded to his wry smile with one of her own

because protest was precisely what she had been preparing to do.

"Before you protest, Iellieth, allow me to say—in your presence and by your side, it is possible for me to believe as much about myself again." He glanced over her shoulder where she was certain Marcon was watching. "You do the same for your companions too, assure them of the truth we can all see that they have forgotten. You awaken the hero inside of them. And a better man inside me." He studied her face while his words sank in. It was somehow more intimate than the kiss that had passed between them, one she still could not say if it would be repeated, if she wanted it to be.

Teodric dropped his hand. "We'll speak soon. I must address my crew. And we'll need to convince Kriega to break with orders, which will be an undertaking all its own."

Iellieth watched after him as he strode across the sand. The warm, steady gaze behind her called her back. She lingered there between them, her past and her future, for a moment longer, soaking in the warmth of the mid-summer sun.

With a slight smile to herself, Iellieth turned back toward Marcon, Quindythias, and Genevieve. They had preparations of their own to make before traveling to the Realms. It remained possible that she and Teodric would both find what they were searching for, would both find their fathers again.

Before they set sail, she and Genevieve had a pair of last tasks to accomplish—bidding their farewell to the stone elves, Beryl in particular, and breaking Reaga's mark from Iellieth. Beryl had promised to help them, a task that would be easier now that the magical storm had repaired

Genevieve's conclave's sacred dagger. Together, they would carve away the invisible mark the great sea dragon had placed within Iellieth's swirling auric field so Reaga couldn't track them across the Infinite Ocean on their way to the Realms.

And once they arrived within the lands she'd been dreaming of for her whole life, they would find the final seal piece, the one bound to earth. A daimon of darkness, Nova, had come to her aid after she'd gained possession of the seal piece of darkness. Before then, an assassin had killed Master Yugo, one of Hadvar's preeminent mages, and tried to steal the seal piece for themselves. She could only expect that the battle for the seal piece of earth would be even harsher—she could only hope that this time, the search didn't end in blood.

CHAPTER 4

BRISERAS

Briseras shot awake from dreams of fire and a vampire attack in the night. She deliberately slowed her breathing and the racing beat of her heart, attuning herself instead to the stillness of Loire's copse within the vast tangle of the Witchwood. Vera snored softly, curled against the back of her knees.

Beyond her bed roll, the creek burbled, the waterfall sighing beyond it, and the susurrus of the leaves whispered overhead. She forced a slow exhale, gathering herself.

Briseras slipped free of the moss blanket the fae had given her and scratched her fingers through the soft, short fur at the top of Vera's head. The wolf would follow her shortly.

She tugged her leather coat over her shoulders, striding out of the trees' shelter and into the pre-dawn dark of the forest clearing. Her silver eyes, transformed by the vampire Malthael's bite years ago, cast the forest in her own internal moonlight. Tiny antlered hares scuttled through the underbrush, darting toward their burrows as a horned owl hooted in the branches overhead.

Vera found her just before dawn at the top of the rocky rise that led to the waterfall. With the first cloud-cloaked rays, Loire emerged from her lover Astrid's branches. She prepared a special tea over a fire and asked Briseras to share a cup with her while they watched the sunrise catch in the trees' upper branches.

Steam curled up from the mug in the fae's cupped hands; her champagne-colored skin was smooth, unlined despite her age. "Steymhorod was not always thus, you understand. Lord Draego has made it so. I know not what he has told you—" The fae turned to study Briseras, her gaze roving from the top of Briseras's head to the mud encrusted on her boots and back to meet her gaze. "He has not yet placed his mark on you, though I sense he desires to. Whichever side you choose, I hope you will allow me to make a case for the Sisters' return. Steymhorod needs the rule of the Archfae."

Was the whole of Steymhorod fighting within itself? How many sides of various conflicts was she supposed to keep up with? "You are speaking in riddles I don't understand," Briseras said. She feigned indifference, staring down at the nails of her right hand. The burns from Nassarq's servant vampires' attack had finally healed, though their flames haunted her dreams still. She and Tybalt had lingered in Loire's glade for long enough. It was time to avenge Everett's death and, she suspected, Lavinia's capture, not to mention the burning of St. Sebastian. It was time for her to hunt down Nassarq and stake him. There would be no blood portal escape this time.

"I speak first of your spirit-mark and the one who gave it to you. Ophelia."

"The druid?" Briseras asked, surprised by the turn in the conversation. How did Loire even know that name?

"Yes, she saved my life." Briseras left unsaid the second half of Ophelia's bargain—death would cling to Briseras, she had said. Having drawn so close, its shadow could not fully be removed, so Briseras would hover between life and death, charged with protecting the living from the monsters of the world. This bargain must be what Loire meant by a mark.

Loire closed her eyes and hummed to herself, stretching her fingertips out toward Briseras. "She did more than that, huntress. It was she who set your path here." The fae's smirk deepened. "Just as it was Ophelia who set a choice upon your path, one that will shape the fate of this realm and realms beyond your imagining."

"Umm . . . I am not here to save a realm. I am here to kill a vampire. Lord Draego has no quarrel with my plan, nor does Nassarq's mage-servant Olya." Briseras sipped the scalding tea, allowing its warmth to spread across her chest as she had hunting in the wilds.

Loire watched her thoughtfully. "Your spirit-friend Everett's assessment of you confirms what my lady, Diannan, has whispered—you are the one we have been waiting for. The one who might return the Sisters to their rightful place, the one who might restore the Fanes." Tybalt's reverence for Loire stemmed from her dedication to one of the four Archfae Sisters who had once ruled over Steymhorod. Loire had told her before that Lord Draego had desecrated the Sisters' holy places and divided their spirits from the land, bringing about the cursed state Steymhorod now knew.

She still had her doubts though—somewhat cursed herself to dwell on the border between life and death, she liked Steymhorod more than any other placed she'd ever been, curses and all. She was learning as much from Loire as she could, especially if what she learned would help her on her own quest. "Fane?" Briseras asked. "You used that word before, attributing this glade to someone else, Diannan."

"The Sister of the Forest, yes. The Archfae whom I am bound to serve though her spirit has been separated from its holy site. I tend the grove in her name, awaiting the day my lady might return."

Briseras nodded, thinking this over. Her mother had taught her to revere the Archfae before Rajas took her away from Haven to train with the hunters. Archfae were localized deities of a sort, from what she remembered. They were closely tied to the land. Her home had once housed Archfae too, before the priests and senators had driven the witches out, killing many and imprisoning the rest in Haven.

"It is not my place to doubt such signs of returning," Loire continued, "though it was Draego who removed the Sisters long ago." Loire shook her head. "You have earned the elf's trust as well, and Tybalt's trust will give you the loyalty of the Vale."

Tybalt trusted her? Briseras looked out in the direction he had gone. As Loire boiled water, he had ventured out of the glade to see if the leszi had tracked them here or if it had passed on to another part of its territory. But surely the fae was mistaken—the elf followed her as a matter of convenience, maybe as a way of thanks for her saving his life in the Ring of Light, but nothing more.

Loire smirked at Briseras. "You are fond of underestimating yourself, huntress." It was a declaration, not a question. The fae closed her eyes, one hand extended toward Briseras. Tiny mushrooms bloomed out of her fingertips. Their spores drifted from the fae to her face.

Briseras leaned away from them, but another puff of spores followed. A soft breeze picked up, and the spores drifted nearer. She sniffed and squinted shut her eyes, but whatever the fae was doing had apparently succeeded.

Loire closed her eyes and inhaled deeply, humming to herself. "You have all the hallmarks of the one we have awaited. You bear the mark of one who walked this land before—Malthael—Lord Draego's former ally and lost friend. And by the silver key you wear, you bear Draego's favor. With his blessing and with the Sisters still separate, still asleep, the creatures of this land will continue to respond to you. Down to the earth itself, Steymhorod has been waiting for you. This destiny is cast into your fate, woven into what must be. Do not try to resist this, Briseras Ravisthinia. Whether the Sisters arise or sleep will be up to you."

Briseras exhaled through her nose, trying to expel the spores Loire had floated there. "Alright, as helpfully cryptic as all of that is, tell me, who are these Sisters you and Tybalt are always speaking of?"

"The Archfae who once governed the lands of Steymhorod. Diannan ruled over the forests, and her sisters ruled over the mountains, rivers, and fields of Steymhorod. Through their rule, these lands thrived. But then the vampire lord grew angry. He took their power for himself and severed from the Sisters their holiest of places." The fae sniffed, wiping at a tear poised in the corner of her eye. "For thousands of years we have waited. I hold watch over my lady's holiest site—the seat of her power. I wait for one who might restore her, restore them all."

As their tea grew cold and the mists rolled out across the forest, Loire met her gaze again, smiling sadly at Briseras. "It is a great deal we ask of one not of our realm. But in its fallen state, Steymhorod cannot save itself. It needs someone with the power of the old ones, someone who remembers our ways. In Steymhorod's returning, you will also create something new."

Briseras set her cup to the side and rose, brushing the dirt off her hands and clicking her tongue to rouse Vera. "I understand your desire to see your land restored, I do." How often had her mother spoken of the past, when the witches of Tor'stre Vahn had been not only free to practice their ancestral magic but sought out, respected, almost revered for their gifts? "But I have a mission here already. Maybe I can see about these Sisters after I've dealt with Nassarq, but the vampire must be staked first, his spirit destroyed." She owed that much to Everett and Lavinia.

She smirked as she pictured the splinter of wood carving through the vampire's bony chest. Nassarq and his servants had bested her twice now. She was looking forward to evening the score.

The fae turned her gaze out to her glade, taking in the sweep of what must have been frustratingly familiar trees if her timeline of her supervision of this glade was accurate. "As you say, huntress, as you say."

ॐ

YVAYNE, NEARLY THIRTY YEARS AGO, IN THE MOUNTAINS OF TOR'STRE VAHN

"She deserves a choice, Yvayne."

"Does she?" The fae raised an eyebrow. "Did you have a choice? Did I?"

Ophelia's eyes burned as she stared back at Yvayne. "That's not the point—"

"Isn't it?" Yvayne raised her voice. It was all she could do not to screech in Ophelia's face. "How much of a choice do any of us have? With this bend in the Weave, the huntress will have everything she needs to be happy in Steymhorod, to be the perfect match for Lord Draego."

"But she won't have chosen him, not fully."

Yvayne shook her head. "We don't know that. The Weave has ways of repairing itself, of filling in where necessary."

Ophelia's expression changed from frustration to one of concern. "Is that what you think happened?" She reached out to touch Yvayne's arm.

The fae jerked out of her grasp. "I don't want to talk about Rowan. That's not what I meant anyway." She exhaled through her nose. "I don't know how long we'll have access to the wheel. Are you prepared to do what's necessary, to take the next step?"

The druid's eyes drifted away behind Yvayne as though she could see some possibility or chance the fae couldn't. She waited so long, Yvayne almost asked her again, but then Ophelia's eyes sparked and she smiled. "I am ready, Varra."

"Only the saudad call me that."

"I like it."

Ophelia's secret smile lingered throughout their ritual, the spell they cast that might save Steymhorod. It was the smallest of changes, one Alessandra and her minions would be sure to miss. Deep in the bowels of Haven, where an impossible romance had blossomed, with promises made and—thus far—kept, a break would have to occur. One that would leave mother and daughter alone against the ravages of the priests' cruelty, their desperation to control their world.

The girl's life would be difficult, her mother's as well—there was no other way to prepare her for what was yet to come. With this first change, the father's fate would fade into uncertainty, but the girl's path would intersect with one trained by the druids, a hunter who roamed the wilds of Tor'stre Vahn. He would take her away, train her, and help her make real the huntress she was born to be.

Near the apex of her training, she would encounter her first vampire of old. The rogue Malthael would sense something in Briseras, some portent of her potential—she was the only one who could reunite him with Lord Draego, return him home to Steymhorod. He would bite her, yes, but he would not turn her. Ophelia would save her life and set her upon her path. Briseras could redeem Xander Rasvan Draego—she and she alone bore the fate-markings of such a possibility, so if someone could, it would be her—and, in turn, he would redeem his fallen lands.

Yvayne wiped the sweat from her temple as they completed their spell. They could not be certain Alessandra would not find the huntress wherever the Weave placed her in space and time. But Briseras would grant them a chance at least to turn the tide in the larger war.

"Well done." Yvayne nodded to her companion. "Have you need of anything else from me? Matters in Caldara move apace—there is another I sense will be returning soon." She bit her lip, hoping Ophelia would know who she meant without asking outright. Yvayne sensed the soul of Lilia-Rowan pressing upon the Weave, seeking to be freed from Astralei. It was early still, the ripples were only just stirring. But whenever her soul returned, the entire fate of the world shifted as well. Ages ended. Empires fell. And new worlds were born.

"No," Ophelia sighed, dabbing at her upper lip. "I can seal the Weave and return to my post." She bowed her head as Yvayne departed for her hideout in northern Caldara.

What Yvayne did not know was that Ophelia waited to do as she had promised. Within the wrinkle they placed in the Weave, she crossed a second thread with that of the huntress. A nobleman whose fate was fraught—by the huntress's side, he might save even more than she could on her own. If she chose the vampire lord, well enough, but she deserved the freedom to select her future for herself. Dictating the fate of others was the purview of Alessandra, not lorekeepers.

Ophelia's grin returned as she closed the knotted thread. This story was far from over—the huntress's choices, she could feel already, would echo through the ages and touch countless realms. Yvayne would understand in time.

She sealed the portal to the wheel and returned the speaking stone to its hiding place. The druid made her way back to her glade, her craggy overlook and waterfall, waiting for the fates she had written to be made real.

CHAPTER 5

IELLIETH

True to her word, Beryl had guided Iellieth and Genevieve through the process of removing Reaga's mark, leaving them only to say their farewells before setting sail.

The stone elf hadn't mentioned lingering emotional effects from the ritual, so Iellieth could only assume it was her own inner turmoil splashing across her perception in the aftermath. The faces of those she'd lost in the course of her journey flashed in front of her. Mara. The druids of her conclave. The entire crew of the *Fairwind*—Galadin. The first mate. The captain.

There always seemed to be a reason, something her friends could use as an excuse for the pall that followed her. The mark's removal would protect those aboard the *Amber Queen* from Reaga, but how to protect them from herself and the danger that hung so close as to drown out her own shadow?

Iellieth hugged her arms around her knees, sitting in silence with Beryl while the stone elf children played a last round of their favorite game with Genevieve. The game consisted of slowly bending one's form like trees caught on a breeze. They called it *teray'ast*, the living tree.

"You mull as though the mark remains," Beryl observed, her pink gaze flashing toward Iellieth while the rest of her remained still. Marcon and Quindythias preferred to linger at the edge of the forest when she and Genevieve visited the stone elves. Quindythias claimed it was to grant her and Genevieve time to bond 'as a mini-conclave,' which she knew he meant as an encouragement, though Genevieve had looked stricken when he'd said it. Iellieth thought it more likely that the statue's forms reminded them of the state she'd found them in and the terrible process that had turned them into crystalline statues in the first place, separating their souls from their bodies, a state held at bay by their binding to her amulet and their proximity to her.

Such is the lot of the Soul Shepherds, Red had said.

She didn't begrudge their connection to her—far from it. But between Marcon's desire to shield her and Quindythias's longing for the adventure and excitement of the world he'd known before, Iellieth couldn't help but wonder how much she was holding them back. She'd learned so much in her training with Genevieve, filling in the holes left by her truncated lessons with Mara.

Ended too soon by Lucien. Because he was hunting Iellieth. Mara had died protecting her, giving her and Marcon time to escape.

It was only a matter of time before the lich found her and endangered her friends again. Left to their own devices, would Marcon and Quindythias have already found the final piece? Would there be a point when she wasn't slowing them down?

"Or as though you could create a mark of your own,"

Beryl added to her initial observation, landing near enough to the mark to surprise Iellieth out of her spiraling thoughts.

By Beryl's reaction, she didn't hide her shock very well—the elf laughed, pleased with herself, her mirth the trickle of pebbles down a boulder. "For centuries, it has been the purview of my people to watch. It saved us from the siren queen, allowed us to keep our home."

The stone-elf children gasped, enamored, as the sea breeze captured strands of Genevieve's hair, tugging it about like the fronds of a willow.

Ever so slightly, Beryl turned her face to the wind. Iellieth tried to imagine the experience of wind across stone. She tucked a loose strand of her own hair back into her braid. That would be the true difference wouldn't it? Not the feeling of the wind, but her ability to feel her body's response.

"The friends I arrived here with are powerful warriors," Iellieth explained. This sense of dread was a slippery tangle of seaweed in her gut. She didn't want to unravel it, nor did she want it to remain. "I fear more than just letting them down, though that would be bad enough."

The pink fronds of moss along Beryl's brow rippled. She waited for Iellieth to continue.

"What if there's a reason Reaga was able to find me? A reason my proximity to the seal piece awakened Alessandra's spell?" She knew Marcon and Quindythias well enough to anticipate what their responses to her concerns would be. Finally speaking them aloud, their weight shifted in her chest, threatening to crack the shelf she'd shoved her concerns back onto.

"Hmm," Beryl answered, the creaking sound coming as much from her chest as her body in her pivot back to face

Iellieth. "Your mentor, she has told you of the power of shadow, has she not?"

Iellieth frowned, nodding. It was a lesson she'd covered in different respects with both Mara and Yvayne.

"You cast yourself into your friends' shadow in your understanding of your role. I cannot advise whether you should or should not, but what I can tell you is this—from the shadows, we must ask ourselves whether we need to move into the light or, as part of your fears, whether we need to embrace the true potential of our inner darkness."

Genevieve loped back over to the pair of them before Iellieth could work out a suitable reply. Beryl's advice seemed precisely the sort of wisdom Yvayne or Mara would dispense. "They'll be expecting us," Genevieve said, peering through the trees back the way they'd come.

She was right about that. Between Kriega's scowling and Quindythias's dismay at the ever-present nature of sand, she wasn't sure who was the most ready to begin their voyage away from the island.

There was really only one suitable reply to Beryl's gift of wisdom. "Thank you," Iellieth sighed, wrapping her arms around the stone elf. A ripple of surprise met her, followed by a wave of sun-warmed heat. Recognizing the wisdom of Beryl's advice was one thing, working out how to follow it was another matter. The journey ahead was sure to give her plenty of opportunities to confront her inner shadows.

"What do you say we stretch our legs one last time?" Genevieve asked as they reached the edge of the stone elves' community. The druid's eyes were already brightening their jade hue, a sign that prefigured her transformation.

Iellieth grinned and placed her palm over the crescent

moon pendant affixed to her glove that allowed her to transform. Embracing her wolf form opened up her senses to the island around them and let her tap into Genevieve's sensory impressions. In some ways it was similar to the sense of connection she'd felt after her initiation ceremony into her conclave. More closely, it felt as though Genevieve had joined their pack of three. "Awoo!" Iellieth answered, raising her face toward the sky. Her hair rippled over her shoulders and fluttered down her back as her spine stretched and shifted.

She shook her fur coat, the scents of salt and stone splashing across her snout. One last run before they returned to the ship and set sail. One last romp before the Realms.

CHAPTER 6

PERSEPHONIE

With the sighting of the spiders, the hands that had been holding Persephonie fast released her. The saudad guards darted off to rejoin their families, helping those less readily abled into the wagons. The low murmur of prayers to Malura drifted out of the wagon nearest her as Persephonie shoved herself up to her feet. Jezebel's attention had turned, searching for the spiders the scouts had seen.

"They come with the storms," she called up to the fae. "Look beneath the threads." An answering growl met her shout for Rennear, and her werewolf bounded into view around the wagons. His beauty in such a form made her breath shorten in her chest—the russet of his fur shone almost gold in the blue light of the threads. She pressed her head against his chest, savoring the warmth of his fur and steady rise and fall of his breath, the solid beat of his heart against hers.

Rennear's chest rumbled, a reassuring growl and promise of protection, and he lowered his head to cup hers beneath the hollow of his jaw, nearly enveloping her entirely in shining red-brown fur. "We will have to help them," Persephonie murmured. "They'll not survive the spiders and the storm on their own."

Around them, the warriors had begun to reemerge from the wagons, taking up defensive positions around the muster. The key was to keep the spiders away from the wagons, for once a wagon fell, it would be lost, and the wagons nearby more vulnerable.

She'd heard, once, of a muster that lost a central wagon upon the threads. One of the spiders had landed in the center of their caravan, dividing them one half from the other. Only a few had survived. They disbanded and slunk off into the wilderness, leaving only their story behind.

"In the rear!" Jezebel shouted, raising their sword overhead. Lightning answered their call—either from the wisps of the clouds that were rolling in around the muster or conjured all on their own.

The guards moved as one, leaving a vanguard behind should the spiders attempt to flank them.

Beyond the muster but increasingly present in her senses, the storm rolled ever closer, as though it sensed the dire threat the spiders already posed and wished to gobble up as many saudad as it could. The stories warned again and again against traveling the threads with outsiders— Gilsen's muster wasn't wrong to blame her for their present fate, but would such a turn of events have occurred had they prayed to Cassandra rather than her shadow before departure?

It hardly mattered now.

Jezebel sent a bolt of lightning from their sword toward one of the spiders that had crawled onto the underside of a thread hanging above them. The spider screeched, scrambling its legs to avoid the lightning.

Smoke twisted off the top of two of its feet where Jezebel's bolt had singed the hair.

Persephonie gasped and backed up against Rennear, his fur a soothing press at her back as the two of them supported the line of guards who were taking aim at the spider. *By Cassandra, let that be the lead spider.* It was larger than any she'd ever heard of, as big around as a wagon.

"Volley!" the first archer yelled.

Their arrows bounced off the spider's thick, hairy hide. It hissed, clacking its pincers together and scuttled closer to the line of defenders. Behind her Rennear growled and bounded forward, joining the thin line of sword-wielders poised before the archers. A second spider's spindly legs whispered over one another as it curled its way up to the top of the fate thread.

Gilsen appeared at her elbow, arriving with the rain. "We need a priestess," Gilsen shouted above the approaching storm. The driving rain slicked his thinning hair to his forehead, coating his skin in pale blue liquid the thickness of milk. He shoved the moisture away, slinging his soaked hand toward the ground.

"Then why did you not bring one?" Persephonie shouted back. Her attention diverted from the argument with Gilsen to where Rennear and three saudad guards faced off against the second spider poised at the rear of the caravan. If the spider threw Rennear, or the guards seized their moment to turn on him—

"Because we have you!"

Shepherd. Marked by Apollo. Blessed of Cassandra. Priestess. The titles swam around and around her head.

A priestess of Malura would surely sacrifice her in this situation, so thank Cassandra Gilsen had trusted her that far even if he had turned on her the moment his fortunes looked bleak.

A third spider scuttled onto the fate-thread opposite the muster. It hissed and spat venom toward the assembled wagons. The venom missed the wagons, but landed on the vine near the center of the line with a loud sizzle. Before her eyes, the vine holding up the muster began to rot away.

Persephonie screamed and pointed, but her voice was lost in the surrounding chaos as the families inside their wagons were doing the same. She sprinted to Gilsen's side instead. "They are trying to bring down the threads so that we all fall." Persephonie pointed to the damaged vine, which crackled as it burned. "You must move the muster," she insisted. Such a step went against most traveling protocols, but the spider's venom was too effective. "We need to shelter in the fate-storm."

There was a certain poetry to the plan—precisely the sort of story Cassandra would weave for her people, running from a present danger toward a more dire one for safety.

Gilsen's mouth bobbed open and shut, but no words emerged.

"Now!" Persephonie shoved him toward the front of the line. The muster boss had grown too used to Dasia's control and was struggling to resume his own leadership role. But they had no time for hesitation.

Persephonie raised her voice above the howling wind that rattled the eaves of the wagons around her, flinging shingles from their carefully nailed placements. "As Cassandra taught us, it is our destiny to travel the threads of fate." She allowed herself a short, relieved exhale at seeing the first wagons move forward. They had several hundred yards yet, but if they could gain the next elbow where the vines twisted onto new paths, the intersections of many fates supporting one another, they would not plummet across the stars when the thread gave way.

"And as such, we and our allies have precisely what we need in order to journey in safety, together." She spoke into being that which she desired—a respite for her friends who longed only to help her people, and the chance to see this muster through to the other side of the fate-storm and whatever lay beyond.

The surrounding storm drowned out Jezebel's voice, but they held their own against the largest spider, supported by a few of the archers.

Rennear wrenched one of the pincers free from the spider he battled, throwing it from the thread and into the starry dark beyond.

Gilsen led the first team of horses by the bridles, tucking them into the swirling mess of the storm. The deep purple of the wind whipped around his clothes, occasionally obscuring him from sight altogether.

Around him, saudad scrambled out of the wagons, following Gilsen's lead and standing between the horses, latching onto one another and the wagon ahead of them to form an unbroken line. Persephonie's throat thickened at the sight, but she continued on in her story weaving—it was very like what Datha would have had them do. "The brave members of Boss Gilsen's muster banded together against their many foes, latching hands onto horses, wagons, and proceeding into the storm."

As those in the rear began moving forward, the guards who had been fighting the venom-spitting spider fell in behind, trying to hold it off.

But they would not be quick enough, not for the final few wagons.

Persephonie darted between the slow-moving wagons and shut her ears against the sounds of panicked children crying from inside.

She needed to find a way to repair the thread.

When she finally reached the spot, her heart sank at the damage the spider's venom had done. The thread leaked a thick, milky substance very like the rain as it decayed before her eyes, turning from bright blue to a brownish black. The damaged section was the color of rot, but smelled of ash and fire.

Persephonie extended her hands toward the thread. What did it mean for a thread to be damaged and rot away? Had spiders always had this ability or was something terribly wrong? "Cassandra, help me," she murmured. A pale purple glow covered her hands and she imagined healing the thread, mending the parts of the weave that had come undone.

The rotting slowed, but the sap continued to drip—she could not stop it entirely.

She crawled closer but an inner sense stopped her. The sickly green venom clung to the top of the thread still, directly where she had been about to place her hand. It drizzled down, undoing the mending she had so carefully wrought.

Her brother Stefan would have known how to collect the venom, but it would chew through any vessel she placed it in. How to remove it from the thread?

The venom continued to eat away at the thread, sizzling and burning as it devoured the fate strand. Persephonie spun back, surveying the line of wagons. They would need to move quickly.

She called to the nearest driver, urging them wide around the thread so there was no danger of the venom splashing onto the wheels. She knelt as near to the edge of the thread as she dared, concentrating on repairing the thread as best she could. Persephonie murmured the stories she'd learned from her datha over the thread, trying to remind it of the interweavings of fate.

The first wagon creaked over the narrow passage, as far from the damaged part of the thread as the driver dared without falling off. Once they were clear, a rider perched on the back of the wagon waved the next in line to cross.

Persephonie turned her attention to the thread itself. She conjured a trio of dragonflies to assist her. They hovered over the damage, raining healing sparkles from their wings onto the thread beyond, a way for Persephonie to disperse the effects of her magic without further depleting her energy.

Behind her, the wagons carefully picked their way over the thread, moving in single file. Murmured prayers hummed a low harmony beneath the wailing storm and dramatic clash of battle all around her.

Rennear and the sword-wielders were gaining the upper hand. The spider had retreated, and they too made their retreat back to the muster. Jezebel and their archers had likewise found a truce with the largest of the fate spiders. It huddled over its legs, arrows protruding from two sunken sockets where eyes had been, leaving only six shining black orbs across its face.

The fae and the archers wove through the wagons, forming a rear guard and retreating over the damaged thread.

The third spider remained across the fate-weave. It trilled its anger at her mending of the thread as the final wagons passed her, the warriors just ahead of it. Rennear had not seen her kneeling beside the edge. She held her mending spell over the thread as the spider reared back. Persephonie cried out to Rennear, to Jezebel for help—the spider darted its weight forward and cast a second spray of venom across the thread.

For a moment, the thread held. The horses of the final wagon cried out in fright. The sizzling worsened as the additional venom eroded the thread even faster than before—faster than she could mend it.

The wagon came parallel behind her, and the weight was too great. Persephonie screamed, flailing, as she fell from the singed end of the thread.

Falling. Falling.

Sluup. A thick, sticky net caught her and the final wagon fast in its grasp. The webbing bounced from the wagon's weight, and the rear wheels crumpled where they'd struck against the web.

The horses screeched, legs flailing, driving themselves deeper into the webbing.

Persephonie shuddered, the hairs along her arms, legs, and back immediately standing on end. *Thread spiders, devourers of the weave.* They were more dangerous than any of the other breeds of fate spiders, feeding off threads of magic and using them to spin new webs.

Falling from the threads was dangerous.

Being snared by the spiders was deadly.

She screamed as one of the spiders skittered into view. The brilliant blue light of the weave all around them shone back against the spider's black eyes. It clacked together its furry pincers, each as thick around as one of her thighs. Two of its eyes had been gouged out by arrows, marking it as the spider Jezebel and the archers had attacked.

From above, Rennear howled, balanced precariously on a thin thread from a different part of the weave, and the family trapped in their wagon screamed.

She struggled, desperate to free herself from the webbing.

The woman in the wagon gathered the children to her side, wrapping her arms as tightly around them as she could. The man positioned himself at the back of the wagon, scimitar drawn.

But they were two against a thread spider, the last of the three who had caught them with the storm.

"Whatever you do, do not touch the webbing," Persephonie called to the man, who was preparing to step out of the wagon, planning to close the space between himself and the spider. While brave, his plan would leave him trapped and unable to help his family. Persephonie could think of no worse fate.

Beyond Rennear, flickering in and out of the black and purple waves of wind that obscured their surroundings, Jezebel flew against the storm, lightning still flickering all around them. They had to be growing tired, and yet they labored on, trying to save her again.

Just before Persephonie could sigh in relief that Juliet at least had stayed in the wagons, a tiny red shape shot down toward Rennear, fluffy tail extended to preserve her balance. "Juliet!" Persephonie shouted. This was no place for a fox.

Tak, tak, tak!

Persephonie gasped as the spider's six remaining eyes fixed her in its stare. This was no place for a saudad either, especially one caught in a web.

She had lost the thread of her story from before—was the weave of fate truly a place to be wielding the magic of story? She wouldn't have a second chance if the first failed.

The spider trilled its victory, preparing to avenge its family, and rushed toward her, gliding over the threads, impossibly fast.

Clang! A metal pot bounced off its armored hide. A second landed against the side of the spider's face with a deep *squelch*, blinding another of its eyes. "Leave her be!" the man in the wagon shouted, balancing in the doorway.

He was risking his family's life to help her.

Tzzt-peew! A bolt of lightning streaked down from Jezebel's upraised sword, singeing one of the spider's legs so that it doubled over, screeching in pain.

Her makeshift family of Rennear and Jezebel would see them all saved.

With a desperate yank, Persephonie freed her arm from the webbing and launched a spray of sparkling drag-onflies into the spider's remaining eyes. The faery creatures were silvered, reflecting the brightness of their surroundings back against the spider and its injured eyes. The spider reared back, trying to capture the faeries with its pincers.

Rennear and Juliet seized their moment to attack.

Her werewolf launched himself from the strand overhead, driving all his weight and momentum into the spider's back and shoving its body against the threads.

It whirled about beneath him, trying to whip itself around and drive its stinger into his fur. Juliet trilled her own battle cry and dug beneath the spider's hide, biting the rear of one of its legs at the joint and causing the spider to convulse in the opposite direction, flinging its stinger away from Rennear.

A shout echoed overhead and a blue lightning bolt shot

down, like a spear into the spider's neck. A weary Jezebel with a crooked wing floated down into view and, as soon as the corpse stopped twitching, perched at Rennear's side upon the spider's body.

"I shall remember this the next time you assure me that I am welcome in an ancestrally saudad place." They sheathed their sword and used it as a lever to pull Persephonie free. She hugged Jezebel tightly, thanking them, and then embraced Rennear and scooped Juliet into her arms. "I told you, the three of you are always welcome among our people when you're with me."

The four of them sheltered beneath Jezebel's wings while they waited for the storm to pass. From beneath the silver-white feathers, Persephonie whispered healing magics, mending the feathers and sinews that had become injured in the fighting. "Your wings—they appear so different here. Fuller." The shards of bone the fae kept curled behind them were impressive, even frightening, but the full breadth of their wings was breathtaking.

Jezebel bowed their head. "One of the few places where Emryc's curse does not hold sway and my wings actually serve a use beyond reminding me of my ancestor's curse—a flightless reminder at that. Such places beyond the curse are rare, cloaked in possibility." The side of their jaw ticked, and Persephonie didn't press the matter further.

As the storm passed, Jezebel carried the family of saudad in pairs over to the rest of the muster, who received them with hugs and tears, quickly making space for the family so they might feel secure. Rennear transformed back into his human form and, begrudgingly, agreed to climb onto Jezebel's back as they scooped Persephonie and

Juliet into their arms and flew the three of them up to join the rest.

Though the reception was not as warm as it might have been, the muster thanked Rennear and Jezebel for their service, with several members praising Gilsen for allowing them to stay when Carnine would have seen them expelled. "She couldn't have saved the fallen family," one of the elders smugly observed. Boss Gilsen thanked her for her sharpness of mind and for serving as their priestess. "I would say 'Malura guide you,' but I do not wish to give offense."

A single remaining dragonfly settled upon Persephonie's shoulder. "You know the one I serve."

CHAPTER 7

BRISERAS

Before Briseras could depart from the fae's side and go after Tybalt, Loire's hand shot out, catching her by the elbow. "There is a stranger in our woods," the fae murmured. Her eyes fluttered shut as she raised open palms to the sky. The wind whispered through the leaves. Loire sank deeper into her trance, and the tree branches shook. "He is injured." Her eyes squinted tighter. "Clutches his neck. Blood drips down his arm."

Finally someone to hunt, someone who could lead her toward her true prey. Loire's description of the stranger bore every mark of one who'd been beset upon by a vampire. Whether he was a victim or a ploy mattered little to Briseras. She wasn't about to let the trail toward her revenge grow cold.

Briseras tore down the hill, grabbing her second crossbow from her pack. "Which direction is he coming from?" she called up to the fae.

The wind shifted in the trees as Loire searched the forest. With eyes still closed tight, she pointed off through the trees. "He is and will be more than he seems, huntress." Her eyes flickered back and forth behind her lids. "Take care."

"I shall," she answered simply. Vera lit out at her side, Briseras's jog a comfortable trot for her wolf. There was no need to tell the fae her truth—it was many years since she'd had need to fear a mere man, even less so a weakened, injured one. If she was to question him about the vampire's whereabouts—or force him to reveal himself as Nassarq's trap in disguise, the trick would be catching him before the bite he'd sustained finished him off or, knowing these woods as she was beginning to, something else found him first.

Briseras read the signs of the forest as she and Vera traversed the rolling, wooded hills. Dry leaves crackled underfoot, an ever-moving campfire of brown and gold. Beyond Loire's grove, the forest was bereft of wildlife—there were no ravens croaking overhead, no startled starlings taking flight. But as her feet carried her deeper into the dark woods, new signs found her—an absence of shadow, a flicker of what passed for sunlight here. Wind whispered through bare limbs. Scratching branches urged her on as though the trees themselves might speak to her if only she knew how to listen. And somehow, beneath her feet, a pulse thrummed. Its rhythm guided her forward.

Vera caught wind of their quarry first. Her nose wrinkled, ears pricked toward the sound. She darted before Briseras and slowed, crouching.

Briseras followed her wolf's movements, sinking low herself. She rolled her boots heel to toe through the fallen brush, careful of leaves and snapping twigs that would alert their prey to their approach. This far from Loire's forested hamlet, the trees were dry, their branches nearly bare. A stiff wind gave the bare branches voices, a scratchy murmur that would help to disguise the rustling of their feet through the fallen leaves.

She and Vera crept to the top of a rise and there, trapped between a rocky hillside and the leaf-strewn hill they had climbed, she found him.

The man staggered at first, unsteadily balancing his weight between his feet. He scanned the rise on either side of the valley, that tingly sense of a creature wary of finding its way into a trap.

She couldn't have arranged a better natural trap for the man herself—the forest had conspired to help her.

Her back to a spindly tree, Briseras observed the man's slow progress through the winding valley. From this distance, even with her sharply honed sight, there was no way to ascertain that he wasn't a thrall of the vampire who'd bitten him, which would make him easier for Nassarq to track. She would have to descend.

A quick nod to Vera—the wolf would follow at her heel.

Briseras jumped to clear the last of the rise and skidded down the piles of leaves. Her cloak billowed behind her, and she slid to a stop a dozen paces before the traveler.

The man wavered in his stance as Briseras's shadow fell across his path. His eyelids fluttered, and his sword arm drifted back and forth as he tried to focus on her.

He wore fine boots, and there was an appearance of wealth in the tiny stitches of his garments, though they had been soiled by blood and his trek through the forest.

His brow raised, and he uttered a soft groan before he collapsed. The brief glimpse of his eyes revealed light brown irises, rich in color, free of red.

Briseras slunk forward, curved dagger clutched at her

side. Blood leaked from the torn flesh at his throat, a wound woven over scars. He'd served as a vampire's meal for months, longer if he was particularly unlucky.

The hair along Vera's back rose as they crept nearer, and a growl fizzled at the back of her wolf's throat. "I know," Briseras murmured. Her own scars had taught her abundant caution where vampires were concerned. Well, caution with all save one. Maybe two, counting Olya.

Briseras glanced up at the hillsides around them, ensuring another hunter hadn't decided to echo her strategy and add her and Vera to the easy meal that had just collapsed in the brush. Jagged trees curled as fangs toward the heavens, but such was the landscape of Steymhorod. She tossed her cloak back over her shoulder so it would remain free of blood and crouched at the man's side, dagger in hand.

Slowly, she extended her hand toward the man's shoulder but stopped as he twitched.

Briseras caught her breath. He was not so far gone as to experience death spasms. His blood was sharp copper on the air, but something else, woodsmoke and the bite of frost—

"Yah!" The pale silhouette of a woman burst free from the man's torso, hands outstretched toward Briseras.

She reared back, slashing wildly at the specter, and crashed into the damp piles of leaves behind her. The ghost's form wavered between her and the man, smoke and water swirling and trying to hold solid.

Possession and vampire's wine—how had the nobleman survived?

Vera raised her nose to the sky and howled. They had faced ghosts before.

"Leave off!" the ghost shouted, its multi-octave voice

echoing across the clearing. It cast anxious looks over its shoulder as it bobbed between Briseras and the nobleman.

Had the ghost been thrown out of the man's body when he fainted? The undead creature was too distracted by its host to pay close attention to Briseras, who used her semi-reclined position in the underbrush to her advantage, slipping her small hand crossbow free from its sheath along her thigh to take aim.

She needed to question the nobleman, certainly, but Briseras had no need of a host-obsessed ghost. "Where is he coming from?" She nodded her chin toward the nobleman, directing the ghost's attention toward him and away from herself once more.

"Leave him alone," the ghost shrieked. Its gaze wavered between Briseras and its host. The man's breath grew more shallow, and the ghost's eyes widened. "He needs—no—leave us!"

The man moaned softly, fully capturing the ghost's attention.

Briseras took aim. The ghost froze in its hovering, its gaze fixed over its shoulder at its felled, groaning host in a pile of leaves.

Briseras should have recognized the tell-tale *swish* of those same leaves, should have seen her own strategy mirrored a dozen paces away.

Just a moment before she let fly her own arrow, a small, jagged rock came soaring toward her head from the nobleman.

Thunk.

Twang.

"Agh!" Briseras's hand flew to her forehead where the rock had struck her. She glared after the arc of her arrow as it flew wide of the ghost, streaking just past the unnatural angle of the creature's thin neck and embedding itself harmlessly into the trunk of a nearby tree.

Blood dripped down her finger from the cut on her forehead.

Briseras cursed under her breath and sprang to her feet. Shadows take the lot of them. Mercy toward a magically captivating vampire lord was one thing, willingly allowing herself to be bitten was something else. But this? Trying to rid a ghost-struck nobleman too weak to even wield his sword of his possessor while he defended his haunting companion?

Rajas would be even more ashamed of her than he'd been when they parted ways for the last time.

"How long have you been under her thrall?" she shouted at the bewitched human. He had the gall to narrow his eyes back at her after preventing her from saving his life.

She wiped the blood from her forehead and stalked closer, curved blade by her shoulder. The ghost's weakened neck would make for the perfect strike point.

"Thrall?" he called back. "She's helping me."

The ghost extended its arms toward Briseras, over-wide eyes fixed on the sharpened edge of her blade. At least one of the pair possessed a modicum of wisdom.

"You'll be free soon enough," Briseras murmured. She strolled past the man's head, backing the ghost against the cliff face, returning the environment to her own advantage.

With another groan, the man shoved himself forward and caught her foot just as Briseras prepared to dart forward and end the ghost. He yanked her off balance, and Briseras crashed once more to the earth. The leaves did little to cushion her fall.

"Gah!" *This man.* She kicked at the possessed man, trying to pin his hand beneath the crushing thrash of her boot to no avail.

The self-satisfied nobleman propped his head on his elbow and grinned down at her. "It seems I've thrown you off balance yet again, huntress—oof."

Briseras elbowed him in the chest as she jerked herself up to her feet. She smirked as he curled up, coughing on the ground.

Vera trotted over and sat at Briseras's side, watching the nobleman intently. At least her wolf wasn't giving the man the satisfaction of believing he was a threat to them.

"Alright, alright, I surrender," he coughed. The man rolled onto his back and raised his hands by his shoulders. The ghost hovered by the cliff, mercifully silent.

Briseras crossed her arms over her chest and followed Vera's example, leveling her gaze at the nobleman. "Where are you coming from?"

He pressed a hand to his lower rib cage and winced. "That is definitely going to bruise." He studied Briseras's elbow from the corner of his eye. "Look, I can tell that we didn't get off to the best start." Another wince as he got to his feet.

"Lord Adrian Calder Jorgan, at your service." He gave a slight bow, careful of his bruised ribs. "And my fiancée, Teela."

Former fiancée, surely, was what the nobleman meant. Perhaps he had struck his head in one of his many falls within the past hour.

Briseras introduced herself and Vera to the addled pair and repeated her question, "Where are you coming from?"

"Ah, that." Jorgan winced. "It's a bit complicated, you see." He took a small step closer, swaying on his feet.

She held up her blade to stop him. His eyes widened, taking in the sharp curve of her shortsword. Sparing the ghost, for now, was as friendly as Briseras was prepared to be. "A simple direction will suffice if you are unsure."

"It's not that I'm unsure," the nobleman snapped, hand to his chest. "It's just, erm, dangerous, for you to be headed back that way alone."

Briseras stared back at him in answer.

His uncertainty deepened as he looked her over. His gaze darted from her array of weaponry to Vera next to her. "Apologies." He scuffed his boot through the under-growth. "It would be dangerous for *me* to go back that way alone—you are obviously the capable sort." He glanced at the ghost and sighed. "Teela knows better than I the direc-tion from whence we've come." He gestured over his shoulder, deeper into the forest. "There's a mist-shrouded tower several days' travel that way." His hand drifted to his neck as he muttered "bastard" under his breath.

Perhaps the nobleman would prove useful after all. "And which vampire is it that held you captive in this tower?" The list of vampiric possibilities was growing disturbingly long. On the side of supposed allies were Lord Draego and Olya. Nassarq topped the list of enemies, with his two powerful thralls close behind.

Another glance at the ghost who was avoiding the nobleman's gaze. "Nassarq," he growled.

Briseras couldn't stop the smile that sparked at the mention of her prey. "I'm going to need all the details you can manage."

The nobleman's face was grim and paler than he'd been moments before. He swayed again on his feet, this time tumbling toward Briseras. She caught him around the shoulders to prevent his head from smacking on one of the roots underfoot. Jorgan flailed for a moment but managed to catch and steady himself with his arm around Briseras's waist. The ghost fluttered uselessly at his side, trying to aid him.

She ground her teeth as she adjusted the nobleman's weight beside her, moving his hand from her waist to her shoulder. "You despise this vampire?"

"More than I can say."

His words rang of truth. The bluster from their initial encounter had faded since he'd mentioned Nassarq's name. "My camp is a few hours' walk from here," Briseras said, turning the nobleman toward Loire's grove. "As you recover, you can direct me toward this tower. My work with the vampire Nassarq remains unfinished."

The ghost piped up beside the trudging nobleman, "You shouldn't go back there, sweetheart. It was a miracle we got out in the first place, and—" She broke off, staring at Briseras. Teela dropped her voice to a whisper, "And you know what will happen if he finds us again."

At first, Jorgan gave no answer, only glared at the earth before his dragging feet. "Many an enemy threatens death, Teela. It is those with the determination and means to make more dire, lasting threats who are the ones to fear." He turned from the ghost to Briseras. "As I'm sure one such as yourself has already put together, Nassarq is precisely that sort of enemy."

A second genuine statement, this one wise. Briseras was surprised but impressed. She clutched the top of her satchel, Everett's journal tucked safely inside. "I am aware of that particular quality of his." Was it Nassarq who had severed the ties of life between the nobleman and the anxious ghost? "But unfortunately for Nassarq, I am that sort of enemy as well."

TWO HOURS INTO THEIR TREK BACK TOWARD LOIRE'S Glade, the ghost had finally abandoned its sullen pout over Briseras's unwillingness to coddle the bloodied nobleman. Rather than slinking away into the forest, which Briseras would have welcomed and then hurried apace away, Teela slid into the nobleman's body and disappeared, leaving the pair of them in relative peace.

"Sorry about the, uh . . ." The man nodded toward the cut on her forehead.

"Don't mention it," Briseras answered. "We both have worse scars than that."

"True enough." He shrugged. An uneasy silence followed and the man chewed his lip. "It's just, most women I've met, well, they would be rather put out by a scratch to their face, you know, and you're, umm—"

Briseras stopped and turned to face the man. An unoriginal observation was sure to follow. She was different than the women he'd known at whatever court he'd happened to come from. Obvious enough from her garb and bearing, though her otherworldly origin would likely complicate matters further. How disappointing that the nobles of Steymhorod were so very like the senators and most of the priests of the Andel-ce Hevran empire.

"Apologies," the man finally said. "My time locked away seems to have dulled my manners."

Yet another courtly possession she'd never found a great deal of use for. Rajas had insisted upon her learning formal means of address and a few courtly customs should she ever need to request aid from a court on behalf of her collective. Thus far, it had never come to that. "What did you say your name was again?"

He repeated it, Lord Adrian Calder Jorgan. Three names and a title seemed excessive given the circumstances.

"Why don't you choose one?"

"Well enough. Would 'Lord' work for you?"

Briseras drummed her fingertips over the hilt of the blade tucked into her bracer. She'd heard of witches in hiding in the wilds of Tor'stre Vahn that could speak to the dead. If such magic had survived the priests' purges, what might be possible in these hallowed, haunted lands? Maybe she could dispatch the nobleman and treat with the ghost instead.

"I'm kidding," the nobleman exclaimed, sensing her irritation. "Jorgan will suit me just fine. And you, huntress? What shall I call you?"

"Briseras." She said it plainly and resumed walking. They'd need to make good time to return to Loire's grove before sundown.

He repeated it after her, as though it might sound different when spoken by his tongue. It did, in a way, though it lacked the added resonance and wonder of Lord Draego's murmur. Was the nobleman from his court? It seemed unlikely. Such a kidnapping would be a stark aggression on Nassarq's part against the vampire lord. Nassarq was cruel and proud but not reckless. The nobleman's accent didn't match Draego's either.

"Before you landed yourself in the vampire's clutches, where were you coming from?"

The nobleman winced and rubbed the back of his neck.

Briseras tried again. "Which court? Or city?" There was still so much about Steymhorod she didn't know, and revealing her origin hadn't gone well thus far.

"I'm not sure you'll believe me," the nobleman answered. He sounded more abashed than she'd anticipated, a strange shift from his former bravado. Jorgan sighed. "I'm not from here, exactly. Nassarq captured me from my homeland in, well, it's called Linolynn."

Briseras halted again.

"It doesn't seem to exist here . . ." His voice trailed off, watching her reaction.

"I'm from—" *Haven*, she nearly said, but there was no need for such a confession so early in an acquaintance, and the priests' prison city was better put behind her anyway. "Tor'stre Vahn," she added quickly, "one of the hunters' collectives. It doesn't exist here either."

Jorgan stared back at her, his mouth ajar. Absently, his hand drifted toward the wound on his neck. He winced as his fingers struck the still-raw flesh. "How did you, ahem, how long have you been here?"

She resumed walking, picking up the pace slightly. Loire would be able to tend to his injury, and Tybalt could help her chart the nobleman's origin before he returned to the Vale. There were notable strategic disadvantages to trading out the elf for the nobleman, though the elf kept insisting that their first priority should be 'returning the Sisters' over 'seeking revenge.' They were still waiting for Otto, her raven, to return with news from Tybalt's allies.

"Over a fortnight now. Not yet two." She was careful to keep her voice neutral. Once Otto returned from the Vale, she planned to send him to Jeremy in St. Sebastian. He had cautioned her on several occasions before she set out into Steymhorod's wilds. *I know you are accustomed to taking care of yourself in such environments, but I urge you to be cautious all the same. There is no other land like this one.'*

For some reason his warning made her mind drift to

the vampire lord who'd led her to the cemetery in St. Sebastian—the true reason *why* this land was like no other. Draego held additional mysteries, additional dangers close to his chest. Some part of her knew that he wished to share these with her and was waiting, but for what sign or signal, she couldn't have said.

The nobleman was watching her curiously out of the corner of his eye. Briseras adjusted the set of her shoulders and turned his question back on him.

"Days and weeks ran together in Nassarq's dungeon," he answered with a shrug.

Dungeon. "Were there others there?" She'd promised Lavinia to help her find her sister, though she hadn't been able to uncover a trace of either since she'd appeared here. It was possible Nassarq held Saige, possible too that he'd captured Lavinia shortly after her arrival. She swallowed the curse that rose to her lips at her own lack of judge-ment when she'd first appeared in Steymhorod—she'd lost the opportunity to attack the vampire when he was injured and would have to contend with him at his full strength within his lair.

"Many." Jorgan shuddered and tugged the shreds of his cloak tighter around his shoulders. "You wouldn't believe the darkness. Enough to make you forget your own name."

Briseras smiled to herself at that. Her mother had been the first to teach her not to fear the dark but to become it. *Beware those who preach only the powers of light, dearest,* she had whispered into the shadows of their prison hut in Haven, tucking Briseras tighter against her side as one of the priests paced past their windows, torch in hand. They'd burned two of her mother's closest friends that morning for reasons her mother refused to say. *The wise witch knows the power that comes from the dark.*

What was it about this land that brought the memories of her mother so close? Memories she'd held apart from herself for years, to hide her pain from Rajas and the others, yes, also to survive.

"I came here looking for a friend," Briseras confided. "Well, a friend's sister. I was hoping she might be there."

"For her sake, she'd be better off dead." No spark of irony glinted in the nobleman's tone, and a stoniness had fallen over his expression. The ghost at his side glared at Briseras as though she'd been the one to sentence its host to imprisonment.

"I'd keep my judgment to myself if I were you," she warned the ghost. The nobleman was too lost in his own memories of the prison to heed her. The ghost quickly took her meaning and hovered closer to its host.

"Come on." Briseras lengthened her strides. "An hour more and we'll have reached Loire's glade."

CHAPTER 8

IELLIETH

The island bobbed away behind the *Amber Queen*, growing smaller and smaller upon the horizon behind them, the sky ahead wide brushstrokes of orange and pink hues. Iellieth steadied her balance, trying to regain her sea legs as she strode across the cabin she shared with Marcon and Quindythias to peer out the door onto the deck instead. "What's Quindythias doing?" she asked Marcon who was leaned against the wall of the ship beside her, staring out the window. He'd decided the best way to regain his sea legs—or his sea stomach, as he called it—was to stay still.

Quindythias found no such limitations necessary. He was bustling about the deck, questioning sailors, a square of parchment and quill in hand. A few of the sailors rebuffed him, waving him off while they attended to their task of getting the ship into the open ocean, but the elf, nonplussed, would simply abandon the one and set himself upon someone else nearby instead.

"He's been asking the more experienced sailors about the Realms," Marcon said. "Before we left shore, he'd questioned a handful of sailors, none of them had ever made it beyond the coastal city, Invae Alinor, the one built into the large cave system at the continent's base, or down the river at Moonsbreak Landing on the western coast but their descriptions of the landscape have made him think of Bastion." A furrow worked its way between Marcon's brows as he spoke. The trip to the Realms was making her companions nervous too.

"The Blade of Bastion, that's what they called him, wasn't it?"

"It was, lady. Being a hero of Eldura was more . . . complex than you'll often find in your storybooks." He turned from the window to stare down at her instead. His voice dropped as he spoke again. "Perhaps that is why we were forgotten." Marcon lowered his gaze.

Before she could second-guess herself, Iellieth reached out and placed her fingertips along the sharp line of his jaw. Gradually, she straightened her fingers to angle his face back toward hers. "Yvayne has been quite clear that you were erased, not forgotten. That is a significant distinction."

"Shouldn't some things be beyond erasure? If they matter enough?"

She hadn't expected the pain behind his eyes. The excitement and confusion of reuniting with Teodric had blinded her to the struggle her protectors were experiencing, the grief of returning to a new world. "I'm sure that's true—"

Marcon held her gaze and leaned closer to her.

"I don't know the exact means of the erasure Yvayne was talking about." The words caught in the back of her throat, jumbled in her mind.

The champion stepped nearer still, so close that a deep

breath would have brought their bodies together. A muscle along the side of his jaw clenched, standing out against his skin before disappearing once more. His tattoos had darkened as he reached for her. His fingertips brushed at the strands of hair that had fallen free of her braid, grazed her neck.

Behind her, the sway of the ship swung their cabin door shut.

Marcon's other arm wrapped around her waist, pulled her body flush against his. "You and I are speaking of two different sorts of erasure, lady." The low gravel of his voice rumbled against her chest, his words echoing deep within her.

Iellieth's breath hitched unevenly between them. She repeated his words to herself. For weeks she had wondered, but now—

"I knew you, from the moment you awakened me within that cave. Not because you have a returning soul, like Red claimed, or whatever your mentor Yvayne would say we are or once were." He shook his head. "I knew you because I've been waiting for you my whole life. The one I lived before and the one I'm living now. Knew you as assuredly as I would a missing part of myself."

His thumb grazed her cheekbone, and his gaze flickered from her eyes to her lips and back. "I am reticent to ask too much of you. I understand you and the captain have a history, just as I know Quindythias and I would return to statues were we to be separated from your side. I haven't said anything before because I fear you feeling trapped again. You make me feel quite the opposite, Iellieth. In more ways than one, you set me free." He took a quick breath, holding her there.

Marcon lowered his mouth to hers. For a moment their

breaths mingled. His lips brushed against hers, sending a rush of tingles across her skin. He held her gaze. "You are everything to me." And then he pressed his lips to hers.

The fluttering thoughts that constantly crowded her mind vanished. There was nothing beyond her and Marcon and this moment.

Iellieth kissed him back. She wrapped her arms around his shoulders, pulling herself tighter against him. At first, he froze, but as her lips beckoned his, as she asked for more, Marcon relaxed. He groaned low in his throat as she opened her mouth, urging him nearer still.

His grasp around her waist tightened. Her hands tangled in the strands of his hair. His touch fell from her face back to her neck, the brush of his skin setting her aflame.

Marcon's lips curled against hers. He broke away from their kiss, eyes bright and staring down at her. "Thank you." He traced the hairline at her temple.

Iellieth used his hold about her waist to steady herself on her feet, slow her breath. She smiled back at him, the distant caw of her flock of thoughts fluttering back, but not just yet. "Marcon—"

"Take your time, lady. I will not leave your side."

Her pulse hammered against the gentle stroke of his fingers against her throat. The way he stared down at her, as though she was a priceless treasure that he would hold on to forever.

The door to their cabin burst open with a swell of orange-gold sunset and a frustrated elf. Iellieth jumped, jarring Marcon's arm from around her waist. He tightened his hold around her hips instead, a muscle in his jaw twitching. Beyond Quindythias, the rigging creaked and sailors shouted to one another.

"I really don't know why they bother," Quindythias huffed to himself as he stomped into the cabin and threw himself down upon Iellieth's bed, his hand draped back against his forehead. "These sailors, so unwilling to share the intimate details of their prior adventures to a *professional adventurer*. A folk hero, really." He twisted his head to glare back at the open door as though even the proximity to the sailors was an insult to his illustrious reputation. "It's not as though they can expect some sort of grand welcome among the elves, who aren't keen on strangers at all. But shouldn't I be able to anticipate something?"

Iellieth pivoted to face Quindythias without moving away from Marcon. Her awareness hovered around the hand upon her hip, his thumb grazing her waist, distracting her from following what exactly Quindythias was complaining about.

"You've been obsessed with the Realms since childhood, haven't you?" He waved the hand that wasn't draped across his forehead toward Iellieth almost in accusation, completely unaware or uncaring of Marcon's arm around her.

"Umm, yes? My father is a diplomat of Thyles Thamor—"

"Which none of these imbeciles have even seen!"

Iellieth glanced up at Marcon, who shook his head and dropped his arm. A different sort of smile than the one she'd felt against her lips tugged at the corner of his mouth now, a special expression reserved for the rantings of his closest friend. "Did someone say something that has upset you, Quindythias? You were happy about going to the Realms this afternoon when we set sail."

"Happy is such a common way of putting it." He

dropped his shoulders as he sighed, blaming the wooden ceiling slats for the utter failings of all his acquaintances aboard the *Amber Queen*, most particularly, it seemed, their lack of appreciation for his emotional complexity.

She pressed her lips together, suppressing a smile. Quindythias and his sensitivity would never recover from being giggled at during one of his moods. "Can you tell me what *is* going on then? A non-common way of saying it, perhaps?"

He huffed once more and raised himself up onto his elbows. "I suppose I can try." The frustration, Quindythias explained, was the burden of carrying so illustrious and possibly misunderstood a history upon his shoulders. "It's easy enough for Marcon to strut about your shiny castle, built upon the ruins of his home."

Iellieth glanced back at Marcon, but the champion was unhurt by Quindythias's casual reference to the destruction of Respite, the ruins of which formed the foundation of Io Keep and Linolynn itself.

"Not all of us have such a clean-cut history. We weren't all recognized for our brilliant contributions at the time we made them."

"Tali complicated that for both of us," Marcon gently reminded him. "Though of course I had a career of honorable service to the Battalion that I set aside to join the forces rebelling against the Cities." He turned to Iellieth. "Quindythias, as you know, sparked an uprising against injustice from within the very heart of his city. The people of Bastion even sheltered us for a time in his name."

"Quite right," Quindythias quipped, his ego soothed.

Iellieth slid forward and sat on the corner of the bed near Quindythias's feet. "Can you tell me what exactly you're worried about happening? I'm sure we can work through whatever it is, together."

He curled his lips into a frown. "What if no one remembers me? All that work as the Blade, and I'm forgotten. Or, worse, vilified? We both know how long you've been waiting and hoping to see your father." Quindythias swallowed and dropped his gaze. "We'll need their help and cooperation to retrieve the seal piece. What if my past gets in the way of that?"

Iellieth's lips parted and closed again. Marcon mourned them having been forgotten while Quindythias feared what would happen if they were remembered. What was she to say to help them?

She grinned instead and flung herself forward, fastening her arms around Quindythias's waist.

He tightened against her embrace, almost tugging himself away, but Iellieth held fast.

A few heartbeats passed and he relaxed, sat up, and patted her on the head.

Iellieth released him.

"I told you what happened to my sister," he murmured, though no one aside from the three of them was near enough to hear. "I just don't know what I would do if something happened to you too. Calixta, she made her choice. You've barely been given the opportunity."

Her eyes watered at the turn of fate that had given her such friends. Iellieth shook her head. "That is the second time today—no." She reached out and tugged Quindythias's hand free from its perch on the bed and held out her other hand for Marcon who took it. His skin was warm, his touch calming. "I want you to both listen to me very carefully. We're not going to keep having this conversation. I choose you."

She met Quindythias's gaze first. He stared back at her like a scolded puppy hoping to still be accepted, perhaps even praised, for its mischief.

Holding Marcon's gaze after such a confession was harder. She wasn't ready yet to give him an answer after what he'd said to her. She hadn't even had a chance to let his words sink in and work through what they truly meant. But she persevered nonetheless. "I choose both of you. I don't care that the amulet didn't give me a choice. Even if it had, I would be standing right here. That is my choice. So whether the elves receive us as returning heroes, enemies, or, more likely, something in between doesn't matter. What matters is that you both know I am precisely where I want to be."

Marcon stared back at her, the intensity behind his bright eyes promising so much, if only she knew how to let herself receive it. Quindythias sniffled beside her. "Well, good. Because we choose you too." He straightened and sighed. "I do hope the elves land on the side of welcoming us as heroes. That would be a nice change of pace from our previous encounters."

Iellieth smiled to herself, imagining her friends being welcomed in the Realms as heroes, showered with praise and flowers as they'd undoubtedly been during the war for Eldura. That the elves would receive her with the same fanfare she doubted, but she would settle for acceptance as a diplomatic ally. Heroism needed to be earned after all, and she'd only just started to prove herself.

CHAPTER 9

TEODRIC

Kriega's commanding voice joined the whisper-crash of the waves, the sounds echoing against the wood panels of Teodric's office on their first full day of sailing for the Realms. With the ship away and their course for the Realms set, he'd shut himself away, stealing a few moments alone. In the stillness, his own personal ghosts appeared. There were two that haunted him. From one, the phantom sting of a whip upon his back, her cackle as he cried out in pain. It was her soft fingers that had rubbed salt into his raw wounds, widening his scars.

His other ghost had been by his side for far longer. The one he'd held at a ball, whose hand had been ripped from his as they tried to flee. She'd screamed in protest as they beat him, begging them to stop.

With both ghosts, there was shame in his memories of their nearness. For Syleste, that he had ever allowed her to touch him, that in his weakness, he had sought solace in the one who had caused him so much pain. Worse, that he'd mistaken that solace for anything other than what it truly was, another of her manipulations.

For Iellieth, his shame was that he'd pushed her away.

Was it for him to decide on her behalf whether or not he was worthy? Or if she did not mind, then why should he?

"It's only because she doesn't know the truth of who you really are," Syleste's ghost that haunted his mind whispered. The phantom memory of her lips brushed his ear. *"She has no idea who you've become. Do you really think she'd keep you within her sight if she knew even a sliver of the horrors you've performed in my name? At my side?"*

Teodric shut his eyes and adjusted his collar by feel, loosening her hold.

Not in this room, he decided. Syleste's ghost was no longer allowed within his cabin—there was only room for one ghost here. One remembered kiss.

He turned away from his map-strewn desk and faced his reflection in the mirror on the back wall. Teodric wasn't blind to the way Marcon looked at her, hadn't missed who had received her on the beach when he'd sent her back after she kissed him. Since then, whether on shore or aboard ship, Marcon had barely left her side, and Teodric had deliberately held himself apart, trying to lose himself in the sailing of his ship and running of his crew.

Kriega was too skilled a first mate for such distractions to be as absorbing as he'd hoped.

Teodric ran his fingers over the slip of parchment folded into his pocket, the letter Syleste had sent with the revenant. The admiral was baiting him, promising she knew where his father was, trying to trick him into doing whatever she wanted, responding to whichever puppet string she pulled.

Not this time, Syleste. Not this time.

She wasn't their admiral anymore.

A muscular frame appeared as a silhouetted shadow behind his mirrored reflection.

"Precisely who I was hoping to see," Teodric said, turning about and waving Kriega inside. Seeing his expression, she shut the door behind her.

The half-orc strutted forward, her jaw set as she spun the top layer of maps toward herself on the opposite side of his desk.

He had thought it would be more difficult to convince Kriega to take the first step in disobeying Syleste's orders, though Darcy, the liaison they'd been instructed to save was buried, along with his arm, on the island they had left behind.

She relinquished the maps and straightened, glowering down at him instead. "How badly do you want to find your father?"

Teodric stammered, caught off guard by her question. He'd assumed she'd arrived to discuss charting their full course, as was their habit. "Of course I want to find him—"

"Not what I asked you. How badly?"

Kriega had lost her entire family before Syleste rescued her from traffickers. He hadn't expected the thought of rescuing his father would mean much to her at all.

Teodric turned away from his first mate and surveyed the wide expanse of windows, revealing nothing but ocean horizon beyond the *Queen.*

"Do you know what I think it will take?" the half-orc growled.

He cast about, finding his cup of wine and downing it.

The memory of her fervor in killing the ship's former first mate flashed back before his eyes.

"We question the right person, one who will squeal. If we're turning on the admiral, we need to be as ruthless as she would be. Make no mistake—there will be consequences." The gravity of her tone said what they both knew—with Syleste, consequences meant blood. "We do what she would do. We hunt down her second-in-command, Henderson, put him to the sword, and cut him until he reveals something we can use against the admiral. She's too strong for us to confront directly. But Henderson knows her better than anyone. If there's a weakness we can exploit, he'll have already considered it for himself."

The violence Kriega was suggesting . . . it wasn't something he could do. He'd already lost his home, lost Iellieth. He'd held on as best he could to his mother's way of life, preserving it for her. He couldn't give up this part of himself to Syleste, could he?

She sensed his hesitation. "If you want to play this game—and that's all it is to her—then you'll have to play on her terms. There's not room for your nobleman's morality in her game."

He knew what Kriega was asking him just as they both knew the crew would need a clear directive if they were to hold their mettle and truly rebel against Syleste after they set sail from the Realms. Could he become the kind of person who harmed others to meet his own ends—making himself more like Syleste than she'd already forced him to be—or was he the kind of son with qualms about what he would do to save his father?

The worst part might have been knowing both the answer and what it should be and not caring as much as he should about the ocean between the two.

Iellieth shouldn't have to be looking over her shoulder for Syleste to appear beyond the concerns that already weighed down her and her companions. That's where he came in. It was time to rid the oceans of the admiral's tyranny, forever.

Teodric ran his hands back through his hair, casting his head back and trying to drop the tension from his shoulders. "Can you think of any other way? Different leverage? If she's expecting us to attack Henderson, he'll be prepared. That's what she would do."

"Aye," Kriega agreed. She hunched and sifted through the maps, pulling one from lower in the stack to the fore and spinning it to face him. "There is one option, outside hunting down her second. Don't know if you'd know it, not being from this part of the sea originally—an island, in the middle of Syleste's territory. She won't set foot upon it and only sends her emissaries ashore."

"That's not so unusual, is it?" Teodric frowned. When he had worked aboard the *Dominion*, Syleste had sent her sailors to raid settlements. For sea battles, she waited until the deck had been subdued before facing the rival captain and putting them to the sword.

Kriega's jaw jutted forward. "It's difficult to explain. Throughout our years together, talking about that island is the only time I've ever seen Syleste look . . . afraid."

That was significant and not something he would ever have associated with Syleste. By reputation the admiral was fearless. But the reality of standing by her side with an impending bloody conflict was worse—he would have expected some sort of nerves, excitement, maybe trepidation. Syleste betrayed none of these. She simply waited, as though the victory she sought was already decided, inevitably hers, she only had to wait to see in what form it arrived.

In a way her nonchalance inspired confidence, if not in individual crew members' belief that they would survive but their ship, their friends would. The money that had been promised to their families upon their demise would reach its intended destination. And if they fell, the admiral would see their body down into the embrace of the Deep, the great sea serpent, as storied and ancient as Azuria itself.

"Do you know where this island is?" The best plan he'd developed so far involved taking the crew to Syleste's island like she'd ordered, where she kept her treasure horde. Where she'd kept him imprisoned, tortured him, for months before allowing him back aboard the *Dominion*. She'd be waiting for him there.

"No." Kriega scowled, staring out at the endless waves of blue beyond them. "She kept it one of her closest secrets. Henderson knew. I was wise enough not to ask, but that much I gathered from their conversations." Her glare intensified. "He knows the nature of this artifact she has us searching for as well. What it is and, more importantly, what it does."

Teodric's stomach twisted, as though a rag of icy water had just been squeezed in the center of his gut. How quickly they'd returned to her second-in-command. *Henderson*. Syleste's most trusted, longest-serving captain. He was the one who'd overseen Teodric's prison sentence, carefully selected each humiliation. Unbidden, an image flashed before his eyes—himself holding a knife to Henderson's throat, ordering Kriega to subject him to the eagle, a slow death sentence in which his innards would be cut out of him and left to bake in the sun, his blood dripping into the sea as he expired, bound and in excruciating pain.

"I don't . . ." Teodric shut his eyes, shoving back the memories from the prison, what he had worked so hard to forget, to keep at bay.

"I know what he did to you," Kriega murmured, her voice low. "What he had the others do too." If he didn't know her better, he could have very nearly caught a note of pity, even concern in her voice. But he did know Kriega, and such a sentiment wasn't going to come for him from the half-orc. "He more than deserves whatever you would see him face."

Teodric's jaw tightened. Deep in the prisons, his body aching, his throat raw from screaming, he'd made himself a promise. One day, he would see an end to Syleste's torments. To Henderson. He would spare anyone he could from such a fate.

He crossed behind his desk, idly sorting through the maps they'd been poring over all afternoon. "What you're proposing would promise untold dangers for our crew. The repercussions, should we fail . . ." Taking on Henderson by themselves—it was as sure a death sentence as his plan of taking them to Syleste's stronghold, Isla de Hossa.

Kriega nodded, rising from her hunch over the table and stretching her arms back. She sighed, shifting her weight onto one hip. "She'll kill us all, eventually. They know that. Have known since that Darcy chap lost his mind and the elf did him in. Just as you and I know what she'll have in store for us. But you've seen it a dozen times on the ships she takes—they decided to die by the point of the sword rather than live on at her whim, rather than sail beneath a flag that's brought so much death and pain."

Teodric resisted the urge to study Kriega's features.

That she was saying these words aloud was unbelievable enough. That she meant them—unthinkable. And yet here they were. Both cast aside by Syleste. Both ready to find a new way forward.

Their planning stretched all the way to twilight. Kriega had a relatively certain idea of where Henderson was making port, one Ambrose should be able to confirm. Syleste and the *Dominion* were planning to spend a month or two on her island, leaving Henderson vulnerable if they were able to pull off the sneak attack Kriega had devised.

Henderson knew their ship, so they couldn't pretend to be a merchant in distress and bait him into an attack. They'd have to use the captain's hubris against him, convince him that it would be worthwhile to either take them on directly or pretend to ally himself with them for a while. And the only way to do that was to make certain he believed they had what he wanted more than anything in the world—Syleste's artifact.

Teodric stood with his arms perched on either side of his desk, staring down at the ocean maps. Kriega slumped back in his chair with arms crossed, a near-empty bottle of wine beside her, boots propped on the corner of the desk.

"The way I see it," Teodric said, "we've one of two options to make this work. We return to Nortelon and spread word far and wide that we've found her artifact, against all the odds, or we make our way to *Lagon des Morts* and hope they're still off the western coast."

Kriega groaned as he mentioned the floating pirate haven. "What could you want with a bunch of washed-up pirates and thieves?"

He'd heard stories about the *Lagon* from Ambrose back in his earliest sailing days and hadn't been able to discern if the navigator was trying to trick him into believing in such a place or if it was real. Legends of the *Lagon* went back centuries. It was said to be founded by the cursed pirate captain of the *Dragon's Keel*, an old rival of Syleste's who, rather than risk his crews in an all-out war against the admiral, decided to take another path. He sheltered in a cove and began drawing other ships to him and his cause, a united Infinite Ocean where pirates fought together, regardless of whom they served.

Over decades, the *Lagon*'s fleet had grown. They'd bound barges to pirate ships, crafted entire docking systems along the sides. The *Lagon des Morts* rivaled the size of a small island now, with trade centers, inns, taverns, and even a below-decks market all its own.

The more he thought on it, the more he liked the prospect. "How many enemies do you think she's accumulated there?" His smirk grew. "If we were looking for someone with information about this island and its denizens, looking to plant false information with Syleste and Henderson's spies, where better to go?"

He'd tried to visit the *Lagon* once while on leave but had been called back to Nortelon to tend to his mother instead. If even a fraction of Ambrose's stories of the *Lagon* were true, the *Lagon*'s sheer size, the way the ships floated together, with smaller barges hoisted above the water to keep their decks level with the larger ones—it captured his imagination, made him feel that, if by some miracle he survived this, he might be able to find a way to belong upon the sea.

There would be no returning to a nobleman's life for him, not after everything he'd done in Syleste's name. There was no future in which he helped his father reclaim the Adhemar estate, in which he settled down to measure out a life for himself and whatever community they had left there. It had likely been taken over by Duke Amastacia already, a quite different turn of events than what he and his parents had so optimistically, so foolishly hoped for.

If they did find his father, would Frederick even recognize his son? Maybe it didn't matter. They'd take a page from the captain of the *Lagon*, find somewhere that would accept them for who they were and make the contributions they could to its future. Nortelon wasn't so bad—his mother could be happy there if his father could return. And with the admiral dead, there'd no longer be a threat hanging over Mama's head.

You won't make it back from this, the voice in his mind seethed. He shut his eyes again, blocking it out. It would be there, waiting for him when he said goodbye to Iellieth in five days, knowing he was seeing her for the last time. Whatever he and Kriega decided—Nortelon or the *Lagon* —their fate was sealed. In all likelihood, he would be leading his crew to their doom.

CHAPTER 10

PERSEPHONIE

On the other side of the fate-storm, the winding threads emptied onto a harsh, windswept land-scape. They had arrived in the Negative Planes. The sky overhead was the color of ash, and the glow of a distant sun cast the landscape in shades of harsh red. Whatever had existed here before, whatever cultures or landscapes this land had once held, had been washed away, leaving only wind-sculpted clay in its wake.

After the battle with the fate spiders, Persephonie and Boss Gilsen had reached an uneasy peace, made easier by the return to the planes—Jezebel and Rennear would no longer provoke danger by being outsiders. "How long is the journey to New Orison?" Persephonie squinted across the barren wastes. A thick, muddy trail wound through piles of clay and sculpted arches. In the distance, small, spiky plants clung to low hillsides.

"Only a few days, borrowed priestess."

Her reputation among the muster remained strained, though a few of their members, particularly the family she'd saved, had taken to presenting her with small tokens of thanks. She'd already had to empty her pockets once of her growing collection of carved totems and treasured crystals. Before using any of them, she would clear their energy with smoke, asking Cassandra to wash away the clinging shadows.

She did not tell her companions that she feared what Datha and her brothers would think when they learned where she had gone. She had sent her shadow raven to her datha a few days after receiving his, but she had not had time to send a second and tell him of her plans. If she had, would they come after her? Datha would not risk the muster on such a dangerous quest, but it would be equally dangerous for him, her brothers, and Velkan to set out on their own without the protection of the rest of the muster.

The gray clouds stretched on overhead. "I have never traveled to the Negative Planes. I wasn't sure what to expect." The disappointment weighed down her voice. The patches of darkness across the Shadowlands were frightening, as were some of the wilds of the Brightlands, but the liveliness of such places captivated her. She'd expected something similar with the location of the saudad's promised homeland. Anything, really, besides a wasteland.

"Hmm." Gilsen crossed his short arms over his belly. "In the making of New Orison, fashioning a home, certain . . . sacrifices had to be made. Once established, the magical pull of New Orison itself, erhm, leeches nutrients and life from the surrounding region." Gilsen thumped his hand against the back of her shoulder. "The good news is, the fate threads have brought us close to home, no?"

Persephonie stared back at him, mouth ajar. The wind tossed clay-tinged dust into her mouth, forcing her to cough and breaking off her conversation with Gilsen. Rennear limped to her side, his jaw clenched tight, a waterskin in hand. Gilsen had returned to the front of the muster by the time she recovered.

Two hours into their journey through the clay, the horses plodding slowly along and wheels sticking in mud, Persephonie was back in the wagon, stitching masks for herself, Jezebel, and Rennear. There she stayed for most of the next three days, massaging the damaged muscles of Rennear's leg and glancing out for a sight of this promised sanctuary for her people. Juliet paced nervously down the length of the crowded wagon, alternately hopping from her lap to Jezebel's to Rennear's.

Finally, something new appeared on the horizon—a strange blue dome loomed out of the endless fields of clay. Masked runners braved the mud alongside the road. "Getting near now," one of them said in answer to Persephonie's questions. "We've ordered a slower muster out of the way and should be there by nightfall."

The mention of the other muster piqued Persephonie's curiosity. In his most recent communication to her, Datha had mentioned that the muster led by his good friend, Boss Emil, had not arrived at their appointed meeting place. She knew he feared they would be yet another muster to have disappeared without a trace. But was it possible Boss Emil's muster was here, in the Negative Planes?

The other muster had been forced off the road to make room for Gilsen's muster to pass them. Their already caked wheels would be further damaged by the near-impassable mud along the side of the road.

Most of the families of the other muster sheltered inside their wagons, though a few looked on from behind the narrow visors of their masks and headscarves. At the front of the caravan, a tall, broad-shouldered man glared at the passing muster, arms crossed over his chest. Three younger men matched his posture beside him—one tall and gangly, one similarly built but on a smaller scale, and the third lean and muscular.

Even with the masks, she would know their silhouettes anywhere.

"Datha!" Persephonie squealed. She leapt off the front of the wagon before the driver could call the horses to a halt.

Her datha straightened at the sound of Persephonie's voice. The moment her feet landed on the red, dusty earth, he tugged free the scarf he wore as a mask to cover his mouth and nose, knelt, and opened his arms wide.

Persephonie sprinted over the mud-caked earth, clay flying behind her feet, and launched herself into her father's arms.

Datha scooped her up and hugged her tightly against his chest. His laugh echoed through both his body and hers as he spun her about and called for her brothers and Velkan to celebrate his Sephie's return.

A few wagon-lengths beyond her father's position at the head of the muster, the wagon she'd been traveling in came to a stop. Jezebel leapt down to help the driver guide the wagon off the narrow road so the last few wagons of Boss Gilsen's muster might move beyond them. Her brothers Felix and Stefan shoved at one another to be the first to get to her. Felix's wide smile carved new contours in the dust covering his mask, and Stefan had somehow grown even taller in their months apart.

Velkan hovered just out of arm's reach, his dark eyes searching. She rushed over to embrace him as Stefan let her go, and Velkan held her tight, his hand pressed into her hair. "I am relieved to see you," he murmured, his voice barely audible beyond the howl of the wind and the groan of mud-caked wheels spattering the edges of the road as the last of Boss Gilsen's muster, save the wagon that had carried them, wound their way to the pale blue dome in the distance, the promised New Orison.

"I am glad to see you as well, Velkan." Persephonie pulled away before he could cup the side of her face. She would have enough explaining to do to acquaint her family and muster with Rennear and Jezebel, and she didn't want to cause Rennear undue distress in his still-weakened state.

Jezebel bowed their head to the driver, thanking and dismissing them—they would find Gilsen once inside the dome.

"Datha," Persephonie called as she stepped free of Velkan's embrace, "there are two someones I want you to meet."

"Two?" Her father did not hide his mirth at her declaration. "You are even more your mother's daughter than I thought!"

For a moment, Persephonie's delight flickered, thinking of her mother's most recent paramour, but thank Cassandra, her datha was too busy craning his neck beyond her brothers to make out the dust-covered figures of Rennear, Jezebel, and Juliet to notice.

Rennear had draped his arm over Jezebel's shoulder, and the fae held him up with their arm around his waist. Rennear stood as straight as he was able on his good leg. The other rested straight out and to the side. Juliet perched before them, daintily licking her upraised front paw.

His transformation and fighting along the threads had

slowed the healing process, as had being confined to the wagons on the road to New Orison. The werewolf-patron-guard was not used to resting.

Persephonie hurried over to them, supporting Rennear opposite Jezebel. A few quick words from her datha were enough to see an alarmed Rennear scooped up from the ground and placed in the back of her datha's wagon. They folded the lower bed down and braced his back against the stacked shelves where Persephonie had always kept her scarves. Juliet settled herself at the foot of the mattress, curling into a fluffy fox sphere.

"They're still there," Stefan said with a smile, indicating her scarf cabinet and elbowing Persephonie in the side as she crawled in to sit beside Rennear on the lower folding bunk.

"Do not say anything important until I return," Cassian called from the back of the wagon as Velkan and Felix sized up Jezebel and climbed into the wagon after them.

Persephonie murmured introductions to Rennear and Jezebel, both of whom studied the wagon's interior with wide eyes.

"Who painted the ceiling?" Jezebel whispered, awe touching their voice.

Seeing her blush in response, Rennear took Persephonie's hand in his.

"Sephie did," Velkan said, his voice sharp enough to make Jezebel flinch away from him as they settled opposite Persephonie and Rennear on the narrow bench that ran the length of the wagon. Velkan hadn't taken his eyes off of Persephonie's hand in Rennear's. His gaze was as fierce as her datha's had been as he'd watched the other muster pass them by.

Beside her, Rennear rolled his shoulders back. Persephonie squeezed his hand tighter, bidding him not to concern himself with Velkan's jealousy. She had mentioned Velkan to Rennear but not in great enough detail for Rennear to know what they had once meant to each other. It felt longer ago than it was, in any case.

All around them, the wagon jostled as Datha and the drivers sought to pull first their wagon and then the others out of the muck that had condensed along the edges of the worn, red road.

Rennear's mouth tightened into a thin line, and he gripped the top of his thigh. Persephonie supported him as best as she was able and propped a second blanket under his leg. "I am meeting your family much sooner than I had believed possible," he remarked with a smile as he adjusted his back against the bench.

Persephonie grinned back and shifted her own shoulders to tuck herself against Rennear's side.

Datha swung himself up onto the back of the wagon and called up to the driver. "I'll be the one to lead us into whatever hellhole we've landed ourselves in," Datha said with a grimace as he thumped the dust from his sleeves, boots, and pants before he climbed inside. The middle passageway, meticulously swept clean multiple times a day during normal traveling conditions, was covered with the same fine red dust that coated every other surface in the world beyond New Orison.

A worried look passed between Felix and Velkan. "Do you think the city itself will be like this, Datha?" Felix asked.

"Bah." Datha waved his hand. "A few hours more and we shall see, but I've no better way of answering you now than when we landed here three days ago with nothing but this wretched road to guide us."

Persephonie smiled appreciatively at her older brother, who had thoughtfully addressed her father in the common tongue so that Jezebel and Rennear might understand. Gilsen had explained the settlement . . . feeding off the surrounding region, but he had not described the landscape of New Orison itself. She would keep what she had learned to herself for now.

"Daughter, please, proceed in telling us about your friends here, and then you can tell your datha all about your adventures."

He nodded as she introduced Rennear and Jezebel. The romantic connection between herself and Rennear she trusted was obvious, though her family's recent run-ins with werewolves made her wait to reveal that aspect of Rennear's story. And of Jezebel's presence, she said simply, "Cassandra saw fit to connect Jezebel's path with mine." The fae had said little more than Apollo had appointed them to protect her and help her along her path.

She clasped her hands beneath Juliet's thin, furry shoulders and angled the fox's head and arms toward her datha. "And Juliet and I found each other fleeing the guards in Andel-ce Hevra." There would be more time, in the coming days, to acquaint her datha with the intricacies of her journey. She wanted to tell him about the castle in the mountains first and the camp they had come across.

But at the moment, Datha was only interested in news about her mother. Persephonie answered in general terms, trying to avoid the particulars of the relationship between Esmeralda and Aylin.

"So your mother isn't seeing anyone now, then?"

Felix caught her eye and hid his smile from their father.

Datha had an enduring place in his heart reserved exclusively for Esmeralda, but her mother would never settle down long enough for the pair of them to reunite.

After a few hours of travel over the rough roads, their driver called back from the front of the wagon, "We are getting close now, Boss."

Her brothers and Velkan murmured their curiosity and drew into a line behind Datha to climb their way up into the front of the wagon.

"Ah—" Cassian corrected them, gesturing to her. "A few months without your sister, and you forget all I have taught you?"

Persephonie glanced at Jezebel, who nodded toward the front of the wagon, and Rennear squeezed her hand. "Go on. We'll be alright here. We caused excitement enough on the way, and I've no desire to spark a repeat occurrence while we're still recovering from the last one."

Without glancing at Velkan, Persephonie planted a kiss on Rennear's cheek and climbed past her brothers and out the window into the front of the wagon. She balanced in the corner on Datha's far side so there would be room enough for all of them to be able to witness their entrance into New Orison.

The large blue dome shone brightly in sharp contrast to the twilight of their surroundings, as though it contained a setting sun somewhere inside rather than the star-studded blanket that had been cast over the red earth. No words passed between the five of them—in all their travels, they had never witnessed something like this.

There was a scratching at the front door of the wagon and Juliet slipped through and leapt into Persephonie's arms. "Do you know what we're looking at?" she whispered into the fox's fur. Juliet stared back at her, implacable as ever. "I'll take that as a yes," Persephonie concluded, returning her attention to the blue dome, larger even than the tallest tower in all of Andel-ce Hevra. At least from the outside, it appeared that the whole of the city could fit inside.

Vague shapes and colors appeared through the pale blue dome, as though Persephonie was staring through a glittering waterfall.

Boss Gilsen's muster had disappeared inside and were no longer visible from the road. Despite their training, the horses stamped nervously, their agitation evident at the strange sight before them.

Datha soothed the horses and called back encouragement to the drivers behind them, addressing the muster from the front of their wagon, his head held high. "For days we have been asking questions among ourselves. Beyond this wall of blue, we will find the answers. And in the finding of them, we will stick together."

Murmurs of assent rippled along the chain of wagons. Persephonie could imagine the drivers echoing Datha's movements, settling the horses, preparing their families. As an added precaution, everyone tucked the wandering children inside the wagons in the center of the column so they would have the protection of those in front and behind.

Datha looked between his children and Velkan. "Ready?" he asked, raising one brow above the others.

Her brothers and Velkan nodded.

"Ready, Datha," Persephonie answered.

She murmured a blessing of Cassandra over them as they approached, her gaze fixed on the wall of blue.

At the base of the wall where it met the road, a ripple began, like a scarf caught in the breeze. It grew taller, stretching wider as well, forming a large archway before them, wide enough for five or more wagons to traverse abreast. The sparkling blue parted as a curtain, revealing wide open, rolling green fields with the grass-tips painted gold in the fading light. The road continued, though the red clay gave way to a worn dirt path, perfectly compacted for wagon travel. In the distance, a herd of sheep grazed before a collection of wagons and, in the valley at the base of the rolling hills, was a town. Glowing lanterns shone out from the town's narrow, winding roads as the twilight that had already fallen beyond the dome settled over the verdant landscape within it.

Boss Gilsen's muster had wound their way off the road and along the hillsides to the left. They had sent a few riders on horseback to speak with the town officials, the column of riders a contrasting line of torches and the dark silhouettes of horses carving their way to the town. After conferring with Felix, Datha said he would consider doing the same but not until they had found a place to stop and rest, most likely waiting until dawn. He brought the drivers near to himself, gathering in a circle so he would not have to raise his voice. "We have traveled many days on perilous terrain, and while it warms our hearts to see so many of our fellows gathered about, we should not let down our guard, not until we know for certain where we are and whom we are among."

The drivers nodded in accord. They lit the lanterns along the tops of the wagons and distributed torches among the muster scouts, her brothers and Velkan among them. The scouts rode out to select a camping ground a few hillsides over from where they'd arrived, following the muster's protocols for traveling and settling in darkness.

"Do you think they were expecting us, Datha?"

Cassian was surveying the terrain, his arms crossed over his chest. "I know not, Sephie, though I wish I did. What we *do* know is that we were not invited here in a traditional sense, nor did we come of our own accord. But if this is where Cassandra's threads have led us, then let us make our way as best we might."

As they traveled over the dusk-hued hills, the wonder of New Orison began to sink over Persephonie, trickling like a buried mountain stream into her bones. For there to be so many of their people in one place—muster upon muster dotting the hillsides, lanterns glowing from wagon clumps as far as she could see . . . "Incredible," Persephonie sighed to herself. The sight was more beautiful than she had imagined it could be.

"Was the first Orison like this, Sephie?" Stefan wondered aloud to her in Saudad as they made camp at the top of the hillside the scouts had selected.

Persephonie blinked to clear her watering eyes. "I like to think so," she whispered, reverence to see so many of their people in one place softening her voice. "I do wonder if they would have known how magical it truly is to be gathered all together, after so many years of being scattered about the planes without a true home beyond the one we bring with us."

"I did not know there were so many of our people left," Datha murmured. Felix nodded beside him.

"We have been thinking for years our numbers were disappearing," Velkan added. "And now we know where everyone went."

Persephonie surveyed the rolling hills. Beyond the town nestled in the valley she'd first noted, on a distant hillside was a sprawling vineyard, the space between the rows cloaked in shadow. She could imagine saudad pickers wandering between the vines in the light of day.

Between their muster and the larger valley settlement, in clumps along the nearest hillsides were collections of what might once have been wagons. Thatched roofs had been erected between them, forming a few shelters and covered pathways, a muster transformed into a spiraling tiny village of its own.

"Datha"—Persephonie wetted her lips, wanting to be sure of her words before she spoke them aloud—"I do not see many true wagons."

Her father frowned as he studied the hillsides anew. For so many of their people to be gathered in one place, there should be roads and pathways leading from one muster to the next, or an appearance of rotation among the settlements. 'It is not our lot to remain in one, stagnant place,' Datha had told her often as a little girl. 'Cassandra's people are like the waters—our movements grant us life.'

"Nor do I, Sephie," Datha answered her, a frown gathering shadows across his brow. "Nor do I." They settled in for the night, making camp as quickly as they could. On the morrow, they would begin uncovering the secrets of the dome they'd found.

Datha appointed a contingency of riders to announce them in the valley town the next morning, what they assumed was New Orison itself, the most sensible next course of action he could see. It was strange enough that they had arrived at twilight and no visitors from the nearby muster-villages had yet come to visit, nor had the town sent anyone out to them. A few times in her life, they had run across a muster only known to one of the elders, especially those with the widest circling routes, but even then, the traditions of hospitality and welcome had held.

Felix and Velkan were among those whom Datha dispatched, much to Stefan's dismay. "You see to your babu," Datha ordered before her younger brother had the chance to complain. He sighed, head hung low as he went to find their grandmother among the clumps of their muster, groups of friends swirling and unraveling only to gather again in a new formation across the hillside as everyone settled into their new location. This, at least, hadn't changed.

While Persephonie helped her datha set up their own camp, several childhood friends came to meet Rennear and Jezebel, newcomers in the muster being relatively rare in the traveling life of the saudad.

"I reckon I am up to capturing almost one in five words of Saudad," Rennear observed as Persephonie returned from one such small gathering of question-bearers.

Persephonie grinned at him as she tossed a heavy quilt she'd toted from the back of the wagon across the line Jezebel had hung between their wagon and the next. A cloud of red dust shuddered off the quilt as it settled on the line. "If those words are 'dashing' and 'handsome' then yes, you are doing masterfully."

Jezebel raised an eyebrow, sensing something else lurking beneath Persephonie's affected ease. "Are you certain those words are not 'stranger,' 'outsider,' or 'dangerous'? That is what I heard."

She shook her head. "You worry too much, and there are some, even in my muster, whose opinions are not worth considering deeply. They would prefer the pair of you to be bandits or spies rather than friends, especially friends of mine."

She'd told Rennear how she'd grown up an outsider among the children of her muster, aside from her brothers and Velkan. And though some of those she'd traveled with as a child had moved on to other musters, it seemed the stories about her and her strange habits, her traveling beyond saudad circles, had spread to the few new partners and friends who had come into her muster's numbers during her most recent absence.

Datha would say that, given time, they would come to accept Rennear and Jezebel just as assuredly as they had accepted her.

Rennear caught her hand before she could slip past to retrieve the next quilt. "I do sense unease in the camp," Rennear muttered, his voice low enough that only she and Jezebel would hear. "I smell . . . concern." He sniffed at the air. "Your father would feign confidence, but he believes something is wrong. What are they waiting for?"

"I have been wondering this as well," Jezebel added before Persephonie could demur.

Persephonie rocked from heel to toe and back, consciously avoiding tucking her hands around her waist. She did not like feeling the need to hide things from Rennear to protect him and her muster both. How much simpler things had been before Aylin's attack against Andel-ce Hevra, before they had guided the Untamed into the hills and met Boss Gilsen. Before Rowan had told her of the wheels.

She sensed too the centrality of the promise of New Orison. Rennear and Jezebel had no way of understanding what such a place would mean to her people, and so they could not fathom the possible danger they were in by virtue of being outsiders. It was not a characteristic they could change or help. It had been hard enough to convince Boss Gilsen's muster to allow Jezebel and Rennear upon the threads, and they had nearly lost a wagon and several saudad as a result. "We will know more when the riders return," Persephonie said. Before then, there was little sense in worrying over the unknown.

Rennear held fast to her arm. "Darling." The reassurance was plain in his voice—we are only trying to help.

Tears welled in her eyes once more. This was the first day in weeks he had been relatively free from pain, and here they were trying to avoid an argument before her entire muster as she waited on her brother and Velkan's return. "People look to me," Persephonie murmured, glancing about. "Because they look to my datha, and he trusts me. I will tell you more as I can but, for now, we stand strong, and we wait."

CHAPTER 11

BRISERAS

The small fire in the center of Loire's Glade crackled, sending sparks up toward the dark gray clouds overhead. Jorgan, Tybalt, and Loire had gathered around the fire already as Briseras and Vera approached from the creek. Briseras joined them at the fire and spread a blanket for Vera behind her. The wolf settled down, tucking her nose into the fluff of her tail.

Upon her return with the nobleman the day before, Loire had received Jorgan more openly than Briseras would have guessed—if he had gained Briseras's trust, the fae had said, then he would have that of the glade as well. Besides, her partner sensed no malice in his bones.

The fae's approval was sufficient for Tybalt's as well and so shortly after Briseras's return, Loire had begun Jorgan's treatment which left him in a deep, dreamless slumber, the ghost hovering close by his side in vigil.

While he'd slept, she and Tybalt had outlined the next stage of their plan to hunt down Nassarq. Tybalt had ascertained that the leszi had migrated to another part of its territory. The elf completed the search the two of them had begun of the area before Loire found them, searching fruitlessly for signs of Nassarq or the Blessed Father. Though the fae was knowledgeable about Steymhorod's history and the wonders of her precious Diannan, the fae was disappointingly unaware of the happenings beyond her glade.

The pair of them agreed that the nobleman and ghost were their best chance of charting a direct route to the vampire's hidden tower. Briseras, Jorgan, and the ghost would retrace the nobleman's steps following his escape from Nassarq's tower, and Teela would attempt to show Briseras where the tower's hiding place was. In case the ghost was listening, Briseras didn't say aloud the secret promise of her plan—since the nobleman had escaped from the tower, there was a chance Nassarq would seek to capture him again. Jorgan was the perfect lure.

Meanwhile, unless Otto arrived before Tybalt set out, the elf would return to the Vale and add to the request for aid Otto had flown there that they needed a contingency of warriors to assault Nassarq's tower and overcome its defenses. The elven rangers did not easily stir from their woods, Tybalt explained, but he would try to convince them. "Loire believes you are an asset to the cause of the Sisters, and the Vale would see their rule returned."

Jorgan had finally awakened around dusk, stiff but clear-headed. Briseras paced twice to the creek and back while Tybalt engaged in pleasantries. The elf told the nobleman of his role within the Vale, how he and Briseras had met in the Ring of Light. He was concluding the tale of the leszi they'd encountered in the woods before reaching Loire's Glade as Briseras drew near. She could wait no more.

Briseras fixed the nobleman in her gaze. "I'm ready."

Jorgan tilted his head to the side. "Oh?"

"Yes." Briseras nodded firmly. "How did you become imprisoned in Nassarq's tower? Arrive here from Azuria? The lot of it."

The ghost floated out of Jorgan's shoulder and hovered beside him by the fire.

The nobleman glanced at the ghost. Its over-large eyes widened as it stared into the flames. "You don't have to stay if the retelling will be too painful for you."

The ghost sniffled, and Briseras stifled a sigh. Had she ever witnessed such codependence between a parasite and its host before? "I'll visit the fae's partner in the woods."

Loire gracefully unfolded herself from the fireside. "I'll accompany you."

Jorgan waited for Loire and the ghost to slip between the trees before beginning his tale. Away from his lingering, undead fiancée, the nobleman's shoulders relaxed and the clinging shadows fell from his face. Did he know the weight he carried for the spirit or had he not yet uncovered that particular aspect of his burden?

The nobleman met her appraising gaze. "I see the calculation in your eyes. Am I a clever, escaped prisoner or a trap from the vampire waiting to spring shut?"

Across the fire, Tybalt stiffened.

"And do you even know yourself?" Briseras added, barely speaking above the crackle of the flames. There was something soothing about having the question spoken aloud—she wouldn't have guessed that.

"It was Teela who engineered my release, Teela who patiently studied the guards, their movements, and worked out a way for me to be free." He looked off to where the ghost had disappeared into the forest. "She didn't give up hope, long after I already had."

Hope—a subject she and Rajas had argued over in the past. He'd claimed the vampire's bite had changed her, had sucked away her belief in their cause. But what cause had they been fighting for? In Tor'stre Vahn, ridding the wilds of terrors so deemed by the priests and senators of Andelce Hevra, the same entities who had rounded up practitioners like her mother and grandmother, who had seen those with promise, like her, raised in captivity. And when they'd snuck away to Caldara, Rajas's one purpose had been finding Fhaona, a mentor whose tracks had long grown cold or had been too skillfully hidden for even Briseras to track her.

"What happened?" Tybalt asked. "Tragedy hangs heavy about you both. What brought you into the vampire's clutches in the first place?"

Briseras tried not to groan as the nobleman explained how he and the ghost had met—while Teela had still been living—how his family had forbidden the match due to her common birth. He'd been sent away only to learn a few months later that she'd married his brother-in-law instead. "Nassarq." Jorgan spat the name as a curse toward the fire. "My sister's husband's brother, who received the estate where I grew up when my sister married."

"No!" the elf gasped, completely immersed in the nobleman's story. He searched about worriedly for the ghost as Jorgan revealed that Teela had died shortly after the nuptials.

"'She's had an accident,'" Jorgan said, imitating Nassarq's low drawl, "said it calm as could be, 'riding alone in the woods. She's dead.' I tore myself from the castle and rode for the mountains. Her ghost found me near the edge of the estate. Tried to warn me. I heard a twig snap, to my right, and then the vampire was upon me."

He shuddered, no doubt recalling that first singe of cold—venom and fangs chomping into his sinews. "I'm a little unclear as to the rest. How I ended up here, when he moved me from one prison to the next."

"But Teela knows?" Briseras asked, trying to keep her voice neutral.

"Aye." He poured a measure of whiskey into his cup. The brightness of his gaze had started to dull. "Or if anyone does, it would be her."

Briseras wasn't in the habit of letting the undead live, whether it was the matter of severing the bond between ghost and host or plunging a stake through a vampire's heart, but she'd willingly given herself to Olya's tracking before she left St. Sebastian, and there were times her mind wandered back to the vampire's teeth brushing her skin even now.

She sipped her own whiskey. Much like the pepperiness of all the wine in Steymhorod she'd tried thus far, there was something curious about the whiskey, a dryness on the back of her tongue and, beneath the earthiness of the peat, an herb she didn't recognize. Was it something particular about the soil of Steymhorod itself? A question for another time.

Briseras studied the nobleman closely as he swirled the amber liquid at the bottom of his wooden cup. There was no hesitation in his speech, no halting of words, either of which might have indicated a ghostly influence over his mind. This lack didn't mean his ghostly paramour wasn't holding him in its sway, but the arrangement between them might be more consensual than those she'd previously encountered. Or, at the very least, whatever unfinished business the ghost still had couldn't be resolved without the nobleman by its side. "Your ghost can remain

—for now." If Teela had special knowledge of Nassarq's whereabouts and tower, the workings of his prisons, she meant to find out.

Jorgan chuckled into his wooden goblet. "Generous of you. It will be a relief to know I don't need to watch over both shoulders in this wretched place."

Briseras almost smiled. "Oh, you'll still need to do that."

"I know what you're thinking." Jorgan eyed her over the rim of his cup. Firelight glinted against the hazel of his irises, darkening their hue. His gaze was steady, considered.

"That you hold your drink better than the elf." Briseras gestured to Tybalt's snoring form on the opposite side of the fire. Half a glass left him composing songs of Loire's beauty and bounty. A full cup, and he fell right to sleep.

"Heh, that's true, though not what I meant." He drained his cup again and settled his weight back on the stump, wrists resting loosely atop his knees.

"Well enough. If you're not a trap, if you truly escaped the tower, now that you're out, what is it you hope for?" She nodded in the direction the ghost had floated before it disappeared between the trees of Loire's grove. "Some sort of resurrection ritual? Will you remain paired with a ghost for all of your days?"

The nobleman winced and searched the trees himself before he answered. "I can't say I have much of a plan, being honest. It remains unclear to me where precisely we are as I've never seen Steymhorod on a map and, yes, I made an extensive study of geography in the past." A white grin flashed across his face. "You finding me has already brought an interesting deviation to what I expected. I thought at any moment, wolves, zombies, a vampire's spawn, would track me down and finish Nassarq's work."

"Vera is still thinking about it." Briseras reached down and scratched the soft fur along the top of Vera's skull. The wolf sighed and adjusted the set of her chin on her paws. "But as far as the rest of Steymhorod goes, you were right to be concerned."

They sat in amicable silence as the fire crackled and one of Loire's favorite owls hooted in the far reaches of the grove. What Jorgan had said about Teela holding onto hope drifted as a wave across her mind. As it rolled in, she thought of Lavinia's tireless search for her sister. As it receded, she turned to herself and whatever Steymhorod had awakened within her, a latent sense she'd yet to fully uncover.

The wave came again and Briseras knew what to do next and who would have answers, perhaps not to the questions she sought, but answers all the same. "Come with me, there's someone I want to show you."

She rose and followed an increasingly familiar path away from the fire, through the damp undergrowth, across a burbling creek, and up a steep, rocky slope to a waterfall.

"Are we going for a midnight swim?" Jorgan called behind her as he paused to catch his breath.

Briseras grinned. "In a matter of speaking." As the nobleman finally caught up to her, out of breath and still weakened from serving as a vampire's meal for weeks if not months, Briseras ducked beneath the waterfall.

The pounding water immediately sent chills over her, but over the last few days, she'd found that the effect helped her body to calm, to embrace the sanctity of this space, where Everett's spirit had taken up residence.

She slicked her hair back and waited for the nobleman.

He emerged on her side of the waterfall soon enough, grumbling about his damp clothes.

"Come on." Briseras strode to the back of the cave.

Jorgan surprised her by latching onto her arm. She jumped and nearly yanked out of his grasp. "Oh, the dark," she murmured. Malthael's attack had sharpened her senses, allowing her to see the intricacies of the cave around her where the nobleman would sense only darkness, the cloak of vampires.

He released a shaky exhale, and his grip loosened slightly.

"Give him a moment," Briseras whispered.

The nobleman hovered close beside her. Memories of Nassarq's prison had widened his eyes and shortened his breath, but he was trying to contain himself, Briseras sensed, for her sake.

A star-like pattern flickered to life against the back wall of the cave, constellations flaring in and out of being as Everett drew his spirit into physical form.

Jorgan stared, open-mouthed, at the shimmering ghost of the folklorist. "You—but—"

Everett's form wasn't as solid as Teela's—Briseras wasn't being haunted. Rather than a floating shimmer, his image took shape against the relief of the rock, like glowing motes of crystal awakened by his presence.

"Save your accusations and listen." Briseras didn't speak above a whisper but there was no need. The cave's echo somehow drowned out the pounding of the falls behind and amplified their voices.

She met Everett's eyes. Each time she'd appeared here over the last four days, she'd expected some sort of condemnation from his spirit, agitation that she hadn't been able to save him. Instead, he offered comfort.

"I wondered why my spirit lingered." Everett studied the nobleman and bowed his head. "And now I see."

"See . . . what?" Jorgan asked.

The folklorist smiled. "The final piece. Briseras can show you in my journal, my work, charting the stories of the hillsides you know well. I sense them, behind your eyes. But new hillsides will call to you, on behalf of the woman you love, before long." Everett chuckled to himself. "Forgive me, speaking in riddles. It is difficult, dwelling between the planes like this. The puzzles fit together differently than one might have guessed. My riddles are worse as I hadn't known what I was waiting for."

Everett turned to Briseras. "You have my journal still?"

She nodded, pressing her hand against the pouch at her side. During their time in the grove, Tybalt had helped her to fashion an attachment by her hip for Everett's journal. He'd been surprised by her request, but his design allowed her full movement and access to the arrows she kept in the small quiver along her thigh. Having it near at hand helped her feel more at ease, lent a sense of purpose to her hunt, one she hadn't realized had been lacking before she passed through the portal of blood.

"Ophelia could tell you better than I—it is she who has wrought this particular twist of fate, after all. Some of the puzzle remains beyond my sight, but I was right to believe that you are at the center of it, Briseras Ravisthinia. A special fate was carved for you, for this." Everett's spirit turned to study Jorgan. "And in secret, Ophelia forged a second, special fate." The spirit returned his stare to Briseras. "In this, even more than before, she wanted the choice to be yours, huntress." Everett smiled. "And so it will be."

Briseras gazed after Everett's spirit as he faded into waterfall mist and slunk back into the starry rock. The sparkling mites of rock across the back surface of the cave winked out, as though the sun had suddenly set upon their glow, leaving her and Jorgan in darkness.

She rubbed her hand across her chest, feeling the folklorist's absence from her side. Briseras sensed that this would be the last time the two of them communed in this way—he would pass on and join James, having fulfilled whatever had kept him loosely tethered to her side. Without speaking further, she turned away from the cave wall and ducked back beneath the waterfall.

As she tossed back her hair, flinging droplets of water from the sky, she hid her face from Jorgan, straightened her lips, composed herself. If Everett's spirit had truly passed on, its bewildering benediction given, it was time for her to continue on as well.

"Who was he?" Jorgan asked as he ducked back beneath the falls and followed her along the path. He jogged to keep pace behind her.

"Someone else I couldn't save."

The nobleman caught her wrist.

Briseras tugged to pull her hand away, but he held it firm.

He raised her arm, waiting for her gaze to meet his. "Take it from someone who ought to know—I'm sure you did all you could and, whatever more we might wish, you can't really ask for more than that."

"I can." Another yank and her hand was free. Their silence held until they returned to camp.

Briseras curled up on her mat around Vera, who formed a perfect wolf-circle, face tucked into her tail. Everett's words echoed through her mind. How had

Ophelia once again manipulated her fate? And what did it mean, that this time, she would have more of a choice?

Around the pain gripping her chest, she sent a benediction of her own to Everett, wishing him peace as his spirit found James in Astralei, where the lovers might dwell, forever, together.

CHAPTER 12

IELLIETH

"I can't believe you're finally going to do it." Teodric leaned his back and elbows on the deck railing beside Iellieth, the ocean wind tugging at the sun-bleached strands of his hair. "It seems like for as long as I can remember, we've been trying to find your father, wondering what he was like."

Iellieth traced the golden threads of her amulet, twirling it between her fingers. Somewhere, out over the blue horizon, her father dwelled in a land she'd only read about. "Did he leave the amulet with my mother on purpose? I remember that was one of our most closely debated questions. Scad was always very concerned about whether or not my father would like him."

Teodric laughed. "As though your father would have any choice." His gaze fell, and his expression clouded. "I remember wondering the same, once upon a time. So much has changed since then." He flicked his head to the side, tossing the hair back from his face. "I want to still be that young, optimistic nobleman who was taken from your side. But I cannot see a kingdom that would send away my family on your stepfather's whim in the same way I did then. Nor can I pretend to have not experienced these last several years upon the sea. The admiral—"

The line of his mouth thinned, and Teodric glared up at the sails. "There's something I need to confess to you."

His mood had shifted so suddenly. A roiling storm descended upon him whenever he mentioned this pirate admiral Syleste. And when he didn't share his thoughts aloud, which happened far more often now than when they'd been in Io Keep together, was the storm still raging internally?

"I want to tell you how I became the captain of the *Queen*. Why . . . why what Kriega and I have to do after we take you to the Realms is so important. It is bigger than finding my father, though that presses sharply upon my heart." Teodric kept his gaze upon the horizon as he told her of the orc settlement Syleste had sent them to raid, believing they might be in possession of a valuable magical artifact she needed. "Only they weren't orcs." His breathing hitched, and his knuckles tightened against the railing. "Syleste had bewitched my sight. She'd altered my memory before. It was an innocent settlement we raided, small, not full of bloodthirsty pirates like I had thought." His jaw clenched, shoulders tightened.

Iellieth fought the urge to take his hand. The were-wolves she'd killed, transformed back into ordinary men and women, flashed before her mind. The faces of the *Fairwind* followed soon after.

"We slaughtered them," Teodric said finally. His shoulders fell with the words. "We took one captive. It's how I found out what had truly happened, speaking to her. Syleste tried to alter my memory again, using the captive's magic to help her somehow. She brought us to Nortelon, where my mother lives."

Iellieth gripped her amulet as though it was her heart. Lady Aurelia Adhemar, Teodric's mother and her mother's dearest friend, banished across the sea because of her stepfather's cruelty. She stepped toward Teodric.

"She threatened my mother." His throat bobbed. "So on her command, I killed the captain who had once been in charge of this ship. I recommissioned it the *Amber Queen*. For our first mission, we set out to retrieve one of Syleste's agents, Darcy, from the port at Andel-ce Hevra. We were to return him to Syleste's island and then continue our search for the artifact." Finally he turned back to Iellieth. "But after his attack of Genevieve and the discovery of another werewolf on our crew, we stopped on the island. And that's where we found you."

He had partially turned toward her at the close of his tale. Iellieth slid forward again, wrapping her arms around Teodric's waist, tucking her chest and head against his. She squeezed him closer to her. His breaths grew more ragged, and she tightened her hold. He thought he had to face all he'd done alone, as though somehow he might be able to absolve himself. Tears pricked against her eyes as the dust of truth settled around her. *As though she would condemn him*, just as he had condemned himself.

Iellieth trailed her fingers over his back. The soft linen fibers of his shirt revealed the swell of scars beneath. "Shh," Iellieth soothed. "None of that is your fault."

Teodric tensed, resisting her still.

"Let it go," she whispered.

He slouched forward then, catching her in his arms and holding her against his chest. He clutched the back of her hair, his other arm completely enveloping her, and held her there. A few shaking sobs rattled against her, but Iellieth held firm, tracing the lines of muscle and scars.

Teodric pulled away only a little and gazed down at her. The tears that brightened his eyes and wet his cheeks were matched by her own. "I'm sorry," he whispered. The gleam in his dark brown eyes, the way he stared down at her, Iellieth knew he was referring to more than the story he'd told.

He closed the distance between them and wrapped his arms around her again, the opposite of what he'd done when they kissed in his cabin. "She's taken so much from me, more than I could ever explain. But there are some things not even she can steal." He gestured to the ship's rigging, to the sterncastle deck where his first mate consulted her compass, one hand draped over the wheel. "This is where I belong. I know that now."

Teodric glanced at her once more. His brow furrowed as he studied her expression. "I'm sorry for not being more understanding at first. I believe you, that what you're doing is important. And I'm sorry, too, for needing convincing about your champions' role in this task you must accomplish. I was jealous." He looked away from her again but didn't turn so far aside as to hide his sudden smirk. "I'm sure that won't come as a great surprise. You tend to sense such things."

The wind changed, filling the sails. One of the lookouts cried from the crow's nest, and Iellieth stared down at her hands. A few days ago, Teodric's jealousy would have set sparks fluttering about her stomach. Now? Now she was grateful for the return of their friendship. And her stomach was certainly aflutter, but not the swirling mess it had been. "You were upset. The admiral—she has no right to threaten you or your family. If I could aid you in a rebellion against her, right this moment, I would."

He shook his head. "No, your task is more critical than my personal revenge. Vendetta might be more fair, but still."

GENEVIEVE

Genevieve slipped through the door of the bunk room and made her way up to the deck of the *Amber Queen* like she had each night since they set sail. And just as she had been the past three nights, Iellieth stood with her elbows leaned against the ship's railing, selenite and garnet in the moonlight, staring out over the water.

Genevieve lowered her shoulders and forced calm breaths of the sea air through her lungs before she approached her fellow druid. Their first days together on the island, she had been so focused on Athena, on trying to find some sort of space inside herself where the sailor and Jade could intermingle, could coexist. Of course she had noticed the bright green eyes, the copper flecks tinged silver beneath the glowing moons. She'd studied the waves of Iellieth's thick red hair. But she'd seen too how the druid studied Marcon and Teodric and had retreated to the sanctuary kept inside herself. Who would cast aside a warrior or a captain for a werewolf?

"Do you mind if I join you?" Genevieve spoke softly, her voice matching the lapping waves against the sides of the ship.

Iellieth glanced at her and smiled. She scooted over a

few inches, as though making room for Genevieve along the railing.

Genevieve leaned down beside Iellieth. Her bare arm grazed the linen fabric of Iellieth's tunic. A silent minute passed as they watched the waves. Ripples lengthened the watery reflections of the moons. From what she'd said before, Iellieth had grown up observing the sea and the moons. For Genevieve, they had been constant guides overhead.

She took another deep sigh and forced the question she'd carried with her from the night before. "What are you looking for, out on the water?" Genevieve studied Iellieth's profile against the dark of the sky. Thin clouds drifted over the stars, erasing and revealing the brilliant patterns above.

Iellieth's lips compressed as she considered Genevieve's question. What would they feel like against her skin, the inside of her wrist, her temple, her neck?

"I'm not sure," she answered. Her hands clasped and unclasped over the water. "Part of me hopes that Nerissa will reappear and say that we've chosen the right path forward." Iellieth had told her about the seawolf who had rescued her from Reaga's attack and led her to the island, to Genevieve.

"And the rest of you?"

"Hmm." Iellieth's fingertips traced the lines of her amulet, something she had done often on the island when they practiced their druidry together. "I've spent my life waiting for my father to find me, or hoping I might be able to visit the Realms. And now that's coming true, but with it comes an adventure I could never have imagined." She grasped the amulet. "Marcon and Quindythias, they have done all of this before." Iellieth turned her gaze to meet Genevieve's. Her eyes shone with the prickling of the salty air. "They know how to do all of this, which decisions to make. But all of it is new to me, and I keep choosing wrong." Iellieth sniffled.

Genevieve stifled the urge to embrace her. Someone else might have said that she would figure it out, that everything would be fine. But they had both lost enough to know the falsehood of such claims. That, among other things, is what drew her to Iellieth's side each night.

She looked away from Iellieth's searching eyes and back to the black line of the horizon. "Do you think they know what it's like, to be the only one of your kind?" The words escaped before she could censure them. A glittering edge of bitterness lingered on her tone. But Iellieth's worry for the champions was misplaced. The task Yvayne had set her, had set them both, was larger than the concerns of the elemental warriors.

"I think they know what it is to be alone," Iellieth murmured.

Genevieve pressed her fingertips into her palms. That was a feeling she knew well. "And to want something that will never be yours?" Jade stirred in her chest. She was pressing deeper than she'd intended, exposing too much.

"From what they've told me, I would say it's more being on the precipice of having everything you'd hoped for, only to lose all of it instead."

She nodded. It was a boon of its own to have your desires in sight. For herself, hadn't she always waited on the edge of what she'd hoped for, knowing it could never be hers?

Genevieve jumped as Iellieth grabbed her hand.

"Come on." She tugged for Genevieve to follow her. "Let's see if we can convince Keever to make us a midnight snack."

BRISERAS

Tybalt laid his hands on Briseras's shoulders before they parted. She and Jorgan would retrace the nobleman's steps through the woods. Tybalt would seek reinforcements from the Vale. "So long as you will have me, huntress, I will fight at your side. The Lady Loire says you are destined to restore the Sisters."

"I didn't agree to restoring the Sisters."

The elf shook his head, smiling as though he knew something she didn't. "Not yet, huntress, but you will. Whatever you would have of me, consider it done."

Tybalt stood before Jorgan next, clasping the nobleman's forearm in his bulky hand and pressing his forehead to Jorgan's. "Watch the huntress well," Tybalt said.

Briseras frowned between them. "Of the two of us, it's clearly him who needs the protection."

"Be that as it may"—the elf smiled—"all seasons turn before long." Pleased with his passing of natural wisdom, Tybalt stepped backward away from them, raising his hand overhead in farewell. "We will find each other again, shadow-walker." He held her gaze. "The seasons change more quickly with a catalyst such as yourself around. Take care, my friend." With a nod, he turned and disappeared into the lush greenery of Loire's borders.

Despite the elf's size, he had traversed the dried leaves of the woods soundlessly, a feat the nobleman beside her had yet to manage.

"I can feel your irritation from here," Jorgan said, keeping his face determinedly forward. "I did not ask you to exchange the elf's company for mine. Teela and I could very well travel on our own to find whatever passes for civilization around here."

"If you made it that far"—she paused to ensure he caught her doubts on the matter—"I believe you would be disappointed in what you found." She had enjoyed the hospitality of St. Sebastian well enough. Briseras smirked. Some parts of it very much so. "If there is a region of Steymhorod catering to nobles and their needs, I haven't yet encountered it."

"But hope still remains, doesn't it, of such a place?" Jorgan lengthened his stride, crunching even more loudly upon the leaves.

Vera glared up at him, her loping gait silent on Briseras's other side.

"Had you seen the creature that chased Tybalt and I into Loire's glade, you would not be so flippant about the dangers of the woods nor the roads of Steymhorod."

"You forget where I am coming from," Jorgan quipped back.

Was he aware that he rubbed his neck, or was it a habit that, once formed, would be difficult to break? The wound along his neck was healing quickly after Loire's ministrations, but the scar it left would still likely be substantial. Briseras didn't often reflect thankfully upon Malthael's bite, but at least the vampire's lasting impression was barely visible rather than a tangle of scars.

"True enough," Briseras admitted. "So tell me, is any of this familiar?"

The nobleman halted and his ghost did the same. Though Briseras was still not enthused at the idea of traveling with an undead creature given to possession, she had agreed that Teela would remain safe from her blade and arrows so long as it and Jorgan helped her find Nassarq's tower. Once she searched the tower for Lavinia and Saige and exacted her revenge upon the vampire for Everett's death, she would escort them to a location of their choosing.

"These woods all look the same to me."

Briseras scoffed—why had she believed he would take this seriously when he resorted to joviality so quickly otherwise? "In my experience with such prey, it is only a matter of time before the hunter finds themselves hunted." One of Rajas's first lessons returned to her—*You cannot find that which you fear.* Perhaps that was what prevented the nobleman from remembering, from seeing the details in one part of his environment over another.

Jorgan scanned their surroundings. "I remember the creek. Endless trees and leaves." He indicated the curving line of the creek that meandered deeper into the woods. "Let's try that way."

It was strange—Briseras's instincts nearly always drove her into the wilds, which would keep them continuing along the creek, but in the case of Steymhorod, she kept feeling the pull of the road, as though something lay at its end, some destination beyond the vampire whom she'd sworn to stake. "I think the road holds what we seek."

Jorgan consented, and a few minutes of silence passed

before the nobleman spoke again, "I was surprised when you agreed to saddle yourself with me instead of the burly elf."

Briseras raised an eyebrow in question—as she was growing used to being the case, the nobleman had more to say on the matter.

"I have been reasoning over *why* you have made the choice you have." He raised a finger. "Possibility the first, you believe Teela and I are the best source of information as to the vampire's whereabouts and you wish to discover and kill the vampire all by yourself. Or share the victory with your wolf."

"No."

From the corner of her eye, the nobleman glanced at her, waiting to see if she wished to elaborate. Briseras kept walking.

He raised another finger. "Reason the second, you're tired of the fae's glade and of the elf's company and so you're taking a break before returning to your special planning sessions with them."

"Also no." It wasn't an entirely unenjoyable way of traversing the woods. Was the nobleman self-aware enough to guess the true reason she'd elected to bring him with her rather than simply taking his directions and going without him and his undead companion?

"Very well. Possibility the third . . ."

The pause was so long Briseras turned from her survey of the woods to examine the nobleman. Had the ghost's control finally taken complete hold?

His hazel eyes danced as he smirked. He lowered his voice an octave, leaning toward her. "Possibility the third, you're smitten with me."

"Mmhmm," Briseras said, laughing. "You should proceed to reason four."

"You're sure that's not it?"

Before she could reply, a giant branch from a nearby tree came crashing down through the forest, striking the ground in front of the nobleman and causing him to dive out of the way.

"Gah!" Jorgan cried as he flew through the air, covering his head with his hands.

Briseras crouched low, searching the trees for what could have caused such a disturbance, but no creatures stirred. She sniffed at the air—damp earth and peat moss. Not so unusual, though this part of the Witchwood was drier than the scent catching in her nostrils. All around them, the forest held impossibly still.

She almost convinced herself she caught a third scent on the air, the warmth and sweetness of red summer berries, but that made even less sense than the damp earth and moss. Briseras shook her head and strode over to the nobleman, taking hold of his shoulder. "Come on, just an effect of walking through an enchanted forest."

The way the nobleman scowled as he rose showed that he didn't believe her any more than she did herself.

"Ha," Jorgan sighed after he'd brushed himself off. "At least we didn't panic and embarrass ourselves. Now, where was I?" Jorgan slid to a stop and crossed his arms over his chest. "I know. You believe me to be either a spy from the vampire sent to lure you into a trap or you're using me, a former captive, to bait the vampire yourself."

The first suggestion had occurred to her, but unless the vampire had promised to revive his undead fiancée and Jorgan had believed Nassarq to be capable of such a feat, the possibility seemed unlikely.

She paused mid-step and turned back. "You are much closer."

"Ah-ha!" he crowed. "Now, let's say you're right and I'm a spy. Don't you feel, especially in my present state, that you could gain the upper hand over me and eliminate me if you needed to?"

A slow smile stretched across Briseras's features. The nobleman had a point. Yes, yes she could. But he still hadn't analyzed her true motivation and what it meant for him and his ghost. Would she be willing to let him be taken if it increased the efficacy of her trap?

The answer remained to be seen.

A few hours' travel deeper into the woodland made for little variety in their environment. They were still surrounded by trees, the creek drifting through the hills. They passed through the craggy rocks and cliffsides where she had found the nobleman and his ghost. Briseras had abandoned asking Jorgan which details he remembered, and the ghost as well. They had taken to quietly bickering while Briseras surveyed the environment, but she had few options but to trust that the nobleman would alert her when they encountered familiar terrain once more.

They tracked his footsteps to an intersection between the creek and their path through the forest but, once they'd crossed, the footsteps disappeared. Briseras quickly ruled out the nobleman having traveled up the creek in his injured state—his boots would have been soaked by the time she found him, and they had been dry.

The press of the trees grew thicker as the cloudy morning faded to afternoon. The creek maintained its steady burble, guiding them along.

Vera stopped in her tracks, the hairs along the ridge of her back standing on end. Her wolf lowered her head, creating a flat line from tail to crown. A growl rippled at the back of her throat.

"Get behind me," Briseras murmured to Jorgan. She crouched beside Vera, slowly withdrawing the crossbow from its holster on her thigh.

The nobleman was too absorbed in his argument with the ghost to hear her or notice Vera's signal. Briseras ground her teeth and shot out her arm, barring his forward progress, costing her precious seconds.

Too late, Briseras spied what had set Vera on edge.

A hulking werewolf, spittle flying from its open maw, sprinted toward them from the dense copse of trees ahead. She fired at the creature, one arrow after another, but the bolts ricocheted off its thick hide, making no indent upon its flesh and only serving to anger the creature more.

It was larger than any werewolf Briseras had ever seen. "Don't let it bite you," Briseras ordered. She tossed aside her crossbow and withdrew her twin curved blades from her back.

Behind her, Jorgan did the same. Tybalt had lent him a sword and Loire had outfitted him with armor she'd retrieved from a long-dead soldier she'd trapped in the encircling vines of the glade. The armor would serve him well enough but wasn't strong enough to withstand a bite from so large a creature.

"And if it does?"

Briseras shook her head. She'd seen hunters taken by a werewolf's venom, their fever-ridden bodies bound to a cart, brought to Andel-ce Hevra, and never seen again. Whether they were killed or caged mattered little to her—a return to the city was as sure as a death sentence either way.

"Great," Jorgan sighed.

Before the creature could close with them fully, Briseras sprinted toward it, Vera close at her side. They split apart from one another, forcing the werewolf to choose. It selected her as the larger target and lunged. Briseras slid along the leaves, narrowly avoiding its maw.

She kept a sword up by her shoulder and managed to slash the werewolf's nose as it tried to bite her, but it was even stronger than she'd feared. The force of its attack slowed her to a stop, and she had to roll away, rendering herself vulnerable.

A cry rose behind her—Jorgan had closed with the werewolf, blade raised by his shoulder.

"Look out!" Briseras shouted—he made his attack too hastily. The werewolf batted him with its claws and sent him flying into a nearby tree. Jorgan bounced off its trunk with an *oof*.

So much for an ally to help her and Vera. She returned her attention to her wolf and their target.

The werewolf pawed at the earth, shaking its head as it snarled and prepared to charge Briseras. She and Vera had trained for precisely such an occasion—they rushed simultaneously at the creature. Vera launched herself through the air and snapped her jaw against its neck, snarling and scratching. It reared up, revealing its belly to Briseras.

She slashed across its chest and down its abdomen. The werewolf threw Vera from its neck with a powerful swipe. Briseras froze as her wolf hit the earth and whimpered. She tried to run toward Vera—precisely what Rajas would have told her not to do—when the creature rounded on her, snapping its jaws.

Briseras screamed back at it and rushed forward, blades crossed against her chest. She leapt into the air and spun as the werewolf reared back, trying to claw her out of the sky. Its paw found her side as her blades met its arm. She severed the limb on either side of its elbow, and the werewolf's forearm and elbow joint flopped onto the leaf-covered earth. Blood spurted from the wound as the werewolf howled—they'd be in trouble if its pack answered its call.

She landed with a soft grunt, sliding over the packed layers of leaves and crouching at Vera's side. Her wolf was bruised and somewhat dazed, but Vera's breaths came regularly, her tongue hanging out of her panting mouth. "We're almost through," Briseras murmured.

Behind her, the nobleman shouted her name in warning. Blinded by rage and pain after she'd sliced off its arm, the werewolf was sprinting toward her, its gait hobbled by its missing appendage.

Another shout from the nobleman, and Jorgan launched himself at the werewolf's head, throwing it off balance before it could lunge at her or Vera.

Briseras scrambled to her feet. Jorgan knocked the werewolf onto its side but slid as he tried to stab it, landing right in front of its jaw. The creature gurgled and growled. A single snap of its fangs, and Jorgan screamed— the werewolf captured the whole of Jorgan's thigh in its mouth.

He screamed again as the creature released his thigh, hand clasped to the wound.

Exactly what they didn't need.

Without thinking, Briseras did precisely for the nobleman what he had done for her—she lunged between the werewolf and its prey before the creature could make its killing strike. It caught the top of her arm in its slathering teeth, clamping tight as she spun back toward it. Spots danced in the corners of her eyes but she'd hunted and trained long enough for her instincts to serve her beyond pain.

Flipping her blade around in her hand, she sliced its jugular, releasing a thick flow of blood all over her side. The creature gurgled and groaned, eyes rolling back in its head.

Briseras cried out as it pulled her down, its jaw still fastened around her arm. Impossibly, Jorgan was there beside her, grimacing as he pried open its toothy maw and grabbed her waist, cushioning her as the three of them tumbled to the ground.

CHAPTER 14

PERSEPHONIE

As the riders' silhouettes faded on their path toward the town of New Orison, Persephonie distracted Jezebel and Rennear from their questions about what her muster would do next by teaching them to block the wagon so it would remain stationary. From the edge of the town, clouds of dust rose. Datha called to her—riders were returning.

The column of riders was larger than the one they'd sent out with Felix and Velkan. "They're coming up from New Orison," Persephonie murmured to her datha, the pair of them watching closely from the head of the muster's circle of wagons. She squinted, searching for a familiar figure among the black-clad riders. "I don't see any of our own among them."

Persephonie rushed back to the wagon, finding Jezebel and Rennear just as they emerged from within. "I need both of you to listen to me," she said, out of breath from the growing panic at the center of her chest. "I cannot explain yet, it is more an intuition than anything else. But we still do not know the full truth of where we are or, more importantly, among whom. There were warnings enough with Gilsen's muster." She paused for breath, hoping they would understand.

Jezebel leaned around her, trying to see the incoming riders. Rennear's gaze was focused on her face, his brow furrowed at her distress.

She would have to say it. "I need the two of you to hide."

"What?" Jezebel snapped. They dodged the push of Persephonie's hands and tried to angle further away from her.

"Please," Persephonie urged. Her gaze darted from Jezebel to Rennear. Jezebel had to help her keep him safe while he recovered. Rowan's magic had healed him, brought him back to her. She wasn't going to lose him again within a day of finding her family.

The fae's eyes darkened as they stared out toward the approaching riders. They nodded grimly, and Persephonie sighed. At least one of them understood.

"Why are you asking me to hide?" Rennear protested as Persephonie gave him a small shove toward the back of the wagon. She was careful not to throw off his balance as his leg was still troubling him after the mountainside attack.

"Not to *hide* exactly," Persephonie answered, chewing her lower lip. "Erhm, more to not be *seen*."

Jezebel huffed behind her, either in irritation or amusement, she couldn't tell.

"Darling, those are quite the same thing," Rennear replied, taking advantage of her nearness to wrap his arm around her shoulder.

The lightness in the face of danger, the expression of affection, both were so like the Rennear he had been before Aylin's attack in the square and before the ambush in the mountains that she couldn't help but smile, some of the tension in her chest alleviated by his ease and warmth. "I think the distinction is more about a particular mindset," she teased back. "Now, please," Persephonie begged as she eased Rennear onto the wagon bench, "whatever you hear, whatever happens, stay here and stay hidden."

Rennear nodded, the weariness he'd been disguising settling over his features as he leaned back against the side of the wagon.

Jezebel blocked her way out of the wagon, their arms crossed over their chest. "If I sense you are in danger, I am sworn by oath to Apollo to aid you."

"By the fates," Persephonie muttered under her breath, shoving past the fae. "I will intercede to Apollo on your behalf and explain that for just this once, I need everyone to trust me instead of arguing with each piece of the plan."

She stopped and spun back around—that had been unfair—the situation they were in was not Jezebel's fault. Persephonie squinted up at the fae, their face obscured by the bright blue of the sky behind them. "There is more than my life at stake here, Jezebel." She dropped her head. "My family—I cannot let anything happen to them. Please."

The fae nodded. "I understand," they pronounced and ducked into the wagon with Rennear.

Her companions settled, Persephonie hurried back to her datha's side. The muster had begun to gather for the riders' approach. Several had come believing the riders to be those they had sent, and two dozen more arrived as soon as they realized the riders were strangers to their muster.

Persephonie had to gently push her way to the front,

angling through couples and groups of friends. Datha nodded to the man beside him as Persephonie arrived who scooted over to allow Persephonie room.

Her heart swelled, and Persephonie wrapped her father's waist in a quick hug. However long she'd been gone, Datha always made it clear that she had a place within the muster. And whatever happened next, at least she was here. Home.

Stefan had not yet arrived from tending to Babu—though with unknown riders approaching, he might remain where he was, a final defense for the elderly women gathered at the center of the muster. It was a habit from the fall of the first Orison—ensuring the survival of their stories, their memories, should the worst occur.

The muttering among the muster fell into silence as the column of riders neared. They moved at speed—the blue of the sky caught in the weapons at their sides, an inauspicious sign.

The riders slowed as they approached the muster, fanning out so that they stood side-by-side in a curving line, spread nearly as wide as the gathering of the muster's members upon the hillside. Though they were outnumbered, the riders had the advantage of their horses' height and mobility.

Butterflies danced at Persephonie's fingertips—she would not be the first to mete out violence, but she would defend her family from slaughter.

"Well-met, strangers," the black-clad rider at the center of the procession of nine called out. "The goddess welcomes her weary travelers home."

Datha's eyes flickered but he resisted glaring at the strange greeting. "The muster of Boss Cassian is pleased to find shelter and hospitality here," he said, hewing close to their traditions.

"Ah!" The man looked almost surprised but quickly shielded the expression. "We have heard of you among other recent arrivals. Boss Emil, I believe he was called."

Datha's calm faltered at the past tense, and Persephonie shifted forward, shielding him. The movement earned her a glare from the riders' speaker.

She decided to meet his disapproval with a challenge. "It is a strange greeting you bring to us," Persephonie answered. "I see no gift, and you bear arms as well." She stared openly at the sheathed scimitars along the riders' sides, the bows and arrows tucked among the horses' saddlebags. If the riders truly came in peace and wished to offer them welcome, they would have presented her and her datha with a cask of wine or mead and some other token of friendship.

"Hold your tongue, girl," the leader shot back. "We would hear from the one who leads you."

Datha growled and stepped toward the rider, whose horse began to paw at the earth. "My daughter speaks for me better than any son—who are you that are so lacking in Cassandra's wisdom?"

Others of the muster scowled or nodded in agreement. Persephonie's absence from the community while she spent time with her mother made her different from most of the muster's members, but not being accepted by children when they were young and being rebuked by strangers were two different things entirely.

Among the newcomers, murmurs arose at Datha's reply. She caught a whisper from one of the riders nearest her: "Ah, it's as Gilsen said. They cling to the old goddess. But they will see."

The leader raised his voice to speak over the others, "We here in New Orison take care to thank the goddess who carved such a home for us within these blighted lands. It is thanks to her bounties that we gather together, to care for one another, each learning a trade or craft, with no need of divisions between us and, more importantly, none of the dependence upon outsiders that has for too long limited our steps and progress."

Persephonie's eyes narrowed. How very like the senators of Andel-ce Hevra they sounded, if only they knew.

Remembering the tokens of Malura within Boss Gilsen's muster, Persephonie searched the scouts for signs of the goddess of misfortune as well. They were numerous, once she began to look. Each scout bore an antlered pendant. A few wore necklaces depicting two dark, closed eyes. And each of their leaders had been marked by a tattoo upon their throat—a black circle with a pillar candle inside. The tattooed candles had been recently extinguished—smoke curled up from the scouts' throats toward their mouths. "They follow Malura, Datha," Persephonie whispered to her father while one of the scouts was speaking. "Just like Gilsen's muster."

Did all the saudad who had gathered here follow the dark reflection of Cassandra, the aspect called the goddess's shadow? Even among so storied a people, Malura had barely survived in legend. Many avoided retelling her stories and speaking her name so as not to draw the aspect's gaze. How had Malura won so many of Cassandra's people to her worship?

Datha's jaw clenched, the only sign he had heard her.

The riders' leader continued, "The ruling council has commissioned myself and my party with welcoming you to New Orison though we understand there are outsiders in your midst." The rider searched the ranks of the assembled muster, hoping to tease out who precisely these outsiders were. Persephonie released a slow exhale as the man began speaking again—they had listened to her and remained out of sight. Rennear's pale complexion and russet hair and Jezebel's obvious fae heritage would immediately single them out as not being of saudad birth.

Persephonie's freckles and the dark red glow of her hair in firelight had often been objects of comment from other musters—others who, like the speaker, wished to single her out for being of mixed heritage, as though it was so unusual for her father to have fallen in love with a woman from beyond their ranks. When she was little, her mother had urged her not to take this to heart when Persephonie had told her about it during her months away from the muster, as the pair of them struggled to survive in the city. Could others like herself and her mother truly be so uncommon here?

The man had continued in his speech while Persephonie's thoughts wandered and she prayed to Cassandra that Rennear and Jezebel would be patient—it was not in Rennear's nature as a soldier nor Jezebel's as her self-appointed protector to hide themselves away. "Tradition holds that within a fortnight of arrival, each muster will determine their ideal settlement location and surrender their wheels. Symbolically, of course."

Murmurs and cries of dismay flitted between the gathered members of her muster. Near the back of the crowd, a few young girls broke away to return to their grandmothers' sides and tell the babus of the man's words. Persephonie knew without needing to look that other girls would quickly arrive to take their place so the grandmothers' information would be complete.

With a swish of her thick tail, Juliet pranced along the front line of her people. She wriggled in her stance before leaping into Persephonie's arms.

The fox caught the speaker's attention. He stopped mid-sentence to stare at Persephonie as though he knew her somehow.

"And why would we do that?" Datha demanded. "Symbolically or no, the wheels are part of who we are."

Her people nodded and many voiced their assent to Datha's sentiments.

"Please, please," the man called, hands raised. He showed no fear in the face of being outnumbered, just like Andel-ce Hevra's guards. He and the other riders must be confident in their use of swords on horseback, then. The leader had not failed to notice how mismatched such a skirmish would be either, though he knew nothing of Persephonie's growing magic. Or of the fae warrior and injured werewolf recovering in their camp.

"The ruling council understands your sentiments. Believe me when I say there have been other musters like yours who have been hesitant to part with the markers of their former lives, but they have all come around in time."

"Or have they been coerced?" one of the older women shouted from the back of the gathering.

The man's jaw tightened, and his horse stamped impatiently, pawing the ground as it had when Datha approached.

There was something strange about the earth here. Lush, verdant grass covered the hillsides, and it bore no markers of the sheep that grazed along the distant hilltop, nor did it bear signs of the disturbance of wagon wheels or herds of horses. Behind their camp, a dense forest stretched over the hills, shielding the base of the dome from sight. Was this what Boss Gilsen had meant when he said New Orison leeched the life from the region surrounding it?

"Not all musters arrive familiar with our ways. And the council understands that not all musters plan their arrival to this place, though they rejoice at each return of our people to our rightful home."

"We should find these other musters, Datha," Persephonie murmured to her father, her words shielded by the shouts of dissent from others in their number.

Cassian nodded grimly.

"The council invites you to explore the lands of New Orison and determine where you would most like to settle. Our industries will be open to you during this time, and you are welcome to take the first steps in learning whichever trades you wish." The speaker gestured to the verdant hillsides, the sweep of his arm taking in the town, the shepherds, and the vineyards. "In addition to surrendering your wheels, you will identify all non-saudad within your midst. *And*"—his gaze narrowed on Persephonie—"should the council deem it necessary, you will identify any of mixed heritage as well. Those who are not *purely* among our own people."

Datha's arm twitched beside her, and Persephonie grasped his wrist.

The speaker had glanced away from them, lifting his chin to better address the muster in its entirety. "Such measures demonstrate not only good will but also dedication to the Lady Malura and her wishes. Cooperating musters desire to be held in her high esteem."

Murmurs quickly rose and faded among the muster at the name of the shadow goddess.

Datha had stiffened beside her. There was a sharp set

to his shoulders and a flexing tendon in his jaw. The speaker was venturing dangerously beyond veiled threats— Datha might have no choice but to attack the mounted riders.

Without moving his head, Datha surveyed the hills between the resting place they'd found and the town in the center of the valley—if matters did worsen between themselves and the scouts sent from this "ruling council," they would be pressed to defend themselves with so many of their own fighters sent away to announce their presence.

Persephonie glanced along the front lines of the muster —others scanned the hillsides and sized up the riders, thinking the same.

"As I have said, we will grant you a fortnight to accept our ways and surrender your wheels," the head rider declared, raising his voice so that anyone listening in the muster might hear, even the babus. His voice lower, he added, "There have been instances where saudad have broken with short-sighted bosses." The speaker tugged at the reins of his stallion as her datha lurched forward, his shoulders back and a growl upon his lips.

Standing tall between his people and the riders, Datha crossed his arms over his chest, and their muster grew quiet, faces pale with rage. Saudad chose their own leaders —an insult to the leader was an insult to the muster at large.

The man smirked atop his horse, his cruel gaze lingering on Cassian. "Let us hope it does not come to that." With a cry, he kicked his horse's sides and spurred him away. The others cantered after.

In the distance, a second band of horses and riders thundered toward their muster. What news her brother and Velkan would have to relay upon their return, Persephonie could only guess at. There was every chance it was just as bleak as what she and Datha would have to share as well.

Persephonie laid her hand upon her datha's upraised arm. She squeezed his thick forearm, hoping to calm him. "Their news may be better, Datha," she said, not believing her own encouragement.

Datha glanced down and wrapped an arm around her shoulder. "Cassandra truly blessed me in the children she entrusted to my side," he said, tears misting in his eyes as he pulled her close. "Do not fear for your partner or friend, my Sephie. Or me for that matter. We will see this put to rights."

Outrage brightened Felix's eyes and tightened Velkan's lips, the ill news they would have to share plain upon their features even before they flew off slowing horses, running to close the distance between the muster's edge and Datha while their horses veered off to the side, froth coating their lips.

Velkan found Persephonie in the sudden press of the muster all around them and hurried to her side. He took her hands in his. "Are you well?" He searched her face, out of breath himself. "We saw the riders and returned as fast as we could." Velkan broke his gaze away to stare across the fields after the first set of riders. "After what we heard in the town, all I could think . . ."

He shook his head, his lips trying and failing to form the words. "Persephonie." He squeezed her hands and met her gaze once more. "I was scared for you before you left the Brightlands for the city. I understand why you felt you had to go, but such dreams Cassandra gave me . . ." Velkan sighed and dropped his shoulders. "Each day of your absence, I have asked her, selfishly, for your return. And now I fear that I may have brought you into the danger she showed me so clearly all those weeks ago." Care clung in deep shadows around his dark eyes.

"Velkan, no, you cannot blame yourself for . . ." Persephonie shook her head. She could not put into words her foreboding sense of what New Orison held for her and her family, for the future of the saudad and the role they had to play in the world. For whatever dangers Rowan's wheels held. She tried again, "For what has happened, what brought us here."

Persephonie sighed, tightening her grasp around his hands in turn. "Just think how I would have felt had I tried to find my way back to you and learned you had disappeared as we feared the others had." She shivered—Cassandra had spared her from greater horrors than the ones they faced at least. "If Cassandra warns us, we must be cautious, but we are not meant to be frozen."

She needed to hear the words as badly as Velkan did. Somewhere here, one of the wheels, or at least its record, lingered. It was up to Persephonie to find and protect it, just as soon as she discovered what exactly it was she was looking for.

CHAPTER 15

IELLIETH

Seven days and seven nights brought the *Amber Queen* to the lichen-covered cliffs on the western coast of the Elven Realms in the inlet that bridged Tor'stre Vahn and the ancient forest lands. A rushing river let out into the shallow harbor, its waters flowing from the mountains north of Shade Rest through Thyles Thamor before cutting west.

Hues of coral and rose painted the edge of the sky as the ship dropped anchor and Kriega called for the boats that would see Iellieth, Marcon, Quindythias, and Genevieve to shore. Logs the former captains had kept recorded several likely hiding places for portals to the Brightlands from within the Realms, and those who received and granted inland passage to travelers from the inlet of Moonsbreak Landing should be able to confirm the most likely route.

Because the three of them would be traveling with Genevieve through the forests, Iellieth turned down Teodric's generous offer to book them upriver passage. If she was going to see this land, she would do it as her heroines had undertaken their own explorations—on foot.

He pulled her aside before they boarded the boats. Her throat was thick as Teodric wrapped his arms around her and bade her to be careful. "I know you face dangers I cannot even begin to imagine but, if I can be selfish, I should dearly like for you to emerge unscathed on the other side of your travels."

"Are you sure I should be the one you're most worried about?"

Kriega called to them from the side of the ship and Teodric waved her off. He made as though to brush at the hair by her ear and thought better of it. Their kiss within his cabin must have occupied his mind as well—they were standing so similarly to how they had been then. "I am sure that you are and have everything you need already." He smiled at her, a tearful gleam brightening his eyes. "But I also know you well enough to know that you won't be the one to put your safety first when it comes to those you care about. And for that, I shall have to content myself with the fact that your tattooed champions know how to take better care of you in a fight than I ever could."

He placed a hand on the side of her face then and kissed her opposite cheek, lingering close to her, his stubble brushing the side of her face before he broke away. "Come." He offered her his elbow like he had done countless times before. In the earliest days of their acquaintance, he had done so as one of her only friends in the entire court. Later, as someone she hoped would be so much more.

"It really has been more special to me than I can say, having you aboard my ship, sharing with you this new life. I . . ." Teodric drew up short before the ladder that had been draped over the side of the ship, the boat floating just below. "Going forward, I will endeavor to make you proud."

Iellieth repeated his promise to herself as she stood beneath ancient trees, holding onto a large wooden pillar anchored in the rocky sand beneath the floating dock outside the settlement of Moonsbreak Landing while she watched Teodric row away. He raised his hand in farewell for her as the sun sank behind the horizon, the shoreline already lost in the shade of the great forest beyond.

As night fell, Moonsbreak Landing came to life, with pale orange torches glowing along the edges of the forest. Wooden walkways very like the one she balanced on wove back and forth between the trees, rope railings providing handholds for their swinging distances over the lower forest floor.

Iellieth craned her neck back, staring up, up, up at the treetops. Even those by the shore rivaled the largest trees she'd ever seen in Caldara, and she knew the inner forests would contain a great many more.

Their arrival and diplomatic papers from across the sea sent first the dock master and then the single inn keeper into a frenzy of activity. They bustled about asking after particulars and names that meant nothing to Iellieth. Should they alert Master Herve Rivven of their arrival or send word directly to the riverside consulate instead?

"Umm, the consulate, I believe, if that is agreeable to you," Iellieth answered, her indecision earning her a poke in the side from Quindythias. "Oof. Yes, the consulate." She drew herself up into her best noblewoman's posture. "Alert the consul that we should like to speak with them in the morning and, if you would be so kind, send word ahead of us to Thyles Thamor so they might receive our diplomatic contingent." Genevieve caught her eye and Iellieth added a request that a skilled navigator be on hand to assist her friend on the morrow.

These arrangements set into motion, Iellieth poked her fingernails into her palms, nervous anticipation welling up from deep within her. She'd made it, finally, to the Realms.

THE INNKEEPER HAD BEEN KIND ENOUGH TO GRANT them her best room near the forest canopy. Not having hosted diplomats in at least five decades, she mused, maybe even six, she wanted to ensure they had the finest experience possible. Quindythias, his mood immediately souring, did not appreciate the half mile of rope bridges that arced through the forest between the main inn and their "special outpost of rejection and forgetting," as he dubbed it two hundred feet into their "trek" toward the canopy room.

Iellieth woke before the sun, sparks flickering at the ends of her fingertips with all the day held in store. She hurried out into the common area with the glowing lantern from her room in hand before rushing out onto the wraparound balcony, hunting the first rays of morning light.

Sunrise in the Elven Realms did not disappoint. Along the exterior of their treehouse the lanterns faded, though the night still pressed close, like a final exhalation of darkness. Through the canopy, she got brief glimpses of stars glittering overhead. And then, visible first along the tops of distant trees and making its way down toward her, the warming rays of the midsummer sun painted her verdant surroundings burnished gold before blazing up overhead.

Even in the middle elevations of the Realms, the thickness of the forest brought a chill to their surroundings. Iellieth darted back to her room to throw on a shawl, crashing into Marcon in her rush. His good-natured laugh at this mishap and its resultant waking of the others led the four of them back down the swinging rope pathways to the core of the settlement itself.

In a quick, lilting Elvish, the innkeeper informed them that a Consul Reyyar would be anticipating their arrival in his rooms in the main tree-lodge and, in the same structure, Genevieve would find the forest navigation expert they had requested.

Iellieth glanced out into the bay, smiling at the sight of the *Amber Queen* still floating there, preparing for a dangerous mission all her own as Teodric went to face his admiral and acquire news of his father. She laid the fingertips of her right hand against her chest and bowed her head over her hand, murmuring a prayer of safety over her friend before his journey. She added to what he had told her the day before—may they both emerge, unscathed, on the other side.

Departing from the inn, she stepped onto the main pathways of the small trading town, itself between fifty and one hundred feet above the forest floor with the river gurgling below. Iellieth stopped short as first one and then a few elves crossed the pathways before her, going about their usual activities for the day.

The elves, in turn, paused at finding newcomers in their settlement, their surprise bordering just on the other side of odd for a town that should often see travelers and traders. They hurried away even as Quindythias called out to greet them. Iellieth sped her own pace to avoid hearing him add this to his gripes about the Realms thus far.

The consulate itself was situated in the center of the settlement on the opposite side of the river from their inn. Far below, white rapids gushed along the edges of the water with ropes down the center of the river rather like those bordering the walkways. Teodric had explained how the upriver passageways worked to some extent, enough that she understood these ropes would be used for barges to pull themselves upriver, a slow and exhausting process for the crews.

Unlike much of the rest of Moonsbreak Landing, the consulate hadn't been built from hewn timber planks affixed into and around a larger tree structure—it had been carved out of a tree itself. Chills raced down Iellieth's arms as she took in the massive tree—the age, the ancientness radiating off of it.

A deep sigh behind her confirmed her intuition. "This is more like what I remember," Marcon said, his voice low, almost reverent. The sounds of the forest and the river faded as they wound away from the river and the rest of the town to enter the structure carved into the towering, wide tree, its branches sprawling all the way across the river.

The branches on the off-river side formed the winding stairway they walked down to one of the glowing archways carved into its sides. It was at the lowest point of the settlement, a design choice Iellieth wished she could ask someone about, but unlike the ropeways above, no elves wandered this low through the old forest.

Taking a few steps nearer, Iellieth gasped, realizing her mistake. An elven soldier slid out from the shadows beside the doorway. His skin was the same gray-brown shade as the tree itself, his hair a rich, dark green, with a moss-like appearance. "You are expected and awaited." The elf bowed his head and led them into a dark corridor lit with the same glowing orbs that graced their canopy treehouse.

"You will find the navigator through there"—he gestured down a narrow, winding hallway that emerged out of one side of the tree and, Iellieth guessed, entered a different part of it. Genevieve nodded and turned down the hallway as the others proceeded down the path toward the center of the tree, Marcon ducking his head to avoid a low-hanging branch across one of the bends. "You must forgive the old one," the elf said fondly, patting the side of the tree as he passed. "No matter how old she gets, she is always trying to regrow back into herself. A metaphor for our realm, perhaps." His tone was neither ironic nor sad, and Iellieth didn't know how to interpret his words.

"Here you are." He slid to the side, revealing lichen-encrusted double doors with intricate carvings beneath the growth. "Consul Reyyar is within."

Hesitantly, Iellieth slid forward as the elf made no move to open the door. She rubbed her palms against her legs—what was the custom in the Realms for knocking and entering doorways? Why couldn't she remember?

Their guide stared straight ahead, seemingly unaware or unfazed by her indecision. Well enough. She knocked softly against the door and waited for a call from within. "Yes, yes, come along." The voice vibrated with age and—she winced internally—maybe a pinch of mirth.

The door scraped at first, dragging over the uneven floor of the tree hallway where the tree was regrowing parts of herself that had been shaven down by both carpenters and footsteps.

Iellieth slid through the doorway and into a library

study straight from her books, complete with a crackling fireplace, an elderly elf lounging in a red armchair, and a dracat—a dragon-like feline, covered in scales and twice the size of even the most engorged of Io Keep's noble pets —lounging along the worn leather sofa placed before the fire.

"Yes, yes, good. Come in, come in," the elf urged. With shaking arms, he pushed himself up to standing, lifted his cane from the side of his chair, and made his way over to them. "Consul Reyyar," he said with a bow, his hand gripping the top of his cane. "You are most welcome to our lands."

"Thank you." Iellieth bowed in turn, relieved when the elderly elf turned back to settle himself in his plush red chair and, with a wave, indicated a sideboard of biscuits, cakes, and tea.

"Whatever you desire, it is yours," he said, smiling to himself as he settled back into his chair.

Atop one of the leaning bookcases—which Iellieth could now see had been almost engulfed by the tree's regrowth—the dracat's spiked tail flicked back and forth as she watched her guests, deciding which of them was worth and who beneath her interest.

Iellieth waited until everyone was settled—herself with a cup of tea, Marcon with tea and a biscuit, and Quindythias with a plate of five cakes—before launching into the diplomatic part of their visit. The elf's relaxed demeanor immediately set her at ease. They were here as travelers and not negotiators after all. "I do not wish to repeat information you already have, nor do I want to leave anything out so, at the risk of redundancy, we are the delegation sent by King Arontis of Linolynn and we're here on a most urgent matter."

She introduced herself and her companions to the consul, who nodded politely at their names, much to Quindythias's chagrin. "I understand the matter we've come to ask for help with is likely delicate in nature." She sipped at her tea, eyebrows raising at the surprisingly earthy undertones in its flavor. Something new to celebrate about the Realms alongside everything else. "My companions and I are on a special quest of greatest importance. We are looking for—well, we hope the Council will help us to find an artifact entrusted to the elves some many millennia ago, before the flood." She set down her cup and leaned toward their now-curious host. "We're looking for a piece of the planar seal that corresponds to the element of earth."

The elderly elf frowned as he nodded. "A puzzling request indeed—most curious. Linolynn, did you say?"

"Yes, that's right—"

With a muffled cry of dismay, Quindythias straightened as the dracat fluttered off its perch and half flew, half leapt to his shoulder, leaning its scaled nose toward his ear. "Apologies," the elf squeaked, trying to keep his back straight without allowing the dracat to come any closer to him.

Reyyar chuckled. "Ah, it is so interesting, hearing about Linolynn once more and noting your heritage mixed between two peoples. Why, I had a friend who went on the diplomatic mission to Linolynn a little over twenty years ago. Hair precisely the same shade as yours . . . Wait."

Iellieth's entire body tensed. Was this diplomat about to say—

"Amastacia, you said?"

She squeezed her hands into fists. "Yes." Iellieth's voice

trembled. Marcon stiffened beside her, and Quindythias broke his attention away from the dracat to observe the exchange.

Tears sprang to the elf's eyes and he clasped his hands together. "The necklace you wear, it was a gift, wasn't it?"

Iellieth wrapped her hand around the amulet, unable to speak.

His smile widened. "By the gods, I never imagined. And to think here I am right in the middle—You wouldn't happen to be the daughter of Dorric Themear, would you?"

The name rolled off the elf's tongue, and Iellieth breathed it in. *Dorric Themear*. "I-I do not know. My mother would not say."

"Ah." The elderly elf shook his head, the smile still tugging at his wrinkled cheeks. "You have his eyes too. How any could mistake it—He will be so very glad, you know."

Iellieth had prepared herself to discuss the seal piece, to negotiate for the elves' blessing to retrieve it. She had not expected the resemblance between herself and her father to be so near that a friend or colleague of his might recognize who she was based on her last name and appearance. With a stifled cry of her own, Iellieth put her face in her hands, unable to believe that she had already found that which she'd sought for so long.

A warm hand weighed against her shoulder, and Marcon scooted closer to her. "If I might speak on Lady Amastacia's behalf for a moment, would you tell us—Is her father well? Is he here or in the city, where she might meet him?"

"Ah, yes, yes, of course. Yes, you would need to know all this and more, would you not?"

Iellieth peeked through her fingers to see the elf settle back into his chair, gazing cheerily at his fire. "Dorric, a fine young lad. Though perhaps young is relative." He glanced at his dracat, who was edging her nose nearer to a panicked Quindythias's left ear. Soft, scale-like feathers covered the joining of its wings to its back. "Even my dear Rilia is young to me, and she turned two hundred decades ago." Consul Reyyar rubbed his fingertips together to call his creature to his lap and stroked her scaled feathers. The dracat arched her back at the treatment and stretched her claws, digging them into the soft wood of the chair's armrest and pricking them back out again. The gesture left several small puncture marks in the armrest which, now that she knew to look for them, Iellieth perceived decorated almost every wooden surface of the dark, polished wood across the entirety of the study.

"I knew your father as a boy, knew his parents, back before Invae Alinor fell to the extremists. He came to see me, after what happened with your mother. One of the landholders here, a quite disagreeable elf by the name of Herve, tried to pin the entire diplomatic undertaking and its subsequent failure upon your father." Reyyar shook his head. "Come to discover, Herve had been plotting with some nobleman in Linolynn and would have diverted any profits to have been made by the Realms, meant to be shared equally among the cities and distributed to the populace as they saw fit." The diplomat grumbled a few choice Elvish curse words under his breath at the audacity of such a move.

"But I don't wish to alarm you," Reyyar corrected himself, holding out his hand upon seeing her reaction to his fervor. "A month of unpleasantness and, I hope you will not be grieved to hear, several years of heartache, but my young friend returned to himself. He spent some time in Andel-ce Hevra, another disagreeable assignment, if you ask me, and is currently on a stint among our far-northerly neighbors, underground with the dwarves of Hammerfell, one of his favorite places." Reyyar grinned again. His every expression spoke of his fondness for her father, though he seemed at times to forget that Iellieth had never met him.

"Oh." Her shoulders fell. "He is not here?"

Marcon and Quindythias were watching her again. Iellieth ignored their attentions and focused on Reyyar.

"No, my dear. I hate to be the one to disappoint you. Such is the lot of a diplomat, as, well, as it seems that you know." He brightened again at this responsibility they all shared.

"I-I suppose that isn't too great a surprise . . ." Iellieth bit her lip, looking down in the same moment the dracat took notice of her and prickled her way over to Iellieth's lap. Rilia shut her eyes as Iellieth scratched at the base of her skull behind her ears and rubbed the scales that grew across the creature's curved forehead. Two tiny bumps, miniature horns, pressed out of Rilia's skull, a unique dracat characteristic she'd never heard of before.

"Shall I write to your father?" Reyyar supplied quickly. "Would you be opposed to him knowing of you? I do not foresee him being able to cut short his tenure with the dwarves but, perhaps, you might travel there once your business here has concluded?"

Iellieth could hardly speak for smiling. Color warmed her cheeks, and bright tears flared at the corners of her eyes. "I would be honored that you would take such a step for me." She squeezed Marcon's hand beside her. Finally, after so many years of wondering, her father would not only know of her existence—he would know that she was trying to find him.

And he'd know that his daughter had followed in his footsteps, a diplomat who traveled to distant lands.

As they finished their tea, the consul told more stories of how the underground city of Invae Alinor had once been, of the uneasy peace between the various powers within the Realms that had been so difficult to achieve and yet was valued by all. Quindythias paid little heed to these stories as the dracat abandoned Iellieth and hovered over his shoulders, twisting herself around and around as she tried to settle on the back of the chair where he lounged. Each time he tried to shift away from the creature, she would give a lazy flick of tail or claw and send the elf jolting in the opposite direction.

"Thyles Thamor is another matter altogether," Reyyar said with a shake of his head. "The council there, whom I will write to on your behalf, they have the ability to advance causes that would unify the Realms, that would address some of the most pressing matters within our borders. The invasion of great shadow creatures that endanger the native biomechos for instance," he mentioned, as though they would know the details of what he referred to. "They might regard our city not as a back-water but as an asset benefiting the whole of the Realms, yet they do not."

He spoke on of other matters within the Realms but waved away further detail when Iellieth asked him to tell her more. "What you need to know to speak to the council I would guess you already know. They're a selfish lot and will be interested in what you can do for them more than the other way around."

The consul squeezed Iellieth's hand in parting, patting

the top of her hand with the other. "Seeing your hope for our lands gives me hope in return, young one. May your road lead you to all you seek."

The dracat hissed at a twitching Quindythias once more before they departed, leaving the champion frowning over his shoulder as he scurried out of the room. "What a disagreeable sort of pet that man has," the elf exclaimed. "Precisely the type of creature that would have been treasured by those ghastly royals of Bastion before a certain champion dispatched them." His confidence emerged for the first time since their arrival as he brushed off his armor and checked himself over for any glaring scratches or fallen feathers. "Though I *do* like being a diplomat thus far. The cakes, I must say, are very nearly worth the unglamorous bits."

Iellieth stood on tiptoes behind him and extracted a feather from his hair that had escaped his notice. She set it carefully upon one of the root-like ledges that poked out through the carved tree wall as they wound their way through the dim, narrow under-tree halls back to the exterior pathway where they'd promised to meet Genevieve.

"Marcon, look!" Iellieth cried as they emerged in time to see a barge working its way upriver. A thin elven woman perched at the top of a stack of boxes piled onto her river craft. Before her, a giant otter perched across the prow, barking as it bounded over the rapids on its way upstream. As the cry echoed back to her, Iellieth peered more closely at the creature—surely she was mistaken . . .

Iellieth gasped. The otter *was* the ship. Its mechanical call had been the first clue that something was amiss, as was its considerable size. Between the creature's rear flippers was a giant spinning wheel, the sort that would be used in a riverside mill. A lead line had been attached to an apparatus at the otter's shoulders, guiding it along the deepest of the river paths.

"I wasn't sure whether or not to believe the old stories." Genevieve sighed, joining Iellieth at the overlook and leaning onto the rope railing beside her. "Biomechos," she said with a nod to the otter-ship, using the same word Reyyar had. Neither Marcon nor Quindythias acted as though the word was new to them—just her. "Many of them are as old as the foundations of the forest, their ancestors dating back to before the flood. Your friends could probably say as much about them as I can, but this is the one place they survived. There were mages called arti-ficers who took care of them before but, as their magic changed or was lost, the creatures adapted, took on more of the natural life of the forest for themselves. The elders whose elders had visited the Realms spoke of living machines, nothing like the workings of the empire." Her eyes shone as she stared after the otter. "I wanted to believe their stories. But seeing it—I don't see how I could have before now."

Iellieth smiled and watched the creature bound up and around rapids, its elven rider perfectly at ease, swaying naturally along its back despite what must feel like trying to ride an impossibly large, wild horse. She thought suddenly of Nerissa, the seawolf daimon who had saved her from Reaga, how difficult it had been at times to stay atop the wolf's slippery hide. "I think that may be just the beginning of the wonders awaiting us."

Her fellow druid smiled back at her. "I certainly hope so."

CHAPTER 16

BRISERAS

"This is not good," Jorgan said yet again, his face pale as he stared at his torn thigh, back propped against a rock.

Briseras clenched her jaw, holding her elbow with her uninjured arm. Putting aside the issue of infection, the werewolf's bite had dislocated her shoulder and torn the muscles, which would take days if not longer to mend.

But they had an even more pressing concern before them. She waited, breath short, for the creature to turn back into its human form. Yet the werewolf remained. For the third time, she searched its neck and chest. No pulse, no breath.

"It should have transformed back by now," she repeated to Jorgan. Standing here before a slain werewolf, she heard again Everett's cries as she slew his transformed partner. The pair of them had watched the fallen creatures transform along the hillside, returning to naked human forms.

She'd performed the slaughter of James as a kindness

and a duty. But she couldn't bring herself now to do the same for herself and Jorgan.

At the next full moon, if the infection was not cured, they would transform into werewolves. And already, from the abnormality of the werewolf's lack of transformation, being a werewolf in Steymhorod seemed to work differently than the lycanthropy of Azuria.

The nobleman paled further as he looked from the creature to Briseras and back, his hands clamped around his bleeding thigh. "What does it mean that it didn't?"

Briseras shook her head, immediately regretting the movement. "I don't know," she admitted through clenched teeth.

Was the creature they'd felled a true werewolf, born in its hybrid form, which prevented its return to a human body as its soul passed on? Or was there something else in the magic of Steymhorod that kept the creature in this state?

Beside her, Vera stirred, whimpering. Briseras raised her finger to her lips and knelt on the earth beside Jorgan, careful to keep her arm still. "I hear it too," she told her wolf. To the nobleman, "Someone's coming."

Those approaching through the forest soon revealed themselves—a group of riders on horseback wearing simple tunics and breeches and armed with curved scimitars.

Briseras withdrew her crossbow, holding it steady as best she could with her one good arm.

The lead rider's eyes widened as they came upon Briseras, Vera, Jorgan, and the slain werewolf. Teela, who had been absent for most of the fighting, had the sense to remain hidden for this encounter as well. The rider, a masked woman, called the others to a halt, gesturing with her fist in the air though her language Briseras didn't understand.

"Vicq, he is here," the rider called back, switching to the common tongue. She dismounted, keeping her hands upraised by her shoulders and her gaze on Briseras. "You have killed this werewolf, no?"

Briseras watched the woman carefully. Her dark hair had been pulled back in a knot at the back of her neck, tied with a dark green ribbon. Her ivory tunic was tucked into high-waisted leather breeches, and the horses were only lightly packed. They must have a camp nearby.

"Yes," Briseras answered simply. Vera's ears pricked forward but she did not growl, and Briseras caught no whiff of damp fur upon the air beyond the musty sweat of horses. The werewolf pack she feared might be nearby wasn't lingering near these riders.

A second rider dismounted, joining the first. This man appeared different than the rest. The others were olive-skinned and dark-haired whereas this man's skin was tawnier, his hair a deep brown with lighter streaks of auburn running through it. Balanced at the bridge of his nose was a pair of round spectacles. He bore a satchel at his waist stuffed full with pages, scrolls of parchment, and a few tomes as well. Immediately, he reminded her of Everett.

The woman pulled down her mask. "I am Aletta," she said, her voice ringing clearly through the forest, "muster boss of the saudad of Steymhorod." She gestured to the spectacled man beside her. "Friend of the muster, Vicq Nightmane." He bowed at her introduction. "We are most grateful to you, brave hunters. This werewolf has been causing a great deal of trouble in this area and, by the look of your wounds, we have tracked him down a little too late. By the look of his, we'll need to track him no more. We are in your debt."

Briseras introduced herself and Jorgan to the muster, remembering Jeremy's mention of Steymhorod's saudad, one of the only bands capable enough to make Steymhorod's roads their home and the only outsiders Mayor Ewald would let—used to let—within the walls of St. Sebastian.

The muster boss sent the scholar forward to speak with them while she organized a party to burn the wolf's corpse. Vicq kept clutching at the bag strap upon his shoulder and shuffling his hands through his papers as though looking for something.

"I-I wonder," the scholar began, "seeing how capable you are—despite injuries, of course, but now that our causes are potentially, or are, actually, in fact, aligned—"

"Jorgan, what's he getting at?" Briseras's shoulder was beginning to swell, and she had no patience for the scholar's roundabout manner. She and Jorgan needed to tend to their injuries, which the muster should be able to help them with from their camp.

"I believe he means to compliment us, Briseras. And now that we are infected, he believes our purposes align."

"Y-yes," the scholar agreed, shaking his head so that the low light of the forest flashed across the round lenses of his spectacles, temporarily obscuring his eyes. "You see, I am a werewolf t-too."

"Too?" Briseras took a warning step toward the scholar, who stumbled back. Jorgan caught her elbow.

"You have been infected, have you not?"

She could only glower in reply—perhaps he had a point. "Go on."

The scholar explained that an upstart rival had stolen

his mate and taken control of the werewolf pack upon Wolf's Head Peak. This new alpha, Kratok, and his warriors had been wreaking havoc across the region ever since, infecting travelers, particularly those unlucky enough to be alone or in small numbers. "Such a practice of forcing the venom, Solane m-must see, is a violation of the Wolf Mother's will. The pack has never—"

"What could your place in your pack have to do with us, whoever this Solane is?" Briseras gritted her teeth as she tightened the bandage around her arm. Even infected, she wasn't going to abandon her quarry to join the werewolves.

"Solane is—was—my mate. She remains the spiritual head of the pack of Wolf's Head Peak and dedicated priestess of the Wolf Mother," Vicq explained.

"Let me help you," Jorgan murmured beside her, balancing on his unhurt leg as he reached out for the bandage.

"I can manage," Briseras snapped, jerking away from him. "See to your own wound."

His lips tightened into a thin line.

"The venom heightens one's anger receptors for the first few days after infection and as the moon reaches her full strength," the scholar said.

Jorgan shook his head. "She's always like this."

Briseras swallowed her retort. She could have easily left him to die in the wilderness, but she hadn't. She *should* have left him in Loire's Glade to fully recover while Tybalt searched the other side of the glade for Nassarq's trail. But he *had* jumped in front of the creature and been bitten trying to help her—even if she and Vera might have avoided the werewolf on their own. That was something.

She struggled with the bandage high on her arm,

recalling the early years of her training when Rajas had taught her the rudimentary healing arts. Briseras grasped one end of the cloth with her teeth and tugged on the other, tightening it until her eyes watered at the pressure on the wound. She most likely would need help settling it back into its socket.

When she raised her gaze back to Jorgan and the scholar, the nobleman was watching her. A smirk spread across his face, and he shook his head before turning his attention to the scholar as well. "In addition to being estranged from your pack, you wouldn't happen to have any special knowledge on healing werewolf bites, would you?"

The scholar sighed. "I have been searching through the Barasov archives with precisely that purpose in mind but, without access to the Wolf Mother Arduenne's blessing upon the mountain fane, unfortunately no, there is little I can do. There's a woman in the camp who had a similar question. I hate having to disappoint you both."

Her gaze locked upon the scholar's face. Loire had used that word as well—fane, one of the holy places of the Sisters and had specifically directed Briseras to seek out Arduenne. Before she could ask after the connection between the fane, Arduenne, and healing her infection, another part of Vicq's speech snagged her attention.

Briseras stepped closer. "A woman?" She ignored the scholar's alarm at her advance. "Describe her." It was unlikely, but while a chance remained that she might have found Lavinia after their separation or her sister Saige, she had to pursue it.

The man described a pale woman with blonde hair and blue paint about her eyes. "She's been through quite an ordeal in her time here," the scholar added, dropping his gaze. "Kratok turned her and he is . . . unkind." Vicq evaded the particulars of what had happened to Lavinia, but Briseras pressed. His meeting with the witch had been fortuitous in Lavinia's case though unfortunate to Vicq's larger purpose. He'd accidentally caught her while in her werewolf state while trying to capture and question one of Kratok's scouts. The saudad had agreed to offer her their protection while she recovered so long as Vicq promised to remove her when the transformation drew near.

Briseras set her jaw. "I need you to take me to her. Now."

Jorgan's brow furrowed but he said nothing. He crossed his arms over his chest and stared at the scholar, waiting for the man's answer.

"We'll have to ask the muster boss, but I'm sure Aletta will agree."

She surveyed the saudad as they divided up the task of clearing the werewolf's remains from the forest, speaking in their own tongue, one to the next. "Aletta," Briseras called. The woman turned toward her. "About that debt—"

All this searching, and she might have finally found her quarry—Lavinia would be a welcome addition to their party, a skilled tracker in her own right, determined to find her sister or, if it was Saige she'd found, she'd have a second pair of eyes to search for the witch.

⁂

HER SUSPICION HAD BEEN CORRECT—THE MUSTER WAS not far from where they'd encountered the werewolf. Two of the riders were generous enough to allow Briseras and Jorgan the use of their horses, which two others would escort back once they'd arrived in camp. Reluctantly,

Jorgan had helped her reset her shoulder before they rode out, her grunt of pain muffled by the branch she'd bitten down upon. The nobleman had paled, looking sick, his color only just returning as they reached the muster.

The setting sun gave rise to a boisterous atmosphere in the camp, whether because of the werewolf's slaughter or an internal celebration, Briseras couldn't have said. Vicq escorted the pair of them to the healer's wagon.

Briseras froze when she glimpsed a woman with familiar white braids inside the wagon. She forced a slow inhale, preparing herself. Steymhorod was more dangerous than the lands they'd left. Even if Lavinia had been a captive of Nassarq's sent to lure her and Everett to his lair, she'd been working against him and was there for the fight that brought them here. But to have been captive of a rogue alpha werewolf . . . Briseras had spent enough time in the wilds to suspect the horrors the witch had undergone.

Lavinia was feverish and burst into tears the moment she saw Briseras, covering her face with her hands. Long, pink scrapes covered the witch's arms and legs, with several puncture marks along her neck as well. The healer had mended the injured skin, but her recovery would still take time.

"The transformation, Briseras—" The witch stared back at her, bright blue eyes wide. "Such pain. I—I don't remember what I did. If I bit someone else—"

"Shh," Briseras soothed, rubbing a damp cloth over Lavinia's forehead and easing her back onto the cot attached to the side of the wagon. "No need to worry about that now. We'll make it right."

She nodded to the healer as the middle-aged saudad woman peeked back inside. The woman avoided Briseras's gaze, murmuring something that sounded almost like a title under her breath as she passed. Briseras stepped out of the wagon, allowing the woman to tend Lavinia again before checking the set of her shoulder.

"Your friend is from the Frostmaw Mountains, is she not?" Jorgan asked. "I recognize her markings though it's been so long, I couldn't name the *teuta* she is from. Her clan, I mean."

Briseras held her jaw tight and clenched her hands into fists. If she had found Lavinia more quickly, she might have prevented this. Had she followed the river a different direction, had the zombies not appeared when they did . . . Such musings were useless. There was one variable she was more than ready to eliminate, however. She'd make sure this Kratok paid for what he'd done and could never infect or attack anyone ever again.

Her eyes had narrowed as she settled upon her revenge —removing each of his teeth and embedding them into his skin seemed a modest place to start.

"Err, Briseras?" Jorgan interrupted her musings, nodding behind her where the healer waited.

"Oh. Right." Briseras settled onto the bench outside the healer's wagon. She straightened her back and nodded to the healer. "If you need to dislocate it again to set it properly, tell me when to hold my breath."

CHAPTER 17

YVAYNE

One moment, Yvayne and Vaxis were traveling from her tree home to the Brightlands, answering a cry for help from the borders of the Autumn Court.

The next, a horde of slavering werewolves surrounded them, ringed by shadow beings, monsters gifted to the false empress of Verrain on behalf of Alessandra as she sought to destroy the daimon. It was one of many attempts against the children of the gods and those of Verdigris.

Before Yvayne could strike them all down, a blade pierced her chest. She gasped for breath, the air wheezing through her punctured lungs. Blood pooled, spilled.

Darkstone. Her vision blurred. Far away, Vaxis screamed.

And a familiar voice whisper-sighed his victory over her.

She woke in a cell lined with darkstones, Vaxis by her side. By the cell's make alone, she knew they had fallen into Lucien's clutches, which meant they were most likely hidden within one of his prisons in the Shadowlands. The purple light that leaked through the cell window high overhead confirmed her suspicions.

The wound in her chest had been healed, but the darkstone blade had left a hole in her armor.

Her insides churned when she thought of where Lucien would take her. An old enmity extended between the fallen guardian and her mother.

The mother Yvayne had left behind in order to protect her.

Her mother Ravenna's one command was that Yvayne never return home. Doing so would bring about her mother's death and set in motion the destruction of their people.

How had she been so careless in setting her portal? The events that led to her imprisonment flashed out of order through her mind. It was the pulse of Rowan's energy that she'd caught that had thrown her off completely. Lucien would have felt it too.

The love Yvayne had carried through the ages would be the same to spell her doom.

"You're scowling again." Vaxis's large emerald eyes blinked across Yvayne's vision as the Brightlands fae leaned close and examined her expression. "What are you thinking about?" Vaxis tilted her head to the side. Amethyst, the fae's firefox, crawled into her lap, turned in a circle, and settled down. The fox's ears pressed against the back of her head as she too studied Yvayne.

With a deep sigh, Yvayne leaned back against the sweaty stone wall of their prison cell. Lucien must have expanded the prisons recently or exterminated their previous keeper. The rock still lived, but with the darkstones embedded into the steel bars of their cell, there was nothing she or Vaxis could do to morph the rock to their will. The darkstones were slowly sapping all the magical stores of their energy.

The fae would know if she lied. Yvayne suspected the fox would too. "I was thinking about her." Yvayne shut her eyes. The heady months she and Rowan had spent together after Rowan had awakened in Faer Haven before she had delved into the founding and work of the Soul Shepherds. With whatever she did, Rowan dove in with her entire heart, her entire being. The refuge she'd made for the champions in the highlands north of Bastion. She'd saved so many, and she'd come so close to saving the two who had rescued her.

Without the sacrifice of Marcon and Quindythias, Yvayne and Rowan never would have met. And what did she do for them in return? The mission they'd set out on with Iellieth, trying to find the final piece of the threshold seal, a magical stone set between the planes. If they could unlock it, they would return to a state of wholeness. They and Iellieth would be free to roam as they pleased.

And she and Vaxis would still be imprisoned here.

"You're sad she didn't come and find you first?" Vaxis's brow furrowed. Her friend knew what it was to have loved and to have lost.

"I'm sure she thought we would be best served if she helped Persephonie."

Vaxis leaned her head against the cave wall. Her fingers busily scratched between Amethyst's ears. "Have you ever wished we could simply let ourselves be happy and do what we wanted instead of always putting a cause first?"

Yvayne sat up to regard the fae. She grinned. From anyone else, such a statement would have pulled the bitterness from the back of their tongue. But from Vaxis, the question was simply another wondering of how their world might have been. "I'm not sure I can begin to imagine what that would be like."

The fae watched her through partially lowered lids. "That was the perspective I was waiting for." Vaxis smirked. "Now, when you're through wishing Rowan could be someone other than who she very much is, can you help me discover how we're going to get out of here?"

Vaxis's early life in the Brightlands had been very different from Yvayne's. She and her sister, Mercedes, were raised communally, but the fae had balked when Vaxis fell for a human man who later died in the wars that raged across the Negative Planes after the fall of the First Age.

Yvayne's memories of her early life revolved entirely around her mother Ravenna. Did anyone still living know what it was to be carved as an aspect of their mother, formed from a single being, bearing the remnants of the magic of Verdigris? Lilia and Lilith both had passed on. Lyric's descendants had been the druids themselves, her magic dispersed. That left Yvayne, daughter of Ravenna, granddaughter of Evelyn, the most powerful of Verdigris's daughters three.

Even as a gar, Yvayne had wondered whether her mother had designed her out of love or carved out a part of herself in anticipation of Lucien's attack. While she was queen of Verrain, her mother's sight had been almost blindingly acute. She could see what would be, what was coming, but her visions were so clear, she could not perceive another way around them.

Yvayne and Vaxis traded their watch posts, allowing one of them to rest while the other waited for Lucien.

It was after one such watch that Yvayne patted her friend's knee as Vaxis rested her head on Yvayne's shoulder. "When Apollo came by my tree, we spoke of what never changes, did we not?"

Vaxis nodded. The dark circles under her eyes flickered in the dim light of Lucien's prison cell. Each day, the darkstones sapped more of their magic, their energy. Even for near-eternal beings, there would be a time when they could bear no more.

"I have known Lucien a long time."

The Brightlands fae raised an eyebrow at Yvayne's understatement.

"What say you to the unchanging nature of our host?" Yvayne whispered. Lucien's self-absorption and pride had guided him through the ages. His obsession with his own advancement rivaled only his obsession with Rowan, especially after she'd freed herself from his soul-bonds. If fate would see his ambition to be Alessandra's right hand put to the test against his desire for revenge, the guardian might finally be beaten.

But she and Vaxis would not have to wait that long.

"The fallen guardian will not be able to help himself," Yvayne continued. "He will threaten our charges"—Iellieth, Persephonie, Genevieve—"taunt them, and when he does, they will learn where we have gone."

Vaxis chewed her lower lip and scratched behind Amethyst's ears. Knowing where they were and being able to do something about it were vastly different propositions, but it was a start.

Each day Yvayne remained here, in such close proximity to her mother, was a day that she placed the remaining lummenfae in danger. The Shadowlands fae could not survive open war with Lucien. Her mother could not bear another battle. Yvayne hoped, fruitlessly, that her mother would remain ignorant of her presence here.

She had broken the one rule Mamaun had given her. She had returned home.

"There's an essential heartbreak to the lives of the fae, Vaxis. One I believe you already know too well." Being back in her home, returned for the first time in millennia, the impossibility of what they were trying to accomplish swelled in her chest. "To be ever-living, until something kills us, with a heart bound to a mortal, even one blessed with apparent rebirth. It is the cruelest difficulty and greatest blessing all at once." Yvayne turned her gaze out over the horizon, its deep purple line just visible through their barred window. She sniffed to clear her nose. "How are we to bear it?"

Vaxis took Yvayne's hand in hers. She had lost both her sister Mercedes and her lover, Brendan. Through thousands of years and near-unimaginable change, they had both lived on without the ones they loved. How did the loss continue to feel so dear, so near at hand, as though no time had passed at all?

When Vaxis spoke, her voice resonated just above the whisper of the wind. "Not bearing the loss would mean letting them go," she said. "Would mean pretending to have loved them less than we did." Vaxis blinked against the tears that clung to her eyelashes. The water droplets stubbornly remained. She glanced up at Yvayne and smiled, a sad, persistent knowing that only those who had experienced what they had could recognize. "We bear it because we don't know how to do anything else. And so we can continue on."

CHAPTER 18

BRISERAS

Thud-thum. *Thud-thum.* The soft forest earth gave way beneath Briseras's driving footfalls. Her large black paws drummed a rhythm that echoed the song of the forest around her.

Not Vera's paws. Hers.

She inhaled cold air through her snout. *Pine. Moss. Damp. Blood.* Briseras changed her course, drawn by the scent of a stag.

She slid to a stop, her tail twitching as she spied the creature across a clearing.

A white stag, a sign of good fortune. To harm one was to court destruction. Saliva thickened along her tongue, and her lips rose, a growl gurgling to life on the back of her throat.

The stag stared at her, waiting. Unmoving. Unafraid. When she could resist no longer, Briseras snarled and sprang forth, darting into the center of the clearing where two impossibly full moons glowed overhead, catching her in their light. The stag disappeared along with its scent.

Briseras abandoned her chase, catching sight of her

shadow instead. She glanced back at her tail and sat upon her hindquarters. This was a dream—it had to be—yet why was she a wolf and not a werewolf in it?

A new scent caught in her nose, the musk of cedarwood and incense with a hint of rose. She spun about and discovered the lithe, muscular form of Lord Draego striding toward her. He had eschewed the cape he'd worn the last time they'd met, wearing only a thin linen shirt and breeches with shiny black boots.

The barest flicker of a smile twitched upon his lips as he noticed her. "You never stop surprising me." He slowed as he approached, appraising her. "It is a most intriguing look for you." The vampire lord circled around Briseras, eyebrow raised. "Are you pleased by your new form?"

With a twist of his hand, the air around Briseras compressed and pulled her upwards. She gasped, suddenly returned to her body and being while remaining within her dream. Before answering Lord Draego, Briseras trailed her hands over her wrists, reassuring herself that she was human rather than wolf.

Draego had been watching her. "Because I have to say —" In a heartbeat he slid closer and caught his arm around her waist, tugging her into his chest. He lowered his lips to just below her earlobe, the chill of his breath making her hair stand on end. "I am far preferential to *this* particular form you take and, were it up to me, I'd never see you leave it nor, for that matter, have you far from sight at all."

Briseras relaxed back into the solid plane of his chest, enjoying the proximity the dream made possible without the danger such closeness to a vampire usually posed. But with one so powerful, was she safe even in a dream? She dismissed the thought. The time for safety had passed long ago.

Draego tilted his nose up into her hair, his chin dragging along the nape of her neck and leaving a trail of goosepimples along her skin. "I have no doubt that your wolf form still smells of lavender." His hand drifted down her waist to her hip, and Briseras responded in kind, tilting her hips back toward him. "Though it cannot possibly be as strong, as intoxicating as it is right now."

Faster than should have been possible yet again, the vampire lord pressed his lips to her neck. Briseras moaned, remembering the rolling pleasure she'd received from Olya's bite. From Draego, what might be possible—

He shot away from her, somehow steadying her and springing more than an arm's length apart all at once. His eyes were two black, swimming pools, gazing at her, tugging her nearer. "Ah-ah." Draego held up a hand to stop her stepping toward him. She'd already stumbled closer without intending to. "Such a time will come, dearest one." Insinuation hung heavy on his tongue. "Let us take one matter at a time."

Draego waved his hand again, and a rough-hewn wooden table appeared beside them, a velvet-cushioned chair on either side. "Please, sit."

Briseras frowned, glancing around the clearing in case something else had changed but all remained as it had before.

He took his seat after she had settled into hers. "Now, tell me—your transformation. Is it one you are happy with? I . . ." Draego turned away from her, staring off into the woods beyond her dream clearing. "I did not see the attack coming, or I might have prevented it." A different sort of shadow clung to his eyes at this confession. Whatever it was made him concerned.

She crossed her arms, studying the forest clearing she'd

conjured in her dream. It wasn't like any forest she'd ever been in before. Not even in her time in the highlands or the depths of the Caldaran wilderness had she seen trees this wide, the branches carefully interweaving like threads in a tapestry. "You're not responsible for my protection."

Lord Draego chuckled to himself at that. "I would not dream of suggesting as much, but I have a vested interest in your wellbeing just as I do in your mission to remove a certain pestilence from my lands." His upper lip curled as he mentioned Nassarq, nearly spitting on the insult to the other vampire.

"The werewolf's attack has diverted my immediate plans to pursue that *pestilence*."

Draego nodded. "I understand. Then the immediate trouble remains—is this a state you want to keep?"

"You asked me that already." Briseras scowled, swinging her gaze toward the vampire. Gods he was hard to look at and impossible to resist all at the same time. How was she to focus on hunting down a rogue werewolf alpha *and* a vampire distracted with such . . . arousal? She crossed her legs for good measure. "Is there a reason why? Is it something you can undo?"

The twisted grin of his answer caused her breath to seize. "There is very little magic I cannot do, Briseras." Again he rolled the 'r's of her name. "Though it is curious you brought us here of all places." Draego gestured to the clearing around them.

She diverted her attention beyond the vampire who, admittedly, exacted a pull so strong she could hardly focus on anything else. Now that he had mentioned it, there was . . . something out in the woods. Waiting for her. Watching.

Briseras slowed her breathing, spreading her hunter's

awareness across her environment like Rajas had taught her to. She searched for a creature like Loire but, no, whatever lingered in the forest felt older, more powerful . . . and less welcoming.

She managed not to jump when she noticed the vampire's attention hungrily affixed upon her face.

"I have not stepped within these woods for an age or more, not since my lands fell into shadow," Draego said, his gaze not straying from hers. "And then to my surprise, she allows me in, because of *you*."

The dream games of guessing were wearing on her patience. "Who?" Briseras sighed.

"You know of her already. The elf you saved, Tybalt, has told you of the Sisters." He seemed nearly as displeased naming them as he did mentioning Nassarq. "The Archfae with whom I used to share rulership of Steymhorod." He shook his head. "A story for another time. Her name is Arduenne, Mistress of the Mountains. Some you meet will call her the Wolf Mother. I suspect given your favored companion that Arduenne has a special task assigned for you as well."

Briseras frowned, trying to put all the pieces together. "I thought you did not wish for the Sisters to be awakened?"

"I do not." His gaze fell, but the slight smile remained, more self-mocking than it had been before. "Nor do I wish for you to remain a werewolf against your will. Though my sight around you is blocked in many regards . . ." He raised an eyebrow at this observation, as though waiting to see if Briseras would suddenly reveal the intricacies of a magical puzzle that she was entirely unaware of before he continued, "There are threads I can see. Your destiny, your necessity within my lands.

And none of these destinies involve your being a werewolf."

Draego's gaze darkened further. "I hope you see why even now my trust in the Sisters falters. Here is Arduenne, trying to take you away from me at the very beginning, while she likewise twists the werewolves' plots to her own ends."

Briseras began to suspect that Lord Draego could not speak more plainly even if he wished to. She would have to do the clarifying herself. "Arduenne *can* change me back from being a werewolf, is that what you're saying?"

"Much more quickly than I can undo the curse, especially given some of my other, pressing concerns along the borders." Draego's expression darkened, but he did not elaborate on what those concerns were. "It is likely she will want you to restore her fane, bring her back, before she removes the curse. I have little doubt that is why she brought you here."

In the silence that followed, Briseras thought over the possibilities. While there were certain advantages she could see in being a werewolf, there were notable limitations too, chief among them the inability to control her transformations, not to mention their connection to Andel-ce Hevra's guards. She stilled the involuntary shudder at the thought of the priests having more control over her than they did already and grasped the underside of her arm, covering over the brand she'd received from them, marking her as one who belonged to Haven.

Draego noted the reaction—how could he not have?—but he did not ask her to explain.

"I have a wolf already," Briseras announced. As she said the words aloud, their sense of surety settled over her.

This was the right path. "I would choose to return to myself."

The vampire lord sighed as the wind picked up around them.

For the barest flash of a moment, Briseras could have convinced herself that a pair of great, glowing green eyes stared at her through the trees before they turned away.

"She is pleased by your choice," Draego clarified. The forest sounds returned around them. She hadn't noticed their absence before, though she should have. He rose, grinning, and offered her his hand. "As am I."

Lord Draego pressed a kiss to her knuckles. "She bids me depart from her domain, though there will be a time when you return." His voice and image faded even as he spoke. "She will show the way before you. Let us keep it to just one of the Sisters though."

Briseras woke with her hand hovering over her face, the lingering pressure of Draego's lips still warm against her skin. At her feet, Vera grumbled in a dream, her paws kicking as she chased unseen prey. Perhaps she dwelled every night in the glade of Arduenne, where Briseras had ventured in her dream.

She smiled to herself and trailed her hand through her wolf's thick fur. Tybalt would be pleased about the connection to Arduenne, and Jorgan would be glad, in his way, that they wouldn't need to stay werewolves if they did not wish to, though Draego hadn't extended the offer to Jorgan as well.

All she needed to do was find a way of telling them the good news without disclosing that it was the vampire lord who had confirmed that Arduenne could help them. That shouldn't be too hard—even if they suspected something, they knew better than to question what she chose to conceal.

CHAPTER 19

IELLIETH

As the wake from the biomecho faded into the river rapids, Iellieth listened intently to Genevieve's account of her meeting with the elven navigator.

The elf had echoed Reyyar's sentiments about the current state of the Realms, especially the isolationist tendencies of the council in Thyles Thamor and the encroaching dangers from the Brightlands. "I wonder if that's what Sariel wanted my help with for his pack," Genevieve said.

Iellieth recalled what the druid had told her of the daimon Sariel's request that Genevieve bring him with her to the Realms, introduce him to a ranger, and see about making his people's case for an expansion of their territory.

"He mentioned trouble with their territory and smaller numbers, though I do not know how I'm meant to protect against shadow creatures that are beyond daimon to manage."

Iellieth laid her hand on her friend's shoulder. "Maybe

Sariel knows something about you that you don't. From your stories, he sounds rather like Yvayne—the way she is so often waiting for us to discover or do something she has already anticipated."

Genevieve grinned at that. "I had never put the two of them together in that way but—oh, good." She leaned around Iellieth, peering down the winding path that hung between the trees and gestured someone nearer.

An elf strode down the hanging walkway toward the four of them, wending his way out of the sprawling oak where they'd met with Consul Reyyar. He was about as tall as Quindythias, though a bit stockier. Like many of the elves they'd seen thus far, his tan skin had a gray hue, like tree bark. As she looked more closely, the veined patterns of bark and branches peeked out from beneath his skin, whisper-imprints of tattoos.

A greatbow was slung on his back, so long that it reached from his shoulder down past his knee. "Are these the three you were telling me about?" the elf asked as he halted on the path an arm's length from Genevieve. His voice was a low baritone with a natural hoarseness, giving him a brusque manner. Whether it was intentional or not, Iellieth couldn't yet discern.

With Genevieve's assent, the elf introduced himself. "Ammon delQueran, ranger."

"Oh, both figures you were looking for in one."

The druid nodded, tucking strands of dark hair behind her ears.

Iellieth quickly gathered that Ammon was a being of few words. He would get along with half of their party then at least.

"Come with me down to the river, and I shall answer your questions on the way."

She glanced at her companions, who were as puzzled as she was.

"The druid tells me you are in need of a guide," Ammon said, more a statement than a question. "She requires a portal to a particular part of the Brightlands, and as Reyyar has just informed me, you have hopes of an audience with the Elven High Council."

"You work quite quickly, to know so much about us."

"The forest spirits have been restless of late, making the route between here and Thyles Thamor even more dangerous for outsiders than normal. If you will have me, I should be honored to guide you to the city." He nodded to Genevieve. "We can find a portal to the Brightlands along the way."

"That would be excellent," Iellieth sighed. Given their mixed reception within the settlement thus far, she had thought they would need to find their own way through the forest.

"Good," Ammon answered simply. He turned and began climbing down the sprawling roots of the ancient tree at the center of Moonsbreak Landing toward the river. The ranger's familiarity with a giant, ancient elven forest was immediately apparent—as was her lack of adaptation to such an environment. How had he begun his descent? One wrong step, and her leg would fall through the tangled root structures.

"He doesn't mean for us to follow him, does he?" Quindythias asked, peering down the ravine after the ranger.

"Come along," the ranger called up to them. He perfectly pivoted his hand and footholds between the roots, making his descent appear as graceful as if the roots were a simple staircase.

"It seems he does," Iellieth answered. She adjusted the straps of her pack and hovered over the edge of the steep slope.

Quindythias grumbled during his descent, though his movements were almost as lithe as their new guide's. He passed Iellieth on his way down and was the first to join the ranger by the river bank.

Iellieth slipped only once a dozen feet from the bottom of the ravine. Marcon peered down at her from above where he and Genevieve were making their descent.

Ammon appeared just behind her and plucked her out of the tangle of roots, keeping hold of her elbow as they completed the descent. "While we await your friends, perhaps I might clarify—I hail from Thyles Thamor and am one of but few remaining rangers. We've dedicated ourselves to restoring the elves to the forests, something those settled in the cities resist. While on one of my patrols, I heard of your arrival. And after meeting your friend"—he nodded up toward Genevieve, who had nearly completed her descent, Marcon just above her—"it seemed only necessary I meet you as well."

"I am glad you did." Iellieth frowned, thumbing through dusty memories of diplomacy lessons to see how she might ask one of her most pressing questions. "Why is it that you were so willing to help us? Was your journey tending back toward Thyles Thamor so soon?"

Ammon shook his head. "As I believe you heard from Reyyar, you have come to the Realms at a dangerous time. I fear our future hangs upon our choices now. A great many new dangers walk our forest, and I am trying to understand them. My hope in seeking out travelers from distant lands is that you might be able to see what my companions and I keep missing. There are poachers, creatures of shadow, wild beasts from the Brightlands maddened by their change in environment. But why?" Ammon's voice fell with his final question. He wasn't looking for her to have an answer, more to be a step on the path of discovery.

Marcon leapt the last several feet down off the ridge, landing easily. No sooner had he brushed the dirt from his hands and rejoined Iellieth than the ranger raised his second finger and thumb to his lips, pressing them together and whistling around them. The sound echoed out across the forest, bouncing away through the trees rather than reverberating back to them. "A ranger's trick," he said with a smirk. "We will need help if we are to reach the city in a reasonable amount of time. They'll meet us on the other side of the river."

"Who is meeting us?" Marcon asked, frowning between the ranger, Iellieth, and Quindythias who was tossing pebbles one by one into the river.

Ammon grinned, throwing back his hood. "Do you hear them? We must make haste."

Without further explanation, Ammon ran along the riverbank, expecting them to follow.

The four of them looked at one another, and Genevieve raised her nose into the air, sniffing. The color in her irises brightened. "Jade senses something approaching." Genevieve squinted, peering up at the other side of the gorge. "A herd of trees doesn't make any sense," she murmured to her inner werewolf.

"A bossy ranger and a suddenly unhinged werewolf." Quindythias raised an eyebrow. "This really is not how I'd hoped the next phase of our journey would transpire."

"If you do not hurry, we'll miss our ride," Ammon called back.

"Has everyone in this time been blessed with a preter-naturally sharp sense of hearing? I am finding this pattern of being overheard when I don't want to be most tiresome."

Iellieth shrugged and took off after Ammon, her boots squelching in the mud. "Come along, Quindythias," she yelled when she noticed he remained where he'd stopped to complain.

"What about the inn?"

"You mean the special outpost of rejection and forget-ting? We're leaving it behind."

AFTER A QUARTER HOUR OF FOLLOWING AMMON OVER the rough terrain along the riverbank, the ranger led them across the river—increasing Quindythias's dismay—and up a winding path through the root-covered gorge on the other side. Behind them, the bends in the river and density of the trees swallowed Moonsbreak Landing.

"Relief is near at hand, druids," Ammon shouted back to Iellieth and Genevieve, who ran beside her. Genevieve's eyes were brighter than they had been, darting quickly from side to side, more Jade than Genevieve, Iellieth was starting to recognize.

A stitch pressed beneath Iellieth's ribs and she bit back her own complaint as she climbed the final tangled stretch of the opposite rise. Surely taking the time to cross the river via a bridge wouldn't have slowed them too much. Just as she was beginning to long for Quindythias's more luxurious vision for their trek through the Realms, Ammon waved her forward to the edge of the tree line.

"You'll want to see. Hurry." Ammon gestured from

behind a giant rotting log, the remains of a fallen tree as big around as the largest trees Iellieth had ever found in Caldara.

Iellieth squatted down at the elf's bidding, crouching to stay low and spider-crawling to join Genevieve beside the elf and peer through a crack in the rotting tree.

She'd thought the otter biomecho ship was a wonder to behold, a remnant of the magic of the old world her friends wanted to describe to her but so much of which fell outside her experience. Though they shared the same world, there had been so much change in the interim, many of their descriptions were difficult for her to fully understand.

But the sight spread out before her was a legend straight from her druid training with Mara. In the forest clearing beyond the fallen tree, a herd of deer-like creatures grazed upon tufts of brilliant green grasses and wildflowers. Only they weren't deer. Their bodies were made almost entirely of bark, with skeletal portions visible at their joints and across their chests. Grasses grew from their necks, as would a horse's mane, and all along their bodies, mushrooms and mosses coated their bark-hide.

"Brachilli," Ammon murmured. "Sacred treemounts who roam between this realm and the Brightlands, near the daimon you seek," he added for Genevieve.

"Sacred to whom?" Iellieth whispered, staring in wonder at the creatures made of earth, bone, and bark.

That barest ghost of the ranger's smile again. "See for yourself."

Iellieth leaned closer to the gap in the rotting log as Marcon and Quindythias settled in beside her.

"Who is *that*?" Quindythias sighed, his wonder-struck tone speaking, for once, for all of them.

A fae-like woman meandered slowly across the field, her hands extended out beside her, palms facing down. She walked with eyes shut, her lips moving in some sort of murmured prayer. Beneath her palms, grasses shot up out of the earth, followed by flowers. In place of a crown of antlers like Yvayne wore, two great horns curved out of her forehead, curling back away from her head before pointing up toward the sky.

Beneath the shade of the forest, the deep blue-purple of her skin took on the etherealness of shadow, enhanced by the iridescent white paint that curved down the center of her face and along her cheekbones and that trailed out further along her mostly bare skin. A sparse covering of flowers hung in delicate threads over her body. Bands of pale blue braids clasped together with bone and rings of silver pooled down her back and over her neck, as though she wore water within her hair.

Ammon murmured something under his breath before pushing himself up to his feet and clambering up the side of the decaying ancient tree. "Hail, water mistress of forest pools," he called from the top of the log. "Hail, keeper of the glades." With a grunt he landed upon the damp earth on the other side of the fallen tree, bowing over his knee in the crouched position he'd landed in.

"Aahhh," the woman exhaled, her voice taking on the cadence of a slowly trickling stream. She was a nymph, by Ammon's formal greeting, which also explained the deep well of magic radiating off of her, its ripples reaching the edges of the clearing. "You are far from home are you not, pinecone?" She said it like a nickname, and Iellieth translated the Elvish for Marcon.

In front of her, Ammon sighed, dropping his head

further. "I come on other matters than those of your cruel friend. There is one in need of your aid."

Iellieth and Genevieve whispered between themselves. The nickname didn't mean anything to either of them, but they agreed meeting the brachilli had been worth the run. If the creatures could be mounted, which Iellieth assumed was the case given their size, it would hasten their trip to Thyles Thamor and speed Genevieve's search for a portal as well.

The nymph wandered closer as they spoke. Her eerily pale eyes—as shimmering as blue selenite—glowed, light refracting from within a cave. "You truly are more than you seem," she said, peering at Iellieth and then Genevieve. The nymph smiled to herself. "Come out, come out, wanderers one and all. Allow us to meet you, to truly see you."

Iellieth had never met a nymph before but, from the impatient set of Marcon's jaw and the starry look in Quindythias's eye, she gathered her friends had. The introductions that followed were less flowery than Iellieth would have guessed, save Quindythias's of himself, and concluded with Ammon explaining his purpose in bringing them to meet the nymph, Nealadora. "You know the dangers of the forest as well as I. These three seek Thyles Thamor, and I should like to acquaint them with our forest before they enter the city. But I am without your special skill in finding portals. Their friend has an urgent cause within the Brightlands, as near to the daimon's territory as possible."

"The portals have grown more unstable of late," Nealadora explained, glancing at Genevieve. "Native creatures like the brachilli are better able to sense their proximity, which they communicate to me."

At that, Nealadora called one of the brachilli forward while Ammon saw to the securing of his pack and tightened his boots. The nymph swung up onto the creature's back before leaning down against the neck of her steed, her body flush against the moss-covered bark of its body. "Would you like to go for a ride, young druids?" she asked Iellieth and Genevieve. The swirling pools of her eyes deepened, and she traced the hollowed stump of the creature's face. "The herd has a sense for knowing where one needs to go."

Iellieth's heart pounded in her chest. She had never imagined that such a creature might exist much less that a nymph would invite her to ride on one. She reached out her fingers and touched the bark of Nealadora's mount. The creature lifted its nose into her hand and snorted, leaning deeper into her touch.

The sparks at her fingertips jolted tingles down the length of her hands. *Yes, yes, yes.* Iellieth smiled and glanced over her shoulder at her companions. Marcon had set his jaw and bore his suspicion as a shield. Though the nymph didn't know it yet, he wouldn't soon forgive Nealadora for suggesting that Iellieth ride away with her without them. Quindythias continued to stare at the nymph, enraptured, his mouth slightly agape. She and Marcon would have to tease him about that later.

Two brachilli trotted toward them from the herd. "Might you call a few others?" Iellieth asked.

"Yes, of course." The nymph beamed. "There are plenty for all."

"Just so long as we don't go *through* a portal," Ammon grumbled in the same moment Marcon grunted a slightly soothed "good."

Ignoring them both, Quindythias strode forward, his

hand clutched to his chest. "We would gladly go wherever you would deign to take us, enchanting mistress of the forest and lady of the glades."

The nymph blinked back at him.

"I don't think you got the titles exactly right," Iellieth murmured to him.

"It's the suggestion of reverence they care about," the elf whispered back. "I'm sure it all means about the same thing."

Ammon stared at Quindythias rather than the other way around. Wordlessly, he shook his head.

CHAPTER 20

BRISERAS

After a full day in the saudad camp, most of it spent by Lavinia's side, Briseras felt the warmth of the saudad wine settle in her belly, the effect heightened by the heat of the fire she and Jorgan had gathered around. A dull throb echoed across her shoulder, but it was nothing compared to the swelling ache that had been present before.

Several glasses of wine and the soothing harmonies of a guitar helped to dull the gnawing realization that she was a werewolf now. *A werewolf.* How many times had she fought rogue werewolf soldiers from Andel-ce Hevra, the enchantments the senators used to control them dulled by either distance or the embedded magic of the wilds?

It's in their nature to dismiss the power of wild places, her mother had told her. The nature of senators and priests to take for granted the magic of Briseras's ancestors, those they'd rounded up and imprisoned, bending their gifts to the will of the empire.

Was she guilty of the same blindness? She'd been warned often of the dangers of Steymhorod and yet here she was, the venom of a werewolf bite surging through her veins. Rajas would be even more ashamed of her than he had been the day they'd parted, forever. But it wasn't her trainer's gaze she imagined dancing over her body, picturing her in a transformed state. It was the dark gaze of her dream the night before.

Long, dripping fangs emerged from beneath a smirking pout, black eyes glittering in her imagination. Briseras shivered, trying to shove away her body's reaction to even the thought of Lord Draego.

Beside her, Jorgan groaned, shifting his leg by the fireside. His wound was healing as well, though between his complaining and his ghostly shadow's useless fawning over him, one would think his leg had been bitten clean off.

"Ah, I am glad you are both on the mend," Vicq called from just outside the circle. He had spent the day with the muster's scouts, searching nearby for any additional werewolves sent by Kratok.

Briseras waved him over and leaned her uninjured elbow onto her knee, fixing the scholar in her gaze. "We will join your cause in reclaiming your position in your pack so long as such a path involves exacting vengeance upon Kratok." Despite the wine-induced haze, she recalled Vicq mentioning his former mate's connection to Arduenne, the same Archfae Lord Draego had told her to seek out. The wine enhanced her visions of a violent pack-order overthrow and dulled her concern about the still mysterious penance that might be involved in reversing her lycanthropy.

She smiled to herself as she ran her fingers through Vera's thick fur. "Un-werewolfing us would be good too," she added, her voice only slurring slightly as she spoke.

The scholar's gaze widened. The knob in his neck

bobbed as he swallowed. "Umm, excellent. Well"—he shuffled the papers in his bag again—"there are two parts to my plan at present. First, if we can convince Solane to turn those loyal to her against Kratok through the influence of, umm, you, we might shift the balance of power enough to remove Kratok entirely. Achieving true stability is a longer-term endeavor . . ."

This man paused for too long when he spoke.

"She'll be happier if you talk about the revenge part," Jorgan added helpfully.

"Ah, yes." Vicq glanced nervously at Briseras before continuing, "There are skilled weaponsmiths in Barasov. Being outnumbered as we are, even if Solane agrees to side with us, I think we will need to devise something, err, special. You seem the capable sort—"

Briseras's mind was already dancing forward, working through the possibilities. Mystique's crossbow was a fine implement, but she sensed there was more that could be forged within this land, waiting just out of reach. "Special weapons are a good place to start. You should draw up a map of your pack's region, possibilities for where Kratok and his scouts will be, weak places where we might make our attack."

"Th-the pack themselves I'd like to leave unharmed. Only Kratok, or him and his closest followers. Solane . . ."

"We'll leave your mate unharmed," Jorgan promised. He carefully avoided meeting Briseras's gaze.

Good. Such a promise I cannot vow to keep.

The werewolf elaborated upon what Briseras had learned from Jeremy about the city: the feud that had caused the flight from Barasov twenty years before and brought about the Blessed Father and the Ring of Light continued on between the Watchers and the Bloodletters.

"Most visitors try to choose one side or another and stay put, but with our journey to the archives, we'll have to make our peace with both." Because the Bloodletters kept careful watch over their gate and didn't let outsiders pass, Vicq added, they'd have to use the Watchers' gate. The one route in and out of the city left the trail to the gate vulnerable to attack.

Jorgan shrugged. "We've survived in Steymhorod this long."

After the scholar left to prepare for their journey on the morrow, several of the muster members sought out the pair of them and Aletta shared that there was a seer in the camp—her mother—who had requested an audience with Briseras.

Around the fire, one of the saudad women leaned closer to Jorgan, whispering in his ear. The nobleman's eyes grew wide at her suggestion. Teela's ghost slipped partially free of Jorgan's shoulders, lending him the unsettling appearance of having a second, spectral head. The ghost echoed its host's surprise before drifting out of Jorgan fully.

He glanced back at Briseras over his shoulder. "Huntress"—a nod—"company, if you'll excuse me." Jorgan took the giggling woman's hand and limped along beside her, Teela floating behind.

Briseras met Vera's gaze. "I agree—we should have killed the ghost the first day."

The wolf grumbled as she lay down at Briseras's feet, smacking her lips as she settled her head atop her crossed paws.

On Briseras's other side, her new companion, the muster boss chuckled. "He is a new acquaintance, no? Not yet aware of what is in front of his eyes?"

"Jorgan does not strike me as exceptionally perceptive," Briseras answered. She rolled her right shoulder, trying to keep it loose in the socket to displace the tension from the left as the healer had suggested. Whatever else Aletta was implying, she didn't care for.

The boss laughed and patted her thigh at this. "Werewolf bite or no, the leader is very funny," she cried to the circle of musicians and storytellers around them. She leaned toward Briseras and lowered her voice. "My mother, she senses that there is one who lays claim to you already, though you remain undecided. That will not last forever. He is determined. Your wolf senses him, even if he does not yet know his name."

"Are you speaking of Vera?" Perhaps the words had grown confused in translation.

"No, no." Aletta chuckled again. "Not *this* wolf. *That* one." She pointed in the direction Jorgan had gone.

Briseras frowned, her mind racing ahead to tell her which other being the boss meant. Jeremy, Rajas . . . or the vampire who appeared to her in fields and visited her dreams.

"I doubt Jorgan cares a whiff for, well, whomever you mean." The conversation was far more personal than she cared to be with a stranger. "Or me, for that matter. We have a common aim, that's all."

The muster boss raised an eyebrow. "Of course." Her grin deepened. "Let us speak of other things. Tell me of your travels through these dark lands."

Briseras spoke of her experience in St. Sebastian and the vampire's attack as well as Olya's rule. She could only hope the children, Vasile and Romina, were faring well with Jeremy's mother. Before they went to speak to the seer, Briseras thanked the muster boss for the care she had taken with Lavinia. "If there is ever a payment I might offer in return, do not hesitate to name it."

The boss agreed, she would.

As the last light faded and the glittering stars emerged overhead, Aletta guided a somewhat wobbly Briseras to her mother's wagon. The remnants of her mother's faith gave her a greater tolerance for seers than other spiritual practitioners, and humoring the boss's mother seemed a small step toward repaying the kindness shown to Lavinia.

Thick incense obscured the old woman from view at first. Briseras coughed, drawing back, Vera whining at her feet.

"Mother, I have told you to at least crack the windows," Aletta scolded. She pulled herself into the wagon and began fanning out the space. "Here—" She extended a hand down to Briseras and pulled her into the wagon. "I will wait with your wolf. Mother," she raised her voice to be heard over the old woman's muttering, "be kind to our guest."

"Kind?" The elderly saudad appeared out of the swirling incense smoke. She was wrinkled and appeared quite short, settled onto her low stool, betraying nothing of the warrior's physique her daughter possessed. "You value truth more than kindness, do you not, Shadow-Touched?"

"What did you call me?"

The old woman laughed to herself. "A name you know, yes? We have a translation of it as well, though it means Awaited One in our tongue. But enough of my ramblings." The seer brushed a swirling orb of the incense away. "My daughter brings you in hope that I might answer the questions which deepen your shadow. Ask me. I know much."

The seer had been the one to request this audience,

but she was not wrong. There were a great many unknowns shading the path ahead. In spite of herself, Briseras hesitated, sensing that, once crossed, this bridge would forever alter her destiny in this realm. She exhaled, decided. "I have my own plans here, plans that grew as I arrived in your camp. But wherever I go in Steymhorod, one of two things, sometimes both, occur. I keep finding those looking to bring back the Sisters who seem to believe that I am somehow destined to do just that. Alternatively, they sense the . . . interest I have sparked in Lord Draego." Her hand drifted to the silver key that hung about her neck, visible for the moment as, at the healer's insistence, she had removed her armor to give her shoulder time to heal.

Her mother had taken her to visit a seer back in Haven. The woman had been badly abused by the priests, and she had requested an audience with Rathenza before she relinquished her spirit back to the earth. Through swollen eyes, the woman had stared at Briseras, hidden behind her mother, just as the elderly saudad woman was doing now. 'She will save us,' the woman had croaked. Behind the bruises, a peaceful expression had settled over her face. 'Though we will not see it, you know it to be true.'

Rathenza had glanced back at Briseras, an expression that, as a child, she couldn't understand upon her face. Picturing it now, Briseras saw resolve, but it could easily be her memory playing tricks. She and her mother hadn't spoken of it again.

"It would be surprising to even the most skeptical for you to have captured the attention of both the vampire lord and Arduenne."

"The Sister of the Mountains." Briseras kept her voice

low but spoke plainly, trying to draw the seer back to the present, to this audience she had requested. "Why her specifically?"

"Ah." The wrinkles across the elderly woman's face deepened as she smiled. "The eldest and most powerful of the Sisters, they whose lands we travel. Though Lord Draego overtook their claim, these land remain theirs. Arduenne exerts her will still. I know you feel it."

"I—" There was no easy way to say what she felt in Steymhorod, the sense of belonging to a land she didn't know, retracing remembered steps she'd never taken.

"The paths you select must be your own, whatever power the old ones would wish to use to influence you." The seer smiled, her wrinkles deepening. "This you know already. Loire is an old friend—for her to share with you her glade speaks well." The seer wafted some of the incense smoke into her nose, inhaling deeply. "I will add to what she told you before and to what you have heard from . . . others." The seer tittered to herself. "When Lord Draego separated the Sisters from their sites of power, he also befouled those sites so the Sisters could not easily be returned. The fanes you know already—holy sites where the Sisters' influence dwells. Each Sister has a priestess or guardian who tends to her domain. Loire, as she may have said, is the servant of Diannan. Others you have yet to meet."

The seer murmured to herself and lifted one of the sticks of incense, swirling it between herself and Briseras. She squinted at the smoke as though watching it for patterns, but Briseras couldn't make out any significant shapes in its twirling. "Your path next intersects with Arduenne, Sister of the Mountains. She has multiple servitors in this land. One watches her heart and another tends her fane. Should you wish to restore the fane, you must first find and cleanse the heart." The woman's head lolled on her neck before her gaze shot up to meet Briseras's. "This choice is still before you. But now, Shadow-Touched, you will know the way."

Her missive given, the woman's milky eyes stared off into the distance, but their gaze was not unfocused. She saw something, an object of great promise, and sighed. "The Sisters have been waiting for you. For myself, I am moved that they would deem me worthy of meeting the one they chose so long ago." She patted Briseras's hand where it rested atop her small table. The old woman's touch was soft and warm.

As she drew her hand away, the seer smoothed the rough-spun silk of her tablecloth. "The other who lays claim to you—you have mentioned him already—he senses the change you will bring to these lands but, somehow, he does not fear it. Already, you spark transformation. Just think where we will be—"

"You sound like Everett," Briseras remarked, surprising herself. She had been trying to keep the folklorist from her mind.

"Ah, your story-weaver." The seer smiled again, this time with a fondness for someone she'd never met. "His spinning lingers over you, though you are right to believe his spirit passed on."

Briseras felt a deep pang low in her chest at the woman's words. Her own knowledge of the passing of Everett's spirit had been weight enough, but having another confirm it—

"He did all for you that he could and you, the same for him, whether you believe so or no. But the fate he perceived the edges of—it is written in the stars above you. So powerful a legacy that came before." The seer's eyes gleamed. "Powerful, too, that you will leave behind."

Briseras's lip twitched at that. She certainly hoped to, starting with Kratok and then Nassarq. "You have been most generous in your time with me." She bowed her head and rose. "I thank you."

Aletta walked her back to the fireside. Jorgan was there, leaning back on his elbows, affecting ease, but clearly waiting for her.

Were he one of the hunters from her collective, she might have made passing mention of what had transpired with the saudad woman and the ghost, though a hunter of her collective would never have allowed a possessive spirit to linger at their side.

He shifted uncomfortably, adjusting the position of his leg by the fire before turning toward her. "Briseras . . . what I said yesterday. I didn't mean it."

She avoided his gaze. Jorgan didn't need her approval for his activities with the ghost, whatever he had convinced himself of in the afterglow of intimate release. Under normal circumstances, such practices were important for hunters, to prevent distraction. "Which thing?"

"Mmm, fair enough." He groaned as he fully straightened his injured leg. "You're not unpleasant to travel with or unduly filled with anger. I—I wasn't myself, when I said that."

Briseras glanced over toward the healer's tent, where she could just make out Lavinia's peaceful, sleeping form. Vera shifted in her sleep, snuggling her rump against Briseras's legs for warmth. "It was a tense situation for both of us."

His jaw tightened again. "Is that all you can manage?"

She whirled back to face him, for the moment forgetting the soreness of her swollen shoulder. "And what if it is?"

He stared back at her, the tendons in his neck tightening beneath his scars.

"Well?" she demanded. The judgmental stare was too much. Tybalt hadn't objected to her company and neither had the elite band of hunters in her collective. Not since Rajas—no. He was behind her. And she wasn't going to let this nobleman try to fill that particular void, try to convince her she had some sort of internal failing. "What is it you want from me?" Briseras finally exclaimed.

Jorgan opened his mouth, and before he spoke, she knew the words that would emerge. *Nothing. I want nothing from you.*

She nearly screamed at him. *Say it.*

"I want you to let me in."

"What?"

He frowned after he said it, recognizing by her shifting expression that his confession was as much a surprise to her as it was to him. "I—I want you to let me be something more than a nobleman you found in the woods who was nearly killed by a vampire. I can help you, Briseras. I want to kill Nassarq, more even than you do, I think." He sighed and scratched at the back of his head, ruffling the neat tie of his hair. A few thick strands fell free at his neck. "But I want to help you too."

"Help me do what?" Her voice was sharper on the final word than she meant it to be, and the nobleman flinched but held his ground.

He watched her for a moment, then a grin flashed over his face. "Heh. I don't think *you* know yet. But I'd like to be there, when you find out." Before she could answer, he added, "And not out of pity. I can help you."

There was a surety to his voice that she believed. It was true that he was unlike the hunters of her collective; his training had been of a different order, but it was there. They had work still to do to understand one another, but perhaps he was right. "You want to help me," she repeated.

"I do."

The ghost pouted, bobbing at his side, but Jorgan didn't spare his undead fiancée a glance as he awaited Briseras's answer.

"Well enough."

His grin returned, wider this time. "What now then?" He opened his arms to take in the muster around them, his eyes bright as though seeing the gathering for the first time. "Is there anything we can do for your friend?" He nodded his chin toward Lavinia.

"Their boss has given me permission for her to remain with the muster while we travel into Barasov. We'll need to be quick about it. They'll turn her out before the full moon."

Jorgan's brow furrowed as he considered this information. "It is strange that they're missing a moon here, isn't it?"

"Strange indeed."

The frown passed, and a lightness returned to the nobleman's gaze as he stared down at her. "What would you say to some mead and a meal?" He grumbled as he pushed himself up to standing and then reached down toward her. "Join me?"

Lavinia was sleeping soundly, and the muster had kept her safe thus far. Briseras put her right hand in Jorgan's, bracing her injured arm against her side as he pulled her to her feet. His grin widened as he tucked her arm around his waist and clasped her to his side. "Normally I'd go fetch your food and drink myself with such an offer, but seeing as I'm recovering from being hobbled, I'm in need of your kind assistance."

She debated for a moment, not having experienced such closeness with someone since Jeremy had immediately taken an interest in her back in St. Sebastian, though this was different still—something about the nobleman reminded her of her hunters back in Tor'stre Vahn, those she'd traveled with and trained.

"Not all of us can be so self-sufficient as you," Jorgan murmured in her ear as his thumb lightly grazed the base of her sling, which she should be able to remove on the morrow. The mirth faded from his expression. "I'm sorry I wasn't able to avoid being bitten and even sorrier that you were. I hate that you were hurt." He held her gaze. "I promise to do everything in my power to prevent anything of the kind from happening ever again."

Briseras's lips parted, but she didn't know what to say. The intensity behind his gaze—he was truly grieved she'd been bitten and injured by the werewolf's claws, something Rajas would have immediately started lecturing her about. In St. Sebastian, Jeremy had tended to her so carefully after the attack, but he hadn't taken personal responsibility for her becoming injured in the first place. Had he been the one to save her from the flames? That night was still a blur.

Jorgan continued to watch her, waiting for her answer.

"It wasn't your fault," she said as much to him as to Jeremy, thinking of the attack, what she'd always wished Rajas would say to her when she was grieving the loss of one of her hunters. Injury and death in the wilds weren't always a matter of mistake. Wounds and loss were inevitable, weren't they?

The nobleman's expression didn't change, but Jorgan grasped her free hand and raised it to his lips, planting a kiss along her knuckles before gently placing her arm back by her side. "I'm not sure that's true, but my vow stands all the same." He nodded toward the table of food and drinks as one of the saudad pulled out a stringed instrument by the fire. A woman joined the musician, humming along with the opening chords before she began to sing. "Come on. We're in for a memorable night."

Briseras gripped Jorgan's waist to help him balance, and they hobbled together to the plates of thinly sliced meat, bread, and berries. A little boy started chattering to Jorgan right away, filled a goblet for each of them, and cleared a place for them by the fire.

She wasn't sure where the ghost had gone, but she could sense from Jorgan's ease at her side that Teela, for the present, wasn't nearby. Jorgan propped himself up on the ground beside her, his shoulder nearly touching hers and hands spread behind his back. The little boy kept their cups filled, and Briseras found herself leaning into the warmth of the nobleman by her side, remembering many such nights among her collective, the hunters celebrating togetherness and survival. Most days, that was all anyone needed, and such remembrance, as Jorgan said, made for a memorable night. She leaned her head against the round muscles of his shoulder and closed her eyes, allowing herself to drift away into sleep.

CHAPTER 21

IELLIETH

Afternoon wore on into evening as they rode the brachilli north through the forest toward a portal that would take Genevieve to her daimon pack and leave the remaining four of them less than two days' hike to Thyles Thamor. The creatures were uncommonly fast, Ammon had told Iellieth as they rode, shortening their trip by two days at least due to their speed and navigational skill.

Iellieth tapped at her brachilli's withers, urging it alongside Ammon. "There was something curious you said to Nealadora this afternoon that I wanted to ask you about," she began. "When you mentioned taking us to Thyles Thamor, you said you wanted us to know these lands. What exactly did you mean?"

Ammon nodded to her. "A fair question. Even so new to the Realms as you are, you will have spent more time in our great forests than the council members have for many centuries."

"Why do they not spend time in the forests? Are there . . . other creatures in the forests? Wild biomechos?

Or something more dangerous?" The phrase 'wild biome-chos' sounded strange in and of itself, but she didn't want to offend the ranger by calling them what she would have said had she run into one outside of Linolynn—monsters.

"You are hitting upon the problem already." Ammon leaned back in his seat upon the mount, his body swaying easily with its gait. "Tell me, in Linolynn, who does your king rule over?"

"The nobles, scholars, clergy, merchants, farmers, servants—everyone really."

"Mmhmm. And what of, say, the horses?"

"The horses? Like the soldiers ride?"

"Please don't tell me that there are no wild horses across the sea. You'll ruin my already biased opinion of distant lands."

Iellieth laughed at that. "I can set your mind at ease there. I do not know their number, but there are several herds of wild horses that call Linolynn home."

"Ah." Ammon held up his hand to make his point. "And that is where the recent council, over the last few hundred years, has diverged from precedent. It is one thing to recognize that one does not rule over the fae—they are beyond taking orders from any they consider to be the short-lived peoples, even if elven lifespans seem long compared to human ones. But what I and a few other like-minded souls would have the council understand, have them recognize anew, is that they do have a responsibility over the wild places just as much as they do those with set borders. The Moonsbreak River, for instance, runs south from the mountains, and pools in the floodplain outside the city."

He leaned closer to Iellieth. "We've divided an inge-nious riverway system of gondolas I believe you will enjoy.

It's the best mode of transportation across Thyles Thamor, but you shall see that once we arrive. For today"—he sighed—"for today, the idea is this—though the High Elven Council cannot control or even really influence the flow of the river, its concerns are theirs because they depend upon it."

"And so, in a similar way," Iellieth added to show she understood, "the concerns of the animals, both the biomechos and the"—she gestured at the brachilli herd they rode in the center of—"well, whatever they are, should be the concern of the council as well."

Ammon placed his hand over his heart and bowed his head. "I thank you for hearing me. They will not, but I shall take this as a victory all the same."

He clucked his tongue and urged his mount ahead, giving Iellieth and Genevieve time to ride together before their parting.

A few hours later, Nealadora brought her mount to a stop in front of a dense copse from which emanated a warm purple glow. "The portal is just through here."

Iellieth's amulet heated in response. "I hope you understand." She wrapped her hand around the amulet and turned to Genevieve. "I can send Marcon or Quindythias into the copse to ensure you are well. But I fear my amulet will redirect me if I get near a portal not made by Yvayne."

"Jade knows we are safe with them." Genevieve smiled, her eyes glowing a brighter green, a signal the werewolf-druid was deeply in touch with her inner wolf. "And if Nealadora can show us where Sariel's pack resides, we should be able to return quickly, maybe even make it to Thyles Thamor before you leave."

Nealadora dismounted from her brachilli and gestured for Iellieth to do the same, then she placed her hands upon

Iellieth's shoulders. "Many disturbances, great and small, come to life in the forest that lies beyond you, Iellieth Amastacia."

Iellieth bit her lip, staring back at the nymph who, in this moment, reminded her of Mara. "I don't understand what you're trying to tell me."

The nymph smiled back at her. "No, but you want to. And that is the key."

Nealadora turned her attention to Genevieve. "A different life and different choices lie ahead of you, wolf-druid. For a time, your paths will part, but you will return to new friends one day."

Iellieth shook her head at Genevieve. "I am glad that for once it's not just me."

A knowing smile bloomed on her new friend's lips. "That makes two of us. Ophelia was always speaking in riddles to me too." Genevieve frowned. "I hope this is what she wanted me to do. She said she wanted me to find Yvayne, but then I found you. Maybe helping the daimon and the creatures of the Realms is actually the path she foresaw for me all along."

Genevieve's confused indecision was a feeling Iellieth knew well. How much of her recent path—what had occurred in Caldara, the ocean crossing, finally making it here to the Realms—had Mara foreseen? Genevieve still looked uneasy. "I'm sure she would be proud of everything you've done," Iellieth said. "And Yvayne would come find us if she needed us, or if she needed to redirect our paths."

"Yes, I'm sure you're right."

The nymph poked her head between them, interrupting their line of sight. "You are ready, then, for what the forest asks?"

"Ammon will lead us to Thyles Thamor and then, if the

council agrees, we will acquire the seal piece of earth," Iellieth ventured, hoping that was what the nymph was looking for. She didn't specify what would happen if the council *didn't* agree.

"I believe the forest holds an even more promising destiny for you than that. You, a curious adventurer wandering through an underground tunnel. The spirits of the realms, a slumbering primordial, waiting to be awakened."

Iellieth's eyes widened. That was certainly a more dramatic plan than what she'd been hoping for. "I have heard similar stories before, but they involved dragons." It had been a battle with a dragon, Braemorn, that led to Marcon's capture and his long imprisonment in the form of a statue.

"Dragons are but one possibility." Nealadora smiled to herself, the frightening turn in the conversation as benign as a stray cloud drifting past the sun. "The primordials are children of the titans. They can take differing forms, depending upon the titan and their other parent, if there is one."

"Wait, I think there's been a mistake—"

Nealadora turned to Genevieve, acting as though Iellieth hadn't spoken. "I will escort *you* to the Brightlands. The daimon will be waiting for you, long-anticipating a shapeshifter's return."

The watery cadence of Nealadora's voice soothed Iellieth's concerns. Perhaps she was right. And Genevieve's confidence had grown in their time together on the island, the week on the ship, and their journey through the Realms, despite Quindythias's suspicions that she might suddenly erupt into her werewolf form. He'd finally stopped nervously eyeing her or, worse, asking her about it.

Her fellow druid met her eyes. "I am ready for this," Genevieve said, as much to herself as to Iellieth and Nealadora. She pursed her lips, decision settling along her brow. Genevieve laid one hand on her stomach and a second on her heart. "Jade and I both are. And I gave Sariel my word."

Iellieth's heart quickened as she imagined Genevieve's rescue by the striking daimon she had described. One day, she would travel to the Brightlands, but she still had much to see in the lands of the elves, a place she had dreamed of for so long.

The two embraced, and Iellieth squeezed Genevieve's hand. "If I see Yvayne first, I will tell her where you've gone." Iellieth grinned. The fae likely already knew or would soon.

"As will I," Genevieve answered. Her eyes were lighter. She was likely thinking the same thing.

Nealadora pressed her deep blue hands on either side of Iellieth's cheeks. Her touch was as cold as river water. "Forget not my warning, Iellieth Amastacia. The forest and its denizens are not always as they seem." A far-off look spread across her features, her gaze drifting away. "The land you have envisioned is near to what this land ought to be. But few remain with the wisdom and strength to still see it." The nymph blinked, her silvery-blue eyes fixing on Iellieth. "They will need you to help them remember."

Before she could ask for clarification, the nymph clicked her tongue and swung back up onto her waiting brachilli. With a sigh, the creature waved its head, signaling to the rest of the herd, and Nealadora and

Genevieve rode off into the depths of the forest. Iellieth's own steed paused at the edge of the clearing before she vanished into the trees.

Iellieth raised her hand in farewell. She would miss the brachilli. They made for strange and intriguing mounts inside the elven forest.

She jumped at Quindythias's sudden appearance beside her.

"Well," the elf said, his arms crossed over his chest, "that was an odd experience, but I am glad to have won the heart of a nymph in this new era I have come to save."

She bit her lips together, glancing at Marcon and Ammon.

Marcon paused before following Genevieve to the portal and clapped his friend on the back. "Let's hope she doesn't take the separation too hard," he said.

Quindythias nodded. "The first few months will be difficult, I'm sure, but the daring deeds we perform inspired by her request and trust should ease her pain."

GENEVIEVE

Genevieve turned back at the mouth of the portal, her hand raised overhead. Marcon was there to see her off. He placed his hand upon his heart and bowed his head, a habit from his military days. She inclined her head as well, thanking him silently for his help. *Keep close watch over her*, she wanted to say. *So much depends upon the three of you*. But he knew this and more already, and she didn't want to impose.

Ammon was there as well. Genevieve placed three fingers to her lips, the druidic symbol of thanks, a tradition shared by the rangers of the Realms. He had been surprisingly open to her cause on Sariel's behalf, so much so that she began to question why Sariel had not asked the rangers himself. Ammon was planning to guide her friends on their mission, and he would leave word in Thyles Thamor with the rangers there who would receive her if he hadn't yet returned.

Nealadora and the brachilli herd had already passed through the portal. She would be the last.

"Ready, Jade?" Genevieve whispered to her wolf.

She placed a steadying hand between her ribs, her center, where she and the wolf melded.

"Alright, here we go." Genevieve strode forward, the purple light flickering over her, bathing her skin in its glow. Three steps in, and the light was all she could perceive, so bright her own hand would have been invisible to her. Five steps in, and the light intensified further. Had it been like this the last time?

Seven steps, and Genevieve's muscles began to burn. Something wasn't right. The light thickened, solidified.

It grew darker as well. The strands developed an amethyst glow, pooling like oil over water, then mixing, a deeper dye.

Eleven steps and she was crawling, panting for breath. "Jade, help me," she groaned.

Her inner wolf pressed claws through her fingers and out of her toes, allowing Genevieve to dig into whatever earth passed between the portals.

The deep shades of purple spun faster. Soon they were all she could see.

For one brief moment, the pressure released, and

Genevieve found herself suspended in Astralei—the world of stars—with no earth or sky to hold her.

She gasped and lurched forward, tumbling down worn stone steps, the purple-black whirl of a portal behind her.

Genevieve lay on her back, catching her breath, pressing her hands into the broken pebbles around the stone.

Once her head stopped spinning she rolled to her side, then carefully onto all fours. *Where are we, Jade?*

The wolf whimpered. She didn't know.

The deep purple glow of the portal shone out across a dark gray stone courtyard, with a stone road spiraling off of it. A black forest of spiky winter trees stretched up toward an amethyst-hued sky filled with unfamiliar stars. Deep, glowing blue-green valleys unfurled beyond, darker than any sea she'd ever seen.

In the distance, blocked by the portal, sounds of horses' hooves clacked over the road. They were too exposed where they were.

Keeping low, Genevieve crept toward the forest, watching behind her so she could spot the front of the approaching caravan as they passed before the portal's light. That same swirling light should block her and Jade from view.

She didn't have to wait long.

A team of black horses with manes of curling smoke marched along the road, pulling a train of metal cages behind them.

Her stomach twisted as they approached—she placed her hand over her mouth to still her gut. She was close enough that they would hear if she retched.

Stones jutted out from the smooth metal of the cages,

catching the light of the portal and absorbing it rather than reflecting it back. Darkstones.

She wiped the sweat from her brow, digging her still extended claws into the earth to hold herself in place and resist the urge to run.

Each of the three cages held a being—in the first, a fae with bright red hair sat hunched with her arms wrapped around her head. Her shoulders were shaking as she wept. A creature with green fur, *a fox*, Jade supplied, curled at the fae's feet.

In the next—Genevieve swallowed her cry of surprise —a beautiful silver wolf, no a daimon. The creature turned its head and she emitted a sob. A daimon with golden eyes. *Sariel.*

Genevieve closed her eyes, sending her thoughts to the wolf as he had taught her. *"Sariel, it's me. Genevieve."*

But she may as well have sent her words into the stones themselves. He couldn't hear her.

Torches shone from the rear of the final cage and Genevieve doubled over, crumpling onto the earth. A fae with sepia-hued skin and deep blue hair reclined against the back of her cage. An antlered crown balanced atop her head. Darkstones littered her cage and cuffed her ankles, wrists, and neck, but the fae betrayed no pain.

Genevieve's eyes blurred. *Varra Yvayne.* She'd found her. How, she didn't know.

A giant winged shape swooped overhead, talons as long as her calf poking out from its curved feathered feet.

But the head was not that of a bird—yellow-green eyes glowed against the gloam all around him. Stars peeked meekly through the holes in his wings. It was a figure she'd never met, but she knew him from Iellieth's stories. Lucien.

The fallen guardian cawed as he circled again, flapping his wings against the caravan of horses, who whinnied in fright and picked up their pace. Genevieve sprinted after them, more afraid of them slipping from her sight than she was of being seen.

They wound their way along the stone path toward a jagged mountain peak ahead—the elegant spires of an ancient castle jutted off the mountainside. Most of the battlements had crumbled with age. The few that remained standing glowed inwardly, lit by glittering purple fires.

This wasn't the Brightlands—she would have remembered the stars. Between the black of the forest and amethyst of the sky, Genevieve knew where she was and what she had to do.

Though she hadn't planned it, she was in the Shadowlands to save her friends.

CHAPTER 22

PERSEPHONIE

After the initial tense encounter with the riders from New Orison, Persephonie and her muster settled into their routine. There were repairs to be made to the wagons and special tending to the horses. She shared as many of the skills required for extensive travel with Rennear and Jezebel as she could. In those moments, the low thrum of danger that radiated off of New Orison itself faded almost entirely from her perception. Almost.

In the stillness of early morning or at night, around the communal fire, when she should have been able to rest and share stories with her babu, the threat seemed more dire.

On the morning of their third full day in New Orison, Persephonie stretched her arms overhead, gazing up at the strangely blue sky of the dome, the impossible sanctuary it promised her and her people. She wouldn't find the truth of what was going on by waiting within her muster for it to appear in front of her. No, whatever was transpiring here, she would have to travel into the center of town to find out.

She spun slowly about, waiting for Rennear and Jezebel to join her as they'd planned.

Velkan approached her instead, his head tilted to the side. "Where are you going?"

"Into town," she said, trying to suppress her impatience. She thought it better to allow his feelings for her to run their course rather than try to talk him out of them.

Velkan took a step closer to her. "I'd rather you not go alone."

"Rennear and Jezebel are coming with me."

"I would rather you have one of *our* people go to town with you." Velkan scowled, glancing away from her. "I'm worried I will sound just like them, even though they're the ones I'm worried about."

His concern was obviously genuine, and whatever he was dancing around had upset him. "Just like who? What are you saying?"

"There's something very wrong here, Persephonie. Anyone who would consider you an outsider among your own people, your home—" His hands balled into fists. Velkan was usually more worried than her brothers when she went to spend time with Esmeralda, even before they had a romance, but this was the most distressed she'd ever seen him. "If you show up in town with two people they genuinely believe to be outsiders, people they don't have any qualms bullying because they think their goddess somehow makes it right . . ." Velkan sighed. "It's dangerous, is what I'm trying to say. Let me and Felix come with you."

"Stefan is going to be put out that you did not include him," Persephonie teased, trying to lighten Velkan's mood. The priests wanted them to be afraid, wanted them to feel uncertain and unsure. She recognized it in the bullying manner of their guards, the way they pecked at any who were slightly different from themselves, how they tried to control that which was no business of theirs, like her muster's wheels.

Their fear-mongering was exactly counter to the feeling of ease and trust that Cassandra wished for her followers to have, knowing that she held the threads of their fate and wished them well.

Velkan answered her with a smirk. "Only if someone tells him."

"Very well." Persephonie bounced onto her toes and looked around for Rennear, Jezebel, and her brother. "I will allow the *four* of you to accompany me, though you cannot slow me down or complain. Agreed?"

Velkan bowed his head. "Agreed."

Several minutes later, Velkan had already violated their agreement in the amount of time it took him to get Felix ready to travel to town.

"Your brother insisted on coming with us?" Rennear asked, wrapping his arm around her waist and tugging her against him.

"Something like that." Persephonie rested her head against Rennear's chest and closed her eyes, relaxing into the heat and feel of him. Each day, Rennear returned more to himself. The recovery was slow, but he *was* recovering. The spiders' attack and his transformation had temporarily slowed his progress. In all the excitement, he hadn't taken special care of his leg while in his werewolf form—she wasn't sure he'd even remembered he was injured while he was a werewolf.

She didn't want to repeat Velkan's concerns to Rennear. He was discouraged enough by his injury, and hearing that

Velkan didn't believe he could assist her if there was trouble in town wouldn't help matters.

Jezebel turned toward the four of them and glanced down at Persephonie. "Are we ready then? I've a great curiosity to see this improbable town." Their great bow stuck out over their shoulder, an additional, unbroken horn paired with the uneven set on their forehead.

"Finally, yes." Persephonie led the way forward, careful of her pace so Rennear would be at ease without it seeming like that's what she was doing. Jezebel fell into step beside her, just as she'd hoped they would.

"I have been wondering, Jezebel. You've spent the majority of your life in the Shadowlands, yes? And that is where Apollo makes his home?"

"Yes to both, though I hope to prevent you from ever needing to visit the latter," Jezebel answered, their expression darkening.

Why was it that every time she spoke with someone today, they became upset for no reason that she could discern or anticipate? "Erm, why I ask is that I was wondering how often you have traveled beyond the Shadowlands into the Negative Planes themselves. Boss Gilsen said that was where we are, but I am still trying to understand where in their vast expanse we might be. I was wondering if it might be apparent to you, if something might be familiar. Any clues we could look for."

She had never encountered a story, from any place, that involved a dome-covered region surrounded by barren fields of caked clay but, if Jezebel had traveled somewhere similar, they might be able to triangulate their location and plan their exit.

"I am afraid I cannot assist you. My travels never extended as far as the Negative Planes, so they remain unfamiliar to me. I had hoped that Emryc's curse might not reach this far but—" The fae waved their hand back toward their wings. The bony protrusions stuck out over their shoulders, the feathers vanished once more. "I do not know if that's an encouragement or not."

"Hmm," Persephonie answered. "Much of New Orison confounds my senses. Perhaps it is a good thing that the curse still touches you and your wings." Where there were saudad without wheels who worshipped the goddess of misfortune rather than Cassandra, any number of reversals seemed possible. She smiled up at the fae, squeezed their elbow, and the five of them set off down the hill.

The road down to the town itself was an hour's walk from their muster's camp, though it took longer with Rennear's injury. Velkan helpfully elbowed Felix whenever he began to complain of the delay, and Persephonie only had to remind him once that he was welcome to turn back should he wish.

They passed through a field of lavender, the pale purple shafts waving in a soft breeze, one of the first Persephonie had noticed—it was oddly still through the rest of New Orison. "Jezebel, do you see that? Could whatever protects this space from the heavy winds outside be allowing in a slight breeze?" She squinted out toward their entry point, a distant speck at the end of a winding road marked by tall grasses, but the blue of the sky overhead obscured any glimpse of the red clay desert outside the dome.

Persephonie tiptoed through the lavender fields and up to a small, walled garden where a young saudad woman grasped the arm of her babu and guided her outside for a rest in the sun. Felix called her back before she could pass near enough to call out to them but, from her vantage point at the top of a low rise, she found an extensive herb garden, large enough to stock an apothecary, and bordered by a large kitchen garden. She couldn't help but note that the hedges, house, and garden layout all perfectly concealed the herbs from easy sight of the town itself, but perhaps she was being paranoid.

Ten minutes more brought them to the perfect vista to look down upon New Orison itself. Despite all her misgivings, upon seeing it, the breath caught in Persephonie's chest and her eyes watered. *This* was what they'd been missing, what they'd lost.

The rolling hillsides contained within New Orison's dome coalesced in a twisting valley, one carved out by the river that must have once stretched through this region. The saudad who had first settled here had built the town up into the valley's side, with the riverbed forming one border of the settlement, though a few structures dotted what had once been the waterside, including a windmill on the opposite end of town. A few old wagon paths wound their way out of the town, but they disappeared into the fields beyond, their pattern in the grass the lingering legacy of when New Orison's residents had traveled by wagons that had been transformed into stationary dwellings.

The other remnant of the saudad's past travels were the buildings on the outskirts of the town itself. There, the rounded shapes of wagons with their clay tiled roofs joined onto stone structures, some of which had been formed atop wheel-less wagons, others built directly into the embankment. Stone steps had been chiseled from the valley as well, bridging the distance between the buildings' foundations or the edge of a wagon as the case may be.

As they drew closer, other areas of the town came into view. One section relied more heavily on wagons for its construction than the others and had more of a residential appearance in its design, at least if Andel-ce Hevra was any point of comparison. The wagons had been stagger-stacked atop one another, three stories high, with thatched pathways joining what would have been the carriage fronts. The effect was of small porches joined by thatched wooden railings, with wider walkways on the upper floors that shielded the lower from winds and rain.

Had there been a time when such protections were more necessary? It had yet to even rain much less storm in their days here thus far. And while it had been summer when they left the mountains, autumn was well on its way here.

Nearing the town, the pressed dirt of the road gave way to carved stone and cobbles. The rocks were smooth, either worn down with time or pulled from the riverbed. Moss clung to the edges of the pathway.

Life within the town of New Orison resembled the settled existence of many of the places Persephonie had visited with her muster or the markets she and Esmeralda had frequented. People bustled to and fro with baskets on their hips on their way to see friends to complete the day's errands. A boy in a knit cap hurried by, pushing a cart filled with fresh bread. Inside the lower level of the stacked wagon buildings, clerks worked behind tables while above, drying laundry caught on the breeze between the structures. Though the accents in Saudad were more varied, it was so very like approaching her own muster at twilight or in the busyness of the morning as everyone prepared for their day.

Persephonie gazed about in wonder, meeting Velkan's glance. His grin was a burst of sun on an already fine day. "I didn't want to spoil it for you." He leaned closer, keeping his voice low. "But from that first day when we rode down here, I knew you would love it. I couldn't miss you seeing it for the first time."

He and Felix pointed out the spots of interest they'd managed to uncover during their brief foray into the town the day of their arrival—the butcher, a candle sculptor, a wooden repairs shop specializing in trinkets and instruments. "There's a tavern just there," Velkan said, pointing toward the center of town, where the main, curving street opened onto a square.

Two streets broke off from the square, leading back to the largest structure set against the riverbank. Though she'd seen larger structures in Andel-ce Hevra, there was a dark, pooling gravity to the steepled tower. "That's their temple," Felix said with a shudder. "Something creepy about it, with that barren patch beyond."

"Let's start with the tavern," Persephonie proposed, to enthusiastic assent from her companions. Rennear had grown pale from their exertions, and she was beginning to regret not taking the horses into town. Given their hostile reception thus far, she had worried the horses would be held until they turned in their wheels, and neither horses nor wheels could readily be replaced. She didn't think matters had soured to the point that the followers of Malura would attempt to restrain them, but if they were too eager to take advantage of Rennear's weakened state . . .

Seeming to read her mind, Rennear appeared at her side and squeezed her hand. "Shall we?" He grinned down at her. "I cannot help but think of our first full day together, exploring Andel-ce Hevra."

The memory warmed her chest and eased her concerns. It did little good to anticipate possible disasters she could not prevent, particularly by worrying about them. "That was a wonderful day," she answered, echoing his smile. "If this is half as diverting, I will be in very high spirits."

Velkan and Felix led the way to the tavern, leaving Persephonie to savor the intricacies of accented Saudad on the streets around them. Never had she seen so many of her people gathered in one place before.

A mix of architectural styles enhanced the eclectic, cosmopolitan flair of New Orison. Some of the structures that joined the adapted wagon buildings to one another were made of stone, others a mix of stone and wood. Most of the roofs were shingled, alternating between clay and wood.

The buildings around the square, including the tavern Felix and Velkan were so excited about, were all made of stacked stones inlaid with wood. Persephonie shielded her eyes to observe the top of the tavern roof and was delighted to find an open terrace. There must be a staircase inside that led to the third story and the roof.

The tavern proprietor greeted them warmly, and she marveled only a little at Rennear and Jezebel. "We don't see many like, well, either one of you, around here," she said with a sideways grin. "Welcome to New Orison. First drink's on the house so long as you buy another." The fae agreed to that and carried a drink over to Persephonie, who had settled into a round table by the window with Velkan and Felix. With the rare time all to themselves, Persephonie recounted some of the smaller details of her adventure in Andel-ce Hevra, what her experience of living at the top of a tavern had been like.

"I'm not sure Datha would have let you go had he

known you wouldn't be able to stay with Esmeralda," Felix said, sipping on his ale.

Jezebel had brought her a chilled white wine, her preference for midday imbibing. "Was he terribly worried?" she asked.

Velkan pursed his lips. "You know your father. He tries to not be, but how can he help it?" As her brother nodded, Velkan offered a quick apology to Jezebel and Rennear. "But surely the both of you can see—she belongs with her family."

For a moment, Rennear looked pained. He hid the expression behind his mug of mead.

"Perhaps a change of subject, then." Persephonie grinned, trying to hide her own discomfort. "Have we visited all of the musters and sent gifts?"

Her question provoked an argument between Velkan and Felix, who couldn't agree on how Datha had decided to handle the arrival gift for New Orison itself. While they bickered, Jezebel looked about the bar, their nostrils flaring on occasion. Rennear alternated between staring into his cup and out the window.

A few other patrons came in, settling into well-worn wooden booths. They gave a brief greeting to the five gathered at the window table but otherwise paid them no heed. Persephonie took note of this—from a young age, Datha had taught her to read non-saudad establishments and cultures by the behavior of tavern patrons. Do they seem surprised to see someone new? Suspicious or excited? Does your presence make the barkeep uneasy? The patrons' casual greeting spoke to the size of New Orison— they did not know everyone, nor did they expect to.

But it also gave her hope. The patrons didn't react to Jezebel and Rennear in fear. Perhaps this town of her people wouldn't be so inhospitable to her friends as she'd feared.

This feeling, warmed by her first glass of wine and deeply internalized by the second, continued to simmer as they followed the tavern keeper's directions toward the market, swinging first by the temple to Malura at Persephonie's insistence. "We do not have to go inside, but I *do* want to see it," she insisted.

CHAPTER 23

IELLIETH

By mid-morning of Iellieth's third full day in the Realms, the shining lake that lay outside Thyles Thamor glimmered into view. An hour later, the outskirts of the city itself peeked through the dense forest all around them. Great water oaks with draping moss hanging from their branches stretched out over the edge of the water, their spider-legged roots poised over the lake, water echoing sky. As Ammon had indicated, a wide dock ran along the tree line. On one side there were larger crafts, those designed for river runs toward either Shade Rest or Moonsbreak Landing. On the other side of the pier—which was, Ammon explained, buoyed by a series of levees—a collection of gondolas floated on the lake. Once they emerged from the trees, they'd take a gondola into the city itself. "Just a few more hours to go."

"There isn't, say, some sort of preparation space before we enter the city, is there?" Quindythias asked their elven guide.

Iellieth raised her hand to her lips, anticipating where

her friend was going but not wanting to interrupt in case she was wrong.

"Preparation space?" Ammon frowned at Quindythias.

"Yes. We've been bumbling through this cursed forest for days. I'm sure there's grass and dirt and who knows what else clinging to every bit of us."

"Bugs, even," Iellieth added, unable to help herself.

Marcon chortled, but Quindythias was beyond irony. "Yes, precisely, thank you, Iellieth. At least one of us besides me is thinking clearly and has their priorities in order. Speaking of"—he took a deep breath and adopted a grave countenance—"it is possible that I will be a dearly beloved figure, in which case our time will be rather full with my adoring public, and we'll have to work in the council and whatever sub-topics of interest the two of you have been working up the past few days. Something about wolves?"

Iellieth chewed her lower lip to hide her own mirth while Quindythias continued. "The second possibility, naturally, is that I shall be despised, in which case we'll know that distant relatives of the royals of Bastion or some other such agent of Alessandra—either now or in the past—has besmirched my name. Should that occur, it was an honor to travel with the three of you. I will spare you from the bloody bits as best I can."

Marcon shook his head, genuine concern wrinkling his brow. "I really don't think—"

"And thirdly," Quindythias continued, paying Marcon no heed, "the reality may lie somewhere between these two in that I am remembered by some sort of underground movement, rather like the one I led back in Bastion, and am a street hero of sorts." He straightened his shoulders and turned his nose up and to the side, striking a posture any folk hero would be proud to be captured in.

"The third option seems the most obvious choice to me," Ammon said, surprising even Quindythias. Without further explanation, he continued on through the forest, whistling an Elvish tune under his breath.

"I know that song," Quindythias called after him, ruffled at the unruffled response of their guide. "Wait. Are you trying to secretively inform me that it's now a song about me? Written by one of my many lovesick admirers after my passing into statue form?"

A great bellowing roar erupted from the forest ahead of them. The earth shook underfoot, and trees swayed, several falling onto their sides in a great rending of roots.

"Ah!" Iellieth covered her ears to block out the trees' cries. What had been terrified, pained screams in Caldara by the mining camp was, here in the Realms, a deep, resonant bellow of dismay—the cavernous pain of an ancient dirge compressed into a single cry.

Marcon gripped her shoulders and placed her behind him, shielding her from an unseen force.

Ahead of them, Ammon darted back through the trees, waving his arm to the side. "Get down!" Iellieth read in Elvish on his lips. He shouted it again in the common tongue, and Marcon pulled her to the side, driving them both into the underbrush.

With a braying crash, the source of the disturbance thundered into view. As tall at least as the tri-level structures of the Air Ward and at least as broad, a giant four-legged creature, somewhere between a moose and an elk, swung its antlers side to side, its echoing bellow reverberating all around them, so strong as to thrust the underbrush into their faces. Dirt and leaves tangled in her hair.

Just as quickly as he'd reemerged onto the path ahead of them, Ammon leapt out of the clusters of low, bushy growth, arms raised overhead. *"Alais vah,"* he called. Be at peace.

The ranger's appearance only served to increase the towering moose-elk's rage. It stamped toward him, lowering its antlers, which snagged in draping lilac flowers that hung from one of the oaks.

Marcon's hold had relaxed around Iellieth as they watched the moose. She launched herself out of the undergrowth after the ranger, standing by the creature's shoulder. *"Cai-le!"* Iellieth shouted the calming spell. Green sparks shot up from her fingers and into the creature's side.

The spell was more powerful than she'd meant for it to be. Additional sparks sprang up from the forest floor, others emerging in a line as vines from the trees, wrapping around the moose, which struggled against the spell's hold. Iellieth pressed her hands forward—the spell should soothe the moose, not send it into a rage.

"Your magic won't work against them," Ammon shouted over the braying moose, "not in the way you think."

Aside from enraging it further, Iellieth's appearance and spell had been enough to divert the moose from Ammon. As it turned toward her, a shadow crossed over the ranger's face. He quickly withdrew a thick arrow from the quiver at his back, took aim, and shot up into the creature's chest.

Its bray worsened, and the moose stumbled side to side, its knobby joints quivering underneath it. Marcon and Quindythias leapt out of their hiding places, scrambling away from the moose's uncertain steps. With a final groan, it crashed onto the forest floor, panting. Ammon's arrow stuck out of its chest.

"I was trying to calm it!" Iellieth shouted, sprinting around the injured creature to Ammon's side. What kind of ranger was he, to speak of helping the wild creatures and then shooting them instead?

"Wait." Ammon held up his hand and she stopped a few feet away from him. He stood on tiptoe, searching over the moose before beckoning Iellieth toward the fallen creature. Its breath heaved in and out, but it remained still. "Don't be afraid. It will remain unconscious for a while yet."

Iellieth swallowed her retort, that she was angry, not afraid. Ammon had helped them reach Thyles Thamor and had been open about the nature of the Realms. She could grant him a moment to explain.

"Here," he said, waving her over to its side.

She gasped, freezing in place as the creature's side came fully into view.

In its frenzy, she hadn't seen this side of the moose—three deep gashes ran along its side where its flesh had been cut, recently enough that blood still coated its fur. Beneath the long rents in its side, blood-coated metallic gears slowed their whirring pace. With them, the moose's breath eased as well.

Iellieth doubled back. Ammon's arrow hadn't pierced its hide—the arrow point had spread out after he fired it, forming a six-pointed star across the moose's chest out of which a pale blue light seeped. The light trickled back along the moose's inner gears, the spelled arrow's glow reminding her of Nealadora.

"Poachers," Ammon growled under his breath as Iellieth returned to his side. "They came down from the north around the same time the leaks from the Shadow-lands intensified. If they can catch the biomechos, they'll gut them and steal the gears and parts. They're trying to uncover the magic that keeps them alive." He shook his head, jaw tightening as he looked over the creature. "We've been trying to find out what they plan to use this knowledge for—what sort of unnatural ends they plan to bend this understanding of the alchemists' old magic toward."

"Alchemists?" Marcon asked, coming to stand behind her and Ammon.

"Yes." The ranger paused. "Wait, do you know their magic?"

Marcon glared off into the forest. "I did, once. Not to practice, but I knew of it. The Cities relied on them heavily during the war, especially after they forced the Champions into hiding and needed other ways of accessing the elemental magic."

"Hmm, this is good to know. It is difficult to uncover the plans of your enemy when you have no knowledge of their aims, only their deeds." He placed his hand along the thin bone of the moose's leg. Its breath had slowed to a resting pace, and the blue glow now covered over its inner gears in place of its pooling blood.

"Sharia would be most upset about this," Ammon said, petting the moose's leg. "I'd introduce you to her, my sister, as we arrive but, last I heard, she was chasing down a band of poachers on part of her assignment for her scholarly cult."

Iellieth's absorption with the injured creature before her—the wounded, arrow-magic healing side of a barn-sized moose riddled with gears and something Ammon called sprockets—faltered. "Hold on." She repeated what

Ammon had just said to herself, poachers and a scholarly cult standing out in particular. "What kind of scholarly cult do you mean?" She thought of Red inducting himself into the Soul Shepherds or Yvayne's stories of the lore-keepers. "A cult of scholars or scholars of cults?"

"A little bit of both, I should think," the ranger answered unhelpfully.

More and more by the moment, Thyles Thamor proved itself capable of thwarting her expectations. How had the records in Linolynn failed to capture so much?

"If there's time, I'll outfit the three of you at the lodge. You'll need more specialized weapons if you're to be truly effective in subduing biomechos who've been injured. Their adaptations make them resistant to natural magic."

Iellieth bit her lower lip, leaning toward the creature for a better look while trying to keep her distance lest it should suddenly awaken. Spinning gears poked through the wounds on the creature's side. A jutting bone held the gear in place.

"I'll heal her before we continue on," Ammon said. "We haven't crossed any poachers' tracks on our way here, so she should be safe from them while she heals. Shortly after we make our escape, she'll awaken and return to her herd."

"Herd? There's an entire herd of . . . giant mechanical moose?"

"Heh," the ranger chuckled. "Welcome to the Realms."

CHAPTER 24

BRISERAS

"I believe we found something of yours in the forest," Aletta called to Briseras early the next morning as she emerged from the spare bed in the healer's wagon. The muster boss smiled, gesturing behind her to a towering, muscular elf with a black raven perched on his shoulder.

"Otto!" Briseras exclaimed, rushing toward the pair. "Tybalt." She bowed her head to the elf, who returned the gesture, smiling down at her.

"Well met, huntress. I would ask how you and the invalid have fared but . . ." Tybalt sniffed at the air before him, his nose wrinkling in displeasure. "Ah, so the saudad's report proves true." His brow furrowed. "Are you alright? A rogue werewolf, even alone, is no easy foe."

A yawning groan from behind her alerted Briseras that Jorgan had woken and joined them.

"Loire had a sense you were in danger and sent her fox after me," Tybalt explained. "Otto here arrived back in her glade just before I did, so I thought I would bring him back to you." The elf's easy demeanor flickered at the mention of Otto.

"Did you receive troubling news from the Vale? Something the matter?"

Tybalt's smirk returned. "For a moment I had forgotten who I was talking to." He breathed deeply and shook his head. "The fault is likely mine. In my report to the Vale, I thought it best to be as forthcoming as possible, believing that my enthusiasm for recent revelations would be matched by the Guardians of the Vale and my superiors." Tybalt frowned, staring off beyond the muster to the undulating fields that stretched past the Witchwood's borders and into the parts of Steymhorod she had not yet explored.

"What I interpreted as signs the Sisters may be awakening, perhaps due to your presence"—he inclined his head toward Briseras as Jorgan came to stand beside her—"they were inclined to dismiss." His scowl deepened, crinkling the line of his mouth. "That you have piqued the vampire lord's interest was a particular point of contention."

"Wait, whose interest?" Jorgan interrupted, looking between them.

"Lord Draego," Briseras quickly explained. "He appeared to me in St. Sebastian and gave me a key to help on our journey." She shifted aside her mother's locket and held up the silver key Draego had placed around her neck. "I don't know what it unlocks yet, only that he thought it would help."

Jorgan's mouth bobbed open as he stared from Briseras to the key in her hand and back. "You . . ." His hand drifted to his neck. "You're working with a vampire?"

"Receiving help from," Briseras clarified. "He wants his

lands to be rid of Nassarq and, as we are already working toward that aim, he decided to throw in his lot with us." The deeper aspects of Lord Draego's interest—and her reciprocation—Briseras decided to leave alone. Jorgan already looked more shocked than he would have had she immediately shifted into a werewolf form and donned a flower crown.

"The Vale has not promised their aid but, should we venture there, my superiors would like to meet you." Tybalt sighed. "I thought it best to return to help you as they are unlikely to change their minds even if I appear in person. I am sorry I could not do more."

"It is no matter." Briseras closed the space between herself and the elf and raised her hand for Otto. She winced as the bird's talons scratched her unprotected forearm and brought Otto close. He croaked deeply and then launched himself off her arm to hop onto the earth outside the healer's wagon where Vera stood watch over Lavinia.

Not having the help of the elves was an inconvenience, but more pressing matters than locating Nassarq's tower had presented themselves. In a little over a week, a full moon would appear over Steymhorod, forcing her and Jorgan's transformation if they could not reverse their infection before then. Lord Draego had told her the next step in healing the lycanthropy, reviving Arduenne, and the muster's seer had encouraged her to seek out the heart and restore the fane. Vicq believed the archives of Barasov might contain records that would help her find these remnants of Arduenne.

The scholar's thoughts turned often to his former mate and their eventual intersection with his past pack. Vicq had explained the importance of them gaining Solane's trust ahead of the transformation—in the den on Wolf's Head Peak, she had the means to ease the pain of transformation and allow them to remain in control of themselves, unlike the werewolf who had found them in the forest the day before. It seemed doubtful they would find both the fane and the heart before the full moon. Luck would determine whether Kratok was waiting for them in the den or if they could approach Solane alone. Briseras knew which outcome she was hoping for, but weapons and Barasov stood between her and revenge.

The saudad arranged a meeting place for them to the north a short ways beyond Barasov's borders in a week's time. There, they could join with a recovered Lavinia and travel the remaining distance to the werewolves' den.

Vicq was in higher spirits than he had been the day they met, only stuttering slightly as he introduced himself to Tybalt and, once he realized the elf was amenable to his werewolf disposition, he relaxed further. "It will be nice to have another Steymhorodian around," he remarked to Tybalt as they set out. He questioned the elf about the minutiae of his life in the Green Vale, expressing his surprise that Tybalt did not more often travel to Barasov.

"He doesn't seem very like a werewolf alpha to me," Briseras murmured to Jorgan as they bid farewell to Lavinia and the saudad and set their sights toward the city.

"No, he does not. Or at least not very like any werewolf I've encountered in stories. Nor in fact . . ." Jorgan rubbed the soreness from his leg. "What sorts of weapons do you think we'll find in Barasov?"

Briseras fondly traced the polished stock of her crossbow, the freshly shaped wood smooth beneath her hand. "I have rather high hopes that something spectacular will find us. And depending on the nature of the weapons' appearance, we'll disarm their current wielder and take the weapons for ourselves. Or, should the city prove to be less exciting than described and the weapons reside in a shop for safekeeping, we'll perform a favor for the weapons' maker, showing ourselves indispensable and worthy of armament."

"Of course. What a simple set of possibilities," Jorgan remarked, smirking at her. "I'm relieved you've already worked all the details out."

She let the sarcasm pass, thinking instead of what Lord Draego had told her about her lycanthropy—she could find a cure, though doing so risked an already delicate balance of power. Her quest would begin with Arduenne, the one known as the Lady of the Mountains, and finding the keeper of Arduenne's heart, as the seer had explained. In addition to weapons, she hoped Vicq's archives would indicate where she might find first the heart and then the fane.

❦

THE FOG GREW THICKER AS THEY TRAVELED NORTH, rolling off Lake Barasov, as Vicq explained, and coating the hills nearby.

On their fourth day of travel from the muster, a few hours after dawn, the jagged teeth of the city's walls emerged out of the fog. The land fell away to the north beneath the rolling mist, slipping into the depths of the lake where Vicq insisted ancient monsters dwelled.

A few hazards had nipped at their heels on their journey—zombies lurching out of the fog, traps of mire and bog hidden by forest roots, and a slinking shadow that stalked through branches, always disappearing as Briseras turned back to observe it.

The hair rose on the back of her neck as she spied the city walls. The lake itself protected Barasov's northern half, but the southern curve of the city had only two entrances. The nearest was a winding walkway along the city's southwestern wall. The other, a narrow, arched passageway on the southeast.

"Vicq, what are they trying to protect themselves against?" Briseras glanced at the werewolf-scholar in the same moment a series of yips arose from the forest behind them. Her shoulders rose—she knew that sound. "Worgs!" Briseras called in the same moment that howls and battle cries arose behind them. "Run!"

The drumming of their pounding feet and hurried breaths weren't enough to hide the galloping rhythm of the creatures who had scented them on the edge of the woods. Briseras pumped her arms, Vera sprinting beside her, ears back.

"Mounted wights," Tybalt called from her other side. "They'll be—argh!" The elf lurched forward, clutching at his back. A smooth black arrow jutted out of his ribs, having pierced through the interlocking scales of his leather armor.

"Armed, I suppose?" Jorgan finished for the elf.

Briseras spun back as she ran, firing crossbow bolts at their pursuers. Jorgan prevented her from extracting the second bow from her back. "There are too many of them. We need to make the wall."

Ahead of them, a half-transformed Vicq tugged a curved horn from his pack, blowing into the end of it and alerting the guards along Barasov's wall of their arrival. "If we can make the field before the city, their archers will protect our flank. I think."

"Why aren't you more sure?" Briseras shouted back.

The werewolf half-snarled an incoherent reply and she let the matter go for the present.

As they neared the barren field before Barasov, evidence of previous wight attacks poked out of the earth in a ring around the city—broken arrows, shattered shields. A spear whizzed past her, narrowly missing her freshly healed shoulder and flying beyond Vera. Briseras swore under her breath, furious with herself for not adding to her wolf's protective barding while cooling her heels in St. Sebastian. So long as they survived the wights' attack, their list of errands for Barasov was growing ever longer.

A hundred paces or so across the barren field, Briseras risked a look back over her shoulder. She gulped in a breath and swung back to face the city, no longer bothering with her crossbows. Row upon row of spectral, armored skeletons jangled closer atop their undead mounts. The undulating, cloud-like flesh of the wights was rotting in places where they'd sustained injuries, lending some of them an entirely marred appearance while others merely seemed to glow in the middle of the day. The glowing, greenish gray fur of the worgs clung to rotting, spectral sides where slabs of decaying muscle ground over jutting bones. Though they appeared solid enough, the bones of the undead knights and their mounts were the only support for their armor. The resultant cacophony of metal rang in her ears, pushing them all on faster.

With a second bugle on his horn, Vicq called up to those posted along the wall, hidden behind the narrow arrow slits nicked into the mortar. But his call was enough.

First one then a second volley of flaming arrows came flying out of the walls, singeing the knights and worgs as they struck true. Vicq, then Vera and Otto, followed by Tybalt, Jorgan, and Briseras sprinted across a narrow bridge the fog had initially obscured. Beneath it was a deep, thick moat of sludgy green water. A bell sounded from high in the wall, followed by the clanking of large metal gears below her, rather like the mechanism that controlled the gates in St. Sebastian.

Vicq cried out as the edge of the moat started to tip up before them, shifting the angle of the bridge. He leapt easily over the gap and waved Vera and a croaking Otto over. Tybalt grunted as he heaved himself across, followed by Jorgan, who was muttering to himself. Briseras dared one last look back at the worgs and their riders—even in all her years hunting, she'd never seen such a large, coordinated undead army.

The final glance was costly. She missed her footing with her leap, launching herself from the moat's edge too early so that she careened toward the other side, arms flailing as she yelled.

In front of her, Jorgan reached his arms out, catching her in his grasp and tugging her back over the opposite edge. They crashed into Tybalt's chest, and all three of them fell to the ground.

"Oof," Briseras sighed as she landed, eliciting a groan from Jorgan, whom she'd accidentally poked in the ribs.

"I know, I know," he sighed. "No whining. Just . . . ouch."

Tybalt laid his head back in the grass and laughed, doubling down on the display of merriment while also wincing at the wound on his back. He clutched the arrow in his fist. Blood coated the tip but not the entire arrowhead—his armor had prevented a more serious wound.

A puzzled guard clad in blue emerged from a narrow doorway at the base of the staircase carved into the side of the wall, frowning as he took in the elf with a bloody arrow, Briseras extricating herself from being tangled with Jorgan, and Otto's ruffled perch on Vera's back. "Quite an entrance the lot of you make, eh?" the guard said.

Otto puffed out his feathers and gave a disgruntled croak. Vera nudged him reassuringly with her wet nose, distressing him further. At that, even Briseras grinned.

The guard took down their names as he guided them through the doorway, repeating several times that they had entered Barasov within the Watchers' Ward and, once they passed their vampire test, they would be allowed to proceed deeper into the city. Vicq claimed to the guard that he'd made prior arrangements at the Tepid Water Inn, his voice so steady as he said it that she very nearly believed him herself.

He opened the metal gate on the opposite side of the wall they'd passed underneath and gestured them through.

"Wait," Briseras said, frowning. "What about the vampire test?"

"You've passed it," the guard said with a smile. "I didn't invite you inside the city, but in you came. So now it's safe for me to say, welcome to Barasov."

She parted her lips to reply but Jorgan wrapped his arm around her waist and guided her beside him into the city. "Great, thank you," he called back. More softly to Briseras he murmured, "If he doesn't know such superstitions won't keep him safe here of all places, I don't see any reason to spoil it for him now."

The nobleman had a point. Briseras allowed herself to be led away and slowed to a stop beside Jorgan, gazing at the city around them. Her first impression of Barasov made her chest tighten—cobblestones lined winding streets, which concealed any dangers that lay out of sight. The buildings were built close together, with laundry lines stretching overhead. The windows hung open, letting in the crisp autumn air and venting the smoke from tallow candles to the outdoors. Unlike in much of St. Sebastian, mottled glass panes shimmered within most of the window frames.

It was the sound that saved her—the bustle and chatter that had set her on edge when she first arrived in St. Sebastian but that reminded her far more of her time with Jeremy before the attack.

She must have paused for a considerable period—Jorgan was staring at her quizzically, and Briseras shook her head. No need to relive the past, even if it haunted her still. She didn't want to explain that settlements were difficult for her. Enclosing walls reminded her of her childhood in Haven.

Before he could ask her to explain, Jorgan's past floated its ghostly head out of his shoulder to an immediate scolding from Vicq who threw his hands up to the sky. "It'll be a wonder if we're not immediately thrown out to be fed to the wights," he lamented. The scholar had overcome any fear of them during their travel to the city, and an alternately jovial and exasperated wolf was just beginning to emerge.

"So"—Vicq clapped his hands together, ignoring Jorgan's glower—"seeing as we're on the Watchers' side of the city, why don't the three of you find a spot at an inn. There are a few old friends I'd like to check in on, and I need to clear out the room I've been letting near the market but, this afternoon, we'll have a go at entering the

Lorespire and then find our way to visiting the weapon-smiths first thing tomorrow?"

Not knowing enough to argue for a different plan, they agreed and parted from Vicq with plans to meet him deeper in the city that afternoon.

The inn was easy enough to find and aptly named—The Watchers' Eye—a somewhat rundown establishment in the center of the Watchers' territory with a bustling tavern on the lower story where agents of the Watchers met with one another to exchange information and make deals of protection with their clients. Briseras nursed an ale while she watched a few of these negotiations take place.

As she'd suspected, most of the need for protection arose from the feud itself. Traders wanted their goods to be able to pass safely from one end of the city to the other, a privilege they had to pay for so the Watchers could protect 'their' merchandise from the Bloodletters. There was probably an inn on the opposite side of town performing precisely the same service for merchants in the Bloodletters' territory.

Tybalt secured a room for them and covered the cost of the three nights they'd be staying before departing to meet up with the muster and proceed into the mountains.

The gleam of success faded from their afternoon at the Lorespire where Vicq's request to access the records was denied. The former alpha grew so angry he started to transform until the equally angry archive guard accused Vicq of having stolen from the archives on his last visit and threatened to call the guards.

The werewolf paled at that and hurried away, leaving the three of them little choice but to follow him. "Ahem." Vicq tugged at the loose collar of his shirt. "I may have . . .

left out the particulars of my relationship with the weaponsmiths and armorers of Barasov."

Briseras crossed her arms and shifted her weight onto one hip.

Vicq wetted his lips, glancing nervously between the three of them and settling on Vera as his audience. Otto was taking the afternoon to rest at the inn.

"Left out what exactly?" Jorgan growled.

"I owe a bit of a debt you see." He pushed a pebble across the stone pathway with the toe of his worn boot.

"To whom?" Tybalt scowled down at the scholar, his jovial mood from earlier having fallen away.

On two previous occasions, it seemed, Vicq had tried to garner support for reclaiming his pack from established forces of protection in Barasov. Not being a city-dweller himself, he lacked the gold necessary to hire such assistance and had attempted to win it by gambling instead. In the process, he had cheated several of the artisans and lost an enchanted set of leather armor that could adapt itself to werewolf transformations to the Bloodletters.

"And what makes you think we'll be able to buy it back for you?" Briseras asked, already suspecting what the manipulative alpha's answer would be. Had his anxiety upon meeting them been an act, or had he grown so desperate he didn't care who he lied to?

Vicq shook his head. "Buying the armor back won't be possible. But *winning* it back is why I brought you all here."

CHAPTER 25

PERSEPHONIE

Low, carved steps led the way down to the temple. Persephonie took Rennear's arm—between his limp and the mead, he was slightly unsteady. "You must not take what Velkan said to heart," she murmured to Rennear as they walked together. "He would never had said that in Datha's presence, and Datha has always said how important it is for me to remain close with my mother."

It took more convincing for her to draw Rennear out of his melancholy, but eventually he met her searching gaze. "What if he's right, Persephonie? What if I've pulled you away from your family?"

She sighed. Trust Velkan to accidentally prod straight into the heart of an already difficult situation. "What if my definition of family is more expansive than Velkan's? And what if my datha understands that too—even if Velkan doesn't?"

Rennear smiled at her sadly and squeezed her hand. Whatever he was about to say was cut off by their arrival in front of the temple or, more accurately, what they found just beyond it.

The temple was easily the largest building in town. Its four stories leered down at them, almost as though the temple itself couldn't draw its gaze away from the gaping hole in the earth on its far side.

To the side, where most temples would have a small graveyard, there was instead a dark, yawning chasm that sank down farther than the eye could see. From some unseen spot deep within its base emerged a sparkling purple glow that cast only the faintest slivers of light up to the edges of the chasm. These slivers flickered like moonlight over disturbed water.

Persephonie wandered closer, drawn to the chasm. No, a fissure. Heat radiated out of it, dry, roiling. It warmed her cheeks but, a step closer, and sulfur burned her nose. She grimaced, wanting to step back, but something about it drew her nearer.

The citizenry of New Orison, for the most part, avoided the area, though a few lingered near. Temple guards stood by, glaring at children who approached with stones. The fissure itself had been roped off. Had someone fallen in? Or jumped?

Instead of layers of hardened clay, there was only rock, slices of shale that had split away from one another and left this hole instead. Persephonie came so close that the rope brushed against her legs. The fissure pulled at her hair and shortened her breath, beckoning her nearer.

Rennear caught the back of her skirt, tugging her away as she inadvertently took a half step forward. "Darling?" His brow furrowed.

Persephonie squinted her eyes shut and shook her head, dispersing the fissure's pull. Sparkles of light and the distant whisper of butterflies' wings traipsed around her fingertips, invisibly beside her ears.

"It's calling to me," she whispered. "To my magic."

"Jezebel," Rennear called sharply. The flush of the mead had faded from his face and he glared at the fissure as though it had done him immediate, personal injury.

With only a glance between them, Jezebel took Persephonie's elbow and tugged her away. "We're going to the market," Rennear announced to Velkan and Felix.

"You must be more careful," Jezebel murmured in her ear. "Did you not see the way the guards were watching you? How they did nothing to intervene?"

"No. What are you talking about?"

"Come on," Jezebel insisted. The fae wouldn't stop tugging at her until they'd brought her all the way inside a teahouse and ordered a hot, strawberry tea and something called a peacock tea on ice. The steaming mug of hot, sweetened tea arrived first.

Velkan and Felix frowned at the teahouse decor—bright teals and purples coated nearly every surface. Shelves along the walls displayed statue after statue of birds. "Can't we return to the tavern?" Felix complained but stopped short at a glare from Jezebel.

"Drink it all," they insisted.

The sugar and berries were sharp on Persephonie's tongue and warm in her stomach. Mixed with the wine, the tea made her feel sleepy, though the arrival of the peacock tea and its splash of cold and soothing herbs helped settle her mind.

"What's happening to me?"

Jezebel shook their head. "I am not certain. But it's something to do with that fissure. Was it calling to you?"

Persephonie took another sip of the peacock tea.

"Do not tell them." An unfamiliar voice whispered inside her mind.

She startled, looking around.

"Shh." Jezebel took her hand in theirs. "Hold still. Wait. It will pass."

A group of the temple guards marched by outside. The streets had grown eerily quiet. Though the guards feigned nonchalance, one glanced into the tea parlor as they passed.

Jezebel leaned across the table, casting a shadow that hid Persephonie from view. "Finish that and tell me how you feel."

It wasn't until she'd finished the last drop of the chilled, deeply pink tea that Persephonie's mind fully cleared. A cold sweat beaded along her back—something at the temple, possibly even the fissure itself, had cast an enchantment on her.

"Do not speak your suspicions aloud," Jezebel said before Persephonie could declare that she had fully returned to herself. There was no additional sign of the whispering voice.

"What is going on?" Felix complained.

"We need to get your sister back to the muster," Jezebel announced. They gave the rest of the group a hardened look, one that would brook no argument.

"But wait." Persephonie bit her lip. It was a feeling she couldn't explain, one different from the urging the fissure had inspired. "I haven't seen the market yet. We should stop by at the very least."

It took some convincing, but eventually Jezebel agreed.

The market was a few blocks away from the center of town. They walked the long way around the central thoroughfare, keeping a row of buildings between themselves and the temple. Persephonie tried to ignore Jezebel and Rennear's heightened attentions and return to her state of discovery and enjoyment, but it was difficult with their constant study of her.

Her supervisors seemed content to allow her to walk a few paces ahead of them so long as she was also clearly seeking to avoid the influence of the temple. She played with the small pouches at her waist as she walked. The sachet of enchanted glitter nearly sparked at her touch, and she thought again of the flashes of light coming up from the depths of the fissure.

On her opposite hip, Persephonie kept a sachet of salt and a stick of charcoal. Shoving her hand into it stilled the remaining static swirling about her thoughts from the fissure—she hadn't realized how greatly it had still been affecting her.

Jezebel had been right. They shouldn't speak of it, not yet, not until they'd put more distance between themselves, the fissure, and the priests who moved like shadows behind the temple walls. Had it been one of them who had cast a spell on her?

Thank Cassandra the market itself came into view. Persephonie sighed, releasing the tension from her shoulders. It was not so different from the market where she had met Rennear in Andel-ce Hevra save that, in this case, each of the stalls arranged about the market's center had once been a saudad wagon.

And every wagon still bore its wheels.

"Oh look," Persephonie exclaimed, rushing over to a table covered with crystals at the edge of the market. "Mama and I have had setups almost exactly like this, especially when I was small and she did not wish to leave me alone for long enough to do a true reading for someone."

A young saudad woman with short, shoulder-length hair streaked through with blue smiled up at her from behind the table. "I recognize in you a fellow soul," she said mysteriously.

Persephonie liked her already.

"Tell me," the woman continued, "what can I help you find today?"

"I should like a collection of stones, the largest and strongest you have, to fasten into protective necklaces, and a few amethysts for safe travels through dreams." An enchanted necklace might not be enough to protect her from whatever lurked at the heart of the fissure, but mages who could wield such mind-influencing magic likely had other manipulations on hand. She tried to remember if anyone in her muster had mentioned strange dreams since their arrival in New Orison—stranger than travel upon the threads tended to inspire—but none came to mind. Still, she would rather be cautious than not.

As Persephonie conferred with the crystal seller, a child sprinted up to a nearby seller and tugged on their tunic, whispering behind their hand into the seller's ear.

"Kessa," the seller hissed as the child sprinted away again. "They're coming!"

The woman's eyes widened. "Help me," she urged Persephonie, frantically throwing a cloth over the table behind her and covering the crystals and cards. She scattered a few bracelets and a necklace on top of the new covering. The jewelry sat at odd angles, but the velvet texture of the cloth held the beaded pieces in place.

Jezebel and Rennear took a few steps forward, standing shoulder to shoulder in order to protect the table from assault. *More likely provoking unnecessary interest*, Persephonie thought, but they were trying. She untied a strand of her own bracelets and slipped several bangles off her wrists, laid them atop the table, and then proceeded to scoop them up to examine them while the woman behind the table stared at her.

Booted footsteps echoed across the square as a contingency of guards clad in black stomped into the market. "You there!" one of the guards shouted, immediately pointing toward Kessa. His three fellows quickly followed after.

"We've warned you before," the guard announced, glaring at Kessa over Jezebel's shoulder. His scowl turned from the seller to Jezebel and Rennear as the pair of them refused to yield their place before the booth to him and his cronies. "Any and all merchandise countervailing the will of Malura will be confiscated. Aren't you nearabout to lose your license?"

Kessa straightened, raising her chin to the assembled guards. "There are a great many goods in the market that have nothing whatsoever to do with Malura. So tell me truly, Landrin, why is it you've come here?" Though she was one market seller against four armed guards, three of whom had the disturbing candle tattoos upon their necks, Kessa stood firm.

Persephonie mirrored Kessa's stance, raising her brow as she looked over Landrin and his goons. Velkan and Felix came running up a moment later. As the balance shifted from even numbers to six against four, the guards relented, reconsidering their position.

"We should have known the half-breeds would find one another," one of the guards scoffed, elbowing his friend in the side.

Velkan shot forward, stopped at the last moment from striking the guard in the jaw by Felix, who tried to play his reaction off as a scuffle between friends.

"Another word and it will be your last," Jezebel warned, shoulder muscles rippling as they tried to keep the bone fragments of their wings in check. Though Persephonie doubted how much of the guards' exchange Jezebel had understood, the guards' tone left no doubt as to their intentions.

The guards' eyes widened, deepening the tattoos along their foreheads, as they truly took in the fae whose irises glowed pure, bright white.

"By Malura," one muttered under their breath, stumbling back.

The four guards looked at one another, removing themselves further from Jezebel. "Don't make me warn you again," the first guard, Landrin, shot back over his shoulder as his friends retreated and he jogged to catch up.

Persephonie let out a slow breath as the guards disappeared on the far side of the market. She wrapped her bracelets back around her wrist and slid her bangles back on while Kessa uncovered the crystals once more and began selecting stones for Persephonie.

"Do they bother you often?" Velkan asked.

"A few times a fortnight." Kessa shrugged. "It's easier for them to pester me, being half-saudad, than the other members of the Feather."

Kessa emphasized the last word and gave Persephonie a meaningful glance. "Wait, what did you say?" She placed her hand against her pocket where her harpy feather resided. Alkona's promise of help when she needed it swelled in Persephonie's chest, a sudden buoy of hope.

Kessa's grin widened. "Meet me at the windmill in twenty minutes." She winked at Velkan, who dropped one of the bangles he was holding in surprise. "Make sure you aren't followed."

CHAPTER 26

IELLIETH

Iellieth and her companions emerged out of the forest on the western side of Thyles Thamor just before dusk. "Ooh," Quindythias sighed, squinting up into the trees at the faery lights that bobbed low across the understory, providing light despite the pre-twilight gloaming made darker by the density of the forest. "I think I may remember this place. North of Bastion, more an outpost than a true settlement, but something about it feels familiar."

Ammon smirked at the elven champion. "I'm glad that for once we may have earned your approval, Master Dark-strider. Mayhap your adoring, underground public will be gladdened to hear their city—and, therefore, themselves—raised from their humble origins in the eyes of their hero."

"There you go with that again." Quindythias stomped after Ammon while Marcon hung back with Iellieth, gazing up with her into the trees.

The initial dockside path was narrow, leading onto a floating boardwalk rather like Linolynn's Water Ward. Sailors lounged near their crafts. A few mended sails or tended to other nighttime chores. On one of the larger crafts, a viol player graced the evening with an ages-old melody from one of Iellieth's favorite folk songs of the elves, one sometimes said to date all the way back to Hugh and Lilia.

Standing there, staring at the outskirts of the elven city, the same emotion washed over Iellieth as when she'd first heard the song—the melody buoyed her up and held her floating, immersed. She'd anticipated arriving in the great elven city for so long that the experience of it felt more like a memory from a dream than her present.

"What are you thinking of?" Marcon asked, his voice low and quiet.

"I just . . . I can hardly believe we're here."

Marcon turned to watch her rather than the lights in the trees and the row of bobbing gondolas beyond the floating boathouse. "One of the first things you told me was how dearly you longed to see the land of the elves."

The lights in the trees blurred as she met his gaze. "And you promised me that you would help me get here."

The viol player arced into the song's bridge, the minor chords recounting Hugh and Lilia's separation, how they'd had to choose their people over one another and, in so doing, allowed for a future for the three realms of life. Hugh had promised Lilia that one day, he would find her again.

Iellieth sniffled and tucked her arm around Marcon's waist. "Let's see about the gondolas we've been hearing so much about."

Quindythias had selected the least understated gondola of the options available, one with a buxom mermaid leaning up and out of the water along the bow, her magnificent tail stretched back to form the stern. The mermaid's hair was pure black, her scales a magnificent, sparkling teal. "This one seemed rather appropriate to me," he announced with a grin of self-congratulations.

The gondolier was a somewhat portly elven male only a few years older than Iellieth herself. He stared after Quindythias in open awe.

"Master Darkstrider has asked me to take you to the center of the city so you might see the council chambers before your important meeting tomorrow."

"Yes, that would be splendid, thank you." Iellieth nodded to the gondolier, who nearly dropped his oar. They'd made prior arrangements with Ammon to wait to announce their arrival to the council until the following morning so they would have a chance to see the city on an unofficial basis before their official diplomatic visit began. His rangers would be more than happy to find them a place in their lodge for the evening, Ammon had assured her.

Leaning around the mermaid at the bow of the gondola, Iellieth could hardly contain her excitement. A narrow channel of water flowed between her and the elven capital, Thyles Thamor.

THEIR GONDOLIER, TANNER, FELL EASILY INTO HIS ROLE as tour guide and divided his attention between Quindythias and Iellieth. The two quieter members of their party didn't seem to mind this oversight. Ammon sprawled along one side of the gondola, his hood raised and hands cushioning the back of his head, and Marcon sat at attention in the center of the craft, on the lookout for danger should it make itself known.

The western portion of the city, Tanner explained, was a more residential district, with treehomes and lodges, where they would conclude their evening tour. Most of the waterways flowed from east to west, though there were a few exceptions for those who needed to move with haste from one side of the city to the other. Because of their special nature, guards supervised these pathways to protect the steady flow of persons and craft around the city.

One of the first landmarks on the eastern side of the city was the sprawling groves of the university. Iellieth sprang to her feet, using the mermaid to steady her as she looked over the rolling hills of the campus. Seeing her delight, Ammon promised to take her there as soon as their schedule allowed.

The university gave way to a roundabout for an open-air market and, beyond that, the temple district, where the elves might honor their ancestors and the deities who looked after them and their lands. "And now we come upon one of my favorite parts," Tanner said, adding a whispery rasp to his voice. She was grateful to see that the elf remained unaware of how his constant asides and adoration were beginning to wear on Quindythias.

The waterway curved around a grove of trees, the park that covered the entire center of the city, Tanner explained, and opened onto a sight that sent Iellieth's hand onto the steadying shoulder of the mermaid—a giant silver tree stretched up in the center of an island, courtyards and tree-lined pathways all around it. The tree rivaled the size of portions of Io Keep. The bark itself glowed like moonlight, shimmering back against the undersides of the silver leaves. Multiple stories of arches trailed up the tree, with room for each of the council members' halls, guest quarters for diplomats, and, at the tree's center, the council chambers themselves. The exterior rooms were graced with balconies overlooking the city.

"What I offer isn't quite as grand as all this," Ammon murmured, his eyes downcast.

"I've had a lifetime of grandeur," Iellieth reassured him. "I'm looking for something different."

"Seeing as you are coming here tomorrow, I could dock us for a bit so you can explore the council's island," Tanner ventured.

An excellent compromise. "That would be wonderful," Iellieth agreed.

A few minutes later, Tanner docked his gondola and gallantly helped her and Quindythias out of the craft. He audibly gasped when Quindythias touched his hand, causing the object of his adoration to jerk away as though he'd been stung.

"We'll explore this area over here for ourselves," Iellieth interjected, tugging Quindythias away before he could scold his admirer.

"Honestly, I am beginning to get a creepy feeling about this place," Quindythias whispered to her. "Or maybe it's only our gondolier. But there's something odd going on, isn't there?"

Iellieth had been so absorbed in taking in the city, she couldn't corroborate his feeling. "I'm not sure. But I believe you. What should we do?"

"Snoop around of course. Drat, I've left my snooping costume back on the boat."

It took some careful maneuvering on their part, but thanks to Quindythias's determination and the alternating glow and shadows of the rows of trees leading up to the various entrances to the Council Tree, the three of them managed to sneak away from Tanner, leaving Ammon behind with the gondolier. Ammon smirked at catching Iellieth crouching behind a bush, nodded to her, and turned back toward the gondola, faking a yawn before settling onto a bench that looked out over the water and the dark silhouetted leaves of the park beyond.

"What are we looking for?" Marcon whispered as they darted into yet another patch of shadow.

Iellieth was no longer certain whether Quindythias was trying to escape Tanner or if he really was looking for something odd going on within the council tree. The shaded path he'd selected led around to the back side of the tree, where a thicker concentration of guards paced back and forth, watching over both the tree and some smaller, walled-off parks behind it. The parks were the first places they'd come across in Thyles Thamor thus far that were protected by gates.

"Let's try over there," Quindythias murmured, indicating the third of the small parks, one without any guards on the outside. As they neared, the reason for the lack of visible guards appeared—they stood in a pair just inside the gate, the archway above them marked with transmigration runes.

Iellieth caught Quindythias's elbow. "That may be the only working transmigration circle in all of the Realms. It's not surprising that the council would have it protected, but good for us to know all the same."

Dark whispers curled beyond the archway, so softly Iellieth convinced herself she hadn't heard anything, but she knew better than to trust such an instinct. She tiptoed closer and the guards didn't react.

From a few paces away, the whispers were still too indistinct for her to make out, and the tongue was unfamiliar as well—Shadyn, perhaps, the language of the Shadowlands.

"Excuse me, miss," one of the guards called as she slid a half step closer still.

Iellieth straightened, faking a bright smile at the guard. "Yes?"

"May we help you with something?" The second guard's accent was even more refined than the first.

She responded in kind with her closest approximation to the formal Elven dialect she had mostly read and only practiced on a few occasions. "I was simply curious about the transmigration circle. Does it attract many visitors? Or bring in many travelers?"

Marcon waited at her elbow, hand drifting slowly toward his sword as he studied her body language. Over her opposite shoulder, Quindythias had paused, holding perfectly still. A tendon tightened in his neck as the sound of the voices recommenced, echoing out from the pause in the guards' speech though they gave no signal they'd heard anything.

The sound wasn't coming from the transmigration circle but from some sort of field in the darkness beyond it. Iellieth narrowed her gaze, certain she'd caught sight of shadowy figures moving in the dark beyond the circular fence.

"A few, miss, though not many. Our council does not look favorably upon those from distant lands whose prying eyes might get them into trouble rather quickly, especially those who are more prone to making judgements than seeking to understand others' ways." The warning was plain enough.

"That is one of the dangers of travelers, to be sure," Iellieth added, trying to keep up her polite appearance.

"If you'll take our meaning then, miss . . ." The guard gestured away from himself and toward the Council Tree.

Iellieth gave a high, false giggle, though its insincerity rang hollow in her ears. She thanked the guards for their assistance and led Marcon and Quindythias away toward a circle of benches she'd spotted on the opposite side of the tree from where Tanner had docked the gondola. She plopped down onto a stone bench and drew her knees up to her chin.

A frowning Quindythias settled down beside her, passing over a wineskin while Marcon stared down at the pair of them, a furrow between his brows. "Was there someone within the circle the guards were protecting?"

"I believe they were beyond it actually." Quindythias nodded toward the fifth archway, the one on the opposite end of their path from the glowing silver tree. Like the third archway they'd just hurried away from, there were no guards before this one either, and though it had a gate, it hung open. But unlike the other archways, this one was living—two elm trees whose branches intertwined overhead, signaling the entrance to a cemetery.

"I believe I've been spending too much time with the pair of you," Quindythias drawled, taking the wineskin back from Iellieth and gulping down a few swallows of the dry red wine he'd acquired in Moonsbreak Landing. "Without thinking, I told our gondola driver my name, and he's been behaving strangely ever since. Unless he always behaves strangely . . ."

"It would be difficult for us to tell, not having met him

before and having Ammon as our counterpoint of reference."

Marcon exhaled slowly as he gazed out across the empty circle, the bare benches around them. "They would have to remember us for our names to be a danger. That or news of our return has reached these shores on the lips of our enemies, in which case they're just as likely to know us on sight."

Iellieth chewed the inside of her bottom lip as she waited for Quindythias to answer. His being remembered was more important to him than he wanted to admit, and he attributed more meaning to the elves' awareness of his legacy than she thought was wise, especially given what Yvayne had said about them being erased, though that had been before they'd uncovered his statue.

Quindythias drained the wineskin, tilted his head back, and pinched the bridge of his nose. "It is a dreadful feeling, this. Being forgotten."

"You aren't—" Iellieth stopped as Marcon shook his head at her.

"At the time, back in Bastion, I told myself that there was a reason I went to so much trouble, a reason I didn't peer too closely at what I was giving up, at the risk I posed to myself and to my parents. But what she said about me was true."

Iellieth leaned closer. "What who said about you?"

"Rafferty. She said I only wanted attention. And though I told myself it wasn't true . . . I fear she was right." It was a name she'd never heard him mention before. There was a fondness in the inflection but different than that he used for the names of his lovers. "She was an airship captain. One of our allies. She helped me in the fight for Bastion, helped me take the steps necessary to bring the city into what it could be."

Quindythias let his hand fall dramatically down by his side. "Helped me bring the city to its knees, no doubt." He pushed himself up to standing and began dragging his feet as he paced back and forth, his hands twitching at his sides.

Iellieth called to him, reaching out her hands, but Marcon took the elf's place beside her and drew her hands back to her side. "Give him a moment," he murmured.

"How could it have been otherwise?" Quindythias's hand shook as he drew it back through his hair, loosening the tight curls that clung to his scalp and causing one side to pouf more than the other. "Had we done right by them, had we been truly on the side of justice, wouldn't it have all turned out differently? Wouldn't—" He sighed and stopped, spinning to face her and Marcon instead. "What went so wrong that of the three surviving elven cities on this side of your world, one of them is under the ground and overrun by zealots and another tries to keep itself separate from the forest of which it is a part? What good can *hiding* like this possibly do for them?"

Voices emerged from the pathway beyond the elm and several figures in hooded robes emerged. They walked in a line toward the circular sitting area where Iellieth and the champions sat, stopping halfway along the path, save one who broke off from the rest, slowly making their way toward the three of them.

Quindythias paid no heed to the figure, too distressed to notice the cloaked form's decisive path.

Iellieth sprang up, causing the champion to stumble back. She raised her hand toward the figure and called out to them to stop, but no sound passed her lips.

She pressed her hand to her throat. No sound, no spells. Eyes wide, she turned toward Marcon, her hand on the shortsword hilt at her side.

The champion had started to rise, already pulling his sword from its scabbard, when a tiny dart struck his neck. Marcon's eyes bulged. His lips parted, white foam burbling along his mouth. He pitched forward, and Iellieth caught him just as a pin-prick struck the back of her neck as well.

Quindythias was on his hands and knees beside her, face contorted, trying to say something. He'd pulled out his own dart and reached for hers. Iellieth's legs gave way beneath her. She cushioned Marcon's fall as she slipped onto the stone, darkness blotting out the silver glow of the tree overhead.

CHAPTER 27

TEODRIC

Before they set sail from the Realms, Teodric called his crew together, everyone from Kriega and Ambrose to Athena and Keever. His first mate had resisted this moment, but Teodric had insisted upon arriving at consensus among the crew if they were to separate themselves from Syleste and seek aid from those she considered enemies upon the *Lagon des Morts*.

"If this is truly to work, we have to prove to them that we're different than she is," he'd argued. "We allow them to make their own choices, to have a say."

It hadn't taken long to convince them. His chest still swelled at the show of faith in his leadership and captaincy. Keever had stepped forward, squinting into the sun, and placed his ladle at Teodric's feet. "We knew you'd be a fair captain, when she appointed you," the goblin said, raising his voice to be heard above the crash of the waves. He stood with only a slight hunch, not cowering away from the exposure of the deck like he normally would. "We never dreamed you'd see us all the way through to our freedom."

There had been cheers to that, a near-unanimous vote, and several days' rapid sailing. Athena had stood at his side as the Realms faded from the horizon. He didn't mention Genevieve, and she didn't mention Iellieth, but there was a togetherness to their loneliness all the same.

The *Lagon* swelled into view their sixth day out from the Realms, its collective masts stretching up toward the pale pink and gold dawn, a day and night's sail from Nortelon. Teodric's plan to rid himself and his crew of Syleste's tyranny hinged upon earning the favor of Aeogan, the captain of the *Lagon des Morts* himself, creator of the floating pirate haven, the visionary who had seen a way for them all to work together.

He called Athena over and directed her to flag their requests via semaphore to the *Lagon*. They directed the *Queen* around to the ocean-ward side where the larger ships docked. A few words from Kriega and the fear-inducing sight of Syleste's flag immediately garnered the attention of the port master, who sent them with a guide into the interior. "Captain Aeogan will want to see you," she had said, her expression grave.

"Will Captain Aeogan be glad to see us?" Teodric asked the agile young man who led their way over decks and across barges, weaving in and out of working crews that gave way to merchants and shop-keepers. Nearer to the interior, the masts had been converted to a series of rope-bridged walkways. Signs for inns and taverns had been nailed to the lower parts of the masts—the *Lagon* was every bit a floating city unto itself.

The agent glanced back at Teodric, eyebrows raised. "I find it best to not try too hard to anticipate the captain's reactions. He is . . . complex in the ways in which he sees the world." The reddened tips of half-elf ears poked out from beneath his thick brown hair.

"Oh." Teodric frowned. That sounded far less promising than what he'd been hoping for. "The port master, she thought he'd want an audience?"

"All crews of the siren queen speak with Captain Aeogan upon arrival."

Siren queen? He'd heard the title whispered a time or two in reference to Syleste, but it was odd to hear her referred to as anything other than the admiral.

Beside him, Kriega stiffened. Her respect for Syleste was deeply ingrained. Even in the midst of their rebellion, she couldn't fully suppress her reaction to a slight against their admiral.

They bounded over and across a series of several smaller ships that had been propped in the air by their bindings to the larger vessels beside them. Their sides had been cut into so as to ease passage between them. Currents of passersby eddied around the three of them, each consumed by business of their own. The narrow points of the prows of the smaller ships granted Teodric a view of the lower decks of the *Lagon*. Where he'd expected to see ocean, he saw instead an echo of the swinging walkways overhead, leading to the keels and holds of the various larger ships.

"Getting close now," the lackey called back. He picked up his pace as they reached a market that stretched along the deck of one of the larger ships, its quarterdeck and captain's cabin transformed into storefronts selling a wide collection of goods and simply called the Emporia. Beneath its sign read the slogan, "Anything at all you need, Jack's the one you'll want to see."

"If you're looking to stay a few days, I'd try the Grotto,

over there." He pointed to an elegant, ancient sailing ship, its hull covered in algae, with a masthead of a beautiful mermaid. Though the outside of the ship made it clear she hadn't sailed in decades, the deck itself was polished and clean. Pairs of sailors and one small crew lounged on the deck, sipping coffee from an assortment of colorful mugs.

Beside the Grotto, musicians prepared for the midday meal at a three-story restaurant, formed from the remains of an old pirate ship with holes blown through the sides that revealed the bars and tables within.

"Have you ever seen anything like this?" he murmured to Kriega, eyes wide as he took in the pirate city. Syleste's island fort and the commerce it hosted were in many ways equal to even a port city like Nortelon. But this? The *Lagon* was something else entirely.

"I came here, once, when I was a girl." The half-orc's scowl said that she didn't want to explain any further.

They passed the Grotto and turned right past its bow. Teodric stopped, staring up at one of the largest ships he'd ever seen. The *Dominion* was a sight to behold, the glimpse of her masts on the horizon capable of inciting fear among even battle-hardened sailors. This ship towered above all the others around it—he'd mistaken the glimpses he'd caught of it earlier for two ships raised out of the water at the center of the *Lagon*. The ship's bow faced them, her three great masts creaking in the midday breeze. Upon the bowsprit was one of the most lifelike figureheads Teodric had ever beheld—a giant dragon curling over and around, mouth spread wide as though it was about to spew poison or flames.

The guide and Kriega both paused and turned back, finding him staring open-mouthed at the ship that had formed an island of pirates around itself. "She is quite impressive, is she not?" The young man smiled, his thin chest suddenly puffed as he looked upon the ship. It struck Teodric then that while their guide didn't have the lean muscles of a lad of the sea, he still carried himself like a sailor, with that insouciance of ease over shifting terrain, his balance as easy as the waves.

"I feel suddenly grateful and envious to have never come across her on open waters."

"You would have to be a great deal older than you are to have managed such a feat. Several centuries or more, to hear the captain tell it."

Teodric broke his study of the ship to observe their guide instead. Though he spoke nonsense, there was no hint of artifice in his expression. "Well . . ." What was one to say to such a comment? "We're at the captain's service, whenever he's ready."

"I think he'll want to see you now."

The lackey led them up the massive gangplank and Teodric rehearsed his offer to the captain—they were prepared to set themselves against Syleste, making a direct assault against her island where she was expecting them anyway. There was no worse place for her to be holding his father.

He glanced at his first mate, who stood straight-backed, gaze forward. She'd follow his lead. For this to work, they had to trust one another.

Two crossbow-wielding guards stood on either side of the top of the plank with another pair stationed by the stern before the captain's cabin. He'd been picturing meeting the captain of the *Lagon* belowdecks, a squeaky lantern swaying and casting flickering light across strained faces, but he now realized the folly of such imagining. Of course Captain Aeogan maintained his original cabin—

how else was he to keep the pulse of the world around him, to walk the decks, consult with his crew, and feel at one with the sea?

Their guide nodded to the first pair of guards and headed straight for the second. On the deck, a diplomat from Cyrinia puffed on a pipe while speaking with an impossibly pale elven woman in long, dark robes, most likely a representative from Invae Alinor, the shuttered elven port at the south of the Realms.

He measured his breath with his steps, elongating his strides to help him be more at ease. The man they were about to meet commanded the ear of the kingdoms of Azuria—what he'd built served as a neutral meeting place. Anything he wished to learn about the workings of the world, it would be possible to discover here. Had Darcy frequented the *Lagon* before settling in Andel-ce Hevra, combing the ships and meeting grounds for gems of knowledge to sell to the likes of Syleste?

The guards stepped aside, pushing open the doors to the cabin, which was dim after the bright sunlight outside. He and Kriega strode into the room, the lackey hurrying before them.

As he blinked to adjust his vision, Teodric froze, breath catching in his chest. His attention should have been utterly captivated by the man lounging behind the most elegant captain's desk he had ever beheld. With tan skin and flowing, thick black hair, he would have been arresting enough, but a pattern of emerald green scales covered the hollows around his eyes like a mask, stretching out toward his cheekbones and enhancing their already sharp lines across his countenance. Dragonkin, they were called in the stories—he'd never had cause, until now, to believe they were real.

But it was the man to the captain's right, standing at a podium, quill in hand, who made him stop short. His wrinkles were deeper, his face tanned by the sun. There was even a bend in the formerly straight nose where it might have been broken. The thick brown hair had a few more streaks of gray, a patch of white by one temple, but it only served to sharpen the glint of the dark brown eyes, the gravity this man had always held. "Agents of Admiral Syleste, aboard the *Amber Queen*," the man said, his voice a low baritone that reverberated in the very depths of Teodric's being. "Tell me, how is it that your interests align with—"

The man gasped, dropping the golden-tipped quill in his hand. It clattered against the wooden podium, the lone sound beyond the creak of the ship and the barges beside her. "Teodric?" the man whispered.

It couldn't be. "Father?"

"I heard it as well as you did," Jezebel repeated to Felix, the fifth time in as many minutes her brother had asked one of them about 'you know, what she said,' referring to Kessa's mention of the Feather, whatever that meant.

"You don't think the windmill was a code too, do you?" Felix asked.

"I think we're going to get uninvited if you keep asking questions," Persephonie said before anyone else could answer. She met Velkan's gaze. Jezebel and Rennear would grow used to Felix in time, but it wasn't always helpful to allow his questions to run on and on. "Stefan is going to be extra mad at you now," she whispered.

Velkan laughed, easing her concerns as they slipped out of the market square and walked down one of the back roads of New Orison, carefully making their way to the windmill as Kessa had asked.

The five of them slowed with the windmill in sight as murmuring voices and plodding footsteps approached.

Persephonie held her breath, preparing a bright spell of

sparkling sapphire dragonflies should agents of the priests appear.

She sighed, relaxing, as Kessa came into view from around the shadowed corner of the winding road.

"These are the ones you were telling me about?" Two men stood behind Kessa. One was tall and blonde, his light hair and curved ears marking him as obviously of human origin. The second had taken a step toward them. He was shorter and stockier than the first, with a strong jaw and severe expression.

"Yes," Kessa answered.

The second man smiled and Persephonie had to stifle a gasp—it completely transformed his countenance as though he'd suddenly thrown off a great weight. At first, she'd believed the taller man to be the leader of Kessa's Feather—Feathers? She would have to ask—but pure charisma radiated off the second man now, precisely the sort that would mark a leader of saudad revolutionaries. "I see what you mean about the motley band led by a striking mage," he said with a nod to Kessa.

Rennear and Velkan straightened on either side of Persephonie, which the leader failed to notice. He reached out for the blonde-haired man's hand and turned about. "If Kessa's new discoveries will come with us," he called back over his shoulder, "I think we can help one another."

"We'll be there in just a moment," Jezebel said, sliding in front of Persephonie to stand between her and Kessa. She was so startled by the sudden appearance of the fae that one of the dragonflies she'd prepared burst from her fingertips, fluttered into the air, and exploded in a shower of sparks overhead.

"Gah! My eyes!" Felix shouted, covering his hands over

his eyes as sapphire glitter rained down over his face and across his chest.

The fae turned, a frown caught between their brows as they stared down at Persephonie.

An invisible butterfly fluttered low in Persephonie's stomach. She was relatively certain she knew the cause of Jezebel's scowl. "Jezebel? What is going on?"

Jezebel's eyes narrowed. "I need to make sure you aren't enchanted."

"I'm pretty certain I'm not—" She stopped short as Jezebel pressed a finger to her lips.

"Wait," they murmured. The fae closed their eyes, not explaining how they planned to uncover the enchantment they feared.

Velkan jumped back as the fae's bone wings appeared from behind their shoulders, swept around Persephonie, and returned to rest behind the fae again. She shivered at the brush of the skeletal wings against her hair. "You are not tainted," the fae said with a measured finality. The frown remained. "I wanted to wait, to give you time and make sure. I felt the power of that fissure, the way it affected you," Jezebel explained. "It pulled you toward itself. If we hadn't been there—"

"But you *were* there." Tensions were running high enough. They didn't need to add hypothetical problems to those they already faced. What must Kessa think, waiting to escort them to the Feather?

"What if we hadn't been?" Jezebel raised their voice, obviously unconcerned with her desire to help everyone stay calm. Their white eyes shot between the other three and then began to search their environs. "We don't know where we are, who we're dealing with. All *I* can tell is that they seem to have a particular interest in *you*." They returned their gaze to Persephonie. "As much as they espouse hatred for outsiders, they seem much more concerned at your lineage than they do mine or Rennear's."

Rennear nodded at that, his brow furrowed.

"That's true, Sephie," Felix added. "Why do you think that is?" he asked Jezebel.

"I could guess, but I doubt my answers would be very helpful at this point. There's more we need to know."

Velkan's gaze hadn't left her through their conversation. "Might I suggest, then, that we ask those who have gathered in the windmill who might have an inclination as to who and what we're dealing with?"

After collecting themselves and knocking at the door, a few casual greetings and yet another pot of tea placed all eight of them together in a rather tight receiving room.

"We are here to learn about the Feather. Erm, Feathers?"

Kessa shook her head.

"Feather," Persephonie corrected herself. "Please."

⚜

PERSEPHONIE WAS DISAPPOINTED TO LEARN THAT THE Feather was not a reference to the harpies she'd befriended while traveling with the Untamed, at least not deliberately.

"That sounds both harrowing and horribly exciting," Kessa said as Persephonie briefly explained the context for her question about the name.

"We nearly called ourselves the Faithful, but then the Malura-worshippers took hold and the term seem too close an association."

"How well do you understand this worship and what it entails?" Briefly, Jezebel mentioned the pull of the fissure, leaving out its hold on Persephonie but, based on the looks Dominic, the saudad and Irving, his human partner, exchanged, they had filled in the gaps for themselves.

"The intricacies of their schemes and their long-term aims, not very well," Dominic answered. "But their history gives us common ground. Word has reached me of your muster's resistance, which is admirable. Such a path has been trod, unsuccessfully before." The leader of the Feather sighed. "From the moment the priests of Malura took hold over New Orison, new musters have arrived. But no one has left."

A bolt of ice jolted down Persephonie's spine. That couldn't be.

Dominic nodded as though he sensed her doubt. "Some, like me, were born here. Others, like your muster, arrived through machinations we do not yet understand." He explained that in recent years, the priests' numbers had begun to grow and with them, their guards and following. "They put pressure on musters such as yours, urging them into falling in line while reveling in the support of musters like Boss Gilsen's. By keeping your muster on the outskirts and showing special attention to Gilsen's arrival, any who are wavering about the priests' cause from within see the merits of their beliefs externally and internally reflected while, watching your muster, they see the dangers of resistance."

"And there *are* dangers to resistance," Kessa added, her expression suddenly grave. It was slight, but the two saudad shifted away from Irving.

Keeping his eyes on the pressed dirt floor of the windmill's interior, Irving rolled up his sleeve.

"My gods," Rennear exhaled, speaking for all of them.

Thick burn scars twisted over one another along the entirety of Irving's forearm. From the stiff way he carried himself, Persephonie suspected there were other scars he wasn't as willing to show. "The muster I came here with was strong. Independent." There was a melodic quality to Irving's voice. As he spoke, Persephonie searched his hands for calluses and, sure enough, found them along his fingertips, precisely where she would expect them to be on a bard.

Irving had found his way to the travelers through his music—Persephonie grinned, pleased with herself—and his infatuation with their stories. One day, as they had been traveling along, their muster had been whisked up from the road and deposited upon the threads of fate, much like Datha had told her happened to them as they left the Brightlands. Irving's muster hadn't been so lucky as Boss Gilsen's had been and had lost nearly half of their number to a storm across the threads.

"Our misfortunes deepened from there. First an illness shortly after our arrival, one that none of our healers could mend. Then there were skirmishes with the priests' guards —this was years ago. They have changed tactics somewhat since then. They locked the rabble-rousers in the prison beneath the temple and executed several a week later for an attempt at escape and violence done toward one of the priests' guards." Irving shook his head. It was clear he didn't believe this story, but Persephonie couldn't imagine there had been many routes of recourse to find the truth.

Irving confessed as much, describing how matters quickly worsened from there. "It ended with them setting the muster aflame. The whole of New Orison came to our aid. And still, so many perished." The ghosts of what he had lost clung to Irving's voice. "Those of us who remained decided to go our separate ways. Trying to stay together was too painful, the reminders too great. And we feared further provocation of the priests." Irving glanced up at Dominic who had leaned into his partner's side and placed his hand upon Irving's shoulder. "Thank you, again, for saving me from the flames."

Dominic pressed his lips to Irving's. "Always, my love, though may Cassandra protect us against such a plight."

Persephonie averted her gaze to grant them a moment of privacy. She hadn't really studied the windmill on their arrival but found it relatively bare of personal effects. The room beyond this one had a bed with a neatly arranged sheet and quilt at the foot. An archway led to a small, shaded kitchen, and the door behind them off the entry held a small wooden tower the likes of which she'd helped Datha build for storing her jewelry in the wagon.

"They've been kind enough to let me settle here with them after my muster turned me out," Kessa said, seeing Persephonie looking over the windmill apartment.

"Oh, I didn't—" She stopped herself. Kessa was simply trying to tell them more about her living situation and express Dominic and Irving's kindness at the same time.

"How long have you been selling jewelry and crystals?" Velkan asked Kessa, diverting her into a conversation between himself and Felix.

"Irving's muster was not the only one to suffer at the hands of the priests, though theirs was the most public punishment. So, what do you say?" Dominic squeezed Irving's knee and looked between Persephonie, Jezebel, and Rennear. "You three seem a capable, experienced lot."

"We . . . are," Persephonie admitted. Though they had not been a band of three—or four, counting Juliet—for long, they worked well as a team. "I am afraid I am not sure what you are asking me." Her mind was still reeling from Dominic's declaration and Irving's harrowing tale. How was she to tell her datha of the fate that awaited them if they tried to depart? Her stomach sank. How was she to see her mother again? "From our arrival, the priests made a foul impression, spurred my datha and our muster toward rebellion. But what are you, erm, we, the Feather, trying to do about it?" Her unasked question hung in the air. *How are we to leave?*

"We?" Dominic smiled again, and Persephonie no longer wondered how Irving had found his way to Dominic's side and more how the priests had managed to retain any of their followers. He leaned toward them and dropped his voice. "Now you understand the significance of our name. *We* are finding a way out." His grin widened. "There's a door on the edges of the dome that the priests don't know about. It's restrictive," Dominic added before Persephonie's hope could flare to full expression in her chest. "It only allows a few out at a time. Sometimes it moves. It's even sealed itself before, locking someone on the outside and trapping them in the wasteland that surrounds New Orison."

Irving glanced at Kessa, who stiffened but didn't waver from her conversation with Felix and Velkan.

"We've chosen to stay, deliberately, and we've been waiting for someone with the means to uncover how the door works and how we can use it to free not just a few, not even an entire muster, but everyone." The saudad's eyes shone with his passion. His gaze hovered over Persephonie. "From what Kessa said, we're hoping that's you."

CHAPTER 29

IELLIETH

With a second prick at her neck, the world came back to focus around Iellieth. It was dark around her, as it had been in the park, but this was the darkness of a subterranean chamber.

A masked and robed figure with long, delicate fingers placed a skull mask over Iellieth's head. She murmured a protest at the gag tied around her mouth, but the figure held their finger gently to her lips. "Quiet," they murmured in Elvish. "You are not in danger. All will be revealed soon."

Two more cloaked figures appeared beside her to lead her forward through a stone passageway and toward a room lit by flickering candlelight. The aroma drifting out of the room was pleasant—beeswax with a touch of honey and . . . something else. Iellieth inhaled. Rosemary. For memory and wisdom, Mara had taught her. Would a secret underground elvish collective—*cult*, her mind helpfully supplied—have the same symbolic intentions for their herbs as the druids?

The figures eased her forward, holding onto each of

her arms. Behind her, two others guided Marcon. The eye-holes in his mask pointed directly at Iellieth. He nodded to her. The angular form of Quindythias appeared behind Marcon.

Wherever the figures had taken them and whatever their plans, they were wise enough to have removed their weapons. Iellieth wiggled her ankle—they'd even found Teodric's dagger in her boot.

"Here we are," the figure in front sighed. She was the one who had bid Iellieth to be quiet. Strands of long blonde hair peeked out from around her mask and hood, draping over her shoulders.

Iellieth's guides led her around the curve of a doorway and into a candlelit sanctuary filled with a dozen hooded elves in robes. At the front of the room was a stage. A broad-shouldered elven man wearing a skull mask like hers sat hunched on the stage, his arms bound behind his back and a gag tied at the back of his head. Iellieth recognized Ammon by his worn, dark brown armor and the set of his shoulders.

Behind him was a long table covered with tapers; they'd been burning so long that wax had dribbled off the candles themselves and now ran down the sides of the table. In the center of the table was a single, small statue. The tiny figure's presence made her question whether or not the table might be an altar, a much more fitting piece of furniture for an underground cult to gather about in any case.

Quiet murmurs rippled through the crowd as the cloaked figures led the three of them to the center of the stage. The two men at Iellieth's elbows pressed at her shoulders, urging her to kneel beside Ammon.

Iellieth's mind raced, although she feigned calm and

cooperation. What sort of spell would allow her to subdue several elves all at once, spread about the room as they were? There was a great deal of struggling behind her as it took four men to do the same to Marcon—they would have needed more had they not behaved so gently toward her.

Ammon had said the elven council was worried about extremist activity in Thyles Thamor, but the way he'd explained it, they seemed to believe he and his rangers were a threat as was his sister's collection of scholars. Whoever this cult was, they seemed far more worthy of concern.

In this strange underground chamber—*church*, she couldn't help but think—the twelve congregants had seated themselves in a circle of wooden stools with the central area between the stools and stage open. No one had produced a ceremonial knife, and none of the robed figures showed signs of being armed.

Marcon inched forward, leaning toward her as the first cloaked figure proceeded to the front lip of the stage. Three masked elves held Quindythias between them— they hadn't forced him to kneel. Iellieth's heart pounded. Mara's circle of green fire wouldn't work—he was too far away and would be burned.

The woman with blonde hair stepped off the stage into the open, central area and the congregants quieted. She raised her hands overhead and heightened the effect. "Darkstriders," she began, "hear me!"

Iellieth met Marcon's gaze, holding her breath.

"We who remember listen," the seated figures chanted in unison. The guards who hovered behind them remained silent.

"Just as our brethren by the sea warned us, those masquerading as our great heroes of old have returned to our shores, conveniently appearing in our hour of need," the figure with the long blonde hair cried. She gestured for the elves to bring Quindythias forward to where she stood on the bare stone floor and tugged back the skull mask covering his face. They hadn't gagged him as they had Iellieth and, she assumed, Marcon. "Would you believe, faithful ones, that fate has seen fit to return our own ancient founder—Quindythias Darkstrider, the Blade of Bastion!"

She tore off her own mask as well, revealing gray-brown skin and delicately formed features. With her full lips and giant eyes, she was absolutely captivating, even clad in a bulky robe. Those seated murmured to one another, with some leaning closer to Quindythias, peering at him through their skull masks.

A second figure stepped forward to join the blonde elf and Quindythias. "You, the faithful, the studied, well know what this appearance means." Her voice was lower than the first speaker's, a grating alto. On Iellieth's other side, Ammon twisted toward the second figure, his slumped posture suddenly stiffer while following her every movement.

The elf brushed a dark braid back over her shoulder, still speaking from behind her skull mask. "As the harbingers of our undoing appear, will you allow them to bring about the ruin of our civilization as transpired in Bastion in the age before?"

Quindythias visibly startled, and he twisted around to peer at Iellieth and Marcon. *He's the savior of Bastion*, she wanted to shout. What were they talking about?

Quindythias's lips parted, his face stricken. "There . . ."

Quindythias's voice emerged in a hoarse whisper. His shoulders had slumped forward.

Iellieth's throat tightened. Her companions had been through enough. Whatever misunderstanding had occurred, they deserved better than this.

Quindythias cleared his throat. "There has to have been some sort of mistake. I-I did not doom Bastion."

At the crack of pain in his voice, Iellieth could sit still no longer. She rolled back from her knees and shot up, rushing to stand with arms bound by Quindythias's side. One of the guards shouted a warning from behind her, and the two speakers turned but neither made to stop her. The one with the dark hair waved off the guards as Iellieth pressed her shoulder into Quindythias's side. Whatever was happening, he wouldn't go through this alone.

"Ah ha," the blonde elf cried, "the druid joins our supposed champion. Is it not fitting that one would now appear, as our own have been stolen from our very woods?"

The seated figures nodded among themselves. A few murmured their assent. Iellieth's mind raced at yet another misunderstanding. Were they determined to interpret every gesture of help as some sort of doom?

The dark-haired elf in the mask shook her head. "All too coincidental for my tastes, Taleria." She lifted her chin to address the crowd but not before one of those seated disrupted their theatrics.

"Let them speak," the seated one said. The speaker had a slight warble to their tone, perhaps brought on by age, though the masks made such conclusions difficult.

"Grandmother," Taleria began.

The old woman repeated her command. "Ask them what they know."

Quindythias turned to Iellieth and nudged her with his

shoulder. The dark-haired elf, seeing this, produced a small blade to a muffled shout from behind her. She quickly slid off the mask and cut free the gag that had been affixed to Iellieth's mouth while, by the scuffling sounds behind her, the guards sought to subdue Marcon.

"You misunderstand my companions and me," Iellieth said. She resisted the urge to rub the sides of her mouth to subdue the lingering feeling of the gag pressing against her skin. "They are not impostors or whatever you would accuse them of." She turned back and met Marcon's gaze and then squared her shoulders and stood tall with Quindythias beside her. "I was there when they were awakened. When they came to life from statues." Her breath came quickly—what were they looking for her to say or explain? Until she understood who these Darkstriders were, she didn't want to share more about her friends than was necessary, but not saying enough might prove more dangerous still.

The dark-haired elf strode forward, placing herself between Iellieth and the seated figure who had spoken. "Even if they are who they say, in the *Book of the Blade*, it says *quite* clearly to 'always test thy enemies and be even more dubious of thy heroes, should they appear.' That is precisely what has happened, precisely what our forebears warned us about. What the true Master Darkstrider warned us of."

"The Book of—what?" Quindythias said. "What are you talking about?"

Excited whispers rippled among those seated. "He does not know." "Of course he does. It's an act." "It's nothing more than one of their agents in disguise."

"Our most sacred text, one of the few surviving records of the War of the Champions," the blonde elf—Taleria—

explained. "We have debated its attribution for some time —a few thousand years, to be more precise—but the prevailing belief is that the Blade of Bastion was the one who inked the *Book of Blades*."

For a moment, Quindythias struggled for words. "This is an outrage!" he erupted. "I never wrote such drivel. I was far too busy—ugh. Marcon can tell you." He waved his arm behind himself. "And why would I have spoken like that? 'Thy enemies?' Utter nonsense!"

The dark-haired figure nodded. "Your protests are understandable and, may I say, quite convincing. An enemy agent would be well aware of the artistic license some scholars took in laying out our guiding code of conduct and compiling the version of the book that exists today. If you *were* the real Quindythias Darkstrider"—her tone left no illusions about the impossibility of such a reality—"I would assure you that there have been centuries of thoughtful debate on the matter."

"Thoughtful debate?" Quindythias sputtered. "I'm standing right here, and I'm saying that the lot of you are completely mistaken. I mean—*some* artistic license?" He turned from one masked figure to the next, still at a loss for words. Finally, Quindythias turned about behind. His jaw dropped open as his gaze landed upon the statue on the table. Iellieth hadn't paid it much heed since they'd arrived, finding the figures holding them captive far more worthy of her immediate attention.

Quindythias stomped over toward it, squatting to glare at the statue's eye level. "Is this supposed to be me?" He reached down and plucked the figure off the table with a loud *plop* as it broke free from the wax. The statue held a blade aloft in one hand and a book tucked into his chest in the other. He returned to Iellieth's side, holding the figure at arm's length as though it might infect him with a disease.

Pointed ears and short, curly hair stood out from a mask, more in the style of a cloth than the skulls that surrounded the room. This close to the statue, Iellieth noticed that it had a much boxier and more muscular frame than Quindythias possessed, almost as though the statue had been modeled on a blend of Quindythias and Marcon. "Ridiculous," he spat, waving it before him. "The proportions alone! I'd scarcely be able to fit through a doorway much less save a city!"

At this last, murmurs erupted around the room. The dark-haired scholar raised her voice to be heard over the crowd, "How intriguing." She tugged back her hood.

Behind Iellieth, Ammon shouted from behind his gag. He froze as they all turned toward him.

The woman in the skull mask drifted away from him toward the center of the circle. She turned her face away and, with a flourish, ripped the skull from her head to reveal a beautiful, striking countenance. "Gathered Darkstriders," she pronounced each syllable slowly in Elvish, half her face still turned toward the shadows. "You will find it no coincidence that we are joined today by my brother, the ranger, Ammon." She waved her hand to the side where Ammon had grown perfectly still. Iellieth checked to see that his chest still rose and fell and that his sister, Sharia, hadn't placed him under some sort of spell. A crackle of unspent magical energy was growing within the room. It fizzled against Iellieth's fingertips, but she couldn't locate its source. "Several moons have passed," Sharia murmured. She twirled to face her brother, and Ammon lurched back.

Ripples of white scar tissue covered the hidden half of

the woman's face. A pale blue eye glowed from the center of the scarred area, a sharp contrast to the dark iris in her non-scarred eye, which was a feature she and Ammon shared.

Sharia returned her attention to those seated. "As most of you know, in the first weeks of my investigation into the missing druids' whereabouts, my scouts and I were attacked by poachers. Only a few of us survived. We were saved by a Brightlands fae on an allied excursion of her own. But in this crossing of paths, the Mother has supplied the answer to our plight."

The seated figure who had spoken before raised her voice over the ripple of murmurs that surged after this announcement. "Speak plainly, Sharia. What do you suggest?"

"The Pilgrimage," Sharia announced simply. "Make the journey to Gaia's Glade."

Iellieth sucked in a breath. A glade named after the titan of earth and the site of a sacred pilgrimage would be precisely the sort of place where the ancients would have placed the seal piece of earth for safekeeping.

Silence had settled over the room at Sharia's challenge.

A single board creaked as Ammon tilted to the side and rose to his feet. At Sharia's nod, one of the guards cut the ties holding Ammon's hands so he could slip off his mask and gag. To Iellieth's relief, the guard did the same for Marcon who rose to stand at Ammon's side.

"You go too far, sister," Ammon announced. "I was as surprised to learn Master Darkstrider's name as any other. Those gathered here are not the only ones sworn to remembrance in the aftermath of the Circle."

The seated figures shifted on their stools at Ammon's

cold glare, which the ranger leveled upon them all in turn save the one who had spoken up before.

"I have no doubts as to their identities or their intentions. Whatever relics, books, or prophesies you possess that speak of arrivals in a time of need, these are the ones foretold."

A wide smile tugged against the scar tissue on Sharia's face. It bestowed a sense of peace to her unscarred features, though it did little to brighten her natural, dark eye. "If they are the promised ones as you have said, then the Pilgrimage will be nothing more than a small impediment for them."

Ammon stiffened. "You do not possess the right to send them to their deaths!" he shouted.

"No," the seated masked figure said. "But the council does." She rose and made a sweeping gesture with her hands. Without a word of protest, those gathered save one hooded and masked figure rose and slid away. "You as well," she said to the guards. "Their magic is no match for my own."

Iellieth focused her attention on the speaker, who was slight and short of stature. She felt into her fingertips, searching for the source of the crackling energy she had sensed. Eddies from herself, a lapping tidepool from Sharia, and—she gasped—a dark, plunging well from the elder.

The masked figure tilted her head to the side, the deep hollows of the skull's eye sockets appraising her. "You have comported yourselves with bravery, something that will serve you well in our wilding lands." She turned the hollow orbs of her skull mask toward Marcon and Quindythias. "Your friend is right to fear for your safety on the journey north. If you are able to impress the council tomorrow with the import of your task as you have impressed those gathered here, your aims will be served alongside our own."

"I don't understand," Iellieth sighed. Were hostility and a mysterious death-sentence journey the reactions of those who were impressed?

"My brother misleads you," Sharia answered, ignoring Ammon's scowl. "The Pilgrimage is the holiest of journeys available to any who visits our realm. Only worthy believers are able to find the path, which is why it has eluded my brother for so long."

Ammon's jaw tightened, but he didn't contradict his sister.

"Our collective exists to right a wrong done long ago," the second masked figure said. Her accent was thicker than any of the others', but Iellieth wasn't familiar enough with the Realms to place the difference. "Our chapter of the Darkstriders is a group of mages who strive to remember the sacrifice chosen by the Sapphire Circle, a conclave of druids who, while well-meaning, brought about the destruction of their world."

Iellieth frowned but did not object. Mara had spoken of the sacrifices of the Sapphire Circle but only briefly. Neither her mentor nor Yvayne had said anything about druids bringing about an end of the world.

"Our origin dates back further than that," the short, elder elf explained. "After the fall of Bastion"—Quindythias flinched at the words, but she paid him no heed—"a secret order rose to a position of quiet prominence with the goal of protecting the city's legacy and ensuring that whatever transpired, our great histories would not be lost."

Iellieth had learned a similar account from Yvayne, but

they couldn't be talking about the lorekeepers. If they were connected to Yvayne's project of preserving the histories, wouldn't they have known that Marcon and Quindythias were neither harbingers nor impostors?

"Through the ages, our enemy's agents have sought to infiltrate our ranks just as we have theirs, so certain precautions were put into place."

"And chief among those precautions was the Pilgrimage," Sharia continued, fervor lighting her dark, pine-green-hued eye. The other glowed the same bright blue it had when she first unmasked herself. "A renegade member of the Sapphire Circle helped the Darkstriders to future-proof their legacy. Should saviors of the Realms ever present themselves, the Guardian at the end of the Pilgrimage would ascertain whether or not they were worthy."

"But we didn't come here to—"

Marcon placed his hand on Iellieth's elbow before she finished proclaiming that they had not, in fact, arrived with the intention of saving the Realms but were instead here to seek the elves' help in saving the rest of Azuria. "We will undergo your Pilgrimage," Marcon said, the first he'd spoken since their capture. "Tell us what we need to do."

CHAPTER 30

BRISERAS

Briseras had to agree that Vicq's plan was simple, if nothing else. Taking advantage of their position within the Watchers' Ward, Tybalt would challenge an unsuspecting Watcher to a drinking contest, win his keys, and gain entry to the Lorespire, where they could research the Sisters and find the whereabouts of Arduenne's fane. The enchanted armor was somewhere in Bloodletter territory. They'd seek it out once they crossed over.

She and Jorgan both held back their objections to this part of the plan. The elf was by far the least likely among them to out-drink anyone, but winning keys from someone in the tavern seemed a reasonable possibility.

"Well enough," Briseras said. "And what about the Bloodletters? How are you going to win your armor back from them?"

"Ah, well they're both easier and harder to deal with, and that's where you come in." Vicq nodded at her, eliciting suspicious glares from both Tybalt and Jorgan. "What the Bloodletters hold most holy is, in fact, blood. So you'll challenge a warrior or two to blood sport, win, and we'll be on our way."

Returning to the tavern beneath their inn after their failed afternoon excursion, Tybalt pulled Briseras aside and confessed his concerns with the plan. "Maybe Vicq is being overeager," the elf said. "We could try asking for keys and see where that gets us."

They'd mostly kept to themselves when they'd first arrived at the tavern but, as far as Briseras could tell, the Watchers primarily cared about gold, a commodity of which neither of the three of them had a great deal to spare.

"Maybe we take a cue from Vicq and see if we can trick or, as you're suggesting, charm a set of keys off one of the Watchers and then sneak into the Lorespire," Briseras added. Tricking or taking felt like a better bet to her than charm, but she wouldn't tell Tybalt to rule it out.

An hour or so later, they were selecting their marks for an initial attempt when a half-drunk guard wobbled over to Briseras's side and pulled up a stool at the end of their table, reminding her of her first night in St. Sebastian.

The guard was more than happy to brag about himself, especially when Briseras was the one asking questions. As the Watcher explained that in addition to his storehouse keys he also had an entry level set for the Lorespire archives, she glanced at Tybalt over the rim of her tankard, delighted with their luck. "So what you're telling me is that the nobles are the ones who run the Lorespire, but no one comes in or out without your say-so—the nobles entrust the entirety of their security to you?"

"Them's who're wise enough to actually wish themselves secure, aye," the man answered with a leering grin.

Briseras smirked into her ale. "Very good to know."

This inebriated, over-confident guard had already proven himself useful, and she had every intention that he would continue to do so, willingly or no. Either way, it got her to the records they needed to uncover the location of Arduenne's fane.

A grubby hand seized her thigh. "What d'you say we ditch yer friends and head upstairs to talk over the details?"

She frowned down at his hand and its grip. The Watcher made her decision as to his fate all too simple, really.

Before the man could draw breath or Jorgan and Tybalt could react, Briseras had unsheathed one of the narrow daggers from the belt around her waist and held its sharpened point to the bobbing apple of his throat. It was one of her three favorite uses for this blade—poking eyeballs, spearing throats, and dismembering small appendages.

The man gasped around the blade point, and Briseras slid the knife's end to the hollow at the top of his throat. A thin trail of blood followed in the blade's wake, droplets pattering one by one onto his lap. She could sever his spine from here or jab all the way into his brain, whichever suited her fancy.

"You were saying?"

Her companions had caught up to her by now. Jorgan seized the man's wrist and wrenched it behind his back, knocking over his own barstool in the process. "You don't get to touch her, *ever*," he snarled. The ring of gold around his iris thickened and pulsed—his wolf was already threatening to emerge.

Tybalt simply crossed his arms over his chest, muscles bulging.

Jorgan's breathing grew more labored, and his lips

bunched together—he was trying to prevent the elongation of his teeth.

Trying to maintain her own façade of calm anger, Briseras flicked her gaze from the guard to the werewolf. She murmured his name, keeping her voice low. Other tavern patrons had already started looking in their direction, and she had no desire for the entire tavern to turn against them in the man's defense.

At the sound of his name, Jorgan met her gaze.

She gave a slight shake of her head, so small she hoped their prisoner wouldn't notice it. "That won't be necessary," she continued, a cold smile spreading over her face as she returned her gaze to the captive guard. "He's going to give us everything we need, aren't you?"

Jorgan growled, low in his throat. The gold of his gaze retreated.

But her concern over Jorgan's transformation had caused her to misread the guard.

The Watcher cursed at her, flailing against Jorgan's hold. He tried to kick Briseras in the side. She elbowed his knee out of the way and sprang out of her seat. Her blade nicked the underside of his jaw, slipping free.

The guard snarled at her and shouted for help. "This bitch and her bastard friends are Bloodletter scum!"

Briseras shook her head, a true smile spreading across her lips. "You really are more interesting than I gave you credit for." She darted forward and stabbed the man through the throat, severing the arteries to ensure he couldn't strike her again.

Blood spurted from the wound, coating the front of her shirt. Jorgan shoved the body away, grunting as he rolled his shoulders back—his wolf was ready to emerge.

She tugged one of her shortswords free from the

sheath on her back and cut off the arm of the next attacker. The man stopped in his tracks, face pale as he stared down at his arm bleeding on the floor.

Freezing wasn't a wise choice in a battle—that had been one of the first things Rajas taught her when she was small.

With a roar from behind her, Tybalt lifted his leg and kicked the man in the chest, sending him sprawling backward into three others who had come to the first guard's aid. Two of them had weapons. One had armed himself with a barstool.

"I'm beginning to like Barasov," Briseras said with a grin to Jorgan.

As one, the three of them sprang forward and restored the tavern to a relative sense of peace. Jorgan and Tybalt left their opponents alive with life-altering injuries, but Briseras saw no need for such heroics.

A blade through the chest ended the life of her newest opponent. He'd never defend someone so unwise as the guard again.

"Keys," she shot over her shoulder to Jorgan.

He let his current victim crawl away, the man's leg broken in multiple places, as he bent and rifled through the pockets of the first guard. The rest of the tavern was in chaos save one couple flirting at the bar and the tavern keeper, who polished glasses and stared out the window onto the cobblestone street.

Briseras tossed a few coins onto the bar top, and the three of them shoved open the side door and stepped out into the fading light of early evening.

After a quick boost into the window to fetch their belongings and Otto, they set out from the ward toward the market, the Lorespire glittering in the distance.

She chewed her lip as they skirted around the market, Vera loping at her side. "You didn't have to defend me from that man, you know," she remarked to Jorgan as they strolled away from The Watchers' Eye. Tybalt complained about the nights they'd pre-paid for, shaking his head as he took in their surroundings.

Should they make their way into Bloodletter territory sooner than planned? How fast would word spread about their disagreement with the Watcher guard?

"I think that depends on what you mean by 'have to,' Briseras."

She slowed her long strides to meet his gaze.

"I know you can handle yourself in a fight. But you shouldn't have to. And I wasn't just going to sit there and let you be grabbed by a stranger who felt entitled to it."

Briseras glanced away, heat rising to her face that she couldn't explain. Among her collective, even the most elite hunters that she had trained herself, such a reaction would never have occurred. They knew she was self-sufficient, and they wouldn't have wanted to get in the way. With Jorgan—and with Tybalt as well—something was different. They wanted to support her, to help, even when she wasn't strictly in danger or in need. She wasn't quite sure how she felt about that.

The need for such questions faded as an irritated guard stepped aside to allow them entry into the Lorespire. She scowled pointedly at the blood on the three of them and the key. Briseras wiped it off the metal and re-presented it.

Within the archives themselves, swirling stacks of books rose up into the glittering heights of the tower, with golden crossbeams serving as shining pathways between them. "You've access to the first floor *only*," the guard emphasized.

Briseras wasn't going to argue. Her grandmother had escaped the burning of her home with three books to her name. They were her mother's most treasured possessions. Two of them and her mother's locket made their way to Briseras after her mother's death. She never learned what happened to the third.

A short woman with a pile of dark brown hair, clad entirely in brown and wearing spectacles quite like Vicq's, squealed when Briseras made her request to learn about the Sisters and their fanes. "It's a pet project of mine, you know." In a rustle of skirts and scarves, the archivist led them to a special side room within the first-floor collection. There was a magical seal on the door, the archivist explained, that preserved the oldest of Barasov's records. "Even from before the fall," she whispered with a wink.

The woman blushed as Tybalt thanked her for her assistance and scurried away.

Jorgan shrugged. "At least we know our evening is spoken for."

The three of them split up across the room. Tybalt was muttering to himself about texts he hoped to find while Teela slumped out of Jorgan and went to pout in one of the corners.

For Briseras, a discarded tome with a faded, whiskey-brown cover caught her eye from the corner of the records room. It was one of the few smaller books within the collection and reminded her of Everett's journal clasped on the side of her thigh. The similarity was apt—*Journal of the Huntress* had been scrawled on a square of parchment and affixed to the front page.

She flipped through diary entries of a woman traveling with her wolf, the record more detailed but not so different from the log she and Vera kept. The writer called herself the Servant of Arduenne and wrote often of her ritual practices in honor of the Archfae.

A few of the pages had stuck together, bound along the edges by a dark brown stain. Briseras turned to the next available page, afraid she would rip the other pages unless she took the time to cut them apart with her blade. It was the final entry of the journal.

I have failed my Lady and my dearest companion both. Luana could not overcome the shadows that befell the desecration of our lady's fane. My sweet wolf has departed and left a monster in her place. Whatever has overtaken her now has ensured that I will not long endure our separation. The tear in my heart weeps even more readily than the one in my side, but it is the latter that will see my end.

If ever there is one who comes after, who might see my Lady shine again, may they know that the Heart leads. Follow it.

I have served as well as I might—I pray my Lady finds her rest—

The end of the final word fell in a scratch down the page as the huntress followed her own benediction.

Had her wolf turned on her? Undergone a sudden onset of lycanthropy, but one for wolves rather than were-wolves? Or had something else transpired between the pair?

Briseras frowned as she looked at Vera, who was padding after Jorgan on his restless rounds through the library. Would the same happen to her and her wolf with prolonged exposure to Steymhorod, or did their origin in Azuria keep them safe?

The night of Nassarq's attack flickered back before her mind—even now, the fear that she and Vera might be separated chilled her blood. She carried the journal to Tybalt to see if the elf noticed any details in the account that might lead them to the mountain fane. But what of the former huntress's missive at the end, to follow one's heart, with special emphasis placed on that word? The seer had urged her to find the heart first. Was that what the writer meant as well? Finding and restoring the heart would allow them to find the mountain fane?

CHAPTER 31

IELLIETH

An uncomfortably quiet gondola ride saw Iellieth, her companions, Ammon, Sharia, and Taleria safely inside Ammon's rangers' lodge, a large wooden structure suspended within a sprawling oak tree near the border of Thyles Thamor, within sight of the stone walls that had been erected around the city in ages past. One of the responsibilities of the city's soldiers was keeping a line clear of forest on each side of the wall so any invading force couldn't use the trees to help them scale the battlements and gain access to the city.

Quindythias lounged on one side of the lodge, speaking animatedly with one of the three leaders of the Darkstriders, a Professor Taleria Tur, historian of the War of the Champions and the fall of Eldura. Marcon and Quindythias flinched each time one of the Darkstriders blithely pronounced the end of their world.

Iellieth's chest tightened—being here in the Realms, the world her champions had lost was becoming ever clearer. When both Marcon and Quindythias had been taken and turned into statues, the war for their world was very much ongoing. For everyone else, that war had occurred five millennia ago.

Sharia was refilling a tankard of dark ale for Marcon and Ammon, gesturing over a map of the Realms and indicating, Iellieth guessed, where the route to the Pilgrimage tended and where the poachers were most concentrated within the forests.

An elven man who rivaled Marcon for height and breadth lumbered in Iellieth's direction, a loping black wolf at his side. Ammon had briefly introduced him to Iellieth—Firan and his wolf, Addah. Firan paused behind Sharia, resting his large hand on her angular shoulder and placing a kiss along her dark hairline. She murmured something back to him before Firan turned away, a grin caught on the side of his mouth, and continued on his way to sit across from Iellieth at the long wooden table and benches on one side of the rangers' great hall.

Firan walked with a limp, one leg near-immobile from an injury he'd sustained from a mozz, the name for the giant moose biomecho that had lurched toward them in the forest. He carried a greatstaff with him to get around the city and had his wolf Addah to help him as well.

"You've had quite a night by the sound of it," Firan said as he settled down across from her, a grumble resounding in his chest as he took the weight off his injured leg.

"That's one way of phrasing it." Iellieth tipped her small glass of wine to him before taking another sip.

He looked troubled, staring down into his own tankard. "I hope you will forgive Sharia her performance. Professor Tur as well."

Iellieth worked her lips between her teeth, chewing over a string of responses without finding the words for any of what she wished to say. "What they did was dangerous," she finally said. "My friends are not harmless characters in stories. And—and neither am I. They act as though we're playthings. Marcon and Quindythias are seasoned warriors, and I am not without resources, even with my weapons taken away." She might have set the entire chamber aflame had she been more assured of her friends' ability to escape without harm. And such a possibility said nothing of the danger that still awaited them on the other side of Sharia's fervent belief in the Pilgrimage.

"I know that. Sharia does too, though she will not be in a hurry to admit it. She's only been back in the city a few days and hasn't truly been herself since the poachers' attack. Ammon has been gone for months. I . . . cannot help but feel they wanted to see some of that danger, to know that when they send you and your companions into the council chamber tomorrow and after, on the Pilgrimage, the High Council will see ancient warriors and will consider, for the first time in ages, joining in the larger fight for our lands rather than fortifying our walls."

The council's supposed ambivalence to the Realms' plight still eluded Iellieth. "And if they do? What then?"

Firan sighed. "That will be up to the council, to show us the sort of elves they are. I have my hopes they will see reason, though they've given us scarce enough opportunity to believe they will."

Iellieth frowned. She'd asked the wrong side of the question. "And if they don't?"

The ranger drained his ale and patted his wolf on the head. "Then the fight they've been trying to pretend isn't brewing will soon lash against their walls." Firan nodded to Iellieth. "I sense that fight in the air around you. Your companions too. Those like Ammon and myself have given decades upon decades of our service, trying to convince them the walls will not be enough. Meeting you, your friends—I know our warnings weren't in vain." He sighed heavily as he rose. "And I know the walls won't be enough."

❧

THE FOLLOWING MORNING, TANNER RESUMED THE apology he'd begun for his role in the Darkstriders' capture the evening before. "I didn't know how frightening it would seem, you know, everyone in robes. The candles. They're scholars. Professors and council members."

Iellieth shook her head, letting the apology wash over her. *Wait*.

Quindythias had gone rigid beside her.

"Did you say there are council members who are part of the Darkstriders?"

Tanner gasped and cupped his hand over his mouth. "No," he lied, his reply muffled by his hand.

"What does that mean for us?" she murmured to Quindythias. Ammon and Marcon had quickly resumed their conversation from the night before, strategizing for both poachers and mechos lying in wait in the forest.

"I'm not sure." A puzzled line formed between Quindythias's dark brows as he gripped and released the dagger handle at his side.

Iellieth had to stop herself from doing the same. She was relieved to be armed again so they might appear as themselves before the council. If the records in Linolynn retained *any* degree of accuracy, which she was beginning to doubt, then the laying down of arms was an important part of the ceremony involved in greeting the Elven High Council, a symbol of friendship, of prioritizing understanding over violence.

"From the moment we got your message back when you met with Consul Reyyar, we've been planning, you see," Tanner continued unabashed. "I'm still quite new to their order. I was overjoyed to be included. The Blade has always been a hero of mine." He beamed at Quindythias, pure adoration upon his face. "And, well, I made something for you too." He wetted his lips and held out a roll of parchment to Quindythias.

Mouth in a thin line, Quindythias took the offering and unfurled it. "What is this?"

"Umm, well, it's just a small something I've been working on." Tanner rubbed the back of his neck and busied himself with directing the gondola through the gradually filling waterway. Their meeting with the council was early, right after daybreak, and most of Thyles Thamor was only just beginning to stir out of doors.

The Adventures of Quindythias Darkstrider had been carefully etched onto the front of the pamphlet. Inside, the parchment pages had been divided into squares, each of which showed a picture of the three of them—and one other figure. The illustrations were done in ink and simpler than portraiture or most paintings Iellieth had seen, but the more pleasing for their difference.

Quindythias flipped through the pages, Marcon and Iellieth leaning over his shoulder to read alongside him. The storyline itself was simple enough to follow—in the narrative the pictures showed, Quindythias saved a dryad from an angry cult of beings who looked like goatmen. The hero of the story then seduced the dryad while his assistant, who looked remarkably like the artist and author, managed to win the heart of the elf's long-haired companion. Marcon, whose head remained only half visible as he seemed to tower over the squares of each page, contributed one word, possibly two, to the book's encounters. By the end, they were mostly sound effects and grunts.

"I'm so . . . eloquent," Marcon said, staring down at the page as he carefully avoided meeting Tanner's wide eyes.

Iellieth laughed aloud when Marcon grunted, exactly like his character in the story, as they reached the conclusion and the hero's sidekick, Tannerias, swept the half-elven maiden off her feet and carried her away.

"I . . ." Quindythias looked from the book to the gondolier and back to the book.

Tanner gave a nervous grin. "I stayed up all night . . ."

Quindythias clutched the pages to his chest. "It's one of the most wonderful things I've ever seen. Thank you."

Tanner blushed, his breaths coming quickly. This morning, he sported a pin on his chest depicting a dagger piercing through an eye; Iellieth had glimpsed a few of the same pins the night before.

The gondolier promised to wait for them at the base of the tree while they made their appearance before the council. They'd left their few belongings at the rangers' lodge. It remained to be seen whether they would receive an invitation to stay at the Council Tree or not.

Quindythias practically pranced toward the sprawling silver tree, where a quartet of soldiers waited at the bottom of an ingenious lift system to escort them up to the council chambers. "I must say, if we're half as successful with the council as *I* have been so far, we shall be well on our way to acquiring the seal piece in no time at all."

Unfortunately, they were not.

"We entrusted the item you seek to the forest long ago," the eldest councilor said with a sigh almost as soon as Iellieth made her request. Her headache from the night before worsened the longer they stood before a semi-circle of elven diplomats. Two of the seven chairs remained empty despite the supposed import of their meeting.

"To the forest?" Iellieth frowned up at the five councilors who had deigned to appear. There was Ammon's mother, Councilor delQueran, who was responsible for seeing to the interests of the people of Thyles Thamor; a thin, excessively pale elf who represented Invae Alinor; a beautiful, surprisingly young elf—Valaexi—who represented Shade Rest; a short, bespeckled elf with spiky hair, Professor Delphinia Idlewylde, who spoke on behalf of the scholars spread throughout the Realms; and an ancient elven woman who oversaw the council. She seemed the least disposed of all of them to offer any help.

Hadn't Red said that each civilization had been asked to carefully guard the seal piece until it was needed? "Are you not worried that the recent movement of forces outside the Realms might pose a threat to the seal piece? Even if they are not seeking the piece for themselves, they might still be responding to its awakening magic." The poachers were organized, but the unnamed monsters from the Shadowlands Ammon had described were just as likely to be roaming toward a powerful magical source as any other motivation that might bring them here.

The eldest council member sneered. "Why would a half-human only recently arrived within our borders, younger than even the weeds of our forest, presume to tell us of the troubles in our lands?" She waved an ancient, wrinkled hand, gesturing for Iellieth and her companions to be escorted from the chambers.

"But you don't understand," Iellieth tried again. "The longer we delay, the greater the danger to all. The seal piece—"

"Has remained safely within Gaia's Glade these many centuries, half-human," the eldest councilor sighed, making it clear that even the act of having to interrupt Iellieth was terribly boring and unnecessary.

Iellieth turned to Marcon, unable to put her distress into words.

The champion gave her arm a reassuring squeeze. "The way is easier with their aid than on our own, lady," he murmured in her ear.

"Anyone who wishes to reclaim the seal piece must first prove themselves worthy, half-human," Valaexi added. Her accent was remarkably similar to the second robed figure's the evening before. "A piece of advice? Don't trouble yourself. I'd hate to think what you might discover."

Iellieth's lips parted but no words emerged as the implications of the elves' words rippled over her. They had been sending travelers into the forest to find the final seal piece? Or had they been treasure-seekers? Agents of Alessandra? The council had thus far avoided mentioning Sharia's Pilgrimage, but the implied danger and their assurance of the seal piece's safety made her wonder whether the trials were one and the same. At the very least, they took place within the same location.

Reckless. There was no other word for it. But saying as much would cause even more harm to their negotiations. "Who has sought to prove themselves worthy?"

"Many have tried before you, half-human," the head councilor answered. "Our memory is long, as is our agreement with the titan. It is not the purview of this council to satisfy your curiosity."

Ammon's mother turned toward the elder councilor. "That may be, Eugenia, but those who would seek the aid of this council must satisfy *our* curiosity. That you travel with my son says much about you, Iellieth Amastacia. More than I believe you could know." He had joined them shortly after the meeting began. At his mother's words, Professor Idlewylde inclined her head in Ammon's direction, though Iellieth wasn't sure why.

"I am curious," Councilor delQueran continued, "as I believe my fellow councilors are as well—what makes you believe you possess something different than those who have come before?"

"You don't need to answer that," Quindythias murmured, low enough that only she could hear. "Let their curiosity work in our favor."

Iellieth nodded to him and rested her hand lightly on his forearm. "I will, in part," she whispered.

She lifted her chin and looked into the eyes of each council member. "In those who already stand before you, you will find that which sets me apart. My companions know the circumstances in which the seal pieces were locked away and know, too, the dire stakes of what will happen should another succeed in acquiring the seal piece before we do." She inhaled deeply and glanced between her friends. "That they choose to travel with me reminds me every day of my own worthiness. I need not prove myself to anyone else."

Quindythias shifted beside her, squaring his shoulders as the council resumed their study of the three of them.

A smirk tugged upward against Valaexi's stoic face, a spark of challenge glinting in her eyes. "There's an ancient saying about the path to Gaia's Glade that perhaps you'll find more useful than your predecessors. *Deep within the titan's sacred glade lies an ancient temple, the heart of which stands outside of time. There, those who prove their worth will find that which they seek.*" Her smirk stretched into a mocking smile. "Continue north, druid, to the temple that stands out of time. If you reach the hidden city, you've gone too far."

Iellieth wetted her lips and nodded. She was more certain than ever that this younger councilor was the same as the second masked figure from the night before. Was the warning actually a hint meant to aid them? "Then with the council's knowledge, we will proceed on our mission. Should the titan find us worthy, will you as well?"

The professor's eyes sparkled and she leaned forward in her chair, smiling. "An excellent notion, that is."

Iellieth stifled a gasp. *This* voice she immediately recognized from the night before.

"What do you say, Eugenia?" the scholar continued, challenge sparkling in her eyes. "If they're good enough for Gaia, are they good enough for us?"

Eugenia's wrinkled mouth pulled down in distaste. "I suppose . . ."

Ammon had spoken true of what they should expect before the council. Maybe their preexisting connection with the rangers had poisoned their case in the eyes of the council. Or, if she was right about two of the council members being secret Darkstriders, perhaps the council's ambivalence was playing right into the Darkstriders' hands. But Iellieth couldn't dismiss the shadow the council's apathy cast over the next part of their mission. What might be waiting for them in the north? What forces might have already tried and failed to recover the piece from Gaia's Glade?

"Excellent!" Professor Idlewylde clapped her hands together, turning her gaze once more to Ammon.

The ranger stepped forward. "If you have further need of them, we'll spend the day at the university. We leave tomorrow at dawn." He spared a final glance at his mother before ushering the three of them outside.

Marcon sighed as the council doors groaned shut behind them. "I would rather we stop for a drink than bury ourselves in piles of books."

Iellieth chewed her bottom lip. Their meeting before the council had utterly failed, and Ammon had shortened their tenure in Thyles Thamor by two days. Had he discovered something that made their return into the wilds more urgent? Or their presence in Thyles Thamor more dangerous?

Traveling with the ranger the past few days, she had already begun to dream of a time, still distant from now, when the three of them might stay in Thyles Thamor. That dream grew hazier now, even with Quindythias warming to his role as a folk hero with a cultish following. He still held the book Tanner had given him close to his chest.

The council had dampened her shimmering imaginings of what their life in Thyles Thamor might be like. Parts of it were an older dream, when she'd planned to join the university, deepening the studies she and Katarina had begun . . . whenever in the future they might put this phase of their adventuring behind them.

To Iellieth's surprise, Ammon grinned. "There's a tavern just outside the university where a few friends are waiting to hear how your meeting with the council went."

He gestured toward the silver archway that led out onto the lift that would take them down to the dock.

Enough time had passed that milling crowds filled the streets of Thyles Thamor. Iellieth took a deep breath. A whole city, for them to explore. "And do not worry, Lady Iellieth. I'll take you to the university straight after."

"I would like that." Then again, new dreams had begun to replace the old. Perhaps their days of adventuring might not come to an end after all. The council meeting had put a damper on any possible plan of continuing in her father's footsteps and pursuing life as a diplomat. But as she'd told that disagreeable Eugenia, with her champions by her side, they could chart a path as-yet unknown, wherever they wished.

CHAPTER 32

PERSEPHONIE

At the end of their first week in New Orison, Boss Gilsen and his muster invited all to attend their burning of the wheels.

The burning started early in the morning, with Carnine making a great show of welcoming a pair of priests and their guards. Twirling plumes of smoke rose with the sun from the great pile of wheels on the edge of the muster's newly permanent position upon the hillsides, with wooden bases supporting the wagons.

Throughout Persephonie's muster, the mood was grim, the morning unnaturally quiet. Datha and the elders had agreed that anyone who wished to join the burning could, even as a gesture of goodwill. But as three more priests and their retinue of guards rode up on horseback, even the most appeasement-oriented members of the muster retreated to within their own camp's borders.

The smoke thickened over Gilsen's muster—with so many wagons, the fire would burn throughout the day and into the night.

Persephonie joined Datha and Felix in watching from a

distance, her shoulders tensing at the sight of the guards. "They will expect a similar show of loyalty from us next," Datha observed.

A few muster representatives approached as well along with another of the priests. They had learned of the priests' number and habits from the Feather. More than five in any one place was an ill sign.

The scent of ash burning in her nostrils, Persephonie turned away. They weren't going to fill her day with fear, however dark their intentions.

"Darling." Rennear gestured for her to come and sit beside him on one of the benches Stefan had formed from logs and a short plank they kept on hand for the purpose. The color had come back into his face over the past week in New Orison. A slight limp remained, and though his hand still hovered at his ribcage, he seemed finally able to take full breaths without wincing.

Persephonie glanced back at her datha and Felix, rapt in one another's conversation. Datha had settled onto a bench similar to the one Rennear was sitting on, his elbows on his knees, making small, decisive gestures with his hands while Felix nodded in agreement. They didn't need her for the moment and, even if they did, she would not be far.

Her family settled, she hurried over to Rennear's side and scooted in next to him. Rennear rested his hand atop her knee and tugged her closer. "Darling," he repeated, leaning closer. He brushed the hair back from her face and peered intently into her eyes. "Do you regret my coming here with you? That business with the spiders, on our way in—you never would have been in such danger had I not . . ." He waved his hand over his leg, stretched out to the side.

"Of course not." What was he talking about? "I do not understand why you ask—what have I done to cause you to feel this way?"

"You have done nothing wrong," Rennear assured her. "Heh." He smiled and shook his head. "Here I am doing precisely what I promised I would not, selfishly occupying your time and pulling you away from your family to serve my own insecurity."

Persephonie tilted her head to the side and studied him. There was an air of jest to Rennear's words, but beneath that, a profound gravity. He had obviously been wanting to share these concerns with her for some time. "Are you unhappy here, Rennear?"

"No!" he insisted, rising from the bench. His mouth twisted but he held his balance. "No. I have only been wondering whether you might be happier were I back in Andel-ce Hevra, or helping the Untamed. Your family— well, you are obviously very dear to them. And Velkan . . ." His jaw twinged as he sought the right words. A soldier's instinct sent his hand twitching toward the dagger at his hip. "Velkan still cares for you a great deal."

Persephonie shook her head, grinning at Rennear's jealousy. "That has been the case for a few years now. Datha says he will move on when he is ready to not be in love with being in love with me."

Rennear chuckled at this, and Persephonie's heart lifted. "Your father is an extremely wise man, something else I envy about you and your family." The shadows returned to his expression as he surveyed the landscape of New Orison all around them. "I don't want what we had to have died on that mountainside with so many of my pack, Persephonie. I cannot tell you how greatly it pained me to be unable to come to your aid, to have put you in danger.

And then it happened again, in our traveling here. If something happened to you—" He sank down beside her on the bench, hands twitching uneasily on his lap as he reached toward her and stopped himself.

For a moment, he raised his gaze to meet hers and then broke away again. "I have borne several unpleasant trials in my years, as gilded as much of my life has been. Over the past days, I have been giving it a great deal of thought. While I would not like to, I could, given time, bear you deciding to part from me, to be more fully with your people. And though I do not claim to understand the sensitivities of the priests here—they are blind at best— what I cannot bear is to invite further danger upon you, nor on your family. If something happened to you because of me, whether by a failing on my part or simply due to my proximity, I would never forgive myself."

His stare out at the billowing clouds that rose over Gilsen's hillside darkened into a scowl. "I have set myself the task of making up to you for what happened in the square."

"You saved me, in the square. Remember?"

His shoulders fell. "Only after you first saved me from myself." He ran his fingers through the tendrils of her hair that had fallen over her shoulder. "You saved me from severing my connection to the person who is dearest in all the world to me." The muscles of his arms tensed against the linen of his shirt.

She unpeeled his fingers from where he was clutching the hewn wood of the bench and wrapped his hand around hers instead, placing it in her lap. "What is it you have decided is going to happen to me because of you? These priests, they discriminate regardless. My mother would say that they fear those who are different because they cannot understand power different than that which they hold, but enough of them for now." She scooted closer to him and draped her legs over his uninjured one. "If you fear for my affections, let me reassure you."

His copper-brown eyes brightened as she closed the distance between them and wrapped her arms around his neck. Persephonie kissed him, leaning her chest against his. She waited for the low sigh at the back of Rennear's throat, for his mouth to open and the press of his lips to harden against hers before she drew back. Shortened breaths panted between them. "Rennear, do not doubt it. You cannot." Persephonie stared into his eyes, the gold of the early morning light catching against the warm brown of the forest she adored. "I love you."

Tears brightened his gaze as he stared back at her. His lips started to form a response but he broke off in a smiling exhale instead. "And I you, Persephonie." He wrapped his arms around her waist and scooped her fully off the bench, holding her up against him. "Where is it in this strange new dome of a place that you and I can be utterly alone?"

Persephonie giggled in reply. Growing up in a muster, it was important to have a sense of these things and to know when to set such concerns aside. "I have an idea," she whispered, nodding to the woods behind them. "I haven't seen anyone going in or out of the forest since we arrived save a few others like us." She raised her brows. "There's a reason, after all, living in such close proximity as we do, that we try to settle by the woods when we can."

Rennear swung her to the side and held her till she untangled her feet from her skirts. He stood up beside her, testing his weight on his leg. "I will follow wherever you take me," he said with a bow.

She laughed again, took his hand, and they scampered off into the forest.

❧

It did not take long for the pair of them to find a quiet, secluded place by a brook that would help disguise any noise. Smooth, moss-covered rocks indicated that whatever had transpired since the dome was formed, the brook had once been much wider, or at least it had once rained more regularly.

Persephonie removed the scarf from her neck and laid it across the mossy stones. Grinning, Rennear picked his way over the rocks to join her. With only a small groan, he settled back on his elbows, gazing up at her as he waited for her to join him.

As she did, Persephonie pressed herself into Rennear's side, savoring the hitch in his breath as her hand grazed up his chest, tracing from linen to skin. She trailed her fingers across his neck and pulled him toward her to resume the kiss they'd started back by the wagons. The kiss after which he'd said he loved her.

The growl of pleasure that was so dear to her was quick to rise from Rennear's throat. He laid her back upon the rocks, mouth pressed against hers and thumb tracing the line of her jaw. When she grew breathless, Rennear broke his lips away, murmuring her name as his lips slid down the length of her neck. He tugged aside her tunic and kissed along her collarbone, his other arm holding her waist, her body locked against his.

They had made love many times before, stealing a few moments alone together back in Andel-ce Hevra, but such opportunities had grown scarce after they'd left the city.

Rennear hummed again, his uninjured leg sliding across hers toward her hips. She rolled her hips in answer, wanting to feel the press of him against her. He caressed her shoulder, slid his hand down her arm.

But now that Rennear had begun to stoke this flame, she found that he was going about it far too slowly, and she would need to take matters of pace into her own hands.

With a delighted chuckle from Rennear, she shifted their weight, rolling him onto his back with her straddling his hips.

He smiled up at her, a hand balanced low around the top of each of her legs, fingertips pressing into her rear. "One of my very favorite memories begins rather like this," Rennear said, referring to the first night they'd spent together.

"Oh does it? And how did that memory work out for you?" One by one, she unfastened the buttons of her tunic and shrugged it off her shoulders.

Rennear's gaze grazed her body, tracing from her face to her shoulders down her chest to her waist and back. His lips parted, watching her as she rolled her hips against his, and his eyes darkened. "Impossibly well," he murmured. Rennear crooked his finger, bidding her to come closer.

She leaned down for a kiss and, lifting her hips from his, began to unfasten the buttons of his trousers.

He was attentive to her throughout, watching her every movement, every expression, as though if he looked away, she might vanish forever. After they reached their successive peaks, Rennear's tracing touch returned to her shoulder, her collarbone, and he rested his hand against her neck, stroking his thumb along her throat. He whispered her name as he did so, drawing her gaze to meet his. "I want you to know, darling, that I meant what I said earlier, that I love you." The bright gleam of his eyes shone, drawing her in closer. "I am yours for as long as you'll have me."

Persephonie snuggled her body nearer against his, tugging the corner of her scarf away from the rock and around her shoulder as she did so. It was much warmer against Rennear than the chilly, damp air. "And if that is forever?"

Rennear grinned. "Then it is forever and I am the luckiest wolf in all the world."

Sorting through the tangle of clothes beside the rock echoed, in reverse order, the enchanting dance of taking each layer off.

Rennear chuckled at the sprigs of moss in her hair, helping her to untangle them from her locks. He allowed her to assist him with his breeches—more because she enjoyed it than because he needed the help.

With her werewolf settled, Persephonie beat her scarf against her knees to drive the remaining flakes of moss from it. *Pat, pat, poof.*

On the opposite side of their clearing, just beyond the creek and not thirty feet from where they'd lain, the silhouette of a man with a large cane and eyes of molten gold appeared in a puff of fluorescent purple smoke.

CHAPTER 33

IELLIETH

Iellieth and her companions were quiet again as the gondola carried them along winding river pathways away from the silver Council Tree. Ammon gave Tanner a gruff description of where to take them, his voice a scraping branch beneath the quiet dip of the oar and burble of the gated river.

"There was a city rather like the council's chambers, wasn't there?" Quindythias asked Marcon. "Silver archways built into the treetops, with bridges formed from branches and glowing lights hanging in the boughs?"

Marcon frowned, thinking back. "Maybe more than one."

Iellieth watched the two of them trying to remember, lips pursed, seeking out the shape of something lost in the dark. Before they left the island, she'd caught Marcon staring up at the rowan tree that had solidified in Loriean-nan's place. What she'd suspected then felt even more true to her now—something had happened to their memories, beyond the severing of souls. Something important had been taken from both of them.

She traced the golden threads that covered the ruby of her amulet. Worse still, though she didn't want to admit it, a tug low in her gut drew her toward that void where something should have been, where it once was—it tugged her toward her amulet just as her amulet tugged her toward them and them toward her.

What they were missing had something to do with how her amulet had been formed in the first place.

Tanner docked the gondola just outside the tavern. A few elves milled about inside, but the wide patio overlooking the river pathways was empty.

As they disembarked, Professor Tur slid out of the beaded doorway, and Firan and Sharia emerged onto the patio, Addah plodding along behind them.

Taleria held out her hand for Quindythias's. "This way," she cooed, leading them through the tavern's dark interior and out again. Tables rough with bark and mushroom-shaped stools decorated the inside of the tavern. Damp moss squelched under Iellieth's feet, giving way to sun-bleached wooden planks outside.

"Tell us all about it," Taleria said, gesturing Marcon and Quindythias over to the table with Firan and Sharia.

Ammon hung back by Iellieth's side. "I know that didn't go as you had hoped," he said.

Iellieth nodded. "You'd warned us. I suppose I shouldn't feel surprised."

"It's funny how alike surprise and disappointment can be at times," Ammon observed. He wandered over to the patio railing. Soft rapids splashed against the wide, wooden columns that supported the patio balcony. In the dock, Tanner reclined in his gondola, his arm draped over his eyes for a nap.

So many questions lingered, but if the ranger wanted to

speak, she would ask them. "You are close with Professor Idlewylde, aren't you?"

A rare smirk creased Ammon's cheek. "I am. I knew her as a child. She supported my interest in restoring the forests, expanding our people's dwelling back to where we belong just as she supported my sister's interest in our histories."

"And in secret societies?" Iellieth ventured.

Ammon sighed. "I'm glad she spoke up for you last night, though we shouldn't have been put in that situation in the first place."

Iellieth bit her lower lip, remembering what Firan had said the night before about the Darkstriders wanting to see the champions of old emerge.

An elf clad head-to-toe in close-fitting black garments slid out of the beaded doorway, a tray of drinks in hand. She handed clay mugs to everyone around the table and then crossed over to Iellieth and Ammon.

"Oh, but we didn't order anything," Iellieth whispered to the ranger.

"A first-timer?" the elf with the tray observed to Ammon. She had pale blue eyes and lavender-hued hair, the colors vibrant in the cloudy morning light against the gray of her skin. "The tavern has a special knack for knowing exactly what you want," she told Iellieth, holding out a mug.

The liquid was clear as she offered it to Iellieth.

"Thank you," Iellieth murmured, taking the mug into her hands. She gasped as it immediately warmed at her touch, steam curling off the mug into the air.

Iellieth looked between the server and Ammon, her eyes wide. She placed her nose over the steam, inhaling deeply. *Impossible*. It was precisely the dark-brewed coffee Dimitri always made for her in Hadvar. "How?"

The server smiled. "These are magical lands. Though the reason doesn't always linger, the magic itself does."

Ammon held his cup up between them. Smoke curled off of it as well, and the earthy scent of tea swirled alongside coffee smoke through Iellieth's senses. "To magical lands," Ammon said.

"To magical lands," Iellieth repeated. Their mugs made a dull *clink* as they tapped the rims together and sipped. Iellieth savored the light oil that clung to her tongue from the ground beans that, through either magic or memory, had appeared in her cup from the other side of the world. What a journey they would have been on, almost as far-reaching as her own had been.

"There's something I wanted to ask you," Iellieth said between sips. She'd been mulling it over since the evening before, waiting for the right moment when she and Ammon could speak alone. "Your sister . . . she says you're not a believer. In the Pilgrimage, I think?"

Ammon nodded as the silence stretched between them which, Iellieth was coming to expect with the ranger. Thus far, she'd always been grateful she'd seen the quiet through to the other side.

"No, I suppose not. There have been times when I've envied Sharia's blind faith, but for me, that's what it would be. What I believe about the Pilgrimage is that it's sent many to their deaths. I try to not be so cynical as to believe that the council uses it as an excuse to avoid confronting the dangers anxious to overwhelm our lands. They live in fear of the spreading empire of Andel-ce Hevra to our west and the portals to the Shadowlands which unleash monsters into our forests."

"Will, umm, your lack of belief impede your ability to get us to the Glade then?" Iellieth didn't want to attempt the trip into the north without the ranger's help, but if Sharia was right and a believer had to show them the way to the Glade, they were effectively without a guide.

"Undoubtedly. But while I have my doubts about ancient pathways appearing in the middle of routes I know well and have walked before, meeting you and your companions has given me an inkling of hope."

Iellieth grinned. "Has it?"

"It's a quite curious sensation," Ammon answered. A sense of ease settled over his shoulders, and he leaned back against the railing, facing their friends and the tavern. "Don't let the council's doubts infect you. Whatever the path before us holds, I will remain by your side. While I have my doubts about the wisdom of my sister's zealots and their precious ancients, I trust the forest. She has taken care of us through the ages. I have to believe she'll allow us to help her now."

Iellieth wanted to take the ranger's words to heart, but the council's adamant doubts and open challenge had left her shaken. Her failings in diplomacy lessons growing up had been an inconvenience. Her blindness to Turdoch's intentions in the logging camp at the beginning of her journey, his goodwill toward those under his power had been a stumbling block, one she'd learned from. Negotiations with King Arontis had gone as well as she could have hoped for. She'd convinced Teodric to believe in her cause and bring her here rather than immediately pursue his missing father.

But what if the council was right and Gaia knew she wasn't worthy? It was one thing to carry the amulet that allowed the champions access to their full selves, bodies and memories. For one of the titans to choose *her*—one who was unable to save Mara from Lucien, who had only survived Alessandra's attack with the seal piece of darkness because of the sacrifice of her friends—wasn't that a stretch too far?

She tucked her doubts away into the corners of her mind. They would be waiting for her, as familiar as her wall of books in Io Keep. And they would keep until after her visit to the elven university, a destination she truly had been working toward all her life.

⁂

A HALF HOUR LATER, ALL THE GEMSTONE HUES OF autumn convened to sway over Iellieth's head above the university courtyards, though it remained midsummer everywhere else in the Realms. The elven students strolled along stone pathways beneath the trees, not even turning their heads to admire the splendor above them. They clutched bark-bound tomes to their chests, some hurrying from one arched-windowed building to another while others took their time, stopping between groups of friends on the meandering paths.

Marcon spied a cart shaped like an acorn with a thatched roof and a wide rectangle carved out of the nut, behind which a fae woman with long, pink ears and magenta hair tended to steaming kettles and a series of mortars and pestles. "What can I do you for, love?" she said, sizing up Marcon and smirking to herself.

Iellieth clenched her teeth together. Stopping for coffees didn't seem like such a good idea after all. The magically conjured coffee she'd had with Ammon was just as perfect as she'd remembered. Marcon ordered for the three of them and turned back to Iellieth, his eyes the same gray-blue as the cloudy sky overhead. "Do you think your father was a student here?"

"I don't know." The idea warmed her insides in the same way the coffee cup did her hands. The timeline of her father's life remained a mystery to her. He'd moved his parents out of Invae Alinor, she'd learned from Reyyar, but had he attended school there or here? "I'd like to think so." She sipped at the steaming beverage but thought better of taking a first gulp till it had cooled a few minutes more.

"Quindythias could actually tell us a thing or two about life as a diplomacy student at an elven university, couldn't you?"

"What?" Quindythias startled as though he'd only just realized Marcon was trying to include him in their conversation. "Oh, yes, it's true." The elf lowered his gaze, strangely sheepish. He inhaled deeply and straightened in his posture. "I know it's probably a great shock to you, Iellieth, but I used to be quite the studious, er, student. That was before we lost my sister."

His voice fell as he spoke of Calixta; Iellieth remembered him telling her that she reminded him of his sister—and that he feared losing her the same way.

Quindythias turned to Marcon. "There is much about this time that I find strange. More than anything else—aside from the lack of airships, of course—it's the lack of loss. There is a heaviness that they lack, though that elder councilor may be an exception." Quindythias furrowed his brow and turned back to Iellieth. "When death occurs at the scale it did in our time, when every family has been marked by loss, it touches every other part of life."

Marcon nodded, his gaze stretching out beyond the

wooded confines of the campus, imagining some impossible vista in Eldura in its place. "The casual way in which the council abdicated their responsibility toward the seal piece seems to me a symptom of what Quindythias describes." The three of them settled onto a bench to observe the students milling about the campus. He lifted the steaming cup from his knee and took a sip. "At first, I understood their lack of caution as a sign of grave apathy toward their people. But I think it's worse than that."

He leaned forward, glancing back at Iellieth. "We're not real to them, lady. Our time. Our concerns. To the council, to many innocently pursuing their lives and dreams here, we are nothing more than a forgotten past."

Quindythias sprang up before Iellieth could answer Marcon. He strode away down one of the curved paths.

Marcon stretched out his arm, gesturing for her to remain where she was. "He'll return shortly."

Iellieth couldn't hold in her reply any longer. "You are real to me." Her throat had tightened as Marcon spoke, but she pushed the words forward anyway. "You're real to Red, and I would say to Yvayne but she carries the past with her. To Teodric and Genevieve and—"

"I know, lady." Ease had crept over Marcon's features as she spoke. "And for that, both Quindythias and I are more grateful than I believe we will ever be able to express."

To Iellieth's surprise, Quindythias reappeared a few moments later, a smiling Professor Tur on his arm. "Would the pair of you like to guess who has been kind enough to offer to show us around the university?" Quindythias cooed. "We have only just arrived in this part of the city and I'm afraid our tour has not extended far beyond that acorn-shaped building that serves coffees."

One of Professor Tur's arms was already draped

through the bend in Quindythias's elbow. "I would like to take you around but I could do with a cup myself first."

"Then please, allow *me* to escort *you*." Quindythias led the professor over to the cart.

Iellieth didn't need to guess at why Quindythias had sought Professor Tur out, or perhaps she had been looking for him. "Was it like this before, when you would visit a new place?"

Marcon grinned watching his friend waving his arms as he spoke, while Professor Tur reacted with animation to every twist and turn of whatever story he was telling. "Perhaps even worse, but yes. There was a time in which we were known entities with quite the reputation. For bravery," he added quickly and then shook his head. "Well, some of us anyway." He recounted adoring crowds throwing flowers at Quindythias's feet, men and women flirting with him in different bars as they traversed the Cities. "Were we to ask him, he'd say he misses such attentions, but I am not certain that's actually true."

He settled his gaze upon hers. "He enjoys your company immensely and tolerates mine." His grin widened at his joke. "I think the fame wore even upon him after a time."

The pair of them had returned while Marcon was speaking. "And such fame was how I was ignominiously captured, of course," Quindythias added, unable to avoid interrupting a conversation concerning himself.

After what Iellieth thought was probably too short a summary of his and Marcon's history for Taleria—she and Quindythias had done away with titles on their trip to the coffee acorn and back—the elf explained the circumstances of his capture and soul-severing. "It seems I had safely locked the memories away—dreadfully painful, having your soul be ripped from your body over the course of several days. But fearing I was being captured again by such beautiful company, I must confess that many of the memories have come back to me."

He recounted how he'd searched for Marcon in Respite after the two of them had become separated. "There were statues of champions in nearly every square," Quindythias added with a wild gesture of his hand. "Several of myself, in fact. But"—he sighed—"alas, I believe it was precisely my fame that led to no one discovering me until dear Iellieth here." He flashed a quick smile in her direction. "You see, it is my belief that I was spirited out of the city *in statue form, disguised* as a statue of myself." Quindythias drew himself up taller as he delivered this revelation, his eyes wide at the drama of his misadventures.

"How dreadful," Professor Tur exclaimed. "And do you remember your time as a statue?"

"Very little," Quindythias said with downcast eyes.

Knowing him as well as she did, it was easy for Iellieth to tell when he was performing and when he was telling the truth. But after their meeting with the council, they all needed a bit of bluster and bravado.

"Quindythias," Iellieth interjected before he could continue, "why don't you have dear Taleria take you on a tour. Marcon and I can wait here."

The flecks of copper in his eyes glowed bright as he looked down at her. "Are you sure the pair of you will be alright without me?"

Iellieth grinned. "We'll do our best to manage."

Quindythias and Taleria strode away, arm-in-arm, leaving Iellieth and Marcon to resume watching the scholars on their various routes along the campus paths.

After the gilded finery of the Council, Iellieth hadn't

been sure what to expect from the university students and scholars. She sighed as she watched them bustling about the wide lawns and pebble-lined paths. Men and women alike wore draped pants that gathered at the ankle or calf, with ankle-high boots or pointed-toe clogs shaped like leaves.

In lieu of the floor-length robes with metallic trimmings favored by the council members, the students and scholars preferred draped shawls, gathered with brooches or tied over tunics, in most cases, though a few wore a heavy-spun knit instead.

Iellieth sipped on the steaming coffee Marcon had brought her, savoring the nuttiness of the flavor, a contrast to the smokiness she had enjoyed a short while before.

The council's alternating ambivalence and disdain lingered over her, a heavy blanket wrapped around her so tightly she couldn't shift it away from herself.

"Ammon said he had a few ideas for our afternoon," Marcon said, glancing down at her. "But I hoped some time here might cheer you."

"It is, immensely."

An elven professor with shoulder-length black hair oiled away from his face walked toward them down the path, a meandering line of students following after him.

"Come along, keep up if you please," the elf called back to his students, who hurried after his long strides. He paused beneath one of the autumnwood trees and gestured up to its branches. "Can anyone tell me, from our readings thus far or your own gathered wisdoms, the origin of these trees?"

A tall young man with gold-tinged hair nearly bumped the student beside him as his arm shot into the air.

"Go ahead," the professor invited.

"Javier Osvaldo claims the trees are a gift from the Brightlands fae, a sign of unity from the Autumn Court."

Iellieth frowned at this explanation. Osvaldo's poetry was as complex as his travelogues were broad, illuminating over a hundred years of rather specific histories, at least from the journals she'd had access to within Io Keep. He had been a favorite for a time as she was deepening her Elvish studies, but the poet's work pulled on earlier folk-lore, weaving symbols of unity into his own conclusions about the flora of his travels.

One of the elf's classmates agreed. "Brigitta vanDe-mark's essays far predate Osvaldo's work and draw compar-isons between both the autumnwood trees and the silver maple, with origins dating all the way back to the flood."

"Both of you are correct to an extent," the professor prodded. "Can anyone tie the trees back to an even earlier tale?"

"The earliest mention of autumnwood trees is from *The Ballad of Hugh and Lilia*."

The entire class turned in her direction. Iellieth's eyes widened—she had said that out loud.

"Ah-ha, a true folklorist in our midst." The professor grinned, clapping his hands and rubbing them together. "Excellently done, fair traveler. And might you be able to remind my students of the circumstances of these partic-ular trees' place within the *Ballad*?"

"Oh, umm, yes, I can." Iellieth rose from the bench and straightened her leather corset, suddenly quite conscious of the fact that she was wearing armor rather than a rainbow array of loomed and woven fabrics like those gathered before her. "The *Ballad* holds that the first trees to appear within this realm—shortly after the legends of the Brightlands, Shadowlands, and our realm diverge—were a gift from Hugh to Lilia during their courtship. Dark forces were advancing across the realms, and we know looking back that the time was coming that Lilia, newly appointed reya of her people, would have to depart for the Brightlands to protect them. But Hugh was still trying to convince her to stay."

The aura of surprise slowly drifted away from the assembled students, replaced by appreciation and curiosity as she continued speaking. Iellieth settled into her story, trying to feel her way through what Katarina would have done in similar circumstances. "He slipped away from the forests he knew, back into the Brightlands, asking the trees' aid in giving a gift that would allow him to express how he felt to the queen of the fae, granddaughter of Verdigris. The forest answered him, giving birth to something entirely new from the borders of the Autumn Court. While the trees share a resemblance to several of the species native to the Brightlands, they are a species all their own, a gift from the Brightlands to their future queen on behalf of her Lycan lover."

"Excellent, most excellent," the professor cried, clapping his hands again. "I cannot think of a more perfect way to conclude our afternoon's studies. So with that, I shall see you all in a few days' time." He glanced in Iellieth's direction. "Would you hold on a moment, please?"

Iellieth nodded, relaying the conversation to Marcon, whose Elvish was more functional than fluent, while the professor spoke with a few lingering students.

As soon as the last of his students had left, the professor hurried toward Iellieth and Marcon, a close-lipped smile accentuating the chiseled lines of his face—in the full glow of his attention, Iellieth quickly understood why two of his students had been so eager to be incorrect and had glared at her for redirecting their professor's gaze. "You must allow me to thank you," he gushed, clasping Iellieth's shoulders and giving each of her cheeks an air kiss, as was common in the Realms.

Marcon bristled beside her.

"Yes, I—well, I had no intention of interrupting your lecture."

"But they needed your assistance," the professor said with a wave of his hand. Following Iellieth's lead, he switched seamlessly into the common tongue so Marcon could participate if he so desired. His studied scowl said he did not.

"And where are my manners?" With a flourish and bow, the elf introduced himself as Professor Adrik Finch, of the university's literature department, with a research focus in cross-cultural narratives.

"That sounds absolutely fascinating!" Iellieth nearly squealed. Her habitual daydream of pacing the grounds of the university campus, cast aside after the meeting with the Council, returned to her more vividly than ever before.

Professor Finch smiled, his eyebrows raised.

"Oh, apologies—I am Iellieth Amastacia and this is my companion, Marcon Colabra. We're here as a delegation from Linolynn."

His eyebrows raised in surprise. "Linolynn you say. Wait, Amastacia?" His fingers tapped against the air before him, and his lips moved without sound, counting and calculating. He smiled to himself and shook his head. "No, no, quite impossible."

"What is it?"

"Oh, it's just"—he gestured with both hands toward her face—"by your hair and eyes alone, you could be the daughter of a very dear friend of mine."

All sound drained out of the world around Iellieth and she swayed on her feet. A deep breath restored her, and she gripped Marcon's wrist in her hand. "And your friend's name?"

"Dorric Themear, of course."

Before she'd had a chance to consider her actions or their consequences, Iellieth had thrown herself forward, wrapping the half-shocked, half-delighted elven professor in a hug. "He is my father. Well, he doesn't know, or he may very soon. His friend in the consulate sent word to Hammerfell."

"Ah, so that is why I did not know about your existence myself." Finch switched into Elvish in his happiness at his discovery. "My dear, he is going to be thrilled beyond words to meet you." He blinked, clearing his suddenly over-bright amber eyes. "And to have such a father—I hope your travels will permit you very soon to meet."

Professor Finch recovered himself and offered Iellieth his elbow for a more detailed tour of the campus, especially the library and the multi-story hall reserved specifically for scholars of literature. One of the classrooms they passed had a prominent map of Caldara on display, with the professor drawing a circle around Hadvar with their fingers, speaking of the poetic history of the Umbral elves who dwelled far below the city.

He and Dorric had been friends since their university days, Finch explained, and Dorric had even stayed with him for a few months on his most recent return to the Realms before the council sent him off for a tour with the dwarves. "I don't wish to intrude upon your plans, but would you care to have dinner with me this evening?"

Marcon cleared his throat from behind Finch.

"Oh, I mean the both of you, of course."

Iellieth hid her smile behind her hand, turning to admire some of the university's greenery. "I thank you, Professor, for the tour, for telling me about my father. But we are due to meet a friend soon, and we've promised to dine with him at the lodge already."

"I see." He bowed his head graciously.

"But perhaps when we return?" She ignored Marcon's scowl.

"That would be lovely." Finch swept into a bow, planting a kiss upon the back of her hand, and excused himself, having deposited her and Marcon back where they'd met. "You're welcome at my lectures any time," he called back as he strode away, adjusting the set of the leather satchel upon his shoulder as he did so.

CHAPTER 34

BRISERAS

Leaving the archives, Briseras, Jorgan, and Tybalt had arrived in the Bloodletters' territory after dark and paid for rooms in the first tavern they found—overpaid if Tybalt's continued grousing was any indication. After encountering the record of the huntress and the destruction of Arduenne's fane, Briseras wasn't entirely surprised to find herself swept away into another dream with Lord Draego. But instead of appearing as a wolf within Arduenne's fane as she had several days before, she found herself in a high tower inside a castle.

There was an oversized fireplace that took up nearly an entire wall, a generous fire crackling at its center. The vampire lord stood by the fireplace, a glass of red wine in his hand. The side of his mouth twisted upward in a smile at her arrival. He looked as though he'd dressed for a special dinner earlier in the day and had doffed much of his finery, leaving a loose tie and vest over a partially unbuttoned white tunic and close-fitting black breeches.

"Welcome to my home." He bowed over his arm as she

appeared at the end of a plush velvet sofa, the fabric a rich shade of burgundy. "I hope you don't mind joining me."

"I . . . I am glad to be here, actually."

He betrayed no reaction, but Briseras sensed a shift in his attention, focusing more closely on her. Lord Draego asked after her time in Barasov, her impression of the city. He waved away her report of the worsening divisions between Watchers and Bloodletters. "They are always quarreling. It is the purview of the nobles to tend to such matters. I try not to frighten them all by getting involved."

She nodded, uncertain how she was meant to react. If he wasn't going to bring up her research, then she would ask about it herself. "A few hours ago, I found a record from the period when the fanes were destroyed."

Draego froze with his glass of wine halfway to his lips, turning toward her instead. "Is that so?"

"You told me once you might share with me the sad story. Would you? If restoring Arduenne is the key to removing my lycanthropy, as you suggested, I would like to understand why you don't want the Sisters returned, their fanes restored, even if you were willing to make an exception for one Sister for me."

"It is possible there are other methods, but curing blood curses takes time." Draego smirked. "I am an expert in such things, likely more so than any other being. I do not wish to keep that from you which you desire to know. I had known them my whole life, the Four Sisters, Archfae who once shared our rule of this realm. As had my ancestors before me, I brought them offerings, consulted their wisdom, tended to their requests. It seems foolish now, looking back, but when my wife, Elena, fell ill, I sought their aid. And they denied me."

His gaze drifted out the tower windows, staring off

into the mountains beyond. "I could not save her, though I tried. With nowhere else to turn, my friends having abandoned me, I learned that her blood curse had passed on to my son as well." Draego's voice thickened. "If I did nothing, I would lose them both. Instead, I bargained with whichever god would listen for the power to exact my revenge upon those who had betrayed me. I promised myself and my son, whatever it took to save his life." His tongue rolled over his fangs. "A god answered me."

Lord Draego spoke of Xarmev, god of undeath, who promised power and immortality, the secret to saving his son. In return for the god's gift, Draego bound himself to the god's service. "While my lands remained my own, I could not share them, as my ancestors had done with the Sisters. And what this god wanted more than anything was blood."

Draego explained how in his fervor to save his wife and at the bidding of the one who had promised to save his son, the armies of Steymhorod swept across neighboring lands, slaughtering as they went. Blood pooled along the earth. His sword drank deeply of his enemies but still he wanted more. "It could not bring back Elena, but my son could be saved. If that meant imbibing the blood of those I had slaughtered, growing the fangs that would drain the life from their throat, I did it."

As for the Sisters, he said, their slaughter was of his own design and volition. "I could not allow such treachery to stand." He shook his head. "Elena's screams were all I had heard for weeks on end. Utter misery. And without explanation, they turned their backs on us. So I did the same." He clenched his hands, released them, and continued, "In the early years of my sole rulership of these lands, I passed my gift on to others—my commanders and confidantes. The first of my kind, I was not yet wise enough to know that such a gift would bring so many . . . complications."

Briseras swallowed, trying to take in his story without panic. Lord Draego wasn't just a powerful vampire, more powerful than any vampire she'd ever heard of. He was the first. The progenitor. "And so every vampire who has ever been—"

"Gained their power and their immortality from me, from my blood. The closer they are to my blood, the more powerful they are." His expression darkened. "That is part of how the vampire you faced, Nassarq, became so dangerous so quickly. He found the blood of one of my oldest friends, one of three vampires—and only three—I turned directly. By imbibing Hugo's blood, he turned himself into a reincarnation of one of the most powerful vampires to have ever lived."

His face fell at the mention of the name she had seen at the bottom of the scroll she and Everett had found in the underground chapel in Nocturne. "For eons, he was one of my most trusted advisers and dearest friends. We had a . . . falling out, one might say. A stranger to our lands took advantage of Hugo's isolation and struck him down. Not even my magic was enough to save him then."

He had lost most of those he loved, just like she had. Though Draego spoke of his wife more often than Briseras would have liked, his concerns spoke to his care for her, even after so long.

"I am sure"—Briseras wrung her hands in her lap, searching for the right thing to say—"she must be waiting for you. Your friend Hugo too. When I, well, nearly died, I saw my family, waiting for me. They seemed . . . happy. At peace." She hadn't told him of Malthael's bite or Ophelia bringing her back. The memories of her mother, her little sister, and the priest beckoning to her from across a river, the serenity upon her mother's face, she who had often looked so strained, lifted Briseras away from her position inside the vampire's castle even while still in the dream.

Glass shattered, and her head shot up. Wine dripped down from the vampire's hand onto the floor. Shards of glass decorated his skin. His shoulders had tensed and risen in a tight ridge along his back.

She sprang out of her seat and started toward him but stopped short as he whirled around.

There was no more amber light within his gaze—shards of onyx glimmered back at her instead. "She cannot be waiting for me," the vampire lord seethed through his teeth, his breathing labored.

"I didn't mean—"

"She will be waiting *forever*." He lifted a second crystal goblet from a tray and flung it against the far wall. "I cannot die," he screamed, stalking toward Briseras. "Don't you understand?"

Her training kicked in, and Briseras backed away from him, fists slowly raising to her shoulders.

She had searched the room upon entry—there were no weapons here aside from the crystal, and bruising a vampire would do her little good. Would violence experienced during a dream harm her upon waking?

The vampire raised his chin and yelled toward the sky, his muscles tensing in his anguish.

The cold stone from the far wall pressed against her back. There was nowhere else for her to go.

Draego locked eyes with her and growled in the back of his throat. Still several paces away, he slashed his hand before him as though seeking to disembowel her—

The room fell away and Briseras woke, breathless, back in the inn that they'd found shortly before midnight in the Bloodletters' territory.

Jorgan snored softly on the mattress beside hers, and Vera had snuggled against her for warmth.

She'd ruined it, destroyed her chance of understanding the vampire lord or . . . what was it exactly she'd wanted from him? What had she been hoping for?

Briseras squinted shut her eyes and shook her head. She didn't want to probe into that particular question and feel any more foolish than she did already. She avoided social situations for precisely this reason. It had seemed only natural to try to assuage some of the pain around his wife's death. She had been dead for millennia. His grief for her still seemed so fresh, his rage at what he'd become to save his son—

She would never see him again.

Briseras released a slow exhale, her heart still pounding against her ribs. That was for the best, wasn't it? She would return to her role as huntress and he to being the ruler of these lands.

She tried to breathe past the heaviness in her chest— each breath shuddered inside her. *Get it together.* Tybalt shifted on his mattress across the room, moonlight casting shadows around his bulky form. Neither he nor Jorgan would accept a simple explanation for breathlessness in the middle of the night, and she had been careful not to tell them about her dreams.

A quick scan of the room, the rhythm of her companions' breathing, returned her to her body, her senses. *It's for the best*, she repeated to herself.

Briseras bit the inside of her lip. If only she believed that were true.

She settled back down onto the mattress, curling her arm around Vera. Almost against her will, her hand fastened around the locket she'd received from her mother. *Please*, she thought to her mother's gods, *please let him give me another chance. Let me explain.*

Sleep was a long time in finding her but eventually it did.

BRISERAS RETURNED TO THE SAME ROOM SHE HAD LEFT, though it seemed that time for Lord Draego had passed as well. The fire had dwindled to shimmering coals. The carafe of wine was empty.

The vampire stood facing the dying fire, his elbow propped against the mantle, fingertips holding up his forehead.

Mountain peaks cast their shadows beneath stars beyond the iron-framed panes of the arched windows.

"I didn't mean to—"

Lord Draego held up a hand, asking her to wait.

Briseras clenched her jaw and sat on the center of the sofa, arms crossed over her waist. Why had she allowed herself to come back here? Could she have prevented this dream-travel, or was his magic so powerful she had no choice?

She twitched her fingers over her linen sleeves. The worst part of it was that she'd wanted to come back. She'd wanted to see him again, to explain herself. What was the matter with her?

The vampire lord raised the crystal goblet to his lips. The last dregs of dark red trickled down the glass—wine, not blood. It left no trace against the crystal. "I owe you an apology, Briseras."

Her skin prickled at the elongation of the syllables of her name, the trilled *r* of his accent.

She straightened on the sofa, striking as self-assured a posture as the plush seat made possible. A huntress through and through, her muscles were tense, prepared to spring away should he turn against her once more.

"You could not have known of my curse and its requisite effects." He cast his gaze from her face to the carved stone floor. "And it was wrong of me to hold you responsible for a work of my own making."

Slowly, he crossed the room, coming toward her. With each step he watched her closely.

She could feel the attunement of his eyes to her every movement and sensed that he was watching to see if she would recoil. But more than curiosity had driven her here. *I am not afraid of you*, she wanted to say, but words would break this spell, and she didn't want to drive him back now that he drew near.

"It's, umm . . . I understand."

"Do you?" At first she thought it was amusement twitching at the corner of the vampire's lip, but his brow had drawn in as well. He had been concerned about her, about bringing her back. Draego stopped half an arm's reach away from her, stared for a moment longer, and sank down onto the couch beside her.

Briseras sat up taller—she wanted to say something. Countless questions darted across her mind but in their stampede, jumbled together into incoherence. The back of her throat was dry.

"I have been waiting a long time for you." His gaze traveled from her eyes to her lips as he spoke.

He didn't mean the time that had passed that evening —he was speaking of something else. "How could you have known to wait for me?" Her thoughts jumped to Everett's mention of Ophelia, the druid manipulating her fate. Was that what he meant?

"It is a special kind of knowing, Briseras. A soul-deep longing. It cannot always be put into words though if you allow me, I will try to explain."

The intensity of his gaze carved a hollow in the back of her throat. She struggled to find an answer, to understand what she wanted to say.

Lord Draego brushed back a strand of hair that had fallen over her face. "My love," he murmured as he leaned closer, so softly she couldn't be certain she had heard correctly. But then his lips were upon hers, and there was no need for thought any more.

CHAPTER 35

IELLIETH

Quindythias appeared at their meeting spot a short while after Finch departed. Marcon excused himself for a moment, saying he would return shortly.

"I acquired a gift for you," Quindythias announced, "before we set out into whatever wilderness Ammon is planning to lead us through." With a flourish, he revealed a rectangular package bound in cloth and twine. The twine held a lush feather quill, the plumage such a dark teal it appeared almost black.

Iellieth's lips parted as she stared at her friend.

"It's a journal. Marcon described your room in Linolynn and all the books you had there, a few of them ledgers of your own design. While we were on the ship, I noticed you were nearing the end of your own journal and thought you might like a fresh one for this new stage of our journey." He grinned fondly when he spied the bundle in her hands. "Perhaps within those pages you can record when we do happen to find your father."

Iellieth's vision blurred as tears welled in her eyes. "Quindythias, I—"

"You deserve that and more." He placed a kiss on her temple and wandered off down one of the university's paths. "I'll meet you by the central fountain when it's time to leave," he promised as he sauntered away, a bounce in his step.

She was still smiling when Marcon found her a few minutes later, a new steaming cup of dark liquid and a collection of small, exquisite flowers in his hands.

In the distance, Quindythias gazed up at the fountain, occasionally dipping his fingers into the waters.

"I see he's recovered himself." Marcon stopped a half arm's reach from where Iellieth stood, his pale gaze fixed upon hers. "Our ideas were similar." He plucked a periwinkle flower with a spray of burgundy, spindle-like petals from the small bunch in his hand and leaned closer, tucking the stem into the braid behind her ear.

"I cannot promise the university would approve of my flower picking." His voice dropped an octave, and his hand lingered in her hair. "But after reaching a place you've wanted to travel to for so long, I thought it fitting you have something to mark the occasion."

Marcon passed her the bundle of flowers, their stems warm from his grasp. Brilliant fuchsia with deep, evergreen leaves brushed against a soft-petaled garnet flower that bobbed with the weight of its golden center, heavy with pollen.

"I have been thinking a great deal of what lies before us, the implications of the Council's ambivalence," Marcon said. "You know that I would spare you the dangers of what we will face in the wilds of the Realms if I could." His eyes danced as he searched her features. "Yet at the same time, I cannot help the swell of gratitude I feel that you should have been the one to find me, that your amulet led you to my side. Perhaps it is an inherently dangerous place to be, but I would not have you anywhere else."

His gaze lingered on her lips, and Iellieth drew closer. "Marcon—"

"There you two are," Ammon called from behind her. Iellieth jumped, finding him so near, and stumbled against Marcon's chest in her effort to save her flowers from being smushed. "Let's see—one ancient warrior of fire, one red-haired druid . . ." Ammon smirked as he pretended to count their small numbers. "Once we acquire our sneaky champion of air, we should be ready to face the forest."

The sneaky champion of air was just then balancing on the edge of the fountain. He wobbled when Ammon called to him and shouted back that he needed only a few minutes more.

While they waited for Quindythias to meander back to meet them, Ammon fondly recounted the last such trip he'd made into the forest. "I met the troupe of children right here and counted them in similar fashion, much to their delight. They had much less an air of my having interrupted them."

"They are less likely to have been in the middle of something important," Marcon murmured to himself, just loudly enough for Iellieth to hear.

"Did you meet them with Firan?" she asked Ammon. Of his friends she'd met yesterday, he would have been first in her list of possible guides for leading children through a wild forest.

"Oh yes, Addah is a great favorite of theirs. The teachers later complained that the children asked for her for over a fortnight after their sojourn through the trees."

Ammon gazed across the campus lawn. "He and I were just meeting, actually. And there's someone who wants to speak with the three of you before we sojourn into the forest."

❦

"YOU'VE ACTUALLY MET HER ALREADY," AMMON explained once Quindythias was ready to depart from the fountain. He'd picked up a game with several of the students in which they placed bets about whether coins would land with leaves or paws up when flipped into the water. His pockets jingled as they walked.

A certain, bright-eyed councilor popped into Iellieth's mind as Ammon led them toward the building she knew from their tour with Adrik to contain magical artifacts.

Iellieth's suspicions were correct. "Oh-ho," Professor Idlewylde called as they appeared in the doorway of a long stone hallway jutting off the main thoroughfare. Colored panes of glass decorated the arched windows that ran the length of the hall, allowing in the light but obscuring the long tables and glass cases that filled the hall. "Our heroes of the day. Yes, yes, welcome in."

Iellieth held back in the doorway. Was Idlewylde mocking them or genuinely glad they'd arrived?

"You, yes." She waved Iellieth in again. "I've much to show you before your expedition and *someone*, in their irritation, has made such an expedition much hastier than it would have otherwise been."

Ammon had already settled himself onto a settee inside the entryway where Idlewylde had a small living area set up before a cold hearth. The university's Estudia Arcania—building of magical studies and works of the arcane—was one of the few stone structures in all of Thyles Thamor besides the wall. "I told the three of you yesterday that you had met two of the leaders of the Darkstriders." He held both arms out toward Idlewylde, his manner more relaxed than Iellieth had seen aside from a few moments in the lodge. "Behold! The third."

Quindythias was the first of the three of them to speak. "What a curious surprise."

"Yes, I suppose it must be. A rather bleak time of it you had this morning with those ninnies on the council. Valaexi is the only one who gives me any hope. And I suppose your mother at times," she added half-heartedly, glancing at Ammon before returning her bright, focused gaze to Quindythias. "But you, my dear young elf, have inspired a fandom that gives me a great deal of hope for the future of our lovely Realms. Something about your story, scholar turned adventurer, resonates deeply with our students, and so Taleria, Sharia, and I set ourselves the task of helping to make real the past, as it were." She tittered to herself. "Who knew we would be so successful!"

Quindythias glanced to Iellieth, who rubbed her hand along his back.

Idlewylde shrugged her narrow shoulders and began ordering them around. "There's no sense in you lying about there," Idlewylde quipped to Ammon. "You three, hop down to the end of the hall and find some charges for your travels."

Ammon smirked as he stood up and motioned for Marcon and Quindythias to follow him. "The charges can be applied to weapons, which will help if we run into more enraged biomechos. It stuns them without harming them," the ranger explained as the champions followed him down the hall.

"An absolute wonder you didn't all perish on the way here," Idlewylde muttered to herself, shuffling toward Iellieth. The wrinkled elven woman was nearly a head shorter than Iellieth, putting her line of sight almost directly parallel with the amulet. "I saw this upon your neck in the council chambers and told Ammon I had to see it more closely for myself." Idlewylde raised a monocle to first one eye and then, flipping it, to the other, mumbling to herself all the while.

She hobbled away from Iellieth toward a long line of shelves that housed a collection of scrolls, muttering as she tugged a few down. The parchment crinkled as she unrolled and rerolled the scrolls, searching for something and growing more agitated the longer it took her to find it.

Iellieth crossed the hall to stand behind her. "Is there anything I can do to help?"

"I swear it was just here," the elderly scholar muttered in reply, continuing in her search.

Her friends listened intently as Ammon went over the intricacies of charges with them at the end of the hall, leaving Iellieth to meander to its opposite side where Idlewylde kept several glass cases atop pedestals. There, magical artifacts dwelled beside crystals and spell implements in a system Iellieth set herself the task of unlocking while she waited.

"Here it is!" Idlewylde declared a quarter of an hour later, tugging a leather-bound tome down from one of the shelves beside the scrolls. Iellieth kept finding herself returning to a fragmented piece of glowing crystal near the center of Idlewylde's collection. She turned from it and joined the scholar at the table opposite the scrolls.

"There was a young woman in Respite whose diary has been of particular interest to us. A witch she was."

Idlewylde nodded to herself as she searched the pages, her sharp fingernail scratching over the dry parchment like a cloak over stone. "We made copies of the most pertinent parts of her journal here—the original resides in the mountains for safety."

Iellieth walked around the table to stand at the scholar's side and look over her shoulder.

"She made a troubling discovery, in Respite," the scholar continued. "The champions had started to disappear. She also found magical gems that seemed to hold immense power."

Reading along for herself, the woman's description of the glittering stones sounded rather like the seal pieces, but there wouldn't have been so many, nor would they have been so small, would they?

"Her troubling discovery, what was it?" Iellieth kept her voice low enough that Marcon and Quindythias wouldn't overhear.

The woman's eyes grew glassy as she followed Iellieth's gaze toward her friends. "It will pain you to learn of it. Are you ready?"

"I don't know how it could be more difficult to hear than much that I've learned and experienced already."

Idlewylde sighed. "The shards the young witch found—they were the shattered remnants of champions. Their souls had been severed, rather like your friends experienced, though likely less prolonged. Marcon Colabra and Quindythias Darkstrider have always been special," she added, a glint brightening her quick-moving eyes.

Iellieth's hand began to shake upon the tabletop. Champions severed and then—shattered? "You mean they . . . they . . ."

"The Cities broke apart the bodies of those they no

longer saw a use for, yes. They used the enchanted remains to power magical elements of their buildings, something rather like our lifts but with remains of a champion rather than magical vines. The remnants were known as soulshards. It's an ancient magic, dating back to the first fight against Alessandra."

Iellieth's knees swayed and she caught her balance on the edge of the table, no longer able to listen to Idlewylde's history lesson. It couldn't be true. It was too horrible. If such a fate had befallen Marcon and Quindythias, and they had been lost to time— "Wait, you said this connects to my amulet. Why?"

The elderly scholar folded her hands at her waist and watched Iellieth's expression, waiting for her to make sense of her questions and assemble them together herself.

Her gaze drifted to the dark shard held in glass across the room, the one she kept returning to.

If, like these shards the witch in Respite had written of, the amulet *was* made from an enchanted stone, something rather like the piece of fire . . . Iellieth's stomach heaved and she turned away from the tome. *Oh gods.* "You're saying it's from a champion of fire?" Her voice cracked on the words and she shut her eyes, willing all around her to stop.

Iellieth hugged her arms against her waist, hoping Marcon wouldn't choose this moment to look over at her. She'd been so touched by the way her amulet linked the two of them together. Yvayne had even told her that the maker of her amulet had been drawn to fire. And all this time—she was wearing part of a corpse formed into jewelry.

She fought back the urge to rip the amulet from her neck and fling it across the sunlit chamber.

A soft, wrinkled hand pressed gently upon her shoulder as the scholar settled her hip against the table beside Iellieth. "Not just any champion of fire." The glint of mischief returned as the scholar once again looked at Marcon.

He was hurrying toward the two of them, a frown caught between his brows.

Iellieth gasped, wrapping her hand around the amulet. What she'd been wearing since she was little—it was a piece of Marcon? "How?" she whispered.

"I would need further study to be certain, but the elemental signature of the sigil is the same as that which your companion bears. As I said, it's an old magic. How the amulet came to be and how it binds not only the two of you together, but awakened his friend as well . . ." Idlewylde shook her head. "That is a part of your story, and his," the elderly scholar concluded, her voice returning to the sing-song reserved for faery tales and moral lessons dressed up in story form. "You will find out when it is time, with my help or on your own. But whatever your amulet's history, however it was forged, what I can glean from it is this—the story stretches farther back than you know."

Iellieth's mind raced, trying to put together all she had learned, what it might mean.

"Lady." Marcon reached out toward her as he approached her side. "Are you well?"

She nodded, stepping closer to lean into his shoulder. Iellieth sighed as Marcon wrapped his arm around her waist. The last time he'd done so, sparks had fluttered about in her stomach but this time, the slow, steady wash of ease his presence so often brought ebbed over her instead. "I think I've been in the Estudia too long."

The scholar bowed her head to the pair of them. "We'll

conclude our meeting for the day. Why don't the two of you go enjoy the sunset? There's a special spot in one of the treetop restaurants. Ammon can show you."

"Are you sure you're alright?" Marcon murmured as he led her out of the Estudia and back toward the acorn coffee hut. Ammon and Quindythias would meet them shortly, charges in hand, and they'd have dinner together before setting out in the morning.

She nodded against his shoulder, still trying to work through her discovery. There would be time, later, to tell him, once she fully understood what it meant and whose story intersected with theirs—the story that had led to the creation of her amulet.

CHAPTER 36

PERSEPHONIE

"Yeep!" Persephonie exclaimed, stumbling back at the sight of the strange man surrounded by bright purple smoke. She fumbled at her half-tied waistband to find the enchanted glitter she had concealed there for precisely such an occasion.

"Ho there!" Rennear called. With the singing ring of steel, he withdrew his rapier from its scabbard and waved it toward the intruder. He took half a step forward, ushering Persephonie behind him.

"Elements be, where in all the planes—" The purple fog cleared, revealing a thin, elderly man wearing a floppy leather overcoat that was covered in thick leather straps that held various contraptions about his person.

Persephonie squinted as she leaned closer, peering around Rennear's attempts to block her from sight. The objects he wore strapped to himself were a mixture of spheres and half spheres, many of which bore slowly spinning sticks inside themselves. The sticks—the size of needles—rotated in set patterns about the severed spheres but each at their own rate, tracing slight, intricate circles within the spheres. Was it a defense tactic, meant to confuse the eyes or distract aggressors?

The man wiped at the shining cylinders he wore around his eyes, a strange form of spectacles made to look almost like armor. The round panes of glass were held in place by thick circles of metal with protruding rivets along the sides. These were connected to leather straps that clung tightly to the man's head. "What—who . . ." He sputtered as he found Rennear and Persephonie opposite him. The eye-glass circles gave him the appearance of an owl, an impression that only increased as the smoke cleared and a few orange beams of sunlight peeked through the evergreens and flashed against the glass panes. "Now where . . ." The man pulled at a flap on his colorful overcoat, which gave a whooshing sound.

Persephonie gasped as a real owl squawked into existence out of the pocket. It flapped up onto the man's shoulder, facing opposite them. Standing between them, Rennear cried out as the owl spun its head back, gazing at them with bright yellow-orange eyes of its own, its head cocked just like the old man's. The owl ruffled its feathers and hooted, adjusting its feet to accommodate its round, heavy body.

They all stared at one another. "It is very unlike the green owl from Andel-ce Hevra," Persephonie remarked. Unless the man kept an entire parliament of owls hidden within the many flaps of his coat or the shining spheres possessed explosive capabilities like Aylin's weapons in the city, she doubted he posed a threat to them. For the moment, he seemed as bewildered as they were, though the owl, for his part, appeared to be quite at ease.

"Ah, Reginald," the man sighed, straightening himself as he nodded to the backward-facing owl upon his shoulder, "there you are. I was beginning to wonder. It seems I may have led us astray."

Reginald the owl merely hooted in reply, unruffled, as it were.

Persephonie had the distinct impression that Reginald's lack of surprise was less that he was an owl and therefore difficult to fluster and more that this strange man had led them astray before, possibly often. She marveled at the way in which the tufts of white hair that poked out along the sides of the man's scalp were so very like the tufted feathers of his owl companion. Had they resembled one another when they first met, or had the likeness formed over time?

"Erm, pardon me." Persephonie rested a hand upon Rennear's shoulder and stood on tiptoe to see around him. "I do not wish to be rude or, erm, to rush you but—who are you?"

The man coughed to clear his throat—small puffs of purple smoke burst from his lips as he did so. "Ahem. That's better. Now"—he stared at Rennear and Persephonie through the shining spectacles—"if you would be so kind, I should very much like to know where I am, precisely, and when as well."

Rennear cast a concerned look back to Persephonie at the man's questions. "I must insist that you answer her question first before we attend to yours." He swirled the tip of his rapier into the space between them.

The owl hooted in immediate reply to this threat. His eyes crossed, staring at the tip of the blade, but Reginald made no move toward them.

"Ah." The man leaned his head back at a dramatic angle —unlike his avian companion, his neck was long and sinewy. "Cornelius Arasmi Morgenstern, temporator extra-ordinaire."

Persephonie frowned and tiptoed forward. "Would you repeat that? Tempora . . ."

"Oh, that is not good." Cornelius met the owl's eyes and shook his head. "Not good at all."

"His accent is quite strange," Persephonie whispered to Rennear. "I have not heard its like."

"Nor I."

"Erhm, perhaps you might, in more detail, explain who you are, and we will answer in turn as best as we may."

The man sighed. "Very well, if we must." He stared down his long nose at Rennear's rapier, crossing his eyes in precisely the same manner as his owl. "Would you mind putting that away first? Reginald and I are rather sensitive to the pointed tips of blades."

Persephonie grinned at this and nodded to Rennear, who did as Cornelius asked. If he ended up posing a greater threat than he appeared he could—which Datha had taught her was always a possibility—she would blind him with glitter and faery butterflies, and they would make their escape.

Cornelius hobbled over toward the creek bed and nimbly leapt over it, landing lightly on the other side. "Now, while I tell you who I am and where I'm from, what would you say to a lovely cup of tea from this, uhh, creek here." He produced a fine white cup from his side that made a plinking sound against the plate he excavated from one of his many pockets.

"I could create an infusion." Persephonie held out her hands for the cup and sprinkled a pinch of an herb mixture she kept in her skirt pocket into the bottom of it while Cornelius pulled two other cups from the pack at his side.

"None for Reginald," Cornelius added. "He won't mind."

A few minutes later, the four of them, counting Reginald this time, settled around the large boulders that bordered the shallow creek.

Cornelius took a dainty sip of his infusion and smiled to himself. "My, that is refreshing." He sniffed the herbal water. "Mint, is it?"

"Yes. And a few sprigs of thyme with dried dandelion."

"Oh, the little yellow bits, I see."

Cornelius had a look about him that indicated he was not a being who rushed in any of his actions save whatever steps of preparation had misled him to New Orison in the first place. Persephonie forced a slow breath, willing herself to wait until he'd had a chance to gather himself before resuming her questions.

But Rennear was not so patient. "It is a lovely infusion, darling." He grinned at her, but his eyes never left the intruder and his owl.

The temporator did seem to be trying quite hard to set both of them and his owl at ease.

"Cornelius," Persephonie began, "while you are getting settled, I can tell you what I know of where we are, though, as to the question of *when*, my own lack of familiarity with our surroundings makes it hard for me to answer." Persephonie bit her bottom lip, worried she'd confused the wide-eyed man further but decided he always looked surprised with a pinch of desperately curious. "We traveled from Azuria to a place called New Orison. I know we are in the Negative Planes, but I don't know *where* exactly." One of the problems with the Negative Planes was their vast scale—an issue the saudad normally subverted by traveling upon the threads, which the priests of New Orison, for the time being, were making impossible.

Cornelius had taken a large slurp of the herbal water and nearly spat it out at Persephonie's answers. "By the hells, Reginald, we've gotten off-track!"

Rennear leaned forward. "Does New Orison's location within the Negative Planes mean something to you?" A note of warning hummed low in his voice, a twinge of the worry he didn't want to share with her about being trapped in New Orison seeping through.

"I'm sure I could find it on the archive maps some-where," Cornelius said uselessly, waving his hand as though accessing these archives would be no trouble whatsoever.

Persephonie studied the temporator's instruments again. Beyond their sheen, could they disclose how this man and owl had arrived within this particular bubble without the blessing of the priests and without using the door the Feather had found?

"I'm not sure how helpful that will be."

Cornelius successfully slurped and swallowed his herbal water this time. "Ah, yes, yes, I understand the trepidation. Perhaps when you better understand the temporators' work, you will have greater trust in our cataloging system. But, before then, I believe I owe *you* some answers." He swept into a low bow over his arm, extending his cup and saucer out before the shiny top of his head. After repeating his name and title, he added, "I hail from Dal'gerra, of course, home world of all temporators. Perfectly dreadful place, though"—he chuckled to himself —"I'm sure you know that already, having arrived within the Negative Planes yourselves."

Rennear shook his head, answering her unasked question even before she'd had time to pose it. Neither of them had ever heard of Cornelius Morgenstern's home.

"You mean to tell me you've never heard of Dal'gerra? What of Naldross, famous—*in*famous—city of thieves?"

"No, that is not familiar either," Persephonie answered.

Cornelius's eyes widened even further behind his spectacles. "Well, what an intriguing predicament I've landed us in, Reginald," he observed to the owl. He leaned toward Persephonie and Rennear, squinting at them. "*Never* go if given the opportunity," he insisted, but then his face scrunched and he began mumbling to himself. "Of course the demons don't always give one a great deal of option do they?"

"Erhm, demons, did you say?" Persephonie smoothed her skirts, trying to push away imaginings of contending with demons alongside the already present threats of the priests.

"Bah," Cornelius laughed. "You're not familiar with either Naldross or Dal'gerra, but you've heard of demons? Ha! What a peculiar place. How fascinating!"

Persephonie could not tell whether the temporator was mocking her or delighted by his current plight, and his sudden swing in mood did not help the matter.

"Being unknown and unanticipated is the lot of a temporator, I fear." He sighed, staring into his empty cup.

"Could I make you some more? And then perhaps you could tell us about your home?"

Cornelius agreed, cheering at the thought of more herbal water as much as anything else. "Traveling through space and time can truly dry out one's sinuses," he complained.

She cast a sideways glance at Rennear. Though his contraptions and mode of travel were exceedingly unfamiliar, perhaps the temporator had more in common with the saudad than she'd realized.

With a fresh herbal water in hand, Cornelius took a measured sip, seeming to want to pace himself his second time around. "I must own," he began, "it is quite puzzling, finding myself here. *New* Orison. I have heard of the old, so that is something. And you are terribly familiar to me," he said, gesturing to Persephonie. "Were you in Orison, before it fell?"

Her eyes widened. "No. I was not." Thank Cassandra for that—what a tragic fate, to have been within her home when the city was destroyed, herself along with it, or to return from travels only to find all the friends and family left behind were now lost forever.

"Hmm," Cornelius puzzled over her again, propping his head upon his upraised fist.

He would have continued in that way for some time had not Rennear interrupted him. "Might we offer you some aid or greater refreshment?" He gestured back toward the way they'd come.

"Oh, yes," Persephonie exclaimed. Here she was, complaining about the lackluster hospitality of New Orison and neglecting proper hospitality herself. "We're sure to be able to find a place for you, and food as well."

"No need, no need," Cornelius said, shaking his head. On his shoulder, Reginald, who was still facing the wrong way and watching with his head turned halfway around, did the same. "I always bring all the necessary supplies with me. Temporator protocol you see." He hobbled back toward the stream, hopped across, and, standing in the center of the clearing, tugged upon one of the ties of his pockets. A small cloth box fell out and plopped onto the ground. Cornelius bent over and loosened the bow from the top of the box. He sprang back—as did Rennear and Persephonie—when the box exploded upward, forming itself into a full-sized tent in which a peculiar man and his owl could sleep comfortably.

"And somewhere in here"—he patted his many pockets —"there'll be stores of food. So don't you worry about me." He grinned and hummed an unfamiliar tune as he wobbled back over to the pair of them, nimbly hopping over the creek once more.

"Now, I do not wish to impose, but I should very dearly like assistance in recovering my original path. I don't suppose there is anything I can help you with in exchange for your aid to me?"

"We are not certain on that front," Persephonie answered, feeling rather like a maiden in a faery tale endeavoring not to be tricked by the Archfae lord of a region she'd accidentally stumbled into. They had agreed only a few days before to help the members of the Feather to find a way out of New Orison, but could Cornelius help with that if he had become trapped here as well? "While I think of something, do you think you might tell us more about your home?"

Cornelius studied her with one magnified yellow-orange eye and then the other. To her relief, Reginald had turned his head back around and now stared into the forest behind Cornelius, though both she and Rennear jumped each time the owl hooted from Cornelius's shoulder.

"I have heard of demons in stories—at least creatures that go by the same name—but even in all our travels, I have never met someone who has encountered them."

"A good reason for that," Cornelius said, nodding. "Most who encounter demons don't live to tell about it."

He settled down into what she recognized as his story-teller's posture. She had one, as did her datha, and it was a relief to see him do something familiar. One bushy eyebrow slowly crept up above his spectacles. "Most, of course, but not all."

Cornelius wove a tale for them of a grand city, run entirely by outlaws, a haven for those who had been expelled from the other mortal settlements, cities, and kingdoms of Dal'gerra, of which there were not many. The vast majority of the world, he said, was ruled by demons. "But Naldross is special. If you're savvy enough to survive there, you'll find the finest inventions—even better, the finest inventors." He smiled fondly, his bright gaze growing distant. "Here I am reminiscing, and you asked me about demons. A great many teeth they have, naturally—"

The temporator's account was more vivid than those she'd heard previously, but his descriptions of the work of his fellow temporators was even more fascinating than the frightening tales of demons.

As Cornelius gestured wildly about with his hands, she noticed a trio of spheres on the belt at Cornelius's waist. Of all the contraptions he wore, they were the only devices that remained still. One bore a slight crack across its rounded face.

"What are all of these devices?" Persephonie asked, studying each of the various contraptions in turn but returning to the three still ones. Upon closer study, it looked as though the devices were connected by small silver threads.

"Ah! The implements of the temporator, my dear." Cornelius beamed, looking himself over. The light flickering through the trees flashed off the glass faces as he wiggled about, gazing at them all. He pointed at the larger set of glass circles enclosed in a gold case along his waist. "Here we have the—well, how helpful will it be to you to know the names of the implements? Do you wish to travel through time?"

Persephonie bit her lower lip. This conversation had been unexpected in its beginnings and was growing more so the longer it went. "Erhm, as a saudad, we already travel through space—not time, so much. But we use the threads of fate?"

"Yes, yes, of course." Cornelius's bright eyes were wide once more and he scrabbled back into one of his pockets, drawing out a notebook and a thin quill which he dipped in a vial of ink embedded within the finger of one of his gloves. "Terribly clever this, is it not?" He grinned widely, and Reginald cooed upon his shoulder.

Persephonie had the distinct sense that when in want of other company, Reginald managed the answers to most of Cornelius's self-apparent questions.

"Now of course I cannot even *begin* to tell you of all the times a slight mis-measurement of impending terrain or the errant flick of a wrist has led to me splashing ink all over myself and any unfortunate enough to be nearby—"

Instinctively, both she and Rennear leaned away from the temporator.

Cornelius laughed to himself once more. "But it seems you have already guessed as much, have you not?"

Was it common for temporators to ask themselves so many questions with the answer implied? It was rather the opposite of Dasia's habit of orders in the form of questions.

"Oh, but you had asked me about my contraptions. Yes, yes, I recall now." He waved his ink-wielding fingers about by his small ears, juggling his thoughts back into order. "It was actually mine and a colleague's study of your threads, in addition to a few other fields of note, that led to our embarking upon the work of the temporator. These connectors"—he indicated the threads she had noticed—"are meant to mimic the threads of fate. That would be the simplest way of putting it."

"Fascinating," Persephonie answered, and Cornelius's expression turned from expectant to exultant. She recognized in his constant gauging of her and Rennear's reactions a habit very like that her datha employed when explaining saudad traditions to curious outsiders. Datha would vary the wording and level of detail depending upon his audience. Cornelius, a true teacher, was doing the same for them.

"While we are satisfying one another's curiosity and speaking of your threads, tell me," he said with a nod to Rennear, "how is it that *you* came to travel across the threads? I mean no offense, but I am a careful observer of all I meet, and you do not have the appearance of one who is of saudad heritage."

"You are correct," Rennear answered with a small nod. His jaw muscles tensed, but he retained his composure. "There were dangers on our journey, but we have weathered them and emerged upon the other side."

Persephonie slid her hand into Rennear's and squeezed. They hadn't even begun to discover how they might leave New Orison as they had been busy enough ensuring their muster and wheels might *survive* New Orison, but Rennear's frustrations with the toils of their trip and the danger he believed he and Jezebel had brought upon Persephonie would reemerge as subjects of concern once they did, somehow, uncover how to leave.

Rennear was still less sure of their impromptu guest

than she was, and continued conversation with Cornelius was not helping matters. She thought it best to return the three of them to less charged ground and to learn more about Cornelius's implements. Persephonie pointed to the three small orbs she had noticed, the three that were still. "And what about these?"

"By the tree!" Cornelius exclaimed. "No wonder I have crashed here!" He undid his belt and stared at the three orbs, his eyes the widest they had been yet. "Are you seeing this?" He showed the belt to Reginald, who simply mirrored his expression.

"A grave development indeed." Cornelius shook his head and sighed over the belt. "I shall have to find some way of fixing it. Tell me, where is the nearest artificer?"

"Erhm . . . artificer?" Perhaps it was Cornelius's accent in the common tongue that was making it difficult for her to understand his request.

"Oh dear." Cornelius explained that he was looking for someone rather like a cobbler or an apothecary who specialized in small trinkets like the ones he wore and with substances that were not quite natural nor magical but had the effects of both.

"That does sound very specialized," Persephonie added. "Perhaps you might tell us more about the three orbs? We may not know an artificer, but we are not without resources." From the purple smoke to the strange reinterpretation of the magic of the threads of fate, the niggling of Cassandra's nudges radiated out from this man and his appearance here.

"I suppose it could not hamper matters. Each of these *orbs*, as you called them, connect to one of the three wheels—space, time, and fate. Seeing the crack upon the wheel of space, it is only natural for one to conclude that such a wheel must be exerting its force upon this region in particular and may in fact be quite nearby."

"Wait—" Persephonie leaned closer to the temporator. "You said the wheels?"

"Yes." Cornelius nodded pleasantly as one would to a child. "And what that means—"

"One of the wheels is here?"

"Precisely. Err, probably. Ah, either way, you're catching on quite fast. What a delight."

She sat back, rehearsing in her mind Rowan's missive that had brought her here and Cornelius's revelation about the wheels. Though she and Rennear had discussed the wheels, and Jezebel as well, the three of them had not made conclusive progress in understanding even what they were looking for.

Cornelius knew.

"You must tell me more," Persephonie said, eyes wide as she glanced at Rennear. "We need to retrieve Jezebel—they will want to hear of this too." With Rennear's agreement, she turned back to Cornelius. "You will be here, yes? You will tell us more of the wheels and their functioning? I was sent on a quest here by . . . someone out of time. Not *out* of time, like dying, but who had emerged from a different point in time?" Cornelius's struggle to explain his own mission and thoughtfulness in not speaking in such a way that they could not understand was doubly impressive to her now that she was trying to do the same.

"Interesting." Cornelius slipped a sliver of meat to Reginald upon his shoulder. The owl gobbled it out of his hand, slurping at the morsel and clicking its beak in an alarming manner. She could tell by his tone that he was not certain if what she had said *was* interesting or not, but he was open to hearing more.

"I must fetch our friend. They should hear of this, and I believe they may be able to help." Persephonie pushed herself up to her feet, dusted off her skirt, and knelt to help Rennear up.

Cornelius rose to see them off. As he did, he hovered quite close to Persephonie, peering at her more closely. "And you're quite sure we've never met before?" He removed his spectacles and stretched them toward her face.

Rennear shifted beside her, positioning his shoulder between her and the strange man.

"My apologies," Cornelius said with a lopsided grin, raising his hands up by his shoulders. "When you've seen as many faces through time as I have, it is a comfort to find even one that's familiar."

CHAPTER 37

TEODRIC

"Father," Teodric repeated. He took a stumbling step forward, unable to believe what he was seeing.

But there, in this sun- and shadows-drenched captain's cabin was the man he'd spent the last several years searching for, the man he'd joined Syleste in order to save.

The sea and years had left their mark upon his father. His lined face was a richer tan, with warm brown streaks standing out alongside the wisps of gray in his dark brown hair.

"My boy." Father recovered from his shock more quickly and rushed forward, arms extended, and caught Teodric in his embrace. He cradled Teodric's shoulders into his chest, his hand clutched at the back of his son's hair. "I didn't think it was possible," his father sighed. He held Teodric out at arm's length, eyes shining.

Teodric flinched under his father's gaze, afraid of what he might perceive, but his father gave no sign of disappointment, only delight and relief. Warm tears clouded

Teodric's gaze as well, accompanying a flood of questions. So near to his mother, had Father gone ashore to Nortelon? Had Syleste ever had him in her grasp or had the letter been a misleading threat? He started more simply first. "I want to know everything. Tell me, how did you end up here?" A pirate haven and the quarters of a storied captain were the last places he'd expected to find his poised, diplomatic father.

"He saved me," Frederick said, his eyes still shining. He'd yet to fully remove Teodric from his grasp, resting his hand upon his son's shoulder. Frederick nodded to Captain Aeogan, and the respect Teodric sensed between them ran even deeper than what had existed between his father and King Arontis, the same king who had sent them across the ocean, who had severed the ties of their family in the first place.

"I'm sure word reached you and . . . your mother . . . of my ship being lost at sea." His voice caught at the mention of Aurelia, but Frederick persevered. "We were beset by pirates, having ventured too far to the south. There's something dark brewing in the Wastes." Frederick shook his head. "But as fortune would have it, they had to stop here to resupply. I was beginning to despair, in the hold—several of my fellow captives had already taken extreme measures to rid themselves of our predicament . . ." Frederick shuddered.

"The bodies were beginning to reek. But then there was a commotion above decks, several cries of dismay, and a man a few years older than myself hurried down the stairs, keys to the cells in hand. A navigator, if memory serves." Frederick began to relax, settling into his tale. His eyes still shone, staring at his son. "He said he was there on business of the captain, ridding the shipyard of the sorts that were not welcome in *Lagon des Morts* and that, if I was willing to apply myself in a useful fashion, he'd have some work for me." His father gestured to the room around them. "I've served as negotiator, scribe, and liaison ever since."

There was a great deal more Teodric wanted to learn about his father's tale, the nature of those who had taken him captive, what he'd discovered in his years of service to Captain Aeogan, the dragonkin who watched them from behind his desk. He wanted to wait to ask but couldn't find it within himself to delay any longer. "Why didn't you come back?" His voice trembled but did not break.

Frederick bowed his head, a tear slipping free from his eyes, darkening the tan of his more rugged complexion. "I suspect for the same reason you're in your current predicament. I owe a life debt to Aeogan"—he gestured toward his captain—"and I knew that departing from his side and returning to your mother's would place her in graver danger than she already was in."

Teodric reddened as a spark of resentment flared low in his stomach. His father answered so simply, a wave of his hand that might brush aside all Teodric had done in service to Syleste. The blood he'd shed, the scars he'd grown.

His father sensed the shift in his mood and spoke more softly, "Our lookouts noticed Syleste's flag approaching. We didn't know what to expect."

"You should still be uncertain." The gruffness of Kriega's voice, the first she'd spoken since their arrival, echoed the concern Teodric had felt at his father's words.

"Your first mate makes a fair point," Aeogan interrupted with a slow wave of his hand. His voice was soothing as a damp spring breeze. "Perhaps she might go now with the liaison who guided you here to arrange for the resupply of your ship. There remain pressing matters for us to discuss."

Kriega gave Aeogan a long look before following the lackey out of the room.

"Of course, Captain," Frederick said. "To make short a longer point, son, whatever Syleste saved you from or coerced you to do, we have reason to believe there was a deeper motive behind it all. She wants, more than anything, leverage over the one they call the dragon king." Frederick's gaze flickered to his captain and back to Teodric. "But that is not my story to tell."

Without his first mate's huffing at the dragonkin, Teodric's thoughts returned to his mother. "Will you go home to her now? Or"—Teodric cleared his throat—"when it's safe?" He hadn't planned on pitching his scheme of violence against Syleste quite so quickly to the captain of the *Lagon*, but finding his father again had scrambled all that had come before.

Aeogan's mouth twitched at the mention of safety, an expression Teodric wanted to find the secret depths of.

His father's hands began to shake, an affliction he hadn't suffered from before his capture. "I-I owe several more years of service to the captain." He nodded toward Aeogan.

Unbidden, a flame of hatred rose in Teodric's gut. He'd blamed Syleste for keeping his father's location from him, possibly even holding him prisoner. And yet it was this man, lounging behind a desk while his mother's mind slipped further and further from reality, who had truly kept his father bound.

The captain's gaze narrowed and he tilted his head, studying Teodric more closely. "A matter which you, your son, and I can discuss," Aeogan said, a deliberate evenness to his voice as though he could read Teodric's thoughts and knew in what direction they tended. "There are a few matters to which we must first attend, if you'll indulge me, Captain Teodric."

He saw little room to argue with the captain whose island he floated upon.

"Do you trust her, your first mate?"

"I do."

"And you've no reason to believe she is a spy, working on Syleste's behalf to keep watch over you and report back?"

Teodric gave the captain a wry smile, focusing all his attention on the seemingly relaxed figure and forgetting, for the moment, his father's presence. "There's something I've noticed in the years I've served Syleste. She leaves her mark on people, whether they want her to or not." He rubbed one of the worst of the scars upon his chest, an uneven circle with a gash through it, the sort of symbol one might use to indicate having one's heart ripped out.

The corners of the captain's eyes narrowed, his gaze flickering back from Teodric's chest to his face.

"She's left several such marks on me, only some of which can be seen. But given my intimate knowledge of these marks and their effects, I have a special knack for sensing them in others." He held Aeogan's gaze. "Both when they're only surface deep, like mine and Kriega's, and when they pierce all the way through." He couldn't pin down, beyond the sense he'd honed in his years trapped with Syleste, why it was he believed the captain was more the latter than the former. The special treatment they'd received upon their arrival, the reference to the siren queen, and Syleste's unwillingness to set foot upon the

Lagon itself, the one place in the ocean over which she didn't claim dominion.

He didn't know Captain Aeogan well enough to know what to expect from the man's reaction if he did understand Teodric's implication. He could toss Teodric into a prison cell or the underground network that ran beneath the ships, whichever would serve his most immediate ends. The captain could dispatch him outright, though Teodric doubted he'd take such an extreme step given the loyal service of his father.

What he hadn't expected was the slow bloom of a grin upon the captain's face, a widening, sickle-split that completely changed the sun-worn features of the man before him.

Aeogan laughed, a quiet chuckle at first, the sort of discreet sound that could be disguised with a cough. But soon enough, he'd thrown his head back and raised a full-fledged guffaw to the thin wooden ceiling slats. "Your father said you were bright." The captain's eyes gleamed an impossible, molten gold, flashing off the scales upon his face. The irises shone like the metallic flecks in Iellieth and Quindythias's eyes, except instead of flecks, the shimmer took up the whole of his iris. In one flash of a moment as Aeogan turned, he caught a second gleam on the back of his irises—a brilliant teal, flat—the sheen of a predator.

"Brave too," the dragonkin added. "Yet even in all I've seen over countless—well, my tale is best saved for another time. Perhaps upon your return. In short, Captain, what I have been waiting for, hoping for, was someone who emerged from her clutches scarred, yes, but fundamentally unchanged. You, Teodric Adhemar, are exactly what we need."

In quick succession, Teodric shared with Aeogan the basic tenets of his plan of open rebellion against Syleste. Captain Aeogan brightened at Teodric's confession. He had precisely what they needed to arrive unscathed.

The plan took shape rather quickly after that. He and Kriega would return to Syleste's island, with the object Aeogan claimed Syleste had been searching for—a magical book artifact, bound in flesh and containing the instructions for a foul, ancient ritual. "Do not worry," Aeogan assured Teodric when he handed over the wooden case that held the cursed tome. "A certain trouble of the heart afflicted your admiral some time ago, binding part of her magic. However much she may wish to, she cannot attempt the ritual contained inside the book. But having it in your possession will allow you to get close enough to her." Aeogan broke his intense gaze from Teodric, his voice suddenly hoarse. "Then, you'll know what to do."

"You seem hesitant," Teodric observed, unable to leave the inner turmoil of the captain unremarked upon.

"When you've lived for long enough, lad, you'll find there are lots of different forms of mourning. Sometimes the loss of what might have been, the death of a long-harbored hope, strikes the most cruelly."

It was Teodric's turn to break from Aeogan's stare this time. The dragonkin inadvertently hit closely to Teodric's recent experience, a still-raw source of pain he'd tucked away within his chest. He cleared his throat, reminding himself of his promise to Iellieth, that he would make them both proud. "I know something of what that feels like."

Aeogan rested his hand upon his side in much the same way Teodric had the deep scar upon his chest. "Take some time with your father. There are preparations that must be made. You will have everything you need before you set sail."

After their meeting, sitting outside the Grotto beside his father, sharing ale and each other's company, Aeogan's words continued to echo in his mind. Was it true that he was unchanged? Or was he only the husk of the man he'd been before?

In the end, his terms with Aeogan had been simple. He would take this Book of Souls Aeogan had kept hidden from Syleste and face her. In return, his parents would earn and retain the captain's protection. His father would be freed from service and, as soon as it was safe and they were able, Aeogan would escort them wherever they wished to go.

Teodric made the terms explicit—Captain Aeogan would do this for his parents whether Teodric lived or died. And one of those outcomes was far more likely than the other.

THREE DAYS LATER, A CHILL SLITHERED DOWN HIS SPINE as he spied her island through the glass—a wild patch of dark green against the horizon. In that moment, he understood Iellieth's frustration with being caught up in the larger plans of long-lived, scheming beings, caught in a spider's web. From the few details he'd been able to glean between the *Lagon* captain and his father, this tension between Aeogan and Syleste stretched back centuries.

Perhaps he should have been more discerning, asked more questions, demanded to know what had come before. There was a glowing optimism to the plan of racing into Syleste's arms, the object she sought in hand.

The scheme's foundation was one only a romantic could form. But the merest glimpse of her base of operations reminded him of what both he and the dragonkin had tried to forget—this story was far from over, and Syleste wasn't done reshaping him yet.

CHAPTER 38

IELLIETH

The first days of travel were as uneventful as a journey through an underexplored elven forest could be. A trio of pixies took up residence in Iellieth's hair the first afternoon. On their second day, Quindythias became entranced by a nymph in a distant pool who, upon closer inspection, revealed herself to be a tall, shapely rock. Naturally, he insisted that the nymph had transformed into a rock after her charms failed to woo him from the path and into the Brightlands—this being a little-known quality all nymphs possess, of course.

Ammon's lips tightened at Quindythias's assertion, and he gruffly insisted upon their return to the path and their journey north.

Iellieth matched her step with Ammon's, her companions holding an amiable silence behind them. "Quindythias doesn't mean any harm. He's curious about the world—I have little doubt that he's always been that way. But coming here was difficult for him. He was afraid of having been forgotten, and while his name and some of his reputation are remembered by people like your sister, I think now he feels more keenly what they lost. And whatever relief meeting the Darkstriders brought him, I'm still not sure his hopes have been answered. He's been somewhat disappointed with Azuria thus far."

Ammon gave her a worried look, but Iellieth's fond smile said what her words hadn't. "Apparently the cities were much grander in Eldura."

"From the ruins that haven't been claimed by the forest, I know that to be true as well."

Iellieth's eyes widened, and she quickened her pace to remain beside Ammon as their path curved uphill.

"Sharia couldn't tell me the temple's exact whereabouts, but I know the remaining ruins well. I've selected the likeliest of them to secretly contain Gaia's Glade, and that's where I'm leading the three of you to."

"Like what Councilor Valaexi said? A temple that stands out of time?"

The ranger nodded. "What Valaexi told you is true—or so the stories hold anyway. There was a time when my faith in our heritage tended more closely toward my sister's fervor and I considered making the Pilgrimage. I nearly undertook it after Firan's injury," Ammon added, anticipating Iellieth's question, "but he asked me to stay by his side instead. If the forest had chosen for him to be more reliant upon Addah and his friends, he said, then he would accept its wisdom." Ammon explained that the forest around the ruins they were headed toward had grown over many of the ancient foundations of what would have been a grand outpost. The scholars like his sister believed that the ancients had also taken pilgrimages like the one the Darkstriders had assigned to Iellieth and her companions to the temple of Gaia, the journey itself serving as a testament to their need and determination.

"Perhaps that was what inspired the council to hide the seal piece there in the first place," Iellieth added. "Tradition already spoke of the import of the journey. And if this guardian Sharia mentioned was already in place, much of their work of protecting the seal piece was taken care of."

Ammon grew quiet at the mention of his sister.

"Have Sharia and Firan always been close?" Iellieth ventured. She couldn't help but think of Quindythias's stories about his own sister and the loss he'd endured. Ammon hadn't said anything about Sharia's injury at the hands of the poachers, so recently acquired. She sensed he would when he was ready.

"When we were small, yes. It is common for elven siblings to drift apart as they age—living as long as we do. Firan and I stayed close, but I know now he kept watch over Sharia as well. While our insular families are important, being part of a communal family matters just as much if not more."

The ridge they had been climbing opened up onto a lush, rolling valley covered in moss. The trees were as wide around as some of the dwellings of the Water Ward back in Linolynn. It was as though the scenes from the books she'd read growing up spread out before her. At any moment, the forest spirit, Ewan'il, might curve around a tree, part giant wolf, part wind given form.

Inured to the forest by his years of traveling it, Ammon had continued answering her question, "And while our culture now is more insular, we retain many of the customs and habits of thought we did when our borders were open and our cities sites of trade and travel." He stopped when he realized Iellieth was no longer beside him and returned to stare out over the sweep of the forest with her.

A few moments later, Marcon and Quindythias joined them as well.

Iellieth filled her gaze with the impossible array of greens. Is this what the pilgrims' path Ammon had described was like, or were the trees smaller and younger then? "This is what you want your people to experience again, isn't it?"

Ammon's voice was hushed when he answered, "The awe that radiates off of you—yes. Even a fraction would bring me no shortage of delight."

She smiled at his words without turning away from the forest. The ranger had started off grave and reserved though he was gradually sharing his thoughts with the three of them, something she was relatively certain he had only done with his fellow rangers back at their lodge. Or the rangers and Professor Idlewylde. The ease she'd sensed settling over his shoulders then had returned to his stance now.

"What do you think that will take?"

"Hmm," Ammon sighed, the sound rough and dry like an autumn breeze. "I have hopes for what might cause such a shift—that as a collective, we would remember who we are, what we are a part of. But there are other possibilities I fear—that disaster might return us to our woods, something happening to disrupt the comfortable life so many live in the city. There are some among our number who wish for such an occurrence, among the young especially, but I would rather awe return the elves to the forest than doom drive them from the cities."

"I have witnessed both sorts of instances in my extensive experience," Quindythias added helpfully, adjusting his pack. "Might we continue onward though? While this view is, erm, large and verdant, I am certain that similar vistas await us. Likely other trees and their . . . roots."

Iellieth held back a giggle as she turned to find Marcon gazing at her. Perhaps like Quindythias, he'd had his fill of the splendor of the view.

"I'm sure you're right. Why don't we press on then?" She resumed her place beside Ammon.

As the afternoon wore on, heavy, gray clouds gathered overhead. Quindythias grumbled behind her, fussing with the folds of his cloak so that his hair would not get wet. "Pointing out that no one will see it aside from us will only worsen his mood," Iellieth murmured to Ammon when he looked back over his shoulder.

The rain began as a series of soft, patting footfalls, as though a stampede of faeries were skipping and then dashing across the leaves overhead. Far below the musical canopy, leaves dumped their overfill onto the heads of those passing below, much to Quindythias's dismay. The forest repaid Iellieth's chuckle at her friend's expense with a heavy cascade that splashed across the whole of her face and front of her scalp, leaving her sputtering in surprise.

"Does it rain like this often?" She raised her voice to be heard over the downpour.

"Before the onset of autumn in particular," Ammon called back.

Iellieth brushed her hair back and wiped the droplets from her face. She could picture autumn in an elven forest —the burnished golds and scarlets mixed with bronze, fallen leaves. Unless a catastrophe delayed their journey, they would miss the changing leaves but, perhaps, in a future year, if she were able to pursue her studies here after all—

Thunder rumbled overhead and she tugged on the hem of her hood. Better save her daydreaming for another day.

"I noticed, earlier, that you seemed somewhat alarmed by Quindythias's story." She blinked the raindrops free from her eyelashes to study Ammon's expression as they walked. "About the nymph. It made me wonder if perhaps such a tale might be true, or possible, at least, in the forest. You have told us of your concerns that the Brightlands and Shadowlands are already blending themselves into the Realms' forests."

The elf nodded. "You are observant, aren't you?" He laughed to himself. "I won't deny what you're asking me, though I'll ask that you allow me to hold my secret a few hours more."

"Of course." They continued on in companionable quiet, leaving Iellieth to observe the trees and reflect upon this newest stage of their journey. Her adventures in the Realms had transpired much differently than Iellieth had always imagined they would—she had met an old friend of her father's, spoken before the ruling elven council, and she was on a retrieval mission for an ancient, powerful artifact that was the key to disempowering their enemy and protecting the future of her world. Very different than advancing her translation studies and finding a new home among her father's people.

They made camp for the evening, and the four of them huddled around a ball of flame Iellieth conjured to float a few inches off the ground to warm their faces and hands from the still-falling rain. She examined the pruned tips of her fingers in the flickering light. Beside her, Marcon reclined on his elbows, his face tipped up toward the sky. Quindythias huddled within his cloak on Marcon's other side, shivering and griping about the foul weather.

"There is a story I have been saving." Ammon scooted nearer to the mote of flame. "One that I hope will cheer the three of you at the end of a long day." Ammon's low, scratchy voice assumed the cadence of the ancient elven tales as he described his own misadventure from a few years ago, when a nymph had lured him away from the path and whisked him off to the Brightlands. There, he'd been a curiosity among the members of the fae courts, paraded by the nymph as one would a rare and prized creature but given little freedom to wander on his own.

"Naturally, I tried to escape to find my way home, at which point the nymph affixed an enchanted collar around my neck and charmed my memory so that I remembered very little beyond my time at her side. From that point, we passed a year and a day, after which she began to miss her glade and pond within this forest. We returned, and she released me. Of course, she kept all my clothes as is the way of the fae. Firan found me, dazed and naked, the next day. Only three days here had passed since he had seen me. I'm a little surprised he didn't tell you this story when we met at the lodge, though there was a great deal transpiring that night." Ammon's gaze darted over to Quindythias, who sat taller and smirked. Iellieth suspected he was thinking about Professor Tur.

While she had a great many questions about Ammon's story, she recognized the practiced cadence of a tale that had been carefully crafted, a tradition she understood was prized and honed among the rangers to entertain one another during their months of travel through the forest.

"This nymph was not Nealadora, was it?" Iellieth couldn't help but ask. Ammon had mentioned a friend of hers to the nymph in passing.

"No, though she takes every opportunity she can to remind me of my embarrassment."

Marcon asked Ammon a few questions he'd been pondering about the charges while Quindythias slunk over to Iellieth's side.

"I would not have them hear me say as much," he murmured, "but I do not think we have as much to fear from the Brightlands as the lands of shadow. Fearsome creatures roam both places, but those of the Brightlands will resent this inauspicious climate. Those of the Shadowlands would find this pleasant, and the trees would provide them with the shelter they require."

"What sorts of creatures roam the Shadowlands?"

Ammon overheard and answered, "Any number of foul, nightmarish beasts. But there are others who pass between the various realms and have managed to find a home in each. The daimon, I believe you know, though with their diminished numbers they travel less than they once did. Herds of centaurs as well—their patrols of their territory take them on a three-year migration between the Realms, the plains of Tor'stre Vahn, and a lowland region of the Shadowlands that is far from hospitable but that they refuse to surrender to the bandits and creatures that would claim it for their own."

Iellieth peered around the fire for a better view of Ammon. She'd read stories of centaur herds as a child and had been dismissed by Linolynn's diplomats and scholars when she asked whether or not they were real. Katarina had assured her that they were and that they were not to be trifled with—fiercely proud and deeply superstitious. She and her brother Aravar had considered an alliance with the centaurs during one of their research expeditions but found such a prospect too troublesome as the stars had not aligned in time. Katarina believed Aravar was particularly unlucky in this regard as the heavens usually arranged themselves to suit her plans.

Ammon and Marcon fashioned a canopy over their sleeping area, and Quindythias took the first watch. Iellieth smiled to herself, thinking of her friends, as the forest rains lulled her into a deep slumber.

CHAPTER 39

PERSEPHONIE

Persephonie pressed at the stitch in her side as she arrived back at the camp, leaving Rennear at the edge of the woods while she rushed through two tellings to help Jezebel gain the appropriate level of enthusiasm and interest in their visitor. She snatched Juliet from her napping place at the back of the wagon, and the three of them darted back toward the forest to meet Rennear before retracing her and Rennear's steps.

But when they stepped back into the clearing where they'd left Cornelius, the temporator was gone.

Her mouth opened and shut again, words failing her. Cornelius had promised he would be here. She turned to Rennear, who looked just as surprised as she did.

Jezebel looked between the two of them, the corner of their lips downturned. "I thought the two of you might be playing a strange sort of prank on me, but you really did expect to find him, didn't you?"

Persephonie nodded. "We should see if he left anything behind." The priests couldn't have taken him, could they? Owls were fearsome hunters, or *most* owls were, which she thought meant they would defend those they traveled with. In Reginald's case, the matter seemed more nuanced.

"Here, by the water," Rennear called. He'd followed a shallow, winding path through the dirt that trailed down to the creek. Rennear took care with his balance and bent to pick a crystal orb from the water.

"Is that . . . a crystal ball?" Persephonie lifted her skirts to cross the creek once more and stood by Rennear's side. Carefully, she took the sphere of perfect crystal from his hand and stared down into it. A faint purple swirl twirled within. "I am not skilled with this form of divination. But my babu is."

They decided to return to the camp and seek Babu's expertise about what they had found. Persephonie glanced back over her shoulder to where the temporator had been. The square lines of his tent and swishing impressions of his loping gait had left a few, faint impressions in the earth around the creek but already, the evidence of Cornelius's presence was beginning to fade away.

"He would probably say such is the lot of the temporator, or something like that," she observed to Rennear. A deeper sadness than she would have anticipated settled low in her chest. Cornelius's life must have been lonely, even with Reginald for company. He'd seemed so cheered by his belief that they'd met before, however impossible that might be. He could say whatever he liked of the nature of the temporator's work—Cornelius wasn't someone she'd soon forget.

As they walked back, Persephonie retraced the threads of her conversation with Cornelius for Jezebel's benefit, the pair of them trying to find some additional clue or significance to his knowledge of the wheels.

"What I *can* say for your strange friend is that he has

proven it is possible to leave New Orison." Dominic had told them before that there had been a few musters, over the years, that had attempted such a feat for themselves. It always ended in disaster—no muster had yet survived, a fact the priests used to deepen their manipulation of those who remained.

Crossing the goddess of misfortune was a perilous prospect in the best of circumstances, and New Orison believed itself to be the seat of her power upon the planes of life.

"That is true," Persephonie admitted to Jezebel. "But has he done so in a way anyone else can follow?"

⁂

THEIR MANY QUESTIONS INSPIRED BY CORNELIUS remained as they gathered outside Babu's wagon that afternoon. The elderly saudad welcomed the three of them inside. She kept her wagon far darker than the sunny interior of Cassian's space. An incense stick sent swirls of smoke up into the corner, where it pooled along the ceiling and slowly drifted out the slatted window.

Persephonie reintroduced her friends to Babu, who insisted she had not had the chance to 'properly' meet them yet. "It means she wants to read your fate-lines," Persephonie explained.

"What about the orb?" Jezebel asked.

Babu stamped the metal-covered end of her cane against the thick wooden floorboards of her wagon. "After," she snapped.

Jezebel straightened and nodded, holding very still until Babu gave them further instructions.

"You first." She beckoned Rennear to sit by her side

with a low table between them, a trio of candles flickering atop its surface. "I see a grave disruption in your childhood, one that forever altered your path," she said, tracing the lifeline that ran across his palm. "There is a shallow record here of what might have been—one you have wrinkled into being through your own wondering—but such paths are not meant to be trod." She patted Rennear's hand and squinted up at him to meet his gaze. "We are much better off accepting who we are than wishing over who we might have been."

Babu's voice deepened as she continued her reading, growing ever more engrossed in Rennear's hand. Persephonie peered over his shoulder, watching her grandmother work. The wolf created a second lifeline, Babu explained, almost as though Rennear was a being of double-fates.

"There is another explanation of such an occurrence," she murmured, studying the three of them in turn. "But I do not know if you are ready . . ."

"She asks you," Persephonie added to Rennear, translating both her grandmother's meaning and her words. "She believes such a revelation may transform our collective understanding of our task—I have told her of the wheels already—but she is asking your permission to reveal to you something that might change your conception of yourself."

Rennear had grown more interested in her nightly tarot readings over their weeks together and had begun asking her to teach him to read the cards for himself. Had Babu asked another member of their muster what she now asked of Rennear, they would have taken a night to sleep on the decision to ensure they were ready for whatever was to be revealed. But Babu never asked unless she believed they were ready.

Understandings of the art of palmistry differed among the saudad. Some believed that certain lines appeared when it was time for their bearer to understand them, others that Cassandra had inscribed her will from the beginning. Babu said it was all of this and more.

"I do not wish to boast, however much I would like to impress you for the sake of your granddaughter, but I am rather confident in myself already," Rennear said to Babu. He had leaned toward her on his stool while she studied his hand, as much to be at eye level with her shorter stature as to observe what she studied.

"That I knew without reading your hand," Babu said, chuckling to herself. "It is good you know it as well."

Babu took his reply as assent and returned to her study of his hand. "My Sephie has met one who has returned— one whose present soul is here already, and yet an earlier fragment remained."

"You are speaking of Rowan, the Shepherd?" Rennear replied.

"Mmm," Babu answered. "Sephie knows the soul in its present form as well. This is Cassandra's sign to me that you are ready."

Rennear looked away from her grandmother to her, a frown etched between his brows. "She speaks of Iellieth also," Persephonie whispered. The back of her throat dried. Whatever Babu was preparing to tell them, it was important.

Babu looked up from Rennear's palm. "You are one such soul, Rennear Ignatius. You are Returned."

"Returned," Persephonie repeated slowly. "He is Returned the way Rowan is the Shepherd?"

Milky white eyes drifted away from Rennear, and Babu sought her gaze as well. "My Sephie has this marker too."

Persephonie wetted her lips, trying to wrap her mind around what Babu had just confessed. "I . . . we—what, Babu?"

But her grandmother ignored her question. "It is this in part that drew the phoenix, the Returned One, to you before." She nodded at Rennear, a small smile on her wrinkled face. "Her soul knows yours." Babu sat back in her chair, settling into the worn contours of its support. "I know not if that is how you found one another, but it may be how this traveler in the forest found the pair of you as well."

Persephonie hadn't yet told Babu about Cornelius, but she was not surprised Babu knew of him—she had always had a sense for these things, one that sharpened with age as her awareness of what transpired around her in her physical environment faded. "He did ask me if we had ever met before," Persephonie murmured, her thoughts still struggling to catch up to what Babu had just said. Rennear was one Returned, which was how Rowan had found them. She knew him, somehow, knew his soul. And the same might be true for Cornelius. "Does that mean some earlier version of me is a temporator, someone who travels through time?"

Babu's crinkly smile wrinkled deeper into her features. "By its very nature, your soul is one such traveler, Sephie. It is an honor to be so closely connected to one who has Returned."

She wanted to speak, wanted to ask more questions of her grandmother, but Babu's revelations—secrets she'd known and yet had concealed—and the strangeness of their encounter with the temporator, what it all meant, swirled around her, filled her senses.

It was all too much. Persephonie breathed deeply, inhaling incense smoke, and began to cough. "Excuse me, Babu," she croaked, squinting her eyes, which had suddenly pooled with burning tears from the smoke. Persephonie pushed past Jezebel and leapt out of the back of the wagon. She lifted her skirts and, scarves trailing behind her, ran into the solitude of the forest.

This time she allowed her feet to guide her of their own accord. She ran in a different direction than the way that she and Rennear had met Cornelius. A great oak tree beckoned to her, its branches having created a tiny meadow of bare grasses and patches of decaying leaves upon the forest floor.

She spun about, sliding down the bark, and settled onto the earth. Persephonie rested her head upon her knees, her arms sheltering her head. Here, in this moment, she didn't need to be anyone beyond herself; she wasn't a previous soul-iteration. Just herself. Just Persephonie.

Her heartbeat and breath slowed, the world reordering itself. A branch cracked in the forest beyond her resting place.

For a moment she frowned—Velkan, not Rennear or Jezebel, picked his way through the underbrush over to her.

He gave her a tentative smile, the one that, a year ago, would have made her short of breath, thoughts blurred all over again. What they shared now, though, the deeper knowing of one another, in many ways was even better.

Velkan settled onto the roots beside her, leaning his head back against the tree, relaxing his shoulders, before he turned toward her.

"Your friends wanted to come after you, Rennear especially. But I asked them to let me. They told me what your babu said."

Persephonie sighed as she leaned back against the tree. The comforting prickle of bark against her back reminded her of countless times she and Velkan had sat precisely like this, trying to understand the world around them over the years. The world kept getting bigger, and however much she grew or learned, it seemed she could never keep up.

"What does it even mean for me to be Returned? *Can* it mean anything? All saudad souls are reborn through time. That is part of how our stories survive. So why does it feel as though Babu is telling me that I am something, or somehow, different? And why does that make me feel sad?"

Velkan turned back to face the forest, arms draped over raised knees. "I've always known you were special, Persephonie. Maybe your babu has just been able to express it in a way you weren't as aware of before?"

"Is that what these priests have been responding to as well? Can they sense this difference?"

"I would not give them credit for such insightfulness, no." Velkan shook his head and selected a twig from the earth beside him, slowly breaking it into smaller halves as he spoke. "They sense that you are a threat to them. I would guess they sense the way Cassandra smiles down upon you especially. You know that she does," he added before she could object.

His twig lying in pieces beside him, Velkan drew a few jagged rocks from his pocket, rubbing them against one another.

Persephonie knew he was right. How often had Jezebel said as much to her as they explained why she had caught the attention of Apollo?

"I see why what your babu said would come as a shock, but I think you may be asking the wrong question. Does it have to mean anything?" Velkan let the words hang between them as she parted her lips to respond but stopped herself. "Your babu has known for some time, possibly the whole of your life. So how much does it really change who you are or how you see yourself?" Velkan turned toward her, his dark eyes warm. "You still seem just like the Persephonie I've always known."

She reached over and took his hand, squeezing it in hers. "That is more a comfort than I think you know—" Persephonie stopped short. The small satchel she'd crafted to hold the orb had grown warm, almost hot against her leg.

Persephonie pulled it onto her lap and gently removed the orb from its purse. What had been a tiny swirl of lavender had darkened and grown. It swirled, twisting through the inner mass of the orb . . . toward the rocks in Velkan's hands. "What are those?" Persephonie murmured. Velkan was always picking up odds and ends on their journeys, but these rocks weren't ones she'd seen before.

"They're from the road we landed on, with all the clay and dust that brought us here." The rocks clacked against one another as he shifted them in his palm.

Velkan tested the orb's response. He brought one of the rocks near the orb and kept the other in his hand. From the center, the spiral split, one half pointed toward his hand, spinning itself tighter. The other half followed the rock as he moved it back and forth just outside the orb's surface.

"There was a strange man in the forest. He left this behind." As quickly as she could, Persephonie explained about Cornelius while Velkan continued to experiment with the orb. "We don't know what it does, but we were hoping it might help us complete the task the Feather set us and find out how to leave this place."

Before Velkan could answer, the alarm sounded from their camp.

"The priests," Persephonie sighed. Velkan's eyes were as wide as hers. She sprang to her feet, tugging him up after her. "We have to get back."

CHAPTER 40

BRISERAS

Following her absorbing dreams that had whisked her away to Lord Draego's castle, Briseras found herself distracted during her second day in Barasov. When she wasn't otherwise engaged by their errands within the city, her fingertips wandered to her lips, the nape of her neck, retracing where the vampire lord had kissed and caressed her in her sleep before returning her to the inn.

The errands themselves occupied the other part of her day, with Vicq hiding around corners while directing them to the best smiths and armorers in the central reaches of the city. Briseras acquired additions for Vera's barding and restocked her stores of crossbow bolts.

Their return to the archives wasn't as promising as Briseras had hoped, though with Vicq's help, they found a few clues as to possible locations for Arduenne's fane.

The next morning, over a hearty breakfast, on Tybalt and Jorgan's side, and several cups of coffee, on Briseras's, they discussed their next steps and how they could recover

Vicq's magical armor from those who oversaw the activity of the Bloodletters, the Red Coven.

By Briseras's third cup, members of the Bloodletters had begun trickling into the tavern from their homes. The Watchers had presented themselves as average city-dwellers, marked by their blue coats.

The Bloodletters betrayed no such modesty. The first three to enter were each as tall as Tybalt, though only one was as broad-chested as the elf. In lieu of day coats or even shirts, they wore a series of leather straps rather like Olya had clothed herself in. The strappy ensemble over close-fitting leather breeches allowed the Bloodletters to show off their scars. Intricate patterns had been carved into their skin—a labyrinthine filigree on one man and a spiderweb pattern on another. Also unlike the Watchers, they wore their weapons openly and seemed to favor longswords and broadswords to the daggers and occasional scimitars she'd witnessed in the ward.

"We definitely should have started our time in Barasov here," Briseras said, eyeing the subtle movement of muscle beneath scarred skin as one of the guards leaned over to talk to the tavern keeper and his son, who scurried back and forth behind the counter.

Jorgan sighed beside her, rolling his gaze up to the thin slats of the wooden ceiling. "Of course you would feel at home here. What do you suppose the ratio is of battle scars to ones carved for, uhh, decoration?"

"There's only one way to find out," Briseras answered, not bothering to break her appreciative study of the guards. Rajas would never have stood for such deliberate self-injury, but she could see the appeal of embracing pain when life involved constant fighting.

Shortly after introducing herself, Briseras's three new

acquaintances—Toris, Brutus, and Glen—led Briseras, Vera, and their companions on a proud tour of the wonders of Bloodletter territory. Outside the tavern, fog rolled off of Lake Barasov, lending a cloaked eeriness to the city streets.

Jorgan gasped behind her as they rounded one turn, climbing down a steep hill into the depths of the Bloodletters' domain. Briseras spun about to follow his shocked gaze—down a winding side street, hanging from a set of thick posts jutting out from the buildings over the middle of the street was a series of bodies. Their arms were bound to chains and hung out to the sides, heads drooping, feet bound together. Scraps of clothing hung from the corpses—

The body nearest to them groaned, and Briseras's gorge rose. The steady *drip*, *drip*, *drip* she'd taken to be a drainpipe of some kind was falling from the prisoner, pooling at his feet.

"Watcher scum," Brutus spat.

"Heh, serves him right, trying to cross the line," Toris answered.

Glen remained silent beside them, observing his visitors' reactions instead.

"I'm surprised Vicq kept his stomach long enough to make and lose a bet with them," Briseras murmured to Jorgan.

The nobleman pressed his hand to his belly and squinted his eyes shut as he turned away. "I'm not sure I'll keep mine."

"This way," Toris called, leading them away from the body-strewn street and down a wide, curving stair instead. As they descended, the Bloodletter waved Briseras over to an outlook.

Her breath caught, this time in wonder. The fog undulated down story after story of the winding stair toward a circular courtyard. One of the great buildings they had wound their way past rose up out of the mists—Highseat, Toris called it, part of the nobles' domain. Across from her, children in pale tunics with red sashes called after one another, laughing as they climbed over and around the fallen archways. Though half the structures had fallen into disrepair, the Bloodletters made use of them anyway, setting up market stalls and open-air dining in the ruins, with apartments and larger shops taking up the established structures.

"See down there?" Toris gestured to the large, round courtyard that the entire ward seemed centered around. "That's where you'll find the coven. If your friend truly gave up something of value, you'll find it there too."

A slightly intoxicated Vicq was waiting for them on the perimeter of the courtyard. Many of those milling about the arches wore leather strap ensembles similar to those worn by Toris and the other guards. Women in flowing scarlet robes stood watch between the archways, granting admittance to those who wished to pass inside. They wore simple gold jewelry along their robes. Others had placed crowns of flowers or bundles of dried herbs in their hair.

"Acolytes," Vicq slurred, following Briseras's gaze to the women poised in the archways. "Their leader, one of the mavens, will decide whether or not we can gain admittance to the sacred pool inside and, from there, determine whether we can win an audience with the Matron."

Brutus had explained some of the coven's structure to Briseras as they descended the staircase to the central courtyard and receiving area. According to the guard, the mavens and Matron possessed significant wells of healing power, which was what brought most supplicants to seek a special audience. Because the witches could only work so much magic in a day, those who weren't among the first chosen for healing would have to either wait or prove themselves above the pool. "You'll see," Brutus said simply.

She caught a glimpse of the pool now through the archway. Further swirls of scarlet robes crossed the court-yard surrounding the basin. Most of the acolytes were barefoot, despite the cold. The mavens, marked by the incorporation of black cloth somewhere on their person, wore leather bands upon their feet, similar to those Bris-eras kept under her boots. Beyond their paths, she could just make out the lip of a sunken bowl that took up nearly half the center of the courtyard.

From above, she'd taken its deep red color to be painted brick. Seeing the injured supplicants being carted away, some moaning on stretchers, others silent and unmoving, she now knew her mistake—it was a pool of blood.

"We wish you well, huntress," Toris said with a nod toward the pool. She and her companions would have to continue forward alone.

After they found him, Vicq resumed his unsuccessful negotiations with one of the mavens.

"You will each make an offering to the Matron," the woman said, gesturing to a stained stone bowl, perched inside the archway they had passed through. The court-yard itself was a few hundred paces across, with the pool of blood a hundred feet wide. One large stone pathway cut across the blood pool at an angle, with several narrower arteries branching off from its sides.

Thin trees with delicately pointed red leaves had been placed at intervals around the courtyard, with small, mortared stones placed around them, patterned to resemble the trees' embedded roots. Red-flowering vines trailed up the courtyard walls, below which families and friends gathered around their invalids, their eyes darting about after the coven members, who each moved with purpose. A few paced in and out of dark, inner archways, their tunnels hidden by the stacked upper layers of the Bloodletters' Ward. They carried clay pitchers to the edges of the pool and poured in blood, departing once their task was done.

An excited murmur passed over the crowd, and those milling about their tasks stopped, turning to the blood pool in the center of the courtyard as a hulking man clad identically to their guides walked along the central pathway over the pool, head bowed and hands clasped behind his back.

"Hurry." The maven waved them forward, gesturing to the bowl. Jorgan was the first to stand beside it, frowning down at the blood-stained knife the maven held out toward him with distaste.

"I'll use my own so long as that doesn't offend." With the woman's assent, Jorgan withdrew a dagger he'd purchased from one of the saudad and sliced into the palm of his hand. Wincing, he squeezed his palm into a fist and spilled his dripping blood into the bowl.

Tybalt followed suit, tugging a dagger from the bracer along his forearm. While they did so, Briseras unbuckled her own bracer to remove the leather cuff and half glove she wore beneath. Hand poised over the bowl, she stopped, dagger extended, when a woman in red robes grabbed her arm. The woman's garb was a mix of onyx and scarlet, and she wore a band of red paint over her eyes, across the bridge of her nose, disappearing into her hairline.

"She has been waiting for you," the witch holding her hand said, tightening her grip on Briseras's wrist. "The special one. He says no blood of yours is to be spilled outside the bowl."

Briseras looked from the woman to her friends and back. Slowly, the woman relinquished her grip, and Briseras pulled her hand back. "Who says?"

The paint along the woman's eyes crinkled. "This, you already know. Come."

She spun on her heel, leaving Briseras and Vera and a confused Jorgan, Tybalt, and Vicq to follow her.

"Briseras, what is she—"

Beyond them, the leather-clad warrior's booming voice interrupted Jorgan, calling for the attention of all those in attendance as the afternoon's spectacle was about to begin. "Here, in honor of the Matron and the sacred spilling of blood, we offer ourselves and our bodies in sport and sacrifice. First challengers, ready yourselves."

The announcement changed the atmosphere of the courtyard. Those clad in red moved more quickly, hurrying to set positions within, while the outsiders, save Briseras's party, craned their necks to better view the central space.

"Such an exception has not been made in living memory, if ever," the woman before them, who introduced herself as the lead maven, explained. "We well remember Vicq's donation to the Matron's coffers and would allow him to win back his offering, once paid in blood, of course."

The werewolf had the wisdom to glance down at his boots again to avoid Jorgan's pointed glare.

"But when the great one spoke to the Matron, he said

someone special would be here, that her blood was not to be idly shed like that of the commoners."

"Hey!" Jorgan protested.

Briseras smirked at that, though Lord Draego might have said he would petition the Bloodletters on her behalf. Their fight from her dream faded further from her mind. Whatever sort of potential lover wouldn't object to their partner engaging in violence, so long as it represented a proper challenge, was one she was interested in entertaining. More than interested, part of Briseras admitted, but her jumping nerves at the growing clarity of the task before her drowned out the thought.

By the time the head maven had finished explaining the Matron's terms, a crowd had gathered, turning the layers of the courtyard into stands of sorts, a crowd half dreading, half anxious for blood sports.

Briseras would be third in line and would face the embedded victor, the announcer himself. No aid would be offered by her friends or any other party. Touching the pool was forbidden and would result in automatic forfeiture.

"Don't worry about me," Briseras repeated to her companions. She'd been sizing up her opponent the moment she understood who she was facing. He betrayed no uneasiness of movement, no sensitivities or existing injuries.

While she admired the warrior's scar patterns, a display of this nature struck her as both excessive and frivolous—fit, perhaps, to entertain the wealthy hordes of Andel-ce Hevra. The bodies of hunters like herself were honed for survival, which meant killing. There was no room for play, no scenario in which their finest warriors would be pitted against one another for a crowd's pleasure, and certainly not as a sacrifice for some sort of blood magic.

The announcer's skill with words and the command of the crowd transformed into pacing and skill with the blade as he dispatched first one and then a second challenger whose unconscious bodies made generous offerings to the pool of blood before they were dragged away. His first opponent had been young and inexperienced, but the second could have easily stood against one of the three Bloodletter guards who had escorted her and her companions through the city that morning.

"Whatever happens," Briseras reminded them, looking pointedly at Jorgan, "let me do this on my own." They needed Vicq's enchanted armor to face down Kratok and his wild pack. She would see that they received it.

"Our final battle," the announcer called. All eyes were upon him in the center of the courtyard. A few beads of sweat gleamed upon his brow, and there were specks of blood on his hands, but he was otherwise unmarred from two rounds of fighting, not even short of breath. Instead, he seemed almost enlivened by the activity. His dark eyes gleamed as he worked the crowd into a fervor, recounting his own great victories.

At the maven's instruction, Briseras had shed most of her armor, permitted only to keep her foot and wrist bindings and the straps that held her blades—no more and no less than the man she faced.

"I know you don't want to hear this," Jorgan murmured into her ear to be heard over the screeching crowd, "but that man is . . . huge."

Briseras nodded. Nearly seven feet tall from what she could tell, well over a foot taller than herself. "Brawny and quick too," she added.

Tybalt squeezed Jorgan's shoulder. "She will be fine."

Briseras tittered as Jorgan wriggled out of Tybalt's hold.

"My final challenger comes forth!" the announcer yelled.

She knelt before Vera and placed her forehead against the wolf's. "Watch them for me," she murmured. A poke from Vera's cold nose said she would.

Cries and jeers echoed across the stone courtyard as Briseras emerged. Many in attendance had noticed the disparity in their size as well and reacted with either delight or concern. She turned her awareness from it until the screams were only a low, droning noise, crickets on a summer hillside. Briseras flexed her fingers, gauged the stability of the stone walkway, and attuned her movements to the beat of her heart as she strode toward her opponent.

Warrior to warrior, there was no need for preamble or additional announcement. As soon as she slid within arm's reach, Briseras spun about, withdrawing the two curved swords from her back and meeting her opponent's broadsword with her crossed swords overhead.

Wrenching her arms down, she dodged out of the way, ducking between the warrior and his extended arms to stand on his other side, the walkway just wide enough for her to squeeze past him without touching or needing to dip over the blood. "Heh," the warrior laughed, "she said you'd be quick."

Slash and dodge, slash and dodge, Briseras took the measure of her opponent, working the large man into a lather as they paced up and down the central walkway. Her own heart had quickened its beat, the opening drum of one pulse nearly meeting the closing drum of the next, but not quite. Still nothing like she felt in the vampire's presence, but such memories were for another time.

Her opponent's breath had sped up as well, which Briseras used to her advantage as she slowly began to press. She tested his balance, darting onto the paths that branched off of the main walkway, each so narrow that she had to balance on the arches of her feet, run on the balls, as there was barely enough room for her foot to rest flat upon the path. This had been one of her predecessors' errors, besides the fact that they weren't trained warriors themselves and so had little business facing the announcer. They were unwilling to use the whole of the space, too worried about falling into the pool of blood to exhaust those they fought.

There were advantages to training in the wilds, fighting to survive rather than fighting for show. Once her opponent began to slow, his energy declined much more quickly. He barely parried one of Briseras's attacks, and she nicked his side with her backward-facing blade as she danced, balancing on the beam, from path to path.

The announcer's jaw jutted forward, and his chest started to heave with each breath. The night they'd arrived, with the Watchers, she'd given no quarter, no mercy. But this man wasn't at cross-purposes with her. A dark shape drifted behind the pillars in the periphery of her vision. Pacing. Almost emerging into the light and then waiting, hidden.

This show was for the Matron's benefit, and so Briseras would bring her out.

On the far end of the pool, a dozen paces from where she'd last seen the cloaked figure, three arteries darted off the central walkway. Her attacker roared, taking her moment's indecision to his advantage. Briseras rolled along the central walkway, staggering backward as she regained her feet. He bellowed again, swinging his sword down from overhead. Briseras's arms shook as she tried to hold off his attack. *Just a moment longer—*

She pulled her body one way as she dropped her arms' resistance, almost but not quite fast enough. "Agh!" Briseras screamed as the tip of the broadsword sliced the back of her calf. Blood poured from the wound though, given the force of the downward swing, she was lucky he hadn't struck her ankle as it would have shattered the bone.

Briseras shoved herself up and risked turning her back on her exhausted, panting opponent to dart back, limping at first, to the spot where the Matron had been before she disappeared into the crowd. Tybalt was smiling, clapping his hands together and shouting encouragement. Jorgan's jaw was set, gaze narrowed; he never took his eyes from her. Vera sat erect beside him, ears pricked up and swishing side to side, trying to detect danger.

The position she wanted gained, Briseras spun back around, narrowly jumping out of the way of a full arc swing. The sword tip's clatter echoed across the courtyard, sending rippling energy up her opponent's arms after the force of the swing. As though they'd coordinated their moves in advance, Briseras ducked beneath the swipe he made at her waist and sidestepped onto one of the narrow paths. Beyond the pair of them, the crowd grew silent— something was happening, but she couldn't take her focus from these final seconds of her fight.

A third swing, this one to throw her opponent off-balance. She skipped behind him, onto the thinnest of the pathways, darting out just far enough that he would need to step onto its edge to get to her. He took her bait, following her onto the path, his balance on his back foot.

Briseras leapt forward, keeping low, and sliced not at the front but the rear leg as he swung the sword around before him, twirling his body after hers. The jump took everything she had—several paces across—and she landed on her injured leg. It gave out beneath her, and she fell heavily onto the central walkway.

Behind her, a slurpy, wet *splash* and a shout of dismay. One breath in. One breath out. With a gasp, the announcer shoved himself up out of the pool, roaring in horror at the blood coating his face, sloshing down his body, slicking over every deliberately placed scar and each cut earned in this arena.

With a blood-covered hand he swiped at his eyes, shaking his head. "Well fought," he panted. "You are unmatched."

She bowed her head to the warrior, though she doubted he could see her, and allowed her awareness of her surroundings to return. To her left, her friends were still; Jorgan looked pale, staring beyond her now toward the center of the arena.

The black-cloaked figure she had been trying to tease out had emerged from the crowd on the opposite side of the courtyard. In the center of the pathway was the dripping pool of blood that had poured from Briseras's calf. Impossibly, floating above her offering, a sword hovered of its own accord in midair.

Briseras had never seen its equal. Long and black, the hilt intricately carved, with a cruel notch on its opposite side, just deep enough to disembowel an enemy unlucky enough to impale themselves along the length of the sword.

A blood-red ruby glinted at the sword's pommel, surrounded by a thin strand of sparkling onyx stones.

"Briseras—seras—eras—seras." Her name echoed on the air. She glanced about, trying to locate the direction of the sound.

When the whispers came again, she knew—they emerged from the sword.

"No!" the Matron screeched. "She is not *worthy*! Their reward has been set already. The sword is *ours*!"

The sword began to vibrate in the air, the ring of its displeasure causing those behind the Matron to cry out and cover their ears.

With a screech, the Matron clapped her hands together, pooling a field of dark energy before her, which she channeled beneath the sword and used to strike Briseras where she sat upon the pathway.

Briseras reared back, every muscle in her body suddenly aflame, her tendons snapping around her bones, spine twisting around over itself.

Shouts rang out behind her. "No! Stop it!"

"Briseras!"

"Let her go!"

But all she knew was pain.

Arms seized her, held her close, kept her writhing body from the pool of blood.

The next Briseras was aware, she was doubled over, retching into the sacred pool of blood and wiping her mouth on her sleeve before Jorgan helped her, shaking, to her feet.

She dragged her injured leg behind her, drawn to the sword as she had been drawn to Lord Draego that night in St. Sebastian. The winter spice of his scent caught on the air, but joining it was the unmistakable copper tang of blood.

"I was His and am now yours, Huntress. Wield me well, and I

will grant you victory unimaginable over your every foe. But with such a promise, I must be fed."

She glanced at Jorgan, who had draped her arm over his shoulder and walked with her toward the floating blade. He stared down the fuming Matron who stood rigidly on the pathway on the opposite side of the sword, but her companion didn't react to the voice.

It was the sword, speaking into her mind.

"I would like a name before our arrangement is complete."

"I am called Ragnar, Huntress. Stretch out your arm and make me yours."

Briseras did as the sword commanded, moving slowly as though through a sludge, her muscles not entirely her own.

Seeing her move toward the sword, the Matron screamed again. "Ragnar is *mine*! By rights it is mine!"

The Matron seized the hilt of the sword, and her resultant scream was just as deafening as Briseras's own had been.

The Matron reared back with the scent of burning flesh, her scream of agony directed now toward her hand. Where she'd seized the sword, Ragnar had burned a hole through the flesh and bone of her hand, singeing the wound shut on either side. A smaller series of burbling burns appeared in a vertical line above the hole, with two smaller holes that dripped blood on either side. The onyxes embedded in the hilt had done their damage as well.

Still screaming, hand clutched to her chest, the Matron stumbled away, her gait uneven as she tried to not disturb the blade floating, by itself, at Briseras's side.

A moment of silence stretched across the courtyard. Beside her, Jorgan smiled. "Is there anyone else? Any other challengers for the huntress? Any others want to try to take her sword?" He grasped her wrist, staring down the few in the amphitheater who weren't avoiding his gaze. Now at the end of the center walkway over the pool of blood, the Matron wept quietly to herself, cradling her hand to her chest as she hurried away to the healers.

"No?" Jorgan shouted.

He grabbed Briseras's wrist and tugged it into the air. "Winner! The huntress, Briseras!"

"Woo!" Tybalt yelled from the sidelines with Vicq clapping by his side. Some of the Bloodletters joined in Tybalt's celebration half-heartedly, glancing about at the quiet figures in red cloaks around them to check their reaction.

Jorgan released her hand and grinned at her. "Well done." He nodded toward the sword that was still floating in the air. "I'm not going to touch it for you, but you deserve it."

She lowered her gaze, unused to receiving such unadulterated praise for so prolonged a period. "We should see about commandeering Vicq's reclaimed prize for ourselves once he's regained control of the pack."

"I've been thinking along similar lines actually." His grin twisted to one side. "I don't think he'll need it, but I suspect we will." For a moment, Jorgan's joviality faltered. "Do you know what happened back there, Briseras? What stopped the Matron when she attacked you?"

Briseras shook her head. Her world had gone dark, the Matron's victory assured, and then . . .

"Tybalt said he saw a shadowy figure on a flying horse above the arena that zapped the Matron with lightning. And Vicq said the sword yelled on your behalf."

She had heard a voice, but it hadn't been that of

Ragnar. Her cheeks flushed, imagining Lord Draego making a dramatic appearance over the pool of blood. She didn't want to tell Jorgan about him, not yet. "There was one thing. A whoosh, like a—" Briseras looked her companion over. "Where's your dagger?"

The nobleman shrugged. "I may have thrown it. Hit too." Jorgan's grin returned. "They're cleaning it off for me, preserving the Matron's sacred blood or something like that. I'll get it as we leave."

"You . . . you threw a dagger into someone's side. For me?"

Jorgan caught his crooked finger beneath her chin and drew her gaze up to meet his. "I'm hoping, eventually, you'll be glad you found me in the woods and didn't kill me on sight. For now, grab your sword and let's get out of here."

CHAPTER 41

IELLIETH

Iellieth picked her way through the forest carefully, following behind Ammon as he led the way deeper into the forest for their third day of travel. The damp earth squelched underfoot with slippery patches of moss coating their path.

Overnight, the rains had abated. Ammon knew, roughly, where they could find the ruins that might hold Gaia's Glade, but the forest could use enchantments to hide its entrance from them, which would add untold time to their journey. The question of worthiness lingered over Iellieth like the moisture on the air—heavy with every breath but unseen. Would there be a challenge to prove themselves? A trial like she'd experienced in the Caldaran forest? A guide like Nova who would appear and help her?

Iellieth's dreams had taken a strange turn in the night; she'd seen shadows, interspersed with bright patches of green. This far north of the city, it might be a residual enchantment from the titan at work in the forest. She wondered if a place of such ancient resonance would retain power and influence over its region and draw travelers near.

The calling intensified as they went. Not as it had when the black oak dryad summoned her. This was something . . . more. The forest thinned, ancient trees giving way to thinner grandchildren down to saplings. Cloud-obscured sunlight filtered down through the branches, and the moss and leaves faded into soft grasses. They were close now.

Iellieth held her breath and stepped forward into a glade. Just beyond the thick line of trees before them, whatever had been calling waited for her.

The grasses rolled silently beneath her feet. Her companions' voices were muffled behind her.

And a flash of bright green—a narrow dart behind a thin star—came pelting out of the darkness.

Iellieth gasped as she took in the fuzzy shape of a sprinting wolf pup careening through the trees. "Wait," she called, running a few steps forward.

At the sound of her voice, the pup's eyes widened and its ears twisted toward Iellieth. The wolf's tiny cry pierced her heart.

As quickly as its short pup legs could carry it, the wolf sprinted toward Iellieth and leapt into her waiting arms. The pup shivered against Iellieth's chest, its eyes wide, breath heaving.

Her amulet warmed and cast a soft red glow across the pup's white fur.

"Lady," Marcon called from behind her.

Iellieth's mind spun. The wolf bore bright green markings upon her forehead like the ones described as running along the backs of the wolves in *Lady of Canis*, a book series she'd read over and over again as a child. At the center of her forehead was the glowing pattern Iellieth had seen in her dreams the night before, a thin green gash with narrow motes darting off of it.

Her companions crashed through the edges of the glade to join her, and a rumbling grew in the distance.

"Something's coming," Marcon warned as she slowly turned around. "We should prepare—" His voice broke off as he beheld the pup in her arms. Marcon brushed his hand against Iellieth's arm as he reached out to introduce his scent to the wolf pup.

"This pup found me," Iellieth explained.

The thundering grew, causing the earth below their feet to quake. Was this what the pup had been running from? An earthquake? Iellieth hunkered over the wolf pup to shelter it from any falling branches. The trees around them swayed.

"Look out!" Marcon dove in front of her and the wolf pup, shield held high.

A whistling object flew toward them and struck the shield with a *clang*. Marcon's arm recoiled at the blow, but he held firm.

"Stay low," he ordered.

She crouched to fully hide herself behind Marcon. "Where's Quindythias?"

Marcon shook his head. "Somewhere in the trees. Try not to look up."

Ammon must have followed Quindythias's lead—the ranger was nowhere to be seen.

Iellieth clutched the wolf pup tight to her breast and leaned against Marcon. They had practiced several different types of scenarios in their trainings together, but not one in which they waited for an enemy to arrive.

The wolf's belly was warm and smooth beneath her

hand, a little girl pup. What was this thunder she was running from? And what about her caused the amulet to respond so profoundly? The warmth had remained though the light faded, just as the glowing green upon the wolf's head dimmed in brilliance, settling as a leafy pattern on her fur.

The answer to the wolf's panic burst out of the forest undergrowth before them.

Flying blue hooves kicked high. They disappeared a moment later as Marcon swung his shield up.

The champion crashed backward into her as the hooves drove down against his shield. Marcon's arm muscles strained.

Over his head, an enraged forest creature with towering antlers and sharpened teeth stared down. "Give it over, human," the creature spit at Iellieth. Red eyes glowed behind the fur covering its face.

The angry creature towered over her and Marcon. What she had taken to be a fur-covered fae and rider was a single being, much like the centaurs she had read about, though all the descriptions she'd ever encountered of centaurs described them as part-elven, part-equine in appearance—and peaceful. Ammon hadn't mentioned a mouth full of canines or a fur-coated face that looked more like a bear than a fae.

Iellieth scowled up at the centaur as Marcon recovered his ready stance. Yet another being in this forest who dismissed the elven half of her heritage.

The centaur was covered in dark blue bear's fur, but Iellieth could see muscles rippling beneath the fur on his torso. His features were large and angular, like those of the fae, and a multi-pronged set of antlers rose out of his head above faun-like ears.

The wolf pup's trembling increased further, quakes running the length of her body.

"What do you want with her?" Iellieth demanded.

The centaur-bear's eyes widened. "You dare speak to me thus?" His booming voice echoed between the trees, and the rumbling thunder grew nearer. He wasn't alone.

"Who are you, that I should address you differently?" Iellieth tossed back. Her hold tightened around the wolf pup. She wouldn't surrender the wolf to this being, whatever reason he offered for trying to reclaim her.

"I am the head of the Hoofheart Clan." He reared up once more, his hooves flailing against the sky. "You will hand over the harbinger to me now or I will kill you and your mate."

Marcon's knuckles whitened as he tightened his grip on his sword. "You will do no such thing."

Earth and fire energy swirled to Iellieth's fingertips. The pup had found her. The forest led them to one another. She had felt its call.

More bear-centaurs clomped out of the trees to join their clan leader. They wielded spears similar to the one jutting out of Marcon's shield, but none of them had antlers like their leader. Some had the semblance of breasts beneath their fur while others—she peered closer —had filed their antlers down, leaving only slight, pointed tips at the top of their skulls.

She needed to try a different tack. "Why are you so interested in this wolf pup?" How could the shaking creature in her arms be a harbinger?

Growls of irritation rippled through the assembled clan, perhaps due to the open disrespect she was showing to their leader. They had surrounded her and Marcon and closed in between the trees. Even if Quindythias and

Ammon attacked from above, they would stand little chance of fending off so many, nearly two dozen.

The leader bared his teeth again and pawed the earth, but he stopped at the sound of a musical female voice.

"It is interesting you should ask such a question," the lilting voice replied.

Iellieth peered through the forest, but none of the creatures present had spoken.

"The Hoofheart Clan has long awaited the arrival of the harbinger, the birth of a white wolf whose arrival signals the end of the age."

Vines rippled behind the leader of the clan, and a fae female, similar in appearance to Yvayne, stepped forward. Where her mentor was violet mist, this fae was sunlight and heat. White-blonde hair shone above her brilliant orange skin. Her eyes were a deep amber with flecks of ruby.

Iellieth held her breath as the fae spoke. Had she come to help them?

The other creatures seemed relaxed in her presence. They lowered their spears to their sides instead of pointing them at Iellieth and Marcon.

"I am Zelphira," the fae said, "an emissary of Titania, Queen of the Summer Brightlands Court." Her white smile caught the glint of dappled sunlight. "I have served Ghol Dustcall, head of the Hoofheart Centaur Clan for several moons now." She bowed to the leader. "Perhaps you might answer his question. Why should they trust you and spare the creature whose howl they rightly dread?"

Iellieth cleared her throat. How much should she reveal to this fae and the assembled bear-centaurs? "My name is Iellieth Amastacia," she began.

A soft groan trickled down from above her. Quindythias already thought she had shared too much.

"My companions—companion and I travel through this part of the forest on a . . ." *Challenge? Quest?* ". . . journey sanctioned by the High Elven Council." It was not exactly a lie, but rather a stretching of the truth, which Quindythias suggested whenever possible. He might forgive her for immediately revealing her identity.

The amber and garnet eyes across from her brightened, and her amulet heated once more, a sharper glow than before.

Iellieth winced as the amulet burned her skin. She shifted its position on her chest without revealing it beneath her jacket. The fae watched her as a predator would her prey.

Beside her, Marcon adjusted his posture, relaxing slightly, but did not lower his shield. He continued to glare at the centaur that had threatened them.

"What is this journey?" Ghol Dustcall demanded.

Iellieth took a deep breath.

"Go ahead, lady," Marcon murmured.

"We seek Gaia's Glade," Iellieth answered, her voice ringing clear across the forest. "We wish to prove ourselves to the guardian waiting inside." From what she'd gathered, there were a few possible reasons a pilgrim might seek to prove themselves to the guardian, though she suspected the most common was recovering the artifact the guardian protected. If the Hoofheart Clan migrated through this region often—the one detail the Caldaran scholars might have gotten right about centaurs—they likely would have run across pilgrims and treasure-hunters searching for the glade before.

The fae's smile deepened. She strode forward and

reached up to grasp Ghol's forearm. "Perhaps this is the mystery the shamans could not solve."

The centaur narrowed his eyes and nodded slowly. "Is she the one you have foreseen, Zelphira?" The deep, grating sound of his voice softened slightly as he spoke to the fae.

Zelphira sighed and turned her gaze to Iellieth and the wolf pup. Her amber and ruby eyes glowed scarlet, bright as fresh-spilled blood. "I sincerely hope so."

CHAPTER 42

BRISERAS

Following Briseras's exploits in the ring, the Bloodletters were so anxious to honor 'the Special One' that, despite Jorgan's initial protests, they ushered her and her companions into their armory. He stopped complaining the moment they stepped inside.

With obsequious bows, the mavens presented Vicq with his armor and choice of any weapon he desired. For Tybalt, magical arrows for his bow and a bandolier of throwing knives. "Exceedingly kind of you, thank you," the elf said, "I left mine back in the Vale."

"And for the wolf who is the second-most favored. Favored by the huntress and so by us, yes," the maven in charge of the armory murmured to herself, bowing and walking backward as she led Jorgan through the armory to select whatever he wished.

"What's the story behind this?" he asked, pointing to a set of dark brown leather armor.

"Enchanted, yes," the witch murmured, her green eyes wide. "A special enchantment for each bearer, one it only shows in time."

"Excellent." Jorgan grinned, pleased with himself. "I'll take this, plus a longsword—a fancy one, if you have it—and a dagger or two." Briseras leaned against the entry door, arms crossed and smiling to herself as she watched them test out the various pieces. He ordered one of the acolytes to fetch the blade he'd thrown and pierced the Matron with, dubbing it the Spellbreaker when once they were reunited.

For herself, Briseras agreed with the weapons' maven that she had already received 'a prize great beyond measure,' though she was happy enough to accept a quiver of poisoned crossbow bolts for a special occasion.

Before they departed, one of the healers whisked in and tended to Briseras's leg, promising it would be returned to full health by the morning, when they were to set out to meet the saudad.

They passed the evening in celebration, with free drinks flowing in from the Bloodletters around them, anxious for the approval of Briseras and her friends.

"Honorary Bloodletters, you lot are," Toris cried, sloshing ale onto the tavern floor.

"And the luckier we are to have them," Brutus agreed.

But Briseras's favorite part of the night was when it was just her and Glen at their table, Tybalt having arranged a line dance in the center of the tavern. The warrior leaned toward her. "Well fought. Well won. Huntress."

"Thank you, Glen." And that was all.

In the morning, Briseras's cure of spiked coffee rallied her companions' moods, and they made their way out of the city, watched over by the Bloodletter guards to protect them, at range, from the wights and worgs. A few hours' travel to their rendezvous spot saw them reunited with the saudad, who received the adventurers in high spirits. Lavinia was more herself, her sharp blue gaze studying Jorgan, Vicq, and Tybalt in turn. She warmed to the elf quickly, as she had to Everett. The saudad paid particular fanfare to Lavinia as the five of them departed, pressing protective crystals into her palm in such great quantities that Tybalt gallantly offered her a leather pouch he kept on his person "for precisely such occasions as this."

Briseras turned back as they reached the crest of the hill that would hide the muster from view. The muster boss stood beside her mother who perched on the front of her wagon. The seer stretched out her hand to Briseras and then placed her fingertips between her brows in a signal, Briseras hoped, indicated a blessing of some sort. "Here we go, Vera," she murmured to her wolf.

Vicq led the way to Wolf's Head Peak.

There were dark moments on the day-long hike. Lavinia haltingly recounted for the others what had transpired after her own arrival in Steymhorod, including her experience with Kratok. Her mood turned still darker as Jorgan, with head bowed, told her that he had seen little of Nassarq's prisons beyond his own cell but that he had no knowledge of whether her sister was there or not.

When she thought no one was looking, Lavinia stared at his neck scars, murmuring to herself. Briseras fought back and forth with herself whether she should say something further, her focus occasionally distracted by Ragnar's requests for blood.

"Were you not sated yesterday?" she challenged the blade.

"Oh yes. I will not need to feed for three days more. But there is always blood to let."

However beautiful and powerful it was, Briseras sensed

the sword would present its own complications to her journey through Steymhorod.

Her meditations on what Ragnar might mean, the different symbols that saved her from the Matron, each reminding her of Lord Draego, all faded away as an orange glow spread across the horizon and the peak they sought came into view.

"Oh," Briseras sighed, stopping in her tracks to gaze up at it. "When you said the name, I didn't quite expect . . ."

"It looks exactly like a wolf's head," Jorgan finished for her.

A muffled cry rang out through the trees ahead, cutting short the shared moment of surprise.

Briseras was the first to spring into action, darting ahead onto the path, crossbow at the ready. Vera kept pace at her side and nudged Briseras off the trail and through the underbrush, leading her directly toward the disturbance.

Jorgan crashed through the trees behind them, his muffled cry of "Wait!" lost by the whipping of tree branches, crunch of leaves underfoot, and greedy panting of the sword strapped to her back.

"Feast, I must feast," Ragnar chanted within her mind.

Vera leapt through a gap between the trees, sliding and snarling to a stop before a mage and a warrior facing off against one another. The one Briseras took for a mage balanced atop a large stone that marked a bend in the path. She wore a long, pale blue robe. Strands of gold thread wove through brunette braids that hung down over her shoulders. A deep, jagged scar marked one side of her face. She turned slowly to take in Briseras and Vera, her hands held up near her shoulders.

Opposite the woman was a hulking man wearing

patches of fur, lending him the appearance of a partially transformed werewolf.

"We have been expecting you both," the robed woman murmured. "Solane welcomes the one who was promised." She nodded to Briseras and Vera, with a second bob of her head as Jorgan jumped through the undergrowth and crouched at Briseras's side. The woman turned to the broad-shouldered man in scant furs. "And the priestess made it clear to you and your leader that you could not come back."

"It's no right of hers to forbid Kratok his mountain."

The woman's dark eyes flashed. "*His* mountain? It belongs to the Wolf Mother and those who serve her." The woman and the fur-clad warrior bore similar tattoos of a crescent moon and howling wolf's head, meant to represent membership in the pack of Wolf's Head Peak, Briseras gathered.

"*Feed,*" Ragnar seethed. With each complaint, Briseras's pulse sped, thumping in her ears.

She and the sword would have to practice together. She would not abide distraction during a fight, however powerful the sword proved itself to be. Yet she couldn't resist finding out. As the werewolf and servant of the priestess argued, Briseras reaffixed her crossbow to her side, freeing her hands to seize the sword should the opportunity arise.

The rival werewolf snarled at the woman's rebuke. "I'll not be told off by a mere pup—" He made to lunge forward.

"Stop." Briseras slid between him and the mage with the high ground. A golden glow gathered about the woman's palms, flaring brighter against the dark backdrop of the forest trail.

The werewolf clacked his teeth at Briseras.

She grinned in reply. *Excellent*, she and Ragnar agreed. Beside her, Vera lowered, preparing to pounce, her lips flickering up in a snarl.

Briseras tilted her head, evaluating the werewolf Kratok had sent. Muscular, relatively agile, but also either unwise or unrestrained. A failing of both training and leadership. "Would you like to be a messenger or a message?"

The werewolf snarled outright as he took her meaning —smart enough for that at least. He lunged.

In a single motion, Briseras slid Ragnar free from her back. He slipped from the sheath as smoothly as falling water.

She sidestepped the lumbering werewolf, gliding the sword along the gap in her furs beneath his muscled ribcage.

Ragnar sliced through the werewolf's flesh, perfectly sharpened, and slurped the creature's blood into itself. Briseras gasped, momentarily thrown. *"More, huntress,"* the blade urged.

This time, its voice returned her to the dance of the blade and the danger of the moment.

The werewolf's shocked yelped still echoed through the trees as Briseras spun back around, the completely clean blade pointed toward her opponent. A bright, crimson streak had appeared along the center of the shaft, where Ragnar gulped the werewolf's blood.

Before her opponent could recover himself and lunge again, he swayed. A frown flashed over his expression, and Jorgan cursed behind her.

Blood poured from the werewolf's wound onto the earth. Already the color drained from his face.

"Feed!" Ragnar screeched.

As one, she and Vera pressed the attack, seizing upon their opponent's weakness. Briseras adjusted her hold upon the blade as she rushed forward, gripping the pommel by her shoulder and ramming the blade into the werewolf's gut.

Vera caught him at the base of his neck, and the pair of them drove him to the earth.

The man wriggled and scratched at her armor. He let out a screech of pain as, within her mind, a low, cruel giggle echoed like a monster's growl within a cave.

"*Better,*" Ragnar praised her, "*good huntress. Much better.*"

With a low sigh from the sword, her connection to the blade dimmed. Briseras's mind was fully her own once more.

The man lay with eyes open, staring blankly at the gray flecks of sky overhead, his flesh many shades lighter than it had been only a minute before.

Warm hands clasped her shoulders and pulled her away from the corpse. Jorgan turned her about, keeping hold of her shoulders while he looked her over, asking if she was alright. At first his voice was muffled, but it gradually grew clearer. "I guess he decided to be a message after all," Jorgan said with a grin.

Vera sat back from the corpse and daintily licked the blood from her paws. She would see to her muzzle in due course.

Briseras let out a deep sigh as the sounds of the forest crashed back upon her ears. Jorgan helped to catch her balance and sought the help of both Tybalt and the robed woman sent by the priestess, one Vicq introduced as a friend.

Tybalt's eyes widened as he took in her and Vera's kill. The glow along the center of Ragnar's blade had turned the hue of wine, and the corpse grew more blanched by the moment.

"One of Kratok's most trusted goons," Lavinia murmured, magic flashing behind her bright blue irises as she glared at the corpse.

"The forest will deal with him," the robed woman said with a grin. "I will help it along." The low chant of her spell called an army of insects and vines to her assistance. Jorgan yelped at the size of the spiders that crept out of the undergrowth, and Tybalt helped him to sidestep a great snake that slithered toward the mage's call.

"We are careful not to add to the number of undead," the mage explained to Briseras. She smiled brightly and gestured for Briseras to tug Ragnar from the body.

Briseras braced herself before tugging the sword free. *"Are you . . . done?"*

A murmured *"mmm"* of assent answered her. She tugged the blade free and jogged after her friends to resume their trek up the mountain to meet the priestess of Wolf's Head Peak.

❧

THE PARTY SLOWED AS THEY APPROACHED THE BASE OF the wolf's head. It was a shape Briseras knew from Vera, that perk in the jaw, narrowing of the nose as a wolf prepared to howl. As Vicq explained with help from the mage, part of the jaw opened up and functioned as a receiving area for the pack's allies as well as a slaughter field for any unwelcome force they weren't able to pick off within the lower woods. Under Vicq's leadership, the pack had used primarily defensive tactics, stationing several wolves at any given time within the forest. Under Kratok, the mage added, the fiercest warriors traveled afield with the alpha, seeking to expand the pack, leaving the den relatively undefended.

"The encounter you just decided on my behalf was intended as one of the first decisive victories of Priestess Solane's new command of the pack," the mage confided. "She will be most pleased to learn of the outcome."

"I am glad," Briseras said simply. Vicq's information had not included what they should expect as they approached the pack's territory, even with the reports from the saudad's scouts. The mage greeted Lavinia with special care, welcoming her to her 'new true home.' Lavinia flinched but eased when Tybalt murmured encouragement to her.

Briseras had not questioned Lavinia's insistence on continuing with them to the peak. "I can recover, avenge myself, and locate my sister all at the same time," she'd said.

As Briseras knew from experience, such declarations were at times easier to say than they were to carry out, though for herself, the path of the hunt had always proven to be rewarding. Seeing the witch's continued unease, Briseras renewed her own vow of vengeance against Kratok. Earning Solane's trust was the key to uncovering the path to Arduenne's fane and the removal of her lycanthropy. Ridding the wilds of a monster was a welcome bonus.

A second brunette mage, the twin of the one they'd met in the forest with a mirrored scar over her eye, appeared at the base of the wolf's head. She bowed her head to welcome the party. "The priestess has been expecting you," she said, gesturing for them to follow after.

A winding stone stair led them through the wolf's

throat, the echo of their boots and weapons bouncing across the stone.

At the top of the stair, upon a wide stone landing, a robed woman with flowing hair was waiting for them. She was half-elven in appearance with dark brown skin and even darker eyes. On either side of her stood an archer and a shifted werewolf, awaiting her instructions.

With a whimper, Vicq took a half step forward then stopped himself. "Solane?" His voice broke at seeing his former mate again.

Briseras hadn't known what to expect from the female alpha, especially after Vicq had proven so varied from their first acquaintance to now.

"Long have I awaited your return," Solane sighed, her voice a wind through mountain trees. Soft, but insistent. The werewolf priestess smiled, tears brightening her gaze. "I knew you would come back to us when you were ready. And that when you did, you would bring her promised one to me."

Jorgan leaned toward Briseras. "Pretty sure she's talking about you," he whispered.

A gleam of mirth flared in the priestess's eyes. "You underestimate the heightened senses gifted by the Wolf Mother. Actually, I mean you both." She spread her arms wide. "Thank you for your service to my acolyte in the forest. On behalf of myself and Arduenne, we are most grateful."

From their research in the archives and confirmed by Lord Draego, Briseras knew that the Wolf Mother was a name for an aspect of Arduenne. Just as the Bloodletters and coven witches spoke of Lord Draego in near-godlike terms, to Solane, the Wolf Mother was her goddess.

Solane's indigo robes swished as she led the newcomers

and her former mate into the deep recesses of the pack's cave. From the open mouth of the wolf's head, they followed her through the first two chambers, where rolls of blankets and small piles of supplies had been neatly arranged across a series of large depressions across the cave, giving the impression that the wolf had hollowed out parts of her skull to make for comfortable sleeping quarters for both wolves and werewolves in their human form. Back in one of the corners, two children played with several wolf pups. Their mother raised her head as Vera entered on Briseras's heels. The two wolves eyed one another, and then the mother laid her head down again. They'd each found the other to be trusted and safe.

"Make yourselves comfortable here," Solane said as she glided down a set of hewn steps in the center of the chamber, resting beneath the one they'd passed through. Behind her and Jorgan, Tybalt spoke reassuringly to Lavinia. Briseras had noted the special care Tybalt had taken of the witch on their hike up the mountain, particularly as they neared the wolves' cave again.

The elf suggested one of the areas at the rear of the wolf's head, where a recess in the cave let out onto a sunny area protected from access by the treacherously steep mountainside but that would allow them to enjoy the fresh air. Briseras had kept close quarters with Vera for long enough to see the wisdom of this plan—an entire pack of werewolves would certainly entail a strong array of smells. It went without him needing to say that the location was the most defensible as it was furthest from the entrance to the cave mouth and, with the exposed outside area, it would give Lavinia a place to shelter, if she wished, when the pack returned.

Having hunted Nassarq by the witch's side, Briseras

had little fear of this being the case—when the occasion arose, Lavinia would want to lead the charge, and Briseras would let her, but the matter could wait for a few days more after which time, Solane had said, the pack would return. "Kratok will feel the absence of his scout and will be eager to reassert his control here." Her information matched with Vicq's tracking and Lavinia's experience—Kratok preferred to have those loyal to him in the pack out and away from the den during the full moon to take advantage of their transformation and spread the Wolf Mother's blessing as widely as possible. The priestess's lips thinned as she said this—her beliefs were different than those of the alpha she'd ousted.

"Might I see the two of you for a moment?" Solane requested, parting from a private conversation she'd had with Vicq around one of the many cavern corners. The echo of his footsteps shuffled off in a different direction as Solane came to collect Briseras and Jorgan.

"When the Wolf Mother told me to expect two who would be of great import to her, she bid me to share with you the innermost sanctum, the place where I perform my worship. Where the Wolf Mother speaks to me."

The werewolf led them through a dark stone hallway, the wall so narrow in places that Briseras had to turn to slide through. Jorgan grumbled behind her, his new array of weapons clattering after him and contrasting sharply with Solane's aura of quiet power.

Solane stepped aside, welcoming first Briseras and then Jorgan into a candle-filled room with a small hole for smoke near the top on one side. Wooden pillars coated in wax of varying shades flickered against a mural backdrop. Just as she had when she first saw Wolf's Head Peak, Briseras froze in awe.

The cavern sloped down toward a glittering mosaic, colorful stones and broken glass that formed the image of a three-headed woman with six arms. Each of her hands carried a weapon, prominent among them a bow and arrow. Her heads were not those of humans or elves but of wolves. The central head stared out at Briseras. Painted into the center of her forehead was a glittering stone with an eye-shaped pattern around it, similar to some of the jewelry worn by the seer she'd spoken with among the saudad.

"The Eye of the Wolf Mother—the Eye of Arduenne— calls to you, does it not, Briseras?" Solane had been watching her closely.

From behind her, Jorgan took a few stuttering steps forward, his lips slightly parted, for once surprised beyond words.

"She said you will be the one to restore her. That with her Eye, all will once again see."

CHAPTER 43

PERSEPHONIE

"The priests wish to make an example of us," Persephonie panted as she and Velkan tore through the forest. Her muster would not have sounded the alarm if they'd sensed the priests had come on a mission of peace.

"You believe they've come back for the wheels? It's only been a week."

"Boss Gilsen's wheels burn now. Perhaps such a display of loyalty has rushed our timeline."

Shouts rose from the muster, but there was no shimmer of magic upon the air, at least not yet.

Velkan kept pace beside her, holding aside the larger branches so they would not catch upon her hair. One of her scarves snagged on a branch, and Persephonie wriggled out of it. Her family needed her.

The camp came into view and with it, the messengers the priests had sent. A line of horsemen stood at the bottom of the hill below their camp. Five of the tattooed guards had dismounted, flanking a single man who raised his voice to address the muster.

The man wore dark gray robes that hung down to his feet, a simple sash about his waist. The sash had been carefully tied so that the embroidered design of an extinguished candle, its smoke curling up the sash to the man's waist, was clearly visible. Across his chest, he bore a large amulet of carved antlers. Thirteen prongs.

A priest.

Two dozen members of her muster had gathered, including her datha and Jezebel. Rennear hovered by her babu's tent and hurried over, limping slightly, when she and Velkan emerged from the forest.

"Go!" she urged Velkan, nodding toward the gathering. Persephonie rushed to Rennear's side, catching her arms around him as he embraced her.

He murmured into her hair how worried he had been. "They sent scouts into the forest. I wanted to go after you, but I knew they would follow me."

Such timing would be too coincidental, wouldn't it? That the priests would have known to send their guard while she was away from her muster.

"Come on." Persephonie tucked Rennear's arm around her shoulder and guided him over to the crowd. The saudad made space for her and Rennear to step forward. She stood beside Velkan on one side of her datha. Opposite them, Jezebel's skeletal wings flicked open and shut. Their jaw was tight with irritation.

"And having welcomed you to these lands in peace, my brothers and I find ourselves concerned that no movement has been made on your part to settle beyond this first patch of ground you have come to, nor have you consulted with the shepherds, vintners, or shopkeepers in establishing yourselves and making contributions of your own to these lands."

"You wield your accusations freely, Hesser." A wobbling alto voice sounded from behind the priest. Datha held back the shouting reply he had been prepared to levy at the priest, peering around the line of soldiers to see who had spoken.

The stooped old woman Persephonie had seen on their way to town a few days prior stepped out from behind the line of soldiers. Kessa and another young woman stood on either side of her—she couldn't be sure from here, but Persephonie believed it was the woman she'd seen with the elder the other day.

"Stay out of this, Novik," the priest shouted, waving his hand in her direction.

Hisses of reproach echoed across Persephonie's muster, and several of the guards flinched, dismayed by the priest's treatment of an elder.

"Tee-hee," the old woman, Novik, laughed. "It looks as though you're surrounded by more as have some sense than you're used to." Novik also wore a robe, a pale blue overcoat that dragged along the tall grasses. She rested her hands, gnarled with age, atop her cane, peering at the priest. Though the priest had to be a decade older than Persephonie at least, Novik's chastisement emphasized his relative youth.

Hesser, the priest, looked about him, trying to regain order among the men. But at Novik's approach, the horses had grown antsy. They stamped, nostrils flaring, and ignored their riders' soothing.

"They've agreed to help me in my fields," Novik added, her dark eyes sparkling with glee, "and they can't very well do that from the far side of the river in the wastes your foul number cannot contain now, can they?" The faint breeze gliding over the fields of New Orison picked up, causing Novik's robes to billow.

"You would lie to one of the priests of Malura?" Hesser cried, puffing out his chest.

Novik only laughed harder, nodding in answer. "Just because something hasn't happened yet doesn't mean it wasn't about to." As she looked back up at the priest, the gleam remained in her eyes, but her smile had faded. "Be gone with you now," she pronounced. Novik waved her hand in the direction of the horses, and the wind rose further, screeching as it cut through the trees and swept up from the valley, coalescing around the line of soldiers.

The already frightened horses bolted, charging in all directions and scattering the priest's guards. The six horses without riders rose up on their rear legs, kicked at the air and, with a whinnying cry, tore away from the camp and down the hill, back toward New Orison.

Hesser's guards shouted and took off after their horses, leaving the fuming, breathless priest alone on the hillside. His jaw jutted forward as he glared down at Novik. She only chuckled again, and he broke his gaze from hers, finding Persephonie in the crowd. His glare was sharp enough that Rennear growled beside her—his wolf snarling its warning at the provocation.

With as much dignity as he could manage, Hesser spun away and stomped off down the hill.

The muster and the three women watched one another for a moment, and then Datha stepped forward. "Grandmother, friends, be welcome." He bowed deeply. "We are in your debt."

Datha helped Novik to the fire at the center of their encampment where she could speak with the muster's elders. She caught Persephonie's eye as she passed and winked. Kessa slid up to her side. "She wants to talk to you later," she whispered. "She knows of our plans."

The elderly saudad recruited some of the available members of the muster to help her with her harvest. "It will not forever keep the priests satisfied, but it should allow you the second week, maybe one after," she explained to Datha and Persephonie. Novik beckoned the pair of them closer. "They have been especially testy of late, on edge about maintaining the appearance of their power."

"Do you know why?" Persephonie asked.

Novik tightened her grip on the head of her cane. "That I do not, child. What I can tell you"—her silvery white eyebrows rose—"is that they are particularly busy the night of the full moon. All thirteen of them stay in the temple, no matter what. So if someone wanted to find out what exactly they were doing, that might be the place to go."

After she worked out an arrangement with Datha, the number of workers she would need on which days and for how long, she recounted the story of a muster that had tried to leave New Orison, that of Boss Emil.

Datha paled. "What happened?"

A dull roar behind her ears drowned out Persephonie's awareness of what was happening all around them. It was his friend's absence from their rendezvous that had started him on this path in the first place.

Novik shook her head. "A fire, the night before they were to leave. They barely tried to make it look like an accident. The guards surrounded the camp, prevented any others from helping, and said it was to prevent the fire's spread. But we all knew." She cursed under her breath and thumped her cane on the ground. "We knew, and naught has been done about it. Until you came along." She raised her gaze to Datha's.

He had sunk onto one of the wooden benches around the fire. Persephonie hurried to her father's side and placed her hands on his shoulders. He wrapped her small hand within his, fully engulfing her palm and fingers. "I feared something had happened when the muster was not here. But this . . ." Datha ran his tongue over his teeth and swallowed hard. "We'll find a way to make this right. It is what Felix has been saying—I told him he was burning too hot, but I was wrong."

The sight of tears streaming down her father's face was more than Persephonie could bear. She slid around to Datha's side and buried her head in his chest. They had been meeting with Emil's muster for decades, a tradition from long before she was born.

"You must help me, my Sephie," Datha murmured to her. "I do not want to ask you to put yourself in danger, but this cannot go unanswered. And you are powerful enough now, with strong friends, that you do not need your datha to protect you anymore." He smiled to himself, sending more tears down his face, which she wiped away for him. "We need you, now, to protect us."

"I will, Datha." Persephonie held her father through the initial onslaught of his grief, each cry for his lost friends, each memory he shared, forming a crystalline barrier around her heart.

She would do more than find out what the priests were doing, more than find a way out for those they persecuted.

For hurting her Datha, for murdering their friends, she

would see whatever they were planning destroyed. Though she couldn't have said how, Persephonie knew the wheel Rowan had sent her to find had a role yet to play in the scheme unfurling within New Orison. And once she found it, she would use this wheel against them.

CHAPTER 44

IELLIETH

The centaur herd thundered away through the forest, leaving Zelphira in the clearing with Iellieth and Marcon. As the forest quiet returned, a rustling overhead drew the fae's attention upward.

"Yah!" Quindythias sprang off of one of the overhead branches, daggers drawn, and flew toward Zelphira.

The fae frowned and stepped out of the way.

Quindythias rolled to avoid a hard landing and leapt up to standing, his dagger tips pointed at Zelphira's throat. "Who are you?" he demanded.

"She is trying to help us—" Iellieth began, but he shook his head.

"Why do you travel with centaurs in the forest?" Quindythias demanded.

Iellieth had been wondering the same thing, but she was more willing to overlook the fae's traveling companions after she had intervened to help them with the wolf pup and the confrontation. The more pressing question, in her mind, was of the foresight Ghol Dustcall had mentioned. Had Zelphira been lying, or was she truly waiting for them? She had never had the chance to ask Yvayne if her long-seeing eye was common among the fae.

"I am Zelphira, as you have just heard, and I am an emissary from the Summer Court of the Brightlands."

Ammon swung down from the trees behind her, making it impossible for Zelphira to watch both him and Quindythias at once. "And what business would Queen Titania have in our forest?" The roughness of his voice was in sharp contrast to the lilting notes of the fae's speech. He stood with half his body turned from Zelphira, hand on the hilt at his hip.

"My business began with the Hoofheart Clan who, as it happens, is traveling through your forest on their tri-annual migration."

Ammon's gaze flicked over to Iellieth's, but she couldn't decipher the look he gave her beyond a lack of trust in the Summerlands fae. "Yes, of course," he said dryly, releasing his hand from the hilt of his sword. He introduced himself simply to the fae, leaving off his familial name and his connection to the high council.

Seeing Ammon make peace with Zelphira, Quindythias's jaw worked back and forth for a moment, and then he shrugged and sheathed his blades. "You're lucky that didn't escalate too far." He wandered over to Iellieth's side and leaned his elbow against her shoulder. "Who have we got here?" He cooed over the wolf pup in Iellieth's arms, wriggling his fingers in front of her round, wet snoot.

The pup had finally stopped shaking after the centaurs had faded into the forest beyond them.

Iellieth scratched the wolf between her ears. "I was

thinking Daphne." The pup could share the name of the heroine who had lived among the wolves.

Marcon smiled brightly at this, and Quindythias groaned and clapped his palm against his forehead. "You cannot seriously mean to keep her?" He stomped away, grumbling to himself. "Four of you I have to take care of now . . ."

Ignoring Quindythias, Iellieth turned to Zelphira. "Does Daphne have a pack? Where is her mother?" The pup seemed quite young still. Her fur was soft and downy, the pads of her toes perfectly pink.

Daphne yipped in the back of her throat. Iellieth resumed scratching her ears and neck, and the pup settled down.

"Let's make camp, and I will explain all," Zelphira said.

Ammon shouldered his pack. "We have several hours still to travel before we stop to rest." He and Quindythias seemed to have some sort of unspoken agreement to make the fae aware that she was unwelcome without going so far as to chase her away.

"Well enough, lead on."

As they traveled north, Zelphira told Iellieth of how she had come to join the ranks of the Hoofheart Clan on behalf of her queen. "They are fearsome hunters, and Queen Titania was hoping I might convince them to extend their territory in the Brightlands nearer to the summer court. A great many terrible creatures have begun expanding territories of their own. We are a peaceful people and are not well set up to defend ourselves in such circumstances."

The fae's story matched with the disturbances Ammon had noticed as well. Sharia, too, had mentioned a Brightlands fae helping her with the poachers. Was it possible that had been Zelphira too? But Iellieth's unease rose as Zelphira laughingly relayed the romantic attachment between herself and Ghol Dustcall. "I'm sure you have found for yourself how simple it is to sway one who bears deep attraction to you." Zelphira feigned amusement when Iellieth said that had not, in fact, been her practice, her false laugh a strained, high-pitched bell that grated against the soft lull of the forest.

"What about the one Dustcall referred to as your mate? I see the way he looks at you."

Iellieth hid the flush that rose to her cheeks at this by adjusting Daphne in her arms. The pup had fallen into a deep slumber shortly into their hike, and Iellieth's muscles were beginning to strain.

Marcon appeared at her shoulder. "Lady, might I help you?" He reached out for the wolf and tucked Daphne against his chest, easily settling her into the crook of his arm.

"Thank you." Iellieth sighed as she stretched out and massaged the inside crook of her elbow and biceps, the tendons gradually loosening from the tension of balancing Daphne while climbing uphill. Zelphira's gaze lingered on her but Iellieth ignored it, walking with Marcon instead and answering his thoughtful questions about Daphne's namesake.

The fae found her again after they'd made camp. Zelphira nodded toward Quindythias and Ammon, who conspired together on the opposite side of the floating campfire orb Iellieth had made. "Your friends are right to be suspicious of me." Her lips pursed, and she stared into the flames. "I have not come here on behalf of my queen alone."

Iellieth ran her fingers along Daphne's bony spine,

ensuring the wolf pup wasn't too close to the fire. "Then why have you come here?" she murmured.

The fae let out a short, bitter laugh, her gaze piercing the forest around them. "I never imagined myself relying upon a half-human and her companions." She crossed her arms over her chest.

Marcon scowled at Zelphira. "Iellieth carries a great weight upon her shoulders, one I fear will only grow heavier as time passes. You would do well to not underestimate her." The constant insults to herself and her capabilities seemed to grate upon him even more than they did her.

Iellieth smiled at the way his olive skin glowed in the firelight, his blue-gray eyes shaded by the dancing flames as he studied her.

"Perhaps you speak true, Marcon Colabra." Zelphira's lip upturned at the corner and she leaned her elbows over the tops of her knees. "Terrors grow across the Brightlands. Forces long dormant have reawakened." She drew a deep breath, and her expression twisted as though she was in pain. "And those of us who stand against them have been attacked, taken, tortured, and worse."

The fire's crackle was the sole sound, the entire forest poised to listen to the fae's story-spell.

Zelphira sighed heavily. She ran her hand down her throat. "My mate Kelvren and I were part of this resistance. We saw our lands changing, shadows pressing where they did not belong, and we joined with those of like minds to do something about it." Her jaw worked back and forth as she observed their reactions.

"I do not know how extensive your knowledge of our land is, half-human," she said to Iellieth. "Among the many fae that walk the Brightlands, I am one of Enid's descendants, the brightfae. My people live in one of four king-doms, each dedicated to a season of the year. The Summer Court is not so passive as the autumn." She spit out the accusation, the orange of her skin darkening. "We were among the first to act."

Iellieth's voice was soft as she spoke into the silence. "To act against whom?"

Zelphira whirled around to face her, the ruby flecks in her eyes blazing. "An enemy you know well."

She recoiled at the fae's ferocity. Marcon instinctively did the opposite, shifting his weight to place himself between Iellieth and Zelphira.

"Forgive me." The fae ran her tongue over her teeth. "Kelvren's fate is not your doing." Her anger abated as rapidly as it had come, replaced by tear-filled eyes. "Alessandra's forces, under the command of Lucien, captured Kelvren and the others. I was the only one who escaped." Her lip trembled as she continued. "I have tried to go back and rescue them, but I cannot manage it on my own, and our forces are spread too thin elsewhere." She drew herself up tall. "If I help you acquire what you seek, will you come with me to free Kelvren?"

The fae explained the scouting mission she and Kelvren had been on, deep in their enemy's lair in the Shadowlands, when hidden shadow-soldiers attacked, whisking away her companions and partner. Quindythias scowled at her throughout the questioning that followed this account. Iellieth still had not been able to ask him what about their new acquaintance set him so on edge. Marcon hadn't yet forgiven her for snapping at Iellieth. Ammon leaned away from the fire, hood over his head, its shadow hiding his expression, but Iellieth knew he was listening. Zelphira's tale connected somehow to a larger conflict spilling over into the Realms—a conflict she felt foolish for not having more strongly suspected Lucien's role within before.

Despite her friends' feigned indifference or simmering hostility, Iellieth couldn't resist the grip of Zelphira's tale. Perhaps her companions had heard many such stories before. Losses were common occurrences in war—she understood that, and they had reminded her often enough. Yet the smallness of Zelphira's request struck her heart. In this one small way, after they acquired the seal piece, perhaps they could help.

What remained was Zelphira's end of their bargain, a barrier the fae anticipated and answered before Iellieth could ask or Quindythias could demand. "I came to the Realms in search of Gaia's Glade," Zelphira confessed, staring into the fire. "I found it. Presented myself to the guardian within."

Iellieth held her breath. Her companions sat frozen around the fire.

"And she accepted me." Zelphira sighed. "But the guardian could not directly aid my cause. She sent me back into the forest to search for allies." At this, the fae's gaze wandered over to meet Iellieth's.

She couldn't hide her wide-open eyes or shortness of breath. "Since you have been to Gaia's Glade once, would you be able to lead us there again?" Sharia had explained that once someone had successfully completed the Pilgrimage, the glade would no longer hide itself from them. Zelphira could take them straight to the glade without risking wandering through the forest.

Iellieth had promised Marcon and Quindythias they would find the seal piece, and Red had urged them to hurry. If Zelphira's story was true, Alessandra's forces were already active in the Shadowlands, advancing across the Brightlands, and trickling into the Realms, gaining access through the portals hidden throughout the forest. Perhaps their cause and Zelphira's were even more connected than she'd at first believed. Yvayne would wish to know of these attacks against fae from the Brightlands if she did not already, and of Lucien's actions in the Shadowlands, the army of creatures he was building. Helping Zelphira would mean more accurate intelligence for her to share with Yvayne who could then better direct the movements of the lorekeepers in their stand against Alessandra.

She straightened. *That* was the sort of choice a true Soul Shepherd would make, someone as hopeful as Red or as brave as Yvayne. A choice elemental champions and heroes of Eldura could be proud of.

"I can," Zelphira answered simply. "Though I should warn you that finding the glade is only the start of the trouble." She nodded to Ammon. "Your guide can get you close, can lead you through the path that lies within the Realms. But once there, your skills of navigation must extend into an ancient fae temple and unlock its magical workings."

Ammon made no objection to Zelphira's claims, leaving Iellieth to decide for herself the degree to which she trusted the fae. His loyalty was to the Realms and the rewilding of his people. This additional test must be what Sharia had meant with proving oneself to the guardian.

Zelphira cocked her eyebrow, looking Iellieth over. "Your power grows, Iellieth Amastacia—I sensed it the moment we met. But do you trust the extent of your powers enough to withstand the forces arrayed against you within Gaia's Glade *and* to have enough power to take whatever action drives you to the guardian?"

Iellieth stiffened at Zelphira's challenge. Neither the elven council nor the Darkstriders had specified in what way she would need to prove herself to the guardian within the glade. The council certainly trusted Gaia's guardian to determine worthiness without a great deal of intervention from themselves, sending seekers to the glade without intervening to offer additional protections to the seal piece's hiding place. The Darkstriders trusted the guardian in equal measure, more as an expression of faith than a matter of convenience. If someone had succeeded in recovering the seal piece of earth, would word have reached Thyles Thamor? Or was whatever guarded the seal piece powerful enough that it had destroyed any who tried to take it for themselves?

Iellieth turned her questions to the fae rather than stirring them constantly within her own mind. "How do you know so much about the magic within the glade when the guardian sent you to find allies?" She left unspoken the deeper question—if Zelphira was willing to reveal this much to those she had just met, how much more was she keeping to herself?

"Similar enchantments exist within the Brightlands," the fae answered simply. "Ancient magics from when the titans dwelled nearer to us—before they shut themselves away." Zelphira pursed her lips, considering Iellieth's reaction. "I did not think such stories had survived here, but among my people and in the long memory of our queen, the tales persist." She turned to Quindythias. "You would find the veneration you seek before Queen Titania and her court, I assure you."

Quindythias's eyes widened, considering, but then he masked his features.

Zelphira returned her smiling attentions to Iellieth. "I

understand your hesitation, but do not let the council and their empty warnings into your head. They are afraid. To the shame of the Realms, they have been overly cautious for far too long." She smiled, and firelight glinted off her white-blonde hair. "Come with me. We will find that which you seek."

Iellieth nodded and took Zelphira's proffered hand. "Thank you. It's a powerful, ancient artifact that brings us to the glade. I want nothing more than to restore my friends to themselves."

The fae accepted Iellieth's brief explanation of the seal piece and its purpose and turned in for the evening, leaving Iellieth and her companions to make plans for turns at taking watch. Quindythias made a point of asking whether they should double the watch with one person supervising the camp and another the forest loudly enough for Zelphira to hear.

Before turning in herself, Iellieth affixed a loose lead around Daphne's neck and went for a short walk, Marcon at her side. The pup's fur glowed, iridescent in the moonlight, and the ivy-shaped leaves along her fur seemed to lengthen and grow.

"I do not know about our visitor, lady." Marcon frowned, gazing over toward their camp. "She knows much already, which alarms me on its own. Why is she so eager to help us instead of finding others who might aid her? The Realms cannot be without capable warriors who could assist her in recovering her partner."

"That's true, and she hasn't won Ammon's trust either even though the forces they arrange themselves against seem to be the same. I cannot help but feel . . ."

"Tell me."

"Does it not seem like a fated meeting? A fae with

knowledge of conflict in the Shadowlands, someone fighting against Lucien, emerges to help save us and a magical, adorable wolf pup from a herd of centaurs." Iellieth scooped Daphne into her arms, extricating the pup from where she had sprawled on the forest floor. Dirt and tiny leaf scraps decorated her round, soft belly.

"But whose fate, and to what end?" Marcon's eyes softened as he stared down at her. "While these are unanswerable questions, she seems overly interested in you, and that, for me, sparks its own set of concerns." His jaw worked back and forth.

For herself, Iellieth was grateful for the darkness that hid the flush of color to her face. "Would it be better, for the time being, to bring her along with us and find out her intentions? If she is an ally as she claims, we'll have assistance in finding the seal piece. And if she's an enemy, we'll have her nearby and be able to learn about Lucien's movements. If she is somewhere in between, which seems the most likely to me, then we're out little more than Quindythias scowling and Ammon avoiding conversation."

Marcon grinned at her jest. "I hope you're right, lady. You know as well as I that our enemy is not to be trifled with."

"I do." What she wouldn't say aloud to Marcon was that such an eventuality was worth the risk if it meant that they were closer to recovering the seal piece and returning him and Quindythias to themselves. They were close now, and the forest had sent them not one but two guides and a wolf pup besides. She intended to see their mission through.

CHAPTER 45

BRISERAS

The mural and the majestic figure upon it drifted through Briseras's dreams that night in the wolves' den. In her dream, she carried the ruby of the eye through dangers, sheltered it against a storm, and presented it at the feet of a woman so very like the one depicted, so powerful Briseras could scarcely bear to look upon her. She recognized the glowing eyes from her dream in the forest. Arduenne. The gemstone pulsed in her hands—like the beating of a heart.

Even with the heart, if her sense of the stone was correct, she still had to find and cleanse the fane, something they wouldn't have time to do before their first transformation, which would occur at dusk the next day.

Jorgan too had been silent and contemplative after their visit with Solane. He watched the sun rise over the hills, arms clasped loosely around his knees. They had a great deal to do to prepare.

Solane spent the day with them, sharing her knowledge of the blessings and gifts of the Wolf Mother while Vicq reacquainted himself with Solane's acolytes, working to regain their trust. With the afternoon sun high over the wolf's head, she sent them out to finalize their preparations, leaving their armor and shoes in the den alongside any excess weapons they carried so as not to risk destroying items of value when they changed shape. Thanks to the blessings of the Wolf Mother, Solane added, they wouldn't really need weapons outside their own bodies at all.

"It's both more true and more disturbing than it sounds," Lavinia added to Tybalt. Since she had transformed before, the full moon wouldn't affect her as greatly, and she could remain by the elf's side through the night of the transformation. Otto would remain safely with Tybalt as well. The two had bonded during their trip to the Vale. The raven perched upon the elf's broad shoulder as often now as he did upon Vera's back.

"What does she mean 'excess weapons'?" Briseras murmured to Jorgan as the priestess turned to tend the incense emitting soft curls of smoke at the statue she kept of the Wolf Mother in the common area for all to share.

Jorgan grinned back at her. "Some people—not you, obviously—carry more weapons than they know how to wield or manage. Or perhaps they're clumsy and tend to lose arrows. I believe that's what she means."

Briseras frowned at the priestess. Perhaps it was because Solane was so comfortable in her wolf form, she found weapons for bipedal, clawless creatures superfluous in comparison to the blessings of the Wolf Mother. "I did know a hunter who carried an extra blade in his boot that he was not skilled enough at throwing to strike through a target's eye. He claimed it was for luck, but it was not enough to save him."

Jorgan started to open his mouth but shook his head instead, and Briseras returned to unlacing her boots.

"I don't much care for the idea of being barefoot." Jorgan wriggled his toes through the holes in his woolen socks.

"For a nobleman, you are not very good at mending," Briseras observed. She wore leather bands around her feet and ankles, additional protection beyond her boots for a rough path or a foe skilled enough to strike at her feet.

"I never had to do my own mending before," Jorgan rejoined. He sounded almost offended.

Briseras didn't blame him. She would have been frustrated as well if her mother had neglected teaching her any useful skills in favor of, well, she still wasn't sure how he had occupied his time besides some schooling and his relationship with the ghost.

"I wish I could mend them for you," Teela sighed wistfully.

She ignored the ghost and rose, tapping her toes against the cold rock of the werewolves' den. "I am ready, priestess."

Jorgan removed the hole-covered socks and got to his feet as well. "As am I."

Solane directed them onto the mountainside above the cave, where loose shavings of pale rock flaked away from the Wolf Mother's head, a worse case of dry scalp than Vera had ever dealt with during a changing season, though the Wolf Mother's likeness, being made of mountain and not wolf, had no hair to hold the rock-skin in place.

The priestess picked her way carefully through the shavings, seeking out the brightest, most opalescent pieces to grind with the mortar and pestle she'd carried with them to the open air atop the cliff. This dust she poured into a tiny, stoppered vial, one for Briseras and one for Jorgan. "Those of us who have transformed before—myself, Vicq, your witch friend Lavinia—can use dried moonsglow flowers to control our transformation. But for yourselves, you will have to descend to the water's edge, pick your flower just before the apex of the moon's journey across the sky, drop the petal into the mixture, add river water, and drink."

Jorgan pursed his lips as he studied the vial. "That seems . . . risky. A great many steps we must get exactly right in a narrow timing."

"Yes," Solane answered, nodding to herself about the mysteries of the Wolf Mother's divine will.

Jorgan exchanged a glance with the ghost, obviously waiting for a more detailed response that was not forthcoming.

"Come along," Briseras called to him, leading the way over the rock face and climbing down toward the river. "We will see you at dawn," she reassured an anxious Lavinia. Her hand drifted to her mother's necklace, looped above Lord Draego's key. She unfastened the two chains, slipped them off her neck, and handed them to the witch. "Will you look after these for me?"

Lavinia nodded, clutching the necklaces in her hand and holding them to her chest. Though Briseras had never explained the significance of her mother's necklace to Lavinia—the one she'd worn for the last fifteen years, brought to her in Rajas's camp after her mother's death—she knew the witch sensed its importance and would ensure nothing happened to it. Remembering Jeremy's reaction as well as that of Tybalt and Jorgan to the key from Lord Draego, she didn't want to explain to the witch how it had arrived in her possession.

Tybalt stood tall behind Lavinia and nodded to the pair of them in benediction. "At dawn," he repeated.

Solane patted the witch's arm, smiling benignly at Briseras and Jorgan as they picked their way, bootless, down the rocky cliffside.

Jorgan grumbled at each prick of rock against his toes.

"I suppose you never hardened the soles of your feet to protect yourself and speed your travels either?" Briseras asked.

"Once again, no," the nobleman answered, a hint of either dejection or irritation in his tone—she'd given up trying to tell the two apart where he was concerned. Jorgan ceased his complaining and followed after her.

Vera slunk down the mountainside and joined Briseras. She followed her wolf's path and hoped Jorgan would have the wisdom to do the same. "I would have thought that some part of nobleman training would involve training with skilled artisans of some kind—isn't the point to be superior to others?"

Jorgan sighed behind her. She didn't need to see the silencing look he passed to Teela to feel its exchange. "I think most nobles would say that not having to do the work of a skilled artisan or a household servant is what makes them superior to others."

Briseras frowned and glanced back at him. Honor through dependency?

He held her gaze. "But you know that's not how I see it, right?"

"Certainly." The path steepened as they broke through the line of trees.

"Then why did you ask such a question," Teela demanded, suddenly appearing before Briseras and blocking her path.

She wouldn't give the ghost the satisfaction of seeing her surprise at its boldness or its appearance. Indeed, Teela seemed to be the only ghost brave enough to make itself vulnerable to Briseras in this manner—the pact she'd made with Jorgan when they met proved more disagreeable by the day.

"Is it truly so offensive that I might attempt to understand something outside my own experience?" She picked her way around the ghost and continued down the path.

Vera ignored Teela entirely, a testament to the ghost's lack of threat.

Jorgan called the ghost back, but Teela ignored him. "It is when you're seeking to assert your own superiority."

Briseras truly stopped then.

Jorgan slid on the rocks behind her, and she reached out a hand to steady him. "She isn't, Teela," Jorgan growled. For a moment, his hand fluttered against the small of her back, a gesture she was relatively certain he meant to reassure her. Jorgan straightened behind her and squeezed her shoulder. "Any perception of inferiority on my part, Teela, is coming from me in light of the rigor of Briseras's training and experience. Don't lay my insecurities at her feet. To my mind, they are entirely justified."

"But we wouldn't *be* in this mess—and you wouldn't be considering maintaining this monstrous form—were it not for her!" The ghost's face had rippled from the narrow points of accusation into an expression of barely constrained rage, glaring not at Briseras but at Jorgan.

Internally, Briseras repeated what Teela had said and whirled around, staring up at Jorgan. "Is that true?" Her voice was soft. "You're considering maintaining your werewolf form . . . because of me?" She had told Jorgan pieces of what she'd learned from Lord Draego, mixing the vampire's revelations with what she'd found in the archives. There was no reason for him to maintain a cursed state outside of his own desire to do so.

Jorgan gazed down at her, a simultaneous darkness and warmth clouding his eyes. "Would that truly be so bad?" The words emerged as a purr that curled in the base of her stomach. His brow furrowed as he waited for her answer. Unease rustled off of the set of his shoulders, but something else too—an intensity, but one she couldn't read.

Briseras shook her head, a slight smile appearing on her lips the longer she considered his proposal. "Of course not. I'm just surprised, is all."

Her companion searched her gaze. "Surprised in a good way?" Jorgan inched closer to her. "Like it's a good idea?" A sideways grin emerged that matched her own.

"I think so."

Jorgan smoothed back a strand of her hair that had caught on the wind. His hand hovered by her face.

"But you don't need my permission or approval," Briseras added quickly. Is that what the ghost had been upset about, accusing her of trying to make Jorgan feel inferior? The undead's reasoning was unsound. Why would she ever wish insecurity on a member of her team?

"I know that."

"Then why—"

"What if I wanted your approval, Briseras?" His closeness, the way he held her gaze, there was a challenge to it, challenge and something else besides. He stepped closer again so that there was little more than a blade's edge between them. "What if more than wanting to be worthy of standing beside you against our common enemy, I wanted to impress you? I have trained. Differently than you, I'll admit. You have Vera already I know, but I could still be an asset, could further enhance your strength and prove to you my dedication."

There were so many questions layered one over the next. The nobleman wanted her approval and, more than that, wanted to remain by her side—is that what he was saying? That after they'd defeated Nassarq, he had some sort of plan for them to continue hunting together? "I . . ."

Jorgan caught her chin between his first finger and thumb, and Briseras's breath snagged in her throat. "Think about it, huntress." His voice had lowered an octave, the purr and its answering curl in her stomach returning. "Your answer is already more than I was hoping for." Jorgan held her gaze for a moment longer before releasing her and sliding past her down the path after Vera.

He passed by the ghost without glancing at her, and Briseras watched him through Teela's smoke-rippled form as he strode easily down the mountain.

She shook her head, allowing whatever had just passed between them to fade away until a later, less charged time. Briseras hurried after him instead, stopping only when they reached the water's edge, waiting for dusk.

THE FULL MOON'S GLOW SLOWLY EMERGED THROUGH THE low, thick clouds that hovered over the spindle of the Witchwood that stretched along the riverbank and crawled up the base of Wolf's Head Peak. As daylight faded to dusk, Briseras sat with arms clasped around raised knees, almost shoulder-to-shoulder with Jorgan, who had just skipped the last of his river rocks across the rippled surface of the water.

"My mother taught me to observe the passings of the

moons, to attune myself to the swell of power Selene brought as she emerged into her fullness." Briseras closed her eyes and repeated her mother's words as much to Jorgan as to herself, "'Night after night, she grows stronger, just as we will one day.'" She shook her head. Such a promise her mother had made—she'd believed so fully in this future, a future that would never come to be.

"What happened to her?" Jorgan kept his voice low, his gaze never leaving the water.

"I don't know," Briseras whispered, hugging her knees closer. "She died shortly after I left Haven. Rajas made sure I never found out exactly what happened." She shuddered. "I'm not sure if that was actually kinder than leaving me to imagine one of many possibilities or not."

The silence stretched between them, but not in an uneasy way. Rather than thinking about her mother, Briseras turned over in her mind the proposition Jorgan had shared with her earlier—what if he relinquished his life as a nobleman and remained a werewolf?

They could carry the moonsglow tincture with them in their travels throughout Steymhorod so his transformations would not be painful. Such a flower did not grow in Tor'stre Vahn—did that render the werewolves' transformations necessarily painful, or was that part of Steymhorod's curse in its fallen state?

"What do you think it will be like? The transformation?" she added at the quizzical turn of Jorgan's brow. In her dreams as a wolf, she sprinted through the forests of Steymhorod, Vera at her side.

Jorgan stared down at his hands. Moonlight cast shadows against the veins that stretched across his tendons and wound up his arms. "I know Solane said the tincture would prevent us from feeling any pain, but I don't see how we could be spared at least a modicum of discomfort in our transformation."

He flipped his hands palm up as though he could find the answer there. "As much as I appreciate that the priestess sees this whole experience as a way for us to 'honor the Wolf Mother'"—the sudden thinning of his lips and sideways glance at Briseras implied that this degree of appreciation was in fact quite small—"I couldn't get a more specific response from her." His voice dropped. "And Lavinia has already been through so much, I didn't want to ask her to share any more than she wished to."

Briseras nodded down at the water, avoiding Jorgan's gaze. Growing up in Haven, experiences like Lavinia's were common occurrences. Perhaps it had been naïve of her to have believed that she had put them behind her. No amount of experience or familiarity with such matters made her feel any more equipped to help the witch. There was nothing she could say to ease Lavinia's pain, though she was looking forward to cutting off the head of the werewolf who had harmed her.

"I want to spill his blood too, you know," Jorgan added.

His eyes widened as Briseras's gaze shot over to meet his. "What? You have that bloodlust look in your eye, more than you normally do." He searched about the river-bank. "Do you think that's part of the transformation as well?"

"I haven't noticed an increase in rage or aggression."

Jorgan bumped her shoulder with his and scoffed. "Yeah, but how would you?"

Briseras scowled back, enjoying these moments of ease before this great unknown they would face together.

"I don't know if I said it before." She glanced down at her toes and played with the frayed end of her tunic, preparing to tug it off over her head so it wouldn't be ruined by the transformation. "But thank you, for jumping in front of that werewolf and trying to save me. Without you . . ." Briseras shook her head. She'd blamed him at first, but neither of them had been paying close enough attention, and she was the trained hunter. "I don't know what would have happened," she whispered.

"You don't need to thank me, Briseras. I—"

Jorgan gasped in the same moment that a sharp, burning pain ripped across her bicep—this couldn't be the transformation. His eyes were wide in the moonlight, ringed in gold.

Thunk. A hollow sound, something striking wood behind her.

Briseras spun about, clutching her arm. Blood pooled over her hand, and an arrow wiggled against its point, embedded in the water oak behind her.

She bared her teeth and wrenched the arrow from the tree. "No weapons," she snarled. Had the priestess set them up?

High-pitched giggles surrounded them, echoing along the riverbank as yellow-eyed creatures slunk out of the grass.

Werewolf-like monsters emerged along the shore, their thin scraps of clothing hanging off of them in tatters.

Briseras gulped—not clothing. Flesh. "They're undead," she murmured to Jorgan.

He growled low in his throat and tugged his tunic off over his head, immediately lowering into a fighting stance. "Not all of them." Moonlight glinted off his muscled chest —the werewolf transformation and his days hunting at her side had already begun returning his body to how he must have looked before being captive in Nassarq's dungeons.

Were the situation less dire, she might have struggled to make herself look away.

But unfortunately for their assailants, she had other things with which to occupy her mind.

An undead wolverine leapt, slavering, from the brush beside her. With a cry, Briseras struck the point of the arrow she'd pulled from the tree through its one remaining eye. Other arrows rained down around her and Jorgan.

He shouted and gripped her waist, tugging her back toward the tree line. "We need the cover," he called.

She searched overhead for a gap in the leaves. They needed the moonlight too.

The giggling barks drew nearer—dozens of creatures clacking their jaws, eager to make them into a feast. Behind the undead werewolves, scouts dressed in furs moved swiftly through the woods. *Agents of Kratok*—he'd made his first counter against Solane. Briseras tugged another arrow from its useless tangle in the branches. "We need to transform," she told Jorgan. Painful or no, they needed the advantages their werewolf forms would give them.

"We need to *survive*," Jorgan corrected.

Teela burst out of the woods behind them, shrieking through the space between her and Jorgan and careening into a wolverine that bounded toward them.

"Just in time." Briseras grinned. The lycanthropy was pulsing through her veins. Any moment now, the transformation would be upon her, and she and Jorgan would see what werewolves could truly do.

She fought with bare feet and her hands, punching and clawing at the creatures as they closed in on them. Vera flew about behind her, ripping out creatures' throats and tugging them down to the ground. All those sessions fighting in the hunters' ring, even defending herself from the acolytes in Haven, were to prepare her for precisely such moments.

In the chaos, she returned to the riverbank, the press of creatures separating her from Jorgan.

"Briseras!" Her name emerged from the undergrowth beyond her, a call as wild as the river rapids. "Your tincture!"

She pawed at the vial around her neck just as claws stretched out of her fingertips. Briseras screamed through gritted teeth as the vial fell onto the damp, silty earth. Her back arched and her arms elongated. She tried to swallow the next scream—the pain so great her vision blurred. The scream morphed into a howl as it left her lips, and she raised her widening jaw to the sky. White, blinding, searing pain—each of her muscles cried out and found no relief.

A soft *squelch* and the *clink* of something shattered beside her. Vera's growl percolated, low in her wolf's throat.

And then a roar emerged, silencing the chaos of the clearing.

Briseras's pulse jumped, her thoughts cleared. A wolf had declared herself alpha, had challenged any nearby to face her if they dared.

She rolled back furry shoulders and shook out her mane. Whimpers of confusion and a few yips of fear shot up around her.

The great wolf growled again and licked the corners of her maw. Undead wolverine, vampire's servant, or werewolf mattered little to her—she would feast upon them all.

Briseras grinned. *She* was the alpha wolf she'd heard. And beneath the goddess's light, she would make her dominance known.

CHAPTER 46

PERSEPHONIE

Several tense days passed in the muster between the priests' visit and Persephonie determining how she would answer. Her plan started simply, with a return to town. She'd waited for the day preceding the full moon, with only two days to spare before the date the priests had set for the burning of their wheels.

As Persephonie, Rennear, and Jezebel crested the hill that led down to New Orison, Jezebel scowled at the rooftops, ostensibly looking for assassins lying in wait. "What are we hoping for, exactly, with this excursion?"

"Mostly an innocent research excursion."

"Mostly?"

"Precisely." Persephonie grinned. "We are going into town to be ourselves, pay a *little bit* of homage to Cassandra, and see how seriously they take their own rules when it comes to only worshipping Malura."

"You're deliberately baiting them?"

"Only a little at first." Persephonie took the lead along the path, Jezebel and Rennear on either side. She'd sent Juliet bounding back along the path to keep her babu company. "I plan to anger them a good deal more once we arrive in the square and still further with the party we are throwing two nights after tonight's full moon."

Her companions looked at one another over her head. True, she hadn't fully explained her plan to them, but the walk to New Orison seemed as convenient a time as any other to do just that.

"Not a burning of the wheels," Rennear clarified.

"Certainly not. I have been going over it with Datha, and we are working on a much better event."

"And so instead of burning the wheels . . ."

"We throw a party so grand that all of New Orison will want to attend, giving ourselves the perfect opportunity to win over the rest of the saudad and show the priests that being without wheels is not as important to the other musters as they believe. Then we get to keep them. And during the party, when the priests believe they are attending a wheel burning and discover they are not, the three of us investigate whatever it is that the priests are doing in the temple with very little danger to the rest of the saudad." It went without saying the danger this would signify for themselves if the priests returned early and they were caught.

Rennear had anticipated her thoughts along those lines already. "But first, today, we are deliberately aggravating the priests in the square."

"Yes. We need to know what we are dealing with, both to prepare ourselves for sneaking into their temple and to protect the muster for the aftermath if we are caught."

"Is that why you look especially, well, Cassandra-y today?" Jezebel nodded to her greater-than-normal number of scarves and pieces of jewelry. She clinked with each step, and her rings tinkled together every time she moved her fingers.

Persephonie patted the set of tarot cards waiting in her pocket and adjusted the strap of the bag of crystals on her shoulder. "Thank you for noticing." If all went according to plan, the priests would notice too. And they would be most displeased about it.

"This reminds me very much of how we met," Rennear said an hour later as Persephonie settled behind one of the booths in the market square. Kessa had explained which ones were usually empty and when, along with the most likely schedule for the priests and their guards' patrol. Unlike what she had at least tried to do in Andel-ce Hevra, this arrangement and its timing would deliberately provoke a response from the guards. The upset that had brought her path careening into Rennear's had been an unintentional provocation.

She spread a dark green velvet cloth over the table top and arranged her cards and collection of crystals across it. The priests had been angry enough at Kessa's display, and Persephonie had chosen hers with care. Of their many ridiculous rules, she selected one that would be easy to break and that ran counter to the cultural practices of most saudad musters, wherever they fell in their worship of Cassandra—the priests had expressly forbidden the use of divination magic outside their own prayers to Malura. Persephonie was going to openly thwart that rule in the middle of the square.

"Fortunes read here! Have your fortunes read here!" Rennear shouted to the square, startling a few of the passersby nearest them. He nodded apologetically. "If they'd been to see you already, you might have been able to warn them that a strange man would shout nearby and disrupt the peace of their expedition through town."

Persephonie giggled at that. Only when she and her mother had been especially desperate, that terribly cold winter in Andel-ce Hevra, had Esmeralda ever tasked her with calling out to those walking by to have their fortunes told and to see their other wares. Jezebel stood tall behind her, remembering to uncross their arms so they would not look so intimidating as a trio of women passed.

How was her mother faring now, in Dasia's castle, with the Awakened preparing for their revolution, having enlisted the Untamed's help? They wouldn't expect her to participate—Esmeralda had never been that kind of fighter. She preferred other methods of disrupting the structures and systems she found overly constricting.

There was little Persephonie could do to help if her mother were in trouble. Nothing, really, until they found a way to leave New Orison.

An older woman and her grandson stopped by the table, and Persephonie performed a reading for both of them. To the little boy, the cards promised adventure, and to the woman, peace for herself and her family. The pair walked away in higher spirits than the ones they'd arrived in.

That pattern continued throughout the morning, reminding Persephonie of why she so enjoyed sharing her gift for reading the signs of fate and feeling the movement of the Weave all around her. When they'd first arrived, she had feared that everyone in New Orison was like the priests—that they would judge her for being of mixed heritage, a fact she could not have helped even if she had wished to, that their prejudice would endanger the friends who risked their own lives and futures to help her and her people.

But such a limited understanding of the world, such limited compassion for others, was only what the priests had wanted her and those like her to perceive. They could pretend all they wished that the rest of New Orison was like them but, as news spread of Persephonie's skill with the cards through the town, the line of those waiting for a reading stretched across the market square, garnering the notice of the other sellers.

The truth of New Orison was that a large number of her people had gathered here and they were looking for reassurance, for answers.

The motivation for their desperate hope became more apparent as a contingency of four guards and one of the priests came marching into the square. They made no move to look about at the other booths but stomped right past the queue to Persephonie's table, glaring down at her and the young woman seated across the table from her.

The guards assembled in a straight line before her table, blocking the woman from the rest of the line. One look from the guards silenced the objections from the crowd.

The first card was already on the table, indicating the woman's past. The Emperor, a sign of self-possession and self-control. "This is a skill you have developed already. You know how to create the terms of the life around you and have experience with maintaining order." Persephonie ignored the presence of the guards, waiting for the priest to arrive, and pulled the second card from the spread before her. King of Cups. "Another card that speaks of balance, but in this case, it is a balance more of art, creation, and possibility. It is also a card of dreams."

Persephonie wetted her lips. Without raising her gaze from the cards in front of her, she searched the crowd for the priest, feeling his proximity but not able to see him for the shoulder-to-shoulder stance of his guards. The cards worked as a reading for the whole of New Orison as well. A past marked by control and order, a present that dreamt of possibility. She knew from experience how profound the third card would be. Cassandra would ensure it was the one she needed.

"Ah," Persephonie sighed, drawing it out and sitting back in her chair. A gleaming light shone from the center of the card. "The Star." For a moment, the danger of her current actions floated away from her. "In your future, there is hope. Relief. Enjoyment, even." The woman returned her smile, blinking at suddenly misty eyes.

"The magic of this card often comes after a breaking away or a falling apart."

The priest shouldered his way through the line of his guards, who adjusted their positions to make room for him. He wore black robes and a dark cap. The sash at his waist faded from white to gray, and the symbol of the extinguished candles rested within the deep billows of his sleeve.

"And what it offers, after this stressed state, is possibility. Life. Where the King of Cups allows us to dream a new world into being, the Star is the promise waiting for us on the other side, after this world has come about." She traced the silhouette of the figure on the card, a woman with flowing hair waiting at the edge of a peaceful sea, staring up into the brilliance of the night sky.

"Enough," the priest growled behind the woman.

Persephonie's attendee had been so immersed in the reading that she hadn't noticed the approach of the guards and priest. She jumped at the growl of his voice and started to rise, but one of the guards shoved her back down onto the stool.

This was the most dangerous part of this stage of her plan, the chance that an innocent saudad would be pulled into the coming conflict between herself and the priests. She'd discussed this possibility with Jezebel and Rennear already, and they'd developed several contingencies for how to intervene to protect those nearby. They had not planned on a crowd of this size, however—a crowd that lingered instead of dispersing.

Ever so slowly, Persephonie raised her gaze to the priest posturing before her table. "Your quarrel is with me, not her."

"It is with both of you, in fact," the priest growled in answer. He tugged a thick baton from the pocket of his robes, clutching it so tightly his knuckles turned white. "With you"—he pointed at Persephonie with the end of the baton, inciting a growl from Jezebel behind her—"and with you"—he held the baton before the woman's face. She shuddered, leaning away from the blunt weapon and into the body of the guard behind her. He took a step back, upsetting her balance upon the stool.

The priest hadn't anticipated the rocking movement and, having missed the soldier's stepping aside, read it as the woman trying to escape. Over and over again, Persephonie would remember what came next, unable to stop the unfolding events.

With a low grunt, the priest struck the side of the woman's head, knocking her to the ground. Persephonie sprang up from her seat, an immediate rush of sparkling blue butterflies at her fingertips.

She shouted and stretched her hands forward, sending

a stream of bright energy at the priest. He screeched as the butterflies swarmed around his head, striking his face with their wings. His skin erupted with blotchy red burns where the faery butterflies struck him. The priest stumbled, tripping on the stool from the woman he'd struck down, and fell back. A bone in his arm cracked as he tried to catch himself.

After the low *thunk* of the priest's baton, chaos reigned within the market square. Saudad ran, shoving past one another in their hurry to escape. People screamed, fell over one another. In the panic, the pen for a herd of sheep was broken, and the sheep bleated, bumbling their way through the rushing crowd.

The other sellers yelled as well, abandoning their booths as tables overturned. One of the guards tried to help the shrieking priest. The other three were caught up in the chaos, torn between establishing order and protecting themselves. One swung his baton, striking at the rushing crowd.

Jezebel sprang over the table and tackled one of the guards before they could attack anyone.

Persephonie's breaths came quickly—she divided her focus half between the butterflies that had now enveloped the priest who writhed on the ground and half, stunned, at the panic of the crowd.

Rennear's voice reached her as through a fog. He clutched her waist and elbow, holding her back from kneeling by the side of the woman who had fallen. A dark ring of blood pooled around the woman's head.

Persephonie leaned into his side, horror seeping over her at what had occurred. "We were supposed to see their magic," she murmured. With her distress, the butterflies grew brighter. They merged one into the next, becoming larger and larger. As three joined together, fangs emerged from their palm-sized faces. They pierced the priest's skin, and he screamed again. The priest sent bolts of dark energy at the butterflies, indiscriminately striking the stampede of saudad nearby.

Rennear moved to block Persephonie from one of the guards, squaring off, rapier drawn, daring the guard closer.

Jezebel seized the struggling guard they'd tackled by the hair and bashed his head into the ground. The guard fell still, and the butterflies flurried over, covering his body as well. The fae stood between Persephonie, Rennear, and the crowd, arms and wings spread to protect them from the press.

One of the priest's dark bolts struck a nearby booth, shattering the wooden legs of the table. Crates of apples fell onto the ground, rolling across the square. Another bolt hit a man as he fled, carving a vicious burn across his arm.

Jezebel turned, shouting an offer of help to the man who'd been struck as the square began to clear. Distant shouts and cries of pain rippled through the town. The fae clutched at a wound across their shoulder. A bright green poison seeped from the slash.

The ring of Rennear's duel with the guard clanged beside her, their weapons a blur of silver.

"Let me help you—"

"Later," the fae called back to Persephonie. Their eyes glowed white, wings stiff and still, a skeletal wall of bone that separated her from the struggling priest who continued to writhe beneath the butterflies' attacks. One of his bolts struck one of the last saudad on the far side of the square, a young woman who stumbled, crying out as the muscle of her right calf melted away. She fell to the ground and began dragging herself away. Her friend doubled back to help her, lifting her up and wrapping the injured woman's arm around her shoulders.

This has to stop. Thoughts of her datha, the implications for her muster, the priests' reprisals, rushed through Persephonie's mind, their roar joining the distant echo of screams. *This is all my fault.*

The two remaining guards turned back toward Persephonie, Jezebel, and Rennear, who continued dueling with the third. The fae shouted as one of the guards shot a crossbow bolt and nicked the bone of their wing. The bolt caught fire, sizzling into ash on the ground by Jezebel's feet. The fae's wing dipped on that side, where they'd been struck with the poison.

Persephonie ducked past Rennear and dove beneath Jezebel's skeleton wing. She rolled on her back, springing into a crouched position, and aimed at a space in the square equidistant between the three guards. She called upon the power she'd availed herself of within Rowan's castle before they'd traveled to New Orison.

A shimmering phoenix appeared, brilliant purple in color. It raised its head and screeched at the sky. Clouds rolled in for the first time in New Orison, answering the phoenix's call. The guards stopped where they stood, crossbows and sword held fast, mouths opened wide as they stared into the sky. Bolts of lightning began to flicker down across the square, striking booths and cobbled slabs of rock.

Answering bolts shot up from the fissure by the temple, and the phoenix squawked. It raised itself up, arcing around the square. The guards took cover as the phoenix shot bolts of lightning out of its beak. They screamed and fled, sprinting back toward the temple despite the fissure's upward-stretching lightning. The phoenix screeched and pursued them.

One of the bolts had struck the priest, leaving a scorched imprint around his body. The spurts of blood the butterflies had caused amidst his burns slowed to a trickle, and the priest fell still, an arm's length away from the woman he'd killed.

"We have to go!" Rennear shouted, suddenly beside her and tugging on her arm. By the look on his face and the roar in her ears, he had been calling to her for some time but in the chaos, she hadn't heard.

"Go, go!" Jezebel urged, falling in behind her and Rennear, whose leg had nearly healed, improving thanks to both her babu and now Novik's ministrations. She had joked with Rennear only the night before that between the two old women, he had no need of her anymore.

That laughter seemed so far away now.

They sprinted down the street, the guards' screams fading behind them. Persephonie found herself tearing toward the windmill. But would their presence prove too great a danger to the Feather? Repercussions would be falling upon her family already—

"In here," a shopkeeper beckoned.

Persephonie slid to a stop and ducked inside the warm interior. Trays of baked goods lined the shelves, with baskets of bread hanging upon the walls. Velkan had brought her a treat from one of the bakeries in town a few days prior, and she'd promised herself she would come back and return the favor. The scent of yeast and rising dough filled her nostrils alongside the tang of cinnamon. She closed her eyes and inhaled, for just a moment allowing herself to escape the horrors they'd just been a part of causing.

The shopkeeper waved them in to the back of the shop. He rolled aside a few bags of grain that rested atop a worn rug in the center of the storage room, revealing a small hinged door to the cellar. "Go down and to the left. Your friends will be waiting for you," the baker urged. The door creaked shut overhead, leaving them in darkness.

A narrow passageway jutted off the end of the cellar, obscured by a series of racks and shelves. Persephonie paused before she passed through, her lips parted as she stared back at Rennear and Jezebel.

She pressed her hands to her temples, trying to block out the woman's blood, the way she fell to the ground. It was her fault. To protect her own muster, to uncover the magic of the priests, she'd put that woman in danger.

She knew the reading she'd performed spoke more to the future of New Orison than it had the woman sitting across from her. But that didn't mean her own actions, her misreading of the risks involved, hadn't cost that woman the future of the Star Persephonie had seen. Now it would never be hers.

Persephonie blew into her palm, conjuring a single, shining butterfly. It bore no fangs, though its wings billowed rather like the tail of the phoenix. The larger spell would dissipate with such a distance from her, wouldn't it? She'd never been a powerful enough mage before now to conjure a creature that remained alive without her direct interaction, one with a will of its own. Something about this place seemed to enhance her magic but in a different way than the static in the air in Andel-ce Hevra. This magic had been latent. Waiting for her to awaken it.

She looked at Rennear and Jezebel in turn, and whispered, "I didn't mean for any of that to happen."

CHAPTER 47

IELLIETH

With Ammon's knowledge of the forest pathways and Zelphira's existing familiarity with the workings of Gaia's Glade, Iellieth and her companions made their way north the following morning, the elemental tug against her spirit growing stronger and stronger.

After a few hours' journey, as the ache from their days of hiking settled back into her straining muscles, a great cliff rose in the distance ahead. Thick vines hung from its surface, with spindly trees poking out of its distant heights.

"What?" Ammon stared up at the cliff face. "That shouldn't . . . We're nowhere near Shade Rest—"

"And the way that reveals itself has done so once again," Zelphira chanted from the ranger's other side.

He frowned at her and squinted up at the cliff.

Iellieth's amulet warmed against her chest, just as it had on the mountainside when she mis-transmigrated. She took a deep breath and pulled the amulet from beneath the leather armor covering her chest, revealing the neck-lace to Zelphira for the first time.

"I hope you're not planning on us climbing our way up there," Quindythias said, straining his neck as he gazed up toward the heights of the cliff.

"The way is different each time," Zelphira answered, that same sing-song resonance to her speech.

No, Iellieth sensed, low in her chest. The way was not to climb, not yet. By her ankles, Daphne yipped at the vines. Marcon strode forward to the spot that was attracting the wolf pup. He pulled back a swatch of vines, revealing yet more vines, where there should have been rock.

Iellieth closed her eyes to shut out her companions' growing concerns, remembering her druidic training with Mara. The enchantment came to her from one of their final lessons—a spell to part the ways. *"Alya lerai,"* she murmured, holding out the amulet as she did so, beseeching Gaia to allow them entry.

Iellieth held her breath, waiting.

With a whisper and a sigh, the doorway of vines peeled apart before them. Some of the tendrils slithered back, the movement like a giant, undulating snake. Others rolled one into the next, a green curtain.

An ancient, primordial forest unfolded before them, the height and breadth of the trees dwarfing the forests of the Realms.

Her lips parted, Iellieth took a step forward, remem-bering Valaexi's words. At the time, she hadn't been sure whether to take them as a challenge, a warning, or an invi-tation. Whatever the councilor had meant, the words fit the ancient forest waiting before her—*Deep within the titan's sacred glade lies an ancient temple, the heart of which*

*stands outside of time. There, those who prove their worth will
find that which they seek.*

"So . . . this seems like what we were probably looking
for," Quindythias observed, rolling his balance onto his
toes then his heels as he waited for everyone else to react.
"Shall we go inside?"

Ammon tugged on Iellieth's elbow, pulling her aside.
"I've made no secret that I do not trust the fae who
happened upon us, and yet we've made better time here
than I could have leading you on my own. Whatever her
subterfuge, I do believe her warning—agents of this
Lucien you've told me about grow more active in the
Realms. I fear a trap springing within the glade while you
are inside, so I will remain here and keep watch."

"No. You've come all this way," Iellieth insisted. "Complete your pilgrimage. Come inside."

Ammon shook his head. "My faith has seen me this far,
for which I am grateful. But I'll not risk your greater
mission and its significance for these lands by venturing
into the glade itself."

Iellieth protested again, but Ammon held firm. Eventually, she relented and left Edvard's statue in his care with
instructions for sending the bird to her should the need
arise.

He grasped Marcon and Quindythias by the forearm
and glared at Zelphira before they passed inside. Before
she went, Ammon pulled Iellieth in for a hug. "Firan
wants to make you an honorary ranger when we get
back. I don't plan to disappoint him by bungling your
return."

She grinned, tightening her hold of the ranger in turn.
"I'll be careful, and I'll look after them too."

Ammon released her, squeezing her shoulders in

farewell, and watched as she joined her friends within the impossibly large forest.

The trees of the Realms had astounded her before but these—they stretched far higher and wider than the Council Tree. From Zelphira's initial descriptions of the workings of the earth spirits, Iellieth had expected she might find herself somewhere akin to the Brightlands, where distinct seasons held sway over different territories.

But as she joined Marcon and fell into step behind Quindythias with Zelphira in the lead, Iellieth recognized what had only been described to her before.

She was walking across Eldura.

Parts of the forest reminded her of the experience she'd had in Red's Cross, returning the piece of darkness to the waiting planar seal. Iellieth shivered, hoping the champions didn't notice—there were still times when she could feel the searing tips of Alessandra's trident piercing her skin.

The way her friends had given up their life energy to heal her from the dark goddess's draining burns—she never wanted to put them through that again.

Was that where the memory forest had been from? The one tied to her soul?

Her companions' reactions were similar states of wonder. Quindythias's lips parted as he stared up at the towering trees above them, many as large around as the multi-level homes and businesses of the Air Ward and a few that would rival the king's summer palace.

Marcon too gazed up at the sweeping branches towering far overhead. They walked slowly, their feet finding the path of their own accord. "I had forgotten what it was like—the ancient forests, those that had survived the war."

Long shadows stretched across the forest floor. It was much cooler beneath this canopy than the forests of the Realms had been.

"What do you remember about them?"

"Hmm." Marcon's gaze narrowed, searching for answers among the branches. "In many ways the characteristics of the forest shaped themselves to fit their inhabitants—or perhaps the other way around. I have a distant memory of a dryad fleeing Alessandra's blight . . . The forests were under threat in my time, like our first mission to Trudid together but at a larger scale."

Iellieth nodded, thinking of Turdoch, her first days with Marcon, the duke's far-reaching hand still holding sway over her fears. So much had changed. "What do you mean the forests shaped themselves to their inhabitants?"

"Quindythias may be better able to explain it. Darkness stretched all around us. Death was a constant shadow. There was a forest, with the battalion . . ." Marcon frowned and shook his head. "It is possible my memory is playing tricks."

She stepped closer to him. Her companions had experienced a great many hardships in the War of the Champions, many of which they did not wish to linger upon. "You can tell me. What did you remember just now?"

Marcon sighed and dropped his gaze. "I remember stalking through a forest that palpitated with fear. It was as if some silent, impossible birdsong was infiltrating my thoughts and those of my soldiers. We were snapping at one another, jumping at the slightest sound in the underbrush. But then we came upon the settlement we'd been sent to attack." His lips thinned into a line, and he inched away from her.

"Tell me," Iellieth whispered, her request even gentler than before. "It was a long time ago."

"The memory has only recently returned. We—we were there to attack a druid conclave. I don't like confessing this to you." He made as if to stride away but stopped himself, turning to gaze down at her instead. "It was shortly thereafter that I broke with the Army of Light, though a few battalion soldiers remained by my side. We made up our own unit, around when I met Quindythias in fact." He searched her expression, gauging her reaction.

Iellieth tried to keep the confusion and hurt from her face. As she'd told him, it was long ago—both Marcon and Quindythias were older than they appeared, not counting the thousands of years they'd spent as statues. The political situation of their world was complex—even with all the stories they'd told her, she still didn't fully understand the different forces that had struggled for power.

"I realized as we drew closer and I felt the fear from the settlement how alike it was to the forest's. The experience in some ways matched the tales I'd heard of the Sapphire Circle and the enchantments they placed around their forest to protect their home from outsiders."

The sacrifice of the Sapphire Circle that the Darkstriders had sworn to remember and to prevent from recurrence had occurred after her friends' souls had been pulled from their bodies, a process her amulet reversed. Even so the mention of the ancient druids sent a chill down Iellieth's neck and crackling energy to her fingertips.

And she wasn't the only being within the forest reacting to Marcon's tale. As he spoke, the trees around them shifted. A cold breeze picked up, slithering through the branches.

Iellieth squeezed Marcon's arm, and they resumed their trek after Quindythias and Zelphira. The elf trailed a few paces behind the fae, his shoulders turned away from her but never fully taking his gaze from her.

"But there were peaceful forests too, were there not?" Iellieth strove to moderate the edge of warning in her voice. Any number of enchantments were possible within the forest but, if she'd correctly sensed the trees' response to Marcon's tale, Marcon might have been more right than he'd realized about the forest's emotional sensitivity and ability to shape itself from memory. "Places rather like where we met Nova?" She softened her gaze, recalling as vividly as possible the dark grove and the daimon who had emerged, touched by elemental darkness and there to aid them.

What would a daimon of earth be like?

Daphne growled softly in her sleep, shifting in Iellieth's arms. She scratched between the pup's ears. Perhaps it would have been wiser to leave her with Ammon—undoubtedly the journey to the seal piece of earth would be dangerous, but something told her to keep the wolf close by.

The forest around them calmed, and Iellieth released a slow breath. Some enchantments would unspool if spoken of aloud, transforming themselves or overtly attacking whoever had uncovered the secret of their workings. This was what Zelphira had meant about the magic embedded within the glade—a series of ancient trials that, if she wasn't careful, would exhaust her magical stores and leave her incapable of retrieving the seal piece itself. That was why they'd accepted the help of their guide.

Red's warnings about Alessandra's desperation, Gaia's attention, and layered enchantments perched like croaking ravens in the trees overhead. Better to try to think of something else. "Did Ignis have a temple like this?" She raised her voice so Quindythias might hear. "And Atamos too?"

Quindythias's expression clouded as he glanced back at her. "There was a temple of rock outfitted with pillars—I believe most had something similar. The corners of the wind were said to meet there. It was a central gathering place for champions of Atamos." He turned away. "Some died there, in his name." The elf quickened his pace and returned to his close observation of Zelphira. His relationship with his titan remained troubled.

The former champion of fire was more open, answering her question as he stared after Quindythias. "Yes and no, lady. By its nature, fire consumes, and so the creation of a natural temple at this scale would endanger any settlement unfortunate enough to be nearby. I am sure that upon the plane of fire, such structures are commonplace."

The sense of awe returned—an entire world dedicated to the element of fire, she could not fathom. This place, this glimpse into a world she had heard so much about, whose tragedies she was trying to right—this was more than she'd ever dreamed of seeing. "I see now why you miss it so much. Why you both do."

There was something primeval about Gaia's Glade. The hearts of the trees thrummed with natural magic. It darted from root to root beneath her feet, the energy so great that she kept checking to see whether or not her hair was standing on end.

Her immersion in Marcon's story and her focus on the forest had distracted her from her awareness of their fae companion. Iellieth's shoulders seized at finding Zelphira so close by.

"You see now why we must do whatever it takes to protect the sacred places like this one, do you not, Iellieth Amastacia?" Zelphira's voice had taken on a strange resonance, as though it was responding to the magic of this place as well. The fae's eyes were a darker red, her skin brighter.

"I do not know that this space is in danger, Zelphira," Iellieth answered slowly, unnerved by the fae's sudden mood shift.

Zelphira forced a tittering laugh. "Yes, yes, of course. And that is not what has brought us here. This way." She called the directive back over her shoulder, leaving Iellieth, Marcon, and Quindythias to exchange confused glances behind her.

"Ancient places tend to hold ancient magic," Quindythias murmured, speaking a facet of Iellieth's observations aloud. "Though it was not something Marcon and I dealt with frequently, I remember the mages' complaints at significant battlefields or sites of great slaughter. However certain you are of your incantations, know that places like this one have a will of their own, a will they intend to see realized."

"What are you telling me?" Iellieth whispered back.

Marcon held a giant leaf frond out of the way ahead. Zelphira had turned aside from whatever course she sensed through the trees and was leading them into a thicket of lush undergrowth. The fae murmured to herself, sensing their path so that Iellieth might preserve her own magical reserves. Dew droplets plonked from the leaf onto the damp earth.

There was something else about the glade, besides

Zelphira's strange shift in behavior and the forest's sensitivity. The splash of dew made it clear. "There should be more noise than this." Iellieth searched the trees overhead and the smattering of underbrush and moss that grew between them. No movement. No birds, no insects, no paths of small animals. There had been nights, sleeping in the forest, when she could scarcely fall asleep for the noise. Between the chittering of bats and hooting of owls at night, and the constant ebb and flow of birdsong during the day, forests were never quiet. Save this one.

She thought back to the forest she'd encountered beneath Red's Cross, the forest of memory. There had been sound near the seal piece—whispered memories of each of the elements. The crackle of a distant fire, a soft breeze through flowers, the gurgle of a shallow brook. But when the four figures appeared, herself and the three previous iterations of her soul, the elemental murmurs had ceased—Alessandra had arrived with the figures as well. But the dark goddess was not silent—her presence conjured a void, a glaring absence of sound that tugged at Iellieth's senses.

There was a hint of that among these trees but from what she could observe, the forest simply seemed to be devoid of non-plant life.

She and Quindythias had passed several nights aboard the *Amber Queen* trying to guess what the quest for the final seal piece would demand of them, what sorts of creatures would lie in wait within the Realms, what magics lay hidden between them and the final artifact they needed to reform the planar seal. But as Ammon kept saying, forests were so much more than the plants that held them. Something else was waiting.

A voice caught on the wind.

"Did you hear that?"

Marcon shook his head. Iellieth quickened her pace and hugged Daphne more tightly to her chest.

The wind intensified, blowing back at her hair and tugging on her armor. "It's the beginning of the test," Zelphira called back as the trees began to wave and shift all around them. "The guardian will determine who you are and whether you can pass." A low rumble rippled across the earth, throwing Iellieth off-balance so that she pitched forward.

The rumble solidified into a voice then, the whispers forming into words that echoed between the trees. "Welcome, Daughter of Verdigris," it sighed, the sound of the final syllable repeating. "Long have we awaited you." Iellieth's breath shuddered, but she continued walking. "Reborn of Rowan"—she forced her legs forward—"returning of Lilia, the blessed daughter of Enid who was a sacred third of Verdigris herself."

Up ahead, a bright green glow beckoned just as it had when Daphne came pelting out of the forest.

Iellieth gritted her teeth against the pressing wind, pushing her way through the pockets of warmth it offered and avoiding the alternate blasts of chill, the wind so strong at times she couldn't progress through.

It grew so fierce she had to squint shut her eyes, trusting in the shapes, the whipping branches of the trees all around her, struggling toward the verdant glow.

With a final push forward, Iellieth leaned against what felt like a full-body spider web. She gritted her teeth against the sensation, and the invisible web broke over her face as the enchantment gave way, opening up onto the heart of Gaia's Glade. Iellieth stopped short, her momentum carrying her forward. She caught herself as though upon a precipice, throwing her weight back to avoid stepping out of the woods and into the clearing.

Before her, many times larger than the underground chamber from which she had mis-transmigrated, was a vast circle of stones arranged together. Moss coated their uneven edges, joining each stone to the next, all a part of the whole. Five low pillars decorated the outer ring of the circle, with a large gemstone glittering at the top of each, their many facets reflecting the light of the low afternoon sun suddenly visible overhead.

In the center of the circle was a raised dais that held a giant rock. Its jagged sides stretched a few stories tall with a large, green gem balanced at its peak. The gem not only caught the sun's light—refracting it across the circle, casting the outer edges in a verdant glow—it also shone of its own accord as though lit from within. An impossibly large statue curled around the base of the dais, reminding Iellieth of the frost giant whom she had accidentally awakened alongside Marcon on Torg's Peak.

She gasped as her eyes adjusted to the clearing's sunlight—beneath a covering of moss and lichen was an enormous statue of a dragon.

Iellieth's breath stuttered at the sight before her, her gaze returning to the glowing gem at the top of the jagged rock. *Lit from within by the seal piece of earth*, the final element needed for them to complete their assembly of the planar seal.

Zelphira hovered at the edge of the circle, gazing hungrily up at the stone. Marcon arrived at Iellieth's side, only slightly winded, his hand resting lightly on her elbow to steady her balance from their sudden stop, the stone of the temple only a few inches away. Quindythias appeared on her other side and crouched low, blades at the ready.

"Remind me of what happened before," Quindythias murmured, eyeing the open expanse of the temple's stones, the forest glade still around its edges.

"The moment I touched the floor of Red's chamber, it transformed into a vast forest. That was when he told me what it meant for me to be a Shepherd. He said I have a recurring soul, and that my amulet is from a previous iteration of that soul." She left out what she had learned only a few days before, that the amulet was somehow a part of Marcon. "Red said the forest remembered me."

Quindythias picked up her retelling. "You ventured into the forest—alone, much to our dismay."

Marcon's grip on her arm tightened. She doubted he would allow such an event to transpire again.

"Inside the forest, I found a circle of six trees, one for each of the elements. And there I encountered an embodiment of Alessandra as an ekhidna alongside spectral forms of my previous soul versions as well as one of me. The four figures each held a seal piece in their hands and walked toward the center of the glade."

"And there," Quindythias continued, "what did you sense from the tree that would have held the element of earth?"

Iellieth's brow furrowed. "Nothing." Her pulse quickened—was that what she had sensed through the forest as well, some aspect of life, missing?

Her breath quickened. All the forest denizens they had been waiting for, the spirits of Gaia she had anticipated, a guardian figure she'd have to impress, absent. And from that tree where the other seal pieces waited—nothing from the tree of earth. "There's something wrong with it." Her voice cracked at the end of her revelation, the truth clawing at her throat. "Something wrong with the final seal piece. That's why no one has acquired it, how it's remained hidden. Part of it is missing."

She turned to Zelphira, hoping to see that the fae was as captivated by the glowing green orb as she'd been moments ago, almost as though she couldn't hear them.

But Zelphira was standing directly before her, both her feet planted upon the stones, and a strange, wide, vacant look in her glowing red eyes. "You've worked it out then," the fae sighed in a voice that both was and wasn't her own. The voice diverged further and simultaneously muttered, "He told me you were smart," and "I knew you'd piece it together."

The hairs along Iellieth's arms and neck stood on end. She knew that voice. It haunted her nightmares. "Lucien."

Zelphira grinned wide. Her arm shot forward and she yanked the amulet from Iellieth's neck, the golden chain breaking at the sudden force.

Iellieth screamed and lunged toward the fae as, on either side of her, Marcon and Quindythias cried out. Her companions arched back, their tattooed runes suddenly glowing bright as scars of moonlight against their skin. Quindythias screamed and fell upon the ground, writhing back and forth. Marcon yelled for her, hand outstretched even as his fingers contorted in pain.

She sprinted out onto the stone circle after the cackling fae. The moment she rushed past the five outer pillars, the earth began to quake.

CHAPTER 48

BRISERAS

Briseras awakened to the feeling of her gorge rising. She had the briefest of moments to gather herself and her surroundings—naked, a dark forest clearing, Vera beside her—before her stomach heaved. She leaned away from her wolf, spilling blood, flesh, and bile onto the earth.

Vera leapt up and trotted a few paces away.

"Ugh," Briseras moaned, trying to catch her breath, but her stomach heaved again. She choked on still more rare meat—*wait*. One roll of her stomach followed the next as she spit a half-gnawed human finger from between her lips. Tears streamed down her face, and she retched again. It was all she could do to keep breathing between heaves.

Vera, helpfully, poked her in the side with her nose, urging comfort the way she would have another in her pack.

Arms shaking, Briseras dragged herself away from the vomit and collapsed onto her side facing away from it. She wiped at her nose with her bare, blood-crusted shoulder, wiped the inside of her mouth with a fallen oak leaf. Where was Jorgan? Lavinia? The last thing she remembered, she had been crouching beside the clear creek as the moon peeked between the cover of clouds. Jorgan had called her name after swallowing his moonsglow tincture. The riverbank had been crawling with undead and wolverines.

One of them had leapt into the space between Briseras and the water. It bared its teeth over a rusty, jagged blade. And then the moonlight had fallen upon her. She groped at her neck—nothing. No dried petals, nor her mother's necklace or Lord Draego's key. Briseras sighed, remembering. She'd entrusted the necklace and key to Lavinia, and the vial for the moonsglow tincture had smashed upon the earth when the undead werewolves attacked.

She gagged again and spit bile onto the earth. There was nothing left for her stomach to disgorge, however many wildlings she'd devoured last night. Briseras rubbed her stomach—it protruded abnormally beneath her ribs despite what she'd cast onto the earth.

An hour passed, marked by the shifting clouds overhead and the cold whistle of the wind through bare branches. Briseras lay stretched across dirt and fallen leaves. Dried blood coated her skin, either from the creatures she'd hunted or from her own transformation, she couldn't say. The wind cooled her feverish skin. Every inch of her body ached. Vera curled up against her, and Briseras tucked her arm around her wolf. "Have you any idea where we are?" she whispered.

Vera grumble-sighed and smacked her lips, adjusting the set of her head upon her paws.

"Neither do I."

Her stomach calmed enough for her to rise, Briseras pushed herself to her feet. Boots, armor, weapons—she'd cast them all aside before she and Jorgan had climbed down into the gorge, where the undead wolverines had been waiting for darkness and for prey. Unlucky them.

The forest had remained still since she had awakened—had it been two hours now? Briseras squinted at the trees. Her blood pounded against her head, each beat of her heart pulsing against the headache that pressed upon her eye sockets and drummed across her temples. She was grateful for the overcast skies of Steymhorod—bright sunlight would be unbearable in this post-transformation condition. She'd only had a few hangovers worse than this, and those had been after unique circumstances.

But the shadows of the daylight gloaming made it impossible for her to discern the time of day or the particulars of her location.

Dragging, clawed tracks had pressed into the earth leading up to where she'd awakened. She had only obscured the last several paces in her stomach upset. Vera's neatly patterned tracks had followed in loping strides alongside her own werewolf prints. She followed them south as the wind changed overhead.

Briseras made slow progress. The bindings she'd been so careful to keep around her feet had fallen into tatters, only just able to protect her arches. She kept one hand against her stomach, steadying her gag reflex as much as possible. Would she be able to eat again for days?

"Water," she mumbled to Vera. Her muscles were tense and sore, and her bones ached from the transformation. Each step was a concentrated effort, and she moved at half her normal traveling pace, if not slower. "We need to find water."

The wolf's ears danced backward, and she emitted a low whine in the back of her throat.

Briseras leaned against a fallen tree. There was something strange about the forest. Branches swayed overhead as the wind picked up, howling through the trees. Dark clouds gathered beyond the spindle tree branches.

It took her a few minutes more—already having resumed her stumbling pace—to realize what was so odd in their surroundings. Birds flocked and called overhead, fleeing the northern reaches where she had awakened. A stag leapt across their path, also darting southward toward the mountains. Except in Loire's Glade, she hadn't seen so many creatures in all the forests of Steymhorod. But all of them were fleeing their habitats, unconcerned with the dangers that lay ahead—an instinct for when the danger behind was far greater than any other they might face.

"Vera, something's coming."

The animals' premonitions and the forest's groans transformed into a fierce windstorm. More than once, Briseras and Vera dove out of the way as a young tree crashed across their path. The storm threw dust and leaves into Briseras's face, choking her and scratching her skin.

She hunkered lower, a hand on Vera's back and the other shielding her eyes.

The branches of a thick oak tree screeched as the storm yanked them from their trunk. They whistled by overhead, flattening saplings before embedding themselves into the frayed branches of other ancient forest sentinels.

Briseras ducked further, arms raised in her hobbling crouch.

They would never reach safety in time. The storm was too great, its reach too far.

She urged her muscles to run, to find her way to safety.

Through everything she'd endured before, her body had answered when she most needed it, when it and it alone could allow her to survive. But no matter her plea, her despair and desperation, her muscles couldn't answer her.

Vera needed to go on. Her wolf could survive.

"Leave me, Vera," she urged. The wolf could find Jorgan and the others. They'd tend to her, understand what had happened.

Her wolf whined and nudged her side, urging her forward.

She tried again, to no avail. "Please," Briseras begged, choking back a sob. But it was no use. Vera would not abandon her any more than she would willingly part from her wolf.

The earth around them began to shake as though the storm were stalking closer toward them, drawn to their scent.

The crash of another giant tree into the forest floor gave her an idea. The holes left behind by the exposed root balls could provide them enough cover. "We'll find a shelter then and hope to survive this."

A twisted feeling in her gut told her that whatever approached was far worse than a storm—no matter how fierce, gales did not move ever nearer in thumping footsteps. A cloud of black dust rose in the direction they'd come from, obscuring the horizon.

Briseras dragged herself forward to the fallen tree, tugging at stray branches and keeping as low as she could, following Vera. The wolf whimpered from behind a fallen tree ahead of them. The pit left behind by the root ball wasn't as deep as she'd been hoping for, but they needed something, now.

She huddled her back into the hollow and hugged Vera into her side, sheltering her wolf from the flying debris as best as she was able.

Curls of dark gray smoke slithered over the forest floor. Vera growled as they inched closer, the newest in the line of heralds of the storm.

At first she thought that there were swirling creatures in the smoke, dark shapes biting and clawing at its edges. But as it drew nearer, she could see that the smoke was tugging roots and branches from the ground, tearing them apart as it absorbed them into itself, doubling its rate of approach. The smoke was so thick it obscured the surrounding forest—making the ruined woods they'd traversed utterly disappear.

The rumble of the earth reached her before the quake. Trying to shield Vera with her body, Briseras cursed as her elbow scraped along the hollow. If only a blood offering would be enough to sate the stalking storm.

Hand shielding her brow, Briseras squinted through the debris to stare back the way they'd come. Another echoing boom and answering quake nearly knocked her onto her side in the hole, but not before she spied the creature causing the storm. A thick, gnarled leg, taking the form of a jagged, petrified tree, twisted and covered in swirling smoke, stomped into the earth. It was tree-like in breadth too—as large as the sacred elms of the ancient druid groves she and her collective had paid their respects to as they traversed the continent.

A sweeping, claw-branch hand swept aside a line of trees, smashing branches and trunks into splinters that flew through the air.

"I'm sorry, Vera." Briseras sobbed into her wolf's fur,

holding her close. She'd failed her wolf just as her body had failed her. Fleeing, taking shelter—it was no use. They couldn't survive the smoke-wreathed tree creature that stalked toward them.

"Briseras."

She curled her arms tighter overhead, huddling against Vera. Though she didn't wish to admit it, she knew why it was *his* voice she heard in the chaos, facing off against a creature whose powers of destruction were beyond her wildest imaginings.

"Briseras." The voice was urgent now, calling for her over the howl of the storm. A horse brayed, the crackle of fire roaring beneath its whinny.

Briseras raised her head, shielding her eyes from the flying debris.

A broad-shouldered man with raven hair and dark eyes atop a black stallion cantered out of the smoke and chaos toward her and Vera. He held a shining silver sword aloft. It glowed as though coated in moonlight, casting a luminous sphere around man and horse. Though the forest roiled and fell, the interior of the sphere was calm. "Back, you beast," the vampire called, raising his voice to the storm. "I repel you and your kind from my lands!"

The horse reared back, kicking at the air between himself, his master, and the giant shadow-tree creature.

The swirling shadow roared, swiping at Draego with its claws.

Briseras gasped as the vampire lord called down lightning from the heavens above, and the skies of Steymhorod answered his call, striking the shadow creature, which stumbled back with a shriek. Draego called a second burst of lightning, buying himself a dozen more paces and easing the edges of its cloud of stinging smoke away from Briseras and Vera.

Draego leapt down from his horse's back, holding his sword aloft. He flexed his arm and cast another burst of lightning. Draego faced the monster as he jogged toward their sheltering place.

"Briseras!" he called to her, his cloak raised against the storm.

Vera whimpered at his approach and nudged Briseras.

She had to be dreaming—or dead. That was where he found her, in her dreams.

Draego called her name again. His brow furrowed as he approached. He cast lightning almost absentmindedly overhead. His stallion whinnied, keeping the monster at bay.

The vampire knelt before her and Vera, reaching out and cupping his hand beneath her chin to lift her face toward his. "It took a while for even me to find you, Briseras." He gave her a crooked half smile. "But find you I did."

His eyes were just as dark, his accent just as spellbinding as it had always been in her dreams. His presence slowed her mind as it had in the graveyard in St. Sebastian, calling her out of her body toward him. Briseras's lips parted as she stared at him. Had the creature's storm knocked her senseless, and this was what she saw?

"You should not be so surprised," Draego cajoled. "I am a skilled tracker in my own right." He ran his thumb softly over her cheekbone.

The horse whinnied again and Draego called back to the stallion. "Just a moment!" He shook his head, staring at her as though he couldn't quite believe she was truly here before him either.

Draego swung his cape free of his shoulders and draped it around Briseras. She hunched forward at its weight and immediately shivered into the fabric. Its silk lining was cold and soft against the abrasions covering her skin, but the protection from the swirling storm was an immediate relief. His green-black gaze sought hers. "Flee to the south. There is a small cabin where you will be safe. I will find you there." He placed his hand below her elbow and helped her to stand. Draego positioned himself between her and the creature as he guided her forward out of the pit left beneath the tree roots.

"Do you promise?"

He froze, watching her, his mouth half open. The surprise fell away. "For you, anything. Do not doubt me." He rubbed his fingers gently beneath her chin, raising her gaze toward his once more. "Were both you and my lands not in such danger, you must believe I would not part from you now that fate has finally provided me the opportunity. But allow me to return to your side a savior of my lands and lady."

His smile made her heart jump in her chest. She still didn't understand why a great vampire lord of a strange, unknown realm would have so singled her out, but she wouldn't argue. "Then I will see you soon." His eyes lingered over her as she hobbled away, south, clutching his cloak around her and looking for the cabin he'd indicated she would find. Her mind raced with thoughts of the shadow creature, what would happen if Draego were hurt, but as she'd learned in her training with her collective, there were times when she'd have to trust her allies and their skill, times when she couldn't help them.

The monster made of storm and shadow was unlike anything she'd ever faced—and in that, the creature was precisely like the vampire lord it fought, the one who had asked her to wait for him.

She didn't need to explain his hold over her to know already that she would do everything and more that he asked. And when he found her, she would make sure this was more than a dream.

CHAPTER 49

IELLIETH

Iellieth sprinted after the fae, throat swollen as her companions' screams of agony echoed out across the courtyard full of towering stones, their pain ricocheting against the woodland edges surrounding Gaia's temple.

"Stop!" Iellieth shouted. She extended her hands, tossing the first spell she could think of before her. Rocks exploded in front of Zelphira rather than the vines Iellieth had tried to conjure. The amulet dangled from Zelphira's right hand, the broken chain clutched in her fist.

Chunks of rock and moss rained down around the fragile necklace but it remained intact. Iellieth gasped for breath, unable to think beyond Marcon and Quindythias's cries as the process that had freed them from their statuesque forms reversed.

She couldn't fail them. Not now. Not when they'd gotten so close.

Zelphira skidded, her balance slipping, and pivoted to run the other way, resuming her dash toward the center of the stone temple.

A sharp *crack* rent the air between Iellieth and Zelphira, causing Iellieth to cry out and fall back, sliding across the stones. Lucien, his lower half transformed into that of a bird with wide vulture's wings spread behind his back soared into view through the portal he'd just conjured.

The world behind him was dark—a swirl of deep purples and blues that flashed away as quickly as it had come.

With a low, croaking caw, Lucien swept down, his taloned feet latching around Zelphira's arms. The fae screamed, her horror matched by Iellieth's behind her. *Gods, her amulet*—her friends' cries echoed across the stone of the ancient temple—an agony the likes of which she'd never heard.

Lucien flew the dangling Zelphira up and into the air, cutting across the temple's expanse, over the dragon's statue to the center where the giant rock rested atop the dais before slowing, wings flapping, to deposit her on top of the stone beside the seal piece.

The trees along the edge of the temple rippled, their branches waving as though disturbed by a fierce wind.

The dais she could leap onto, as it was raised only a few feet off the ground. There was a small gap between the dragon statue's claw and snout where she could access the raised platform without having to scale the dragon itself, but how she would scale the rock in time to prevent Zelphira from stealing the seal piece or her friends from transforming back into statues—

She didn't have to wonder for long. With a screech that rent the air, Lucien dove from the top of the pillar, flying straight toward her.

Lucien squawked as he swooped down, his voice

somehow melded with that of a bird. He lashed out toward her with his talons and Iellieth threw herself out of the way, rolling onto her shoulder like Marcon had taught her and springing up again. He cawed out what sounded like a curse, and static magical energy crackled on the air.

For a flash of a moment, the dragon's statue eye shot open, staring directly at her, the iris shimmering gold.

The iris returned to gray. She was imagining things, and there were much more immediate threats at play.

Lucien flipped about in midair and dove back toward her, carving a low, wide path behind her so as to attack her from behind. Iellieth tossed a spell back at him—just as shocked as he was when a stream of white feathers rather than a spray of acid struck him in the face.

The lich spat out the mouthful of feathers as Marcon shouted her name from the edge of the temple. Lucien croaked once more and latched his claws around her shoulders, scooping her up and into the air. She struggled, trying to free herself, but the fallen guardian held her fast.

Iellieth caught one look over her shoulder as she writhed, trying to remove her armor from the guardian's thick talons. She caught a single glance at her friends below. Quindythias clasped a solid blue arm against his side, his face contorted in pain. Marcon dragged his right leg in a hobbled run, his gaze locked on her. Daphne's fuzzy shape bounded along at Quindythias's side.

She yelped as the talons pierced through the panels of her armor and tore at her skin, scraping deeper with each great beat of Lucien's wings.

As he had with Zelphira, Lucien flapped his wings, slowing their descent. He deposited Iellieth onto the top of the stone, the space just wide enough for her to balance upon without bumping into the seal piece or falling off the edge onto the mossy stone below.

Zelphira was waiting for her, poised in a fighting stance, the amulet clasped tight in her hand. Lucien had placed Iellieth opposite the fae, the seal piece glinting between them. A single shard of the base stone—an obsidian growth beneath her feet rose straight into the air, holding the seal piece aloft. Now that she was close to it, Iellieth could see that a rock and emerald outer layer protected the shattered and remade piece within.

"I had hoped you might be happier to see me," Lucien sighed, stretching his wings as he settled onto a perch at the edge of the pillar between Iellieth and Zelphira. "I'm sure your various allies warned you of my interests here."

Iellieth glared back at him. Marcon and Quindythias's cries had grown fainter with the height, though the wind still tugged at her hair. The ripples of disturbance radiated out from the temple's edges through the forest spread wide as far as she could see. "I may have heard rumors," she shot back at the lich.

Lucien clacked his teeth together, a vulture surveying its prey. "Then you must have worked out what's next."

There was a great *crack* from below and the wind howled more fiercely than it had before. *"Your foe would have you see but one path forward,"* the voice that had spoken to her, known who she was, named her past selves, whispered into her mind.

"Are you the guardian of the glade?" Iellieth thought back to the voice, her mind racing. What had gone wrong that the guardian's protective magics had failed, that she had allowed Lucien through?

"I am."

Iellieth glanced between Lucien and Zelphira, both of

whom watched her intently. They didn't act as though a strange voice spoke within their minds. "I suppose you're going to offer me a trade to coincide with your trick." She didn't bother to keep the bile from her voice. *"He's asking me to sacrifice either my friends or the seal piece,"* she hurriedly told the guardian. *"If there's a way I can save them both, please, tell me."*

"All magic is choice." The low alto voice rumbled across her thoughts, the sound echoing as it had when she first entered the glade. Trees bent toward the ground on the edges of the temple. Branches snapped free, cracking on their way to the earth.

The guardian's answer wasn't helpful. *"Did you send Zelphira to find allies?"* Iellieth thought to the guardian of Gaia's Glade in the same moment Lucien tauntingly answered her challenge.

"I must admit, Zelphira performed her part quite well," Lucien sighed. Puffs of bright green spores fell from the hollows in his cheeks. His talons clawed into the shale, sending long, white scrapes over the obsidian surface. He settled his wings back behind his shoulders, feigning indifference to the gale taking shape around them, but she noticed the growing pallor on his cheeks, the beads of sweat upon his brow. "And an array of choices spreads before you, heir of Rowan. I trust you will not be so foolhardy as to believe there are no additional strings attached, that you can simply have one for the other."

Iellieth stopped herself from asking the most obvious next question aloud. Why couldn't Lucien seize the seal piece for himself? Why would he act as though he was holding her amulet hostage while her friends' souls were rent from their bodies and they were returned to statues in the temple below?

"I sent the traitorous one to find you," the guardian of the glade answered.

Iellieth searched the jagged rock, trying to find a trap or enchantment embedded in the stone that might answer why Lucien needed her to take the seal piece. *"Why me?"*

The guardian chuckled low in her throat. *"The answer you seek requires more time than your friends have. You are as quick-witted as she was. I was right to wait."* A twinge of sadness lingered in the guardian's voice, lightened ever so gently by hope.

Far below, Marcon's cry of pain surged through Iellieth's senses. She needed to act and quickly.

"The longer you take, the more dire your champions' chances," Lucien warned.

"Master, I did all you asked. Kelvren, please, you promised—"

"Enough!" Lucien hissed. His wing cut into the space between himself and Zelphira, nearly knocking her off the edge of the rock.

So that part of Zelphira's story had been true as well. Iellieth met the fae's anxious gaze. Her eyes were wide, pleading. Whatever else she'd lied about, the lich having captured her mate was true. It was likely, then, that he had the druids too, those Sharia and the Darkstrider scouts had gone looking for.

From the corner of her gaze, the golden glow returned below, followed by another crack of rock.

Iellieth held her breath and looked down.

Oh. Gods.

The eye was open below. And it was watching her.

"Are you a dragon?"

The guardian chuckled low in her throat. *"Your compan-*

ions run out of time. The foul one cannot touch the piece—he forfeited the right long ago."

"If I touch it, he'll take it from me, and I have no way of knowing that he'll return the amulet to me in one piece."

"Touch the stone, and I will assist as I can."

Below them, more stones cracked and crumbled. Shale slid and scraped—the stone covering the dragon's scales was wearing away. A great bronze wing shifted in its socket.

She needed to distract Lucien from realizing that the guardian was awakening. "Why did you bring me here?" she hurled at Zelphira. "You put me through precisely what he did to you, and for what?" Scowling, she turned to Lucien, her flood of panic rising alongside her hatred of the pair of them. "You needed me to seize the stone for you? Why?" She smirked, looking over his wings and talons. "Too great a surge of life, perhaps, for one already dead?"

His snarl of acknowledgement was all the confirmation she needed. "Delay any longer and I'll kill them both."

Iellieth leaned away from the seal piece and toward the edge of the rock, eliciting a gasp from both Lucien and Zelphira. She shook her head, resolve settling over her limbs, easing the line of her shoulders. They couldn't see the dragon around the stone, the scales of emerald and teal emerging from the casing of rock. "I won't help you do this. I won't remove it from the glade for you."

"No!" Zelphira shrieked. "Do you know what he'll do to Kelvren? To me? I'll not be thwarted by some half-blood who's only just learned to wield her magic."

"Do you see, Shepherd?" Lucien sighed as though bored by Zelphira's threats. He glanced down at his taloned fingernails and lazily waved them in the fae's direction. "Without your aid, this is what I must resort to. But were you to join me instead, we could rival even the might of Alessandra. The planar seal would be *ours* to command."

An eerie calm fell over Iellieth. "I said no."

"Gah, but you're easier to manipulate than you let on, aren't you? All of you!" Lucien beat his wings in frustration, glaring from Iellieth to the enclosed seal piece and back. "I shall make this simple for you as part of your situation seems beyond your grasp. You must choose—retrieve your amulet and save your friends before the soul-severing is complete, or sacrifice them in your stand against touching the planar seal." He clacked his teeth again. "The hurry isn't mine but theirs."

Distantly below her, beyond the sheets of shale falling from the dragon, any sound drowned out by the wind, a glowing figure crawled across the flagstones, dragging a shiny, red leg. Iellieth's sob caught in her throat. Her own carelessness, her blind trust, was returning Marcon to his statue form and still he was trying to save her.

Lucien followed her gaze and smirked, the seal piece hiding his view of the dragon. "He'll never reach you in time. The same story, I'm afraid, playing out over and over again through the ages." The glint in his yellow eyes shone with pure delight, and Iellieth had no doubts as to Lucien's hand in whatever repeating story he was referring to.

Iellieth straightened, setting her shoulders. The fae was by far the more vulnerable of the two of them. "Give me the amulet."

Zelphira sneered back at her, "Pick up the stone and retrieve the seal piece from inside."

The fae had no way of knowing what had happened when she'd tried to return the piece of darkness to the planar seal, nor what the proximity to the piece of darkness had conjured out of the Caldaran forests. And here, within Gaia's Glade, touching the seal piece would fully release the dragon from whatever spell had bound her in stone below, a process she had to believe was not unconnected from what had happened to Marcon and Quindythias and the other champions sacrificed by the Cities. Was that why the dragon had been waiting for her? Because she was a Shepherd? "I have to be in possession of the amulet in order to unlock the enchantment."

The gemstone atop the plinth glowed brighter, and Lucien clucked his tongue behind his sharpened teeth. "No, no, reborn Rowan. This is not the time for tricks. The magic required is within you, not innate to her amulet." He grinned again. "Ah, an even more intriguing day for me than I'd realized. You didn't know what it was, did you, this precious gift from your father?"

Iellieth squinted into the wind to stare at the lich. Idlewylde had said the amulet came from Marcon—that it matched his sigil of Ignis but that, somehow, it also allowed her to awaken Quindythias as well.

Lucien's eyes glinted, his gaze sharpening as though it could pierce through Iellieth's chest and through her heart. "Would you have found it as precious, I wonder, had you known that it came from one your pathetic champion professed to love and failed to protect? How spectacularly must such a failing have been that he does not even remember her?" Lucien chuckled to himself. "Or perhaps he simply professes care where it suits him and abandons the recipients of affection shortly thereafter. You saw his lack of mourning for poor Lorieannan."

The lich's grin twisted wider. "True ardor is this—Who do you think watched over her amulet through the ages, ensuring it eventually found its way into the possession of her successor so that she might return? Your precious Shepherds? The *lorekeepers*?" He spat out this last, his disdain for Yvayne's organization so intense that the pointed rock quaked beneath them.

There would be time later for her to uncover the significance of Lucien's revelation—it could easily be a lie. But the quaking rock had given her an idea.

"Alright," Iellieth cried, dropping her gaze in feigned surrender. She would have to be exceedingly careful or she would lose everything. The seal piece was damaged—she had sensed as much, or Gaia had shown her—either way.

And Gaia's guardian dragon had promised her aid.

With her shoulders lowered, Iellieth raised her head only slightly, enough to narrow her gaze and focus on the seal piece inside the chunk of green, glowing rock. Small chunks had been carved out of it over time, removed and then rejoined to the crystal—all save two pieces, taken from the heart of the gem. A sliver from the center of the stone was missing, a narrow, jagged piece, spear-like and striated. The second piece had been carved away from the top of the spiked piece in a fashion similar to the shards that had been rejoined—it formed a perfect teardrop shape, sized similarly to the dangling gemstones that decorated heirloom necklaces at court.

As Iellieth focused her awareness on the gem, a series of images flashed before her—a moonstone-skinned fae with purple eyes, looking back over her shoulder at a man with horns before she transformed into a giant, white wolf. A young woman with raven-black hair, sprinting across a verdant field, the sound of hoofbeats drumming behind her. And an elven woman, one she'd seen before, when she faced Alessandra. An elf who looked remarkably like her. The elf threw her head back, garnet hair flying over her shoulders as she raised a hand to her chest. Iellieth's breath caught—she recognized the sigil emblazoned across the elf's forearm, a perfect match for one of Marcon's tattoos, one of the only ones that didn't shift and ripple beneath his skin. *'The elemental signature of the sigil is the same as that which your companion bears,'* Idlewylde had said. Was this the answer? Marcon and her previous soul-iteration—*Rowan*, her mind forced her to admit—bore identical sigils of Ignis? Before Iellieth could finish working through the implications for herself and her amulet, the woman stared up at a spectral Lucien and smiled before bursting into light.

On the other side of the flashing images—spirits somehow imprinted within the stone—Lucien reached out, his face twisted in horror even more terrifying than the surprise followed by panic in the images she'd seen. "No—"

His arms extended to where the woman had been, and Iellieth seized her moment.

With all her might, she kicked the gemstone from the top of the stone plinth. The moment she touched it, the earth rumbled beneath them, and the dragon stretched up onto her feet, raining stones around them as she shook clinging boulders free from her scales.

The creature stood tall, staring down the three of them, her great glowing eyes sizing up Lucien, Zelphira, and Iellieth in turn. *"We meet again, vulture."* The dragon's voice boomed inside Iellieth's mind, louder than the cascade of rock and earthquake beneath them. Zelphira and Lucien both flinched—they heard her too.

Zelphira rounded on her. "What did you do—"

Iellieth launched herself at the fae, throwing herself over the space between them and wrenching the amulet from her hand, sending them both over the jagged edge of the stone.

And toward a yawning chasm that had opened up below where the dragon had been.

The massive stones of the temple shook like rocks beneath a stampede, falling away into a great, black chasm. The seal piece of earth and its emerald casing plunged into the darkness, Iellieth and Zelphira not far behind.

What she'd taken to be a small dais in the center of the temple was instead the lower half of a giant stone tree, its top sawed free with stone roots that stretched deep underground—revealed now that the entirety of the temple was quaking rock and falling boulders, plummeting down into a dark chasm with a shining light at the bottom.

Iellieth tucked the amulet safely inside her tunic as she fell, tightening her leathers around where it rested atop her heart. Whether it would be enough to restore Marcon and Quindythias, she would have to find out.

Zelphira waved her arms, clawing at the sky as she tried to slow her fall. A cry echoed out from above them, followed by a ray of sickly green energy directed at the dragon whose great wings expanded to hold her weight aloft.

The dark shape of a winged creature plummeted toward Iellieth alongside a second beam of bright green.

Iellieth conjured a verdant shield and reflected Lucien's spell. This spell didn't fail—Lucien's ray bounced off the green shield and struck Zelphira instead, transforming her in mid-air into a large reptilian monster. What began as a shriek morphed into a low growl.

Zelphira struck one of the roots and bounced off of it, her alligator-shaped head lolling on a short neck as she fell through several more layers of stone roots.

The seal piece of earth struck against the stones as well. Shards of emerald peeled off the gem as it fell, revealing the damaged seal piece beneath.

The croaking call from above said that Lucien had abandoned his hunt for Iellieth, pursuing the seal piece instead.

Iellieth winced as the enclosing gemstone struck against one of the stone roots, another chunk of its outer covering shattering. She braced herself as a gnarled root loomed ever nearer beneath her. She clutched her amulet in her palm, the one protection she could offer her friends.

The mottled gray surface would be the last thing she saw.

Iellieth's scream cut off as a huge, peridot-green paw scooped her out of the air and tugged her into a copper and emerald-hued chest of scales. She hadn't even realized she'd been screaming as she plunged toward her doom.

"The seal piece!" Iellieth shouted up toward the dragon.

The creature lifted and fell over a dozen feet between its wingbeats, making her stomach churn and causing her breath to hitch every few seconds.

For a moment, she thought the dragon wouldn't answer. They hovered there, between the sprawling stone roots of the tree-temple, an ever-widening expanse opening below them. The darkness swallowed Zelphira. Lucien had tucked his wings against his back, plummeting with his hands outstretched toward the shimmering seal piece just beyond his grasp.

Far below, at the base of the roiling chasm, a shiny mechanism flashed in and out of view as rocks struck upon its surface. A series of twisting circles set within one another spun inside a single great circle, like a flattened version of the movement of the planets she'd seen modeled in the Arcanium of Hadvar. The spinning silver circles exerted an intense pull all their own, drawing the temple's remains down and calling Iellieth too.

She'd thought at first that the enchantment holding the dragon was what had given way and caused the temple to collapse in on itself. But the waves of magic pouring off the silver discs—they not only held the temple together, they held the temple out of time.

The golden gaze hovering above her pulled Iellieth's attention away from the rings' gravity. *"What is most dear to you?"*

Her lower lip trembled, and tears prickled her eyes. "They're not separate. The choices are one and the same. I need the seal piece to save them."

"Hmmm," the dragon answered, *"but what if you already have?"*

"Lady!" Marcon's voice echoed out ever so faintly from above. The roots' cavern wasn't just growing deeper. It was growing wider too.

"We have to get them!" Iellieth exclaimed. "They'll fall!"

"Hold tight."

Her stomach flipped again as the creature beat her wings against the air and lifted them up and away from the network of stone roots.

Their progress was slow at first with the dragon picking her way between the large roots Iellieth had easily plunged past. She balanced on hands and knees atop the dragon's palm, peering between the digits of her talons out into the chaos of the disintegrating temple.

"Over there!" Iellieth called, pointing toward a dangling shape caught upon a large stone root midway between the forest's edge and the temple center where the stone dais remained. The rock had fallen off its center plinth, revealing the circles of life within the stone tree itself.

As the dragon angled her flight toward Marcon, Iellieth searched the falling stone for Quindythias and Daphne. Her throat seized as she spied a slow-moving shape a few hundred feet away. Quindythias clutched Daphne to his chest and was trying to get her to safety.

By his proximity to the tree, Marcon must have kept pursuing her rather than turning back when the temple began to collapse.

The stillness from Lucien's trial atop the jagged rock returned. "Leave me with him, and I'll get us to safety," Iellieth called to the dragon. "Quindythias will need your help."

The dragon bobbed in answer and redirected her flight, beelining for Marcon.

His eyes widened at first, and then a strained smile spread across his features as he spied Iellieth in the dragon's paw.

"Thank you," Iellieth shouted over the wind and the wing beats as the dragon slowed, gently depositing her a dozen or so feet from where Marcon dangled from the stone root, his leg a crystal weight beneath him.

"I will rescue your elven friend and the fuzzy one," the dragon thought to Iellieth.

She tried to spot Quindythias amid the rising dust from the earthquake and falling stone. The dragon would have to hurry. It would take them both to save the champions.

"Careful," Marcon yelled, reaching out toward her

reflexively as she balanced upon the center of the sprawling root.

Iellieth crouched low like they'd practiced, hurrying along the stone surface, her gaze not leaving the champion's.

"You fell," he said simply, his eyes shining. Marcon's runes stood out as glowing welts across his skin.

Iellieth knelt down beside him, trying to discern how best to pull him up to safety.

Below her Marcon sighed as the crystalline covering flaked off his leg and sloughed into the abyss beneath them.

"A dragon caught me."

Marcon grimaced as he pulled himself up, Iellieth holding one of his arms to steady him as he swung up onto the root beside her. "You have a knack for making allies."

An understatement, especially as the dragon had orchestrated their arrival in the glade by sending Zelphira to find them for reasons Iellieth was still working out. "Were you following me?"

A screech from below prevented Marcon's answer.

Lucien pelted up toward the pair of them, emerging from the darkness below with the seal piece clutched in his talons. His putrid yellow gaze seared into hers the moment before he shot past, snatching Iellieth from the root in his talons, one of which impaled itself into her thigh.

"No!" Marcon shouted.

Iellieth screamed, writhing to free herself from his clutches a second time. The piercing talon was blinding white light and pain.

Bright like the woman she'd seen in her vision, when

she clutched the amulet she'd created, the one Iellieth now wore, and burst into light.

Lucien cawed his victory, twirling his hands before him in a sphere, the same motion she'd seen Yvayne use to conjure a portal between spaces.

If he pulled her away from Marcon and Quindythias now, they would turn into statues. She couldn't let that happen again.

Iellieth tightened her hold on the amulet. "Rowan," she murmured, searching for that inner sense of stillness, "help me." Red had said she was a Shepherd and a recurring soul. *Rowan Reborn*, Lucien called her. Whatever else that meant, it had to be that part of Rowan waited inside her.

She sensed another part of her soul's iteration within the amulet itself.

There, instead of the peace she'd thought would help her, she found a raging inferno.

A sea of elemental chaos spiraled within the amulet, with a pain greater than she was currently experiencing.

Multi-colored beams of light shone out around her fist. The emerald ray lit upon the seal piece of earth clutched in Lucien's talons.

The mottled flesh where he touched the piece was covered with burns. Her suspicions had been right before. There was too much life in Gaia's magic for one consumed by death.

Iellieth called to the earthen energy within her amulet and the green of the seal piece pelting through the air beside her. She twisted, reaching out for it, screaming as Lucien's talons sank deeper, but she was so close.

The seal piece answered, beams of light shooting out of its broken and reforged form.

A final vision flashed before her eyes—a red-haired

elven woman, huddled over a stone shape in a sprawling forest. The vision intensified. The shape was the snout of a dragon, its last breath curling out around the elf as the stone rippled over her scales, holding her in place. Solidifying her as the guardian of Gaia's Glade.

Lucien's squawk of pain yanked Iellieth from the vision of the dragon and the elven woman—the one the dragon must have been waiting to return.

The seal piece sizzled in his grasp.

Iellieth murmured the spell for green fire that she'd watched Mara cast in her final stand against the lich before the conclave fell. She carved her hand before her chest, crossing the inside of Lucien's thigh, the spiked protrusion hanging off his backward-facing ankle.

The verdant flames answered her, searing across feathers and singeing flesh.

Lucien cried out, agony scraping along his throat, and he released Iellieth from his grasp in the same moment he dropped the seal piece, sending her and the emerald plunging toward the abyss and the stone roots waiting below.

CHAPTER 50

PERSEPHONIE

"I understand why you're upset, I do," Dominic said two hours later after Persephonie had recounted the events from the square. Irving had left shortly after their arrival to help with those wounded in the attack and to send a warning to Persephonie's family to ready themselves for a reprisal. "But I think you're being too hard on yourself. Acts of violence against New Orison's populace, the selective torching of wagons have happened before." Dominic wetted his lips, his brow darkening. Persephonie suspected he was thinking of the night he'd rescued Irving from the torching of his entire muster, as she was. "Maybe this time, it will galvanize the change we've been needing—"

"No," Persephonie cut him off before he could finish. "It's too dangerous for us to remain here. I know we promised to find a way to help everyone escape, but I have to take care of my family."

Dominic lowered his gaze and nodded. "I understand your sentiments and will not try to convince you further." The clench of his jaw told her how badly he wanted to.

Jezebel was not so lenient. "You are ignoring the larger picture."

"I am not. But I *am* finally conscious of what my responsibility is and what it is not." She turned to Dominic—he had mentioned a door, one unguarded by the priests that could be used as a last resort. "This door you spoke of that leads out beyond the dome, is it large enough to allow a wagon through?" It would be a challenge for her family to travel across the whole of New Orison without interference from the priests. They kept careful watch over the main gate, but Dominic knew of a secret exit.

"Only just large enough to crawl through most times we've managed to find it, and I doubt there's a way to widen it further."

Persephonie scowled, trying to come up with a solution that would save her family from her own recklessness. Rennear wrapped his hand around hers and squeezed. A small comfort, but it was something.

Silence hung for a minute, disrupted by Jezebel. "They're weakened. Now is the time to strike."

"You saw what happened out there," she shouted at the fae. "Obviously I can't do this."

"If that's your conclusion from this morning's events then you didn't see what I saw."

"In what other way could I understand what happened?" Persephonie shot back. "A woman is dead, simply because she wanted me to read her fortune. And she'll never . . . I . . ." Persephonie exhaled and slumped back. It was no use arguing with the fae. In their centuries of service to Apollo, Jezebel had seen more death and suffering than she could imagine, and the two of them would never agree about the sort of sacrifices that were necessary and those that were not in heightened situations.

"We were outnumbered, Persephonie, and still we prevailed. What is more, we learned of their magic and tactics." The fae sighed. They leaned their elbows onto their knees, staring between her and Dominic. "If you want to see change at this scale, if you truly want to save your people, there is going to be a great deal more loss of life than a bystander and a guard." They shook their head. "The priests have been preparing. They have soldiers, a center of power, that fissure in the ground, whatever it is. You'll have a war."

Persephonie squeezed her eyes closed, trying to shut out Jezebel's words with the darkness. Memories of the priest's magic flashed through her mind, her imagination replacing the people of New Orison with her family members. She saw Felix struck down by one of the black bolts, a burn across his thigh that wouldn't heal. Velkan, blood leaking from his temple, felled in his efforts to save her. Her datha crying out in pain, soot-streaked face raised to the sky, holding a limp Stefan in his arms. Persephonie whimpered, tucking herself into a ball.

Between the nature of her goddess and the nature of her gift, she didn't know if what she'd seen was a premonition, a warning from Cassandra of what was to come, or if her guilt over what had happened to the woman, to those simply passing through the market, was getting the better of her. Datha and Babu would know how to help her sort through it, but returning to her muster posed a grave risk to all those who trusted her. Staying away might invite greater danger still.

As before, Rennear anticipated the trajectory of her thoughts. "The most immediate concern before us needs to be the care of your family, Persephonie. Our apologies to the Feather"—he inclined his head to Dominic—"but we cannot help in this larger conflict without taking into consideration the risk of further violence meted out specifically against her muster." His lips curled around his slowly lengthening fangs. "In short, we need to find out what the priests are planning and act to disrupt their next schemes."

Rennear ran his hand through the strands of hair that had fallen free of his topknot, brushing them back out of the way. He faced Persephonie, ignoring the others. "I don't wish to upset you, far from it, but Jezebel is right. We cannot hide in the shadows—the priests have been interested in you from your arrival. We need to find out why."

Persephonie squeezed the bridge of her nose. Nothing she was trying would help. There wasn't a way to block out the truth of her friends' words, no way to undo what had already been done. "Then perhaps we take the fight to them, now." The surprise on everyone's face told her she was on the right path. "They will not be expecting it. Before the party, before the full moon tonight, we act. They will think we are in hiding. That would be the sensible thing to do, to find a place in the woods to disappear and hope they do not harm my family."

She pressed upon the ache in her stomach, the churning pit of fear that had not abated since she'd found her family on the road to New Orison. Persephonie had always loved that, for better or worse, they stuck together. But the danger in this promised to be so great, there seemed little chance Datha, her brothers, Velkan, Babu, her muster would emerge unscathed.

Jezebel was the first to speak. "Then where are you suggesting we go?"

"Back to the temple. We do not wait for nightfall. We sneak in now."

⚜

TAKING THE INITIAL STEPS TO SNEAK INTO THE TEMPLE was less challenging than Persephonie had believed it would be. Dominic had already been preparing for such an eventuality after Novik had uncovered the priests' habit of meeting the night of the full moon. The leader of the Feather had been storing up a collection of dark robes for the purpose. The robes wouldn't stand up to close inspection—they were without the extinguished candle imagery—but they would allow Persephonie, Jezebel, and Rennear to blend into the number of acolytes who tended the temple. Dominic would stay behind in case something happened. Mercifully, he didn't outline what that 'something' might be. More frightening still, Persephonie tried not to admit to herself, was that none of them knew what might transpire if they fell into the priests' clutches.

They spent the latter hours of the afternoon with Dominic, going over the basic layout of the temple. The Feather's agents had made it into all but the innermost parts of the temple, and he sketched out a map for them of the grounds and inner chambers.

Though Persephonie would have preferred waiting until they were further from the windmill to don their disguises, they couldn't risk someone recognizing them and alerting the priests to their presence. Irving hadn't returned or sent news from the healers, which Dominic assured them was a good sign even though his tone didn't match his words.

The more immediate problem was that the New Orison priests were exclusively male.

Rennear smirked at Persephonie as she donned the robe, which pooled at her feet. "*I* wouldn't mistake you, but the priests are less accustomed to breathtaking company than I am." His grin widened as his gaze swept from her head to toe, and Persephonie's pulse quickened. "Less appreciative too, I should think—"

"Alright." Jezebel stepped between them, blocking Rennear's attempt at sweeping her up into an embrace. "There will be time for that after, so long as we're successful."

Rennear winked at her and donned his own robe. Jezebel had to slouch to disguise the bony tops of their wings and found a makeshift cane to make the hunch in their back more believable. The robes seemed little better equipped to hide Rennear and Jezebel's warrior's physiques than her feminine one, but so long as they remained at a distance from others, the disguises should work.

Departing from the windmill and taking side streets through town, the going unnoticed part of the plan fell apart almost immediately as an elderly woman hobbled toward them, asking for their blessing. Neither Jezebel nor Rennear were fluent enough in Saudad to avoid suspicion if they spoke. Persephonie lowered her voice like she had when she was a child, imitating her older brother. "Erm, we have an urgent matter to take care of . . . Please see a front temple attendant . . ."

She'd pressed on Jezebel and Rennear's elbows, urging them forward and away from the supplicant.

The next block over, Jezebel paused to snicker behind

a building. "Temple assistant—you make it sound like a shop."

Persephonie pushed the fae out of the building's shadows and back onto the street. "I said attendant," she protested. Perhaps assistant would have sounded better. She flapped the too-long sleeves of her robe at Jezebel, trying not to trip on the hem. "What am I supposed to call them? Doesn't Apollo have temple attendants?"

"He has a skulk of vulpine which have never failed in their varying duties, so I'm not sure how to answer you."

Of course Apollo had foxlike spirit servants, but that would not help them now. "Ugh." Persephonie rustled her sleeves, trying to free her hands and then abandoning the effort. "Well, unfortunately I do not think the priests here are so lucky or we wouldn't find ourselves on opposing sides."

"True enough," the fae agreed.

They snuck around the back side of the temple, skirting as far around the fissure as possible without stepping out of place from the paths the priests usually tread. Persephonie held onto Rennear's arm as they passed the fissure, risking their ruse. It called to her still, beckoning her nearer, within. She shut her eyes and let Rennear guide her away, not daring to open them again until the bright scent of mint filled her nostrils.

There were gardens on the rear side of the temple with a few gravestones behind. Cascading vines of mint had overtaken one of the beds, draping over the wooden side and snaking their way onto the garden path. Should other means of escape elude them, perhaps she could enchant the mint as a trap to slow pursuers.

The wooden gate creaked as Jezebel opened it for the three of them. Gravel crunched beneath their feet. Persephonie released Rennear's arm to hold onto her robe instead. Now that the path was flat rather than hilly, she'd have to take more care not to trip on the ends that dragged the ground.

As Dominic had indicated, there was a door on the rear side of the temple that had been left cracked. The three of them filed inside and stole down the left-hand corridor, which would lead them deeper into the temple and away from the public spaces.

Persephonie whispered a prayer to Cassandra as they wound through the arched stone hallways. The square floor tiles had been formed from polished clay and the walls were the color of sand, the mortar and stone blending together along well-lit paths. She tugged her hood further over her face at the sounds of approaching footsteps from the hallway adjacent to theirs. It was this part of the temple that Dominic had been less certain of—no member of the Feather had made it further into the lower floor other than to know there were several sets of stairs that led below and that this was where the priests performed their more secretive work.

Instinctively, the three of them tucked themselves against the side of the hallway as the voices neared. There were at least two speakers, talking together in hushed tones. They shuffled through a thick wooden doorway and failed to fully shut the rounded door behind them.

She let out a breath as the priests wound down the stairwell—their voices echoed up to where the three of them hid.

As the voices faded, Persephonie nodded for Jezebel to follow. She and Rennear crept after them. The winding stair led deeper and deeper into the temple, further than Dominic had indicated should be possible. A few hundred feet down, the stairwell split. The main stairwell opened onto a balcony of arched openings that overlooked a lower chamber with a large wooden table. Chairs lined each side of the table, with a single chair at the end. She knew even before she counted—six chairs along each side, with a thirteenth at the head.

They didn't have much time to decide which direction to go—another set of footsteps sounded on the stairs behind them. The three hurried across the balcony. Persephonie could only hope that no guards lay in wait, hidden by the arches. The voices of the gathering priests echoed up from below.

Jezebel gestured them further along the balcony so they could see the room in its entirety around the lower staircase and avoid being spotted by the priest descending behind them.

Rennear slipped behind one of the arches just in time. The priest behind them had a heavy step. It echoed along the balcony. Persephonie shrank in her crouch, hoping he wouldn't spot them.

"Ah, Ludvic," a low baritone called out a few moments later from below. "Was the way clear?"

"None have gathered here who should not be here," the priest named Ludvic answered.

Persephonie risked peering over the brick edge of the balcony railing to take in the room beneath them and immediately regretted it.

She tugged herself back, eyes wide, and met Jezebel and Rennear's questioning stares. A pounding headache had worsened as they descended. She now knew why. Persephonie shut her eyes and nodded to the two of them to look. Even in the darkness, she couldn't stop herself from seeing what was below.

There were indeed thirteen places around the long wooden table. But at the opposite end, nearest the stairs, instead of a chair there was a stretcher, raised up at an angle. And strapped to it, with bindings against his wrists, ankles, knees, chest, and throat, was the priest they'd encountered that morning in the market square. His eyes were shut, and the barest ripples of movement flickered over his chest. He had survived, and they'd brought him here.

Beyond the priest was the cause of her headache. A throb that pulsed behind her eyes. Opposite the opening of the second, smaller flight of winding stairs, the chamber wall had been carved away. The wall itself looked like the largest geode she had ever beheld, revealing facets of sparkling amethyst or another deep purple gem.

A hole had been carved into the floor around the geode. How they had accomplished such a smooth cutting away, Persephonie couldn't say. But one thing was clear— this was the fissure from above. A distant pale blue light shone down from above the geode, mixing with the fire- light from the torches that flickered across the stone's surface.

The hole continued downward, opening onto black depths from which no light emerged.

This was where the priests had built their inner sanctum.

Sounds of shuffling and the groan of wooden chairs echoed up from the chamber as the priests gathered around the table.

Very little of their conversation at the beginning of the meeting made sense to her, but a few minutes in, they came to the matter at hand.

"We won't be enough in and of ourselves, my brothers,"

one of them said. "But the girl—she could revive the wheel."

Persephonie gripped Rennear's wrist and dared a glance over the side of the balcony.

Several of the priests nodded in agreement. They fell silent as the eldest among them stood and raised his hands, capturing their attention from the head of the table, opposite the deep pull of the fissure. "We all know what it will truly take. Each of you have known from the moment of taking your vows. It is the truth foundational to our order, what has been present since the destruction of our first home, the suffering that has brought this place into being. Malura made the path clear to us, her faithful. For generations, we have brought the people of Cassandra here. With the girl's muster and her magic, we are enough, finally. The sacrifice will be all the sweeter offering those who give their worship to the false goddess, she who would lead us astray. You well know what these next steps will take. If any of you are without the forbearance to see our sacred task through, speak now."

Only half the faces were visible and upon them, Persephonie found fear. Resolve. What she looked for was missing—doubt.

A shallow breath whispered up from the injured priest, a wet, clicking sound layered over the low thrum of the fissure.

"Good. With our brother's death, we strike the first chime. With the thirteenth, the people of Cassandra will be no more, and the goddess herself will perish. As they breathe their last, we shall see Malura come into her power, taking the wheel, newly regenerated, for herself."

With their brother's death . . .

The priests showed their accord by banging their fists

onto the wooden table, the explosion of sound startling against the relative calm that had pervaded the chamber before.

The broad-shouldered man paced around his brethren, causing Persephonie to duck beneath the balcony again, only daring to peek out once the pounding reached a roar.

He stood tall behind the injured priest, whose eyes roved wildly from behind closed lids. Beads of sweat dotted the man's brow. Persephonie clamped her hand over her mouth, her stomach a mess of knots. She didn't want to see what came next but knew better than to look away.

'Be brave enough to look upon that which you face, daughter,' her datha had told her from her early childhood. His instruction had saved her from the werewolf attack, had helped her to find her way through hostile cities. And it would guide her now through this new horror among her own people.

The elder priest withdrew a thin dagger from the belt at his waist and raised it high overhead. As the priests around them rose to their feet, adding their voices to the pounding drum of their hands, he dragged the priest's stretcher over to the side of the fissure, which seemed somehow darker than it had before, as though the entire room had been pulled into shadow and the gravity of the fissure had been enhanced.

Even from the balcony it tugged at Persephonie, running invisible fingers through her hair, pulling against the set of her shoulders.

The priest lowered the dagger and sliced the bonds that held the injured priest to the raised stretcher and, in a single motion, he slit the man's throat and dumped the body into the pit in the center of the chamber.

Persephonie pulled back from the balcony and clapped her hand over her mouth in the same moment that Rennear reached for her, his hand wrapping around hers to stifle her gasp. Any relief she'd felt at not being the one to have murdered the priest had utterly faded.

The priests fell silent with the final slice, and the *thump* of the body's entry into the cavern echoed through the chamber. With the low, heavy sound of its fall, the earth rumbled, receiving the priests' first horrific offering. The fires upon their torches flickered, fading. The flames transformed—black with flashes of green, the same shades as the sacrificed priest's bolts and their guards' poison.

They shouted again, likely at a signal from their elder.

Persephonie held her shoulders tight, dreading the moment of hearing the next body strike the cavern floor, but no such sound came. She stared back at Rennear and Jezebel, the three of them still hidden from sight by the shadows of the balcony arches. But they would only remain hidden for so long. They needed to escape.

The rumbling intensified, sending Persephonie crashing onto Rennear, where he knelt to support her. Several of the priests lost their footing and all seemed caught off-guard save the elder who held his dripping dagger overhead still, allowing the blood to fall drop by drop down into the hole.

The elder priest lowered the dagger and spoke again, his voice an octave lower this time, almost a chant that rose above the distant rumble from within and below the walls. "From the moment she arrived, we knew the girl was a necessary evil, but our brother's sacrifice will not have been in vain. No, far from it. My brothers," the priest cried, "our first offering is made. Find the girl and her father. We shall need them before our summoning is complete."

Datha. They threatened her datha. If Rennear hadn't already been covering her mouth, she would have given them away.

Before she could protest, Rennear and Jezebel dragged her away toward the stairs, through the tunnels, and back the way they'd come.

As they burst out into the twilight of the back gardens, Persephonie panted, her mind reeling. "Did you see—"

"Yes," both Jezebel and Rennear answered.

"And my datha—"

"We will protect your father," Jezebel promised, sliding forward. They cupped her hand in theirs. "I promise."

They hid behind a tree and slid out of their robes, stealing along the river's edge until they reached the town borders. From there, they headed back through the fields and toward her muster.

"Do you think Rowan knew?" Rennear asked as they hurried through the evening's shadows, retracing the steps they'd taken that morning.

Persephonie could hardly think. *They want my datha. They want me. And they'll use us to kill all of our people. In Malura's name.*

There was kindness behind Rennear's questions, something to divert the direction of her thoughts, help her feel like it was possible for them to avoid this catastrophe. "I don't see how she could have . . ."

The truth came with her next rapid breath, sinking into her chest as surely as that third tarot card's promise for New Orison, for the saudad. "But Cassandra knew. That's why she sent us here. To stop them."

The priests' plan was even worse than she'd feared. The

final offering was not to be only her or even her and her datha—it was her people. All of them. And with them, Cassandra herself.

Since she had met them, Jezebel had hinted at her being special to the goddess Cassandra and therefore to Apollo as well, almost teasing her with a suggestion that she could one day be Cassandra's chosen. The weight of that implication settled over her shoulders now. She didn't need the title or the recognition. But she would see her people saved from this.

It wouldn't be Cassandra's reign that came to an end with the fall of New Orison. Far from it.

Behind them, Rennear groaned. His arms tugged to the side at an unnatural angle as though he was being restrained. His back arched and mouth widened. The golden brown eyes she loved stretched wide. "It's not. Possible," he groaned. With a roar, Rennear reared back, fur bristling along his neck.

"Go," he urged, his gaze rising to the full moon overhead.

"But you're not cursed!" Persephonie cried.

She turned her gaze up toward the moon, her eyes widening. In a land meant to break the curse of the saudad, did other broken curses re-form? They hadn't planned around the full moon because it didn't spark Rennear's transformations, or it hadn't before. Blazing through the deep blue of the bubble above them, the two moons hung in the sky. The lesser moon shone down weakly, very near full. Beyond it, shining through the heavy clouds was the greater moon. Selene. Ruler of the werewolves. Shining at full strength.

Whatever else the priests had done with their sacrifice, they had weakened the protections set around New

Orison, lessened the shield from the dome. "Go!" Rennear urged again.

Jezebel tugged at Persephonie's waist, and the two sprinted past Novik's cabin and toward the muster. They had to warn everyone and hope Rennear could make it to the woods. The last time he'd transformed against his will, he'd nearly attacked Persephonie and her mother. They couldn't risk him bursting into the muster in an unstable state. She once again held his needles in the pocket of her skirt—it was too dangerous for her to tell if the silver would change him back. Or—the true implication rattled in her chest—he might be vulnerable to silver now, a second broken boon.

A consequence very like one devised by the goddess of misfortune.

She and Jezebel made it back to the muster. The werewolf's cry rent the still air of the night, echoing out from within the trees.

Persephonie slid to a halt outside Datha's wagon and rapped her knuckles against the door, a crackle of nerves and wood upon the night air. Jezebel's panting behind her played harmony to the pounding of her heartbeat. At any moment the priests might launch their attack against her muster, her *family*, just as at any moment, Rennear might lose control of himself as a werewolf, like that day in the market in Andel-ce Hevra, only now—

Datha swung open the arched wooden door, a tunic slung over his head and one shoulder. "What is—Sephie?" His eyes widened as he looked between her and Jezebel. "Are you hurt?" He leapt out of the back of the wagon and grasped her shoulders, searching her for a sign of what was the matter before she'd had a chance to answer.

Behind Datha, Felix poked his head out of the wagon.

"They're coming." Her breath still came too quickly, too loudly, in the silence that followed. Persephonie shook her head, shutting out what she'd seen and focusing only on what was immediately before them. "The priests. They mean to sacrifice us to Malura."

Velkan slid out of the wagon behind Felix and jumped down. Moonlight cast shadows over the contours of his bare chest. "Whatever you need, we'll do it." He was always quick of wit and foot in a crisis.

Datha clapped his hand against Velkan's shoulder, just as he would have done to one of his own sons. "Aye." He leveled his gaze with hers.

"I-I don't think we can leave, not in time anyway." Despite the growing knot of panic in her throat, her focus still darted away from her, following after Rennear's retreat into the woods.

"So we fight them," Felix answered. "How?" He jumped down from the back of the wagon as well and straightened beside his friend.

Between the muster and the village center, a lantern flared to life in the apothecary's cottage, though it had been dark when the three of them passed before.

You are not alone. The sentiment reverberated across Persephonie's chest.

Cassandra?

The reverberation stilled, its warmth seeping through her, settling in the center of her body. She would take that as answer enough.

"We need the apothecary's help," Persephonie told them, pointing toward the bobbing glow of the lantern, a floating speck against the black hillsides of New Orison.

"We'll go," Velkan promised, nodding to Felix and launching into action before Persephonie had time to think through her plan or its implications for those dearest to her. The pair of them yanked on tunics and boots and sprinted down the hill, their shadows blending into the cresting waves of the tall grasses.

"And what of your datha, Sephie?" His low, soothing voice called her back to what she could influence, to those she could help and protect. Velkan and Felix knew how to take care of themselves. Usually.

Datha towered over her, steady and solid when all she loved lay under threat.

Persephonie threw her arms around Datha's waist and squeezed herself tight against him. She'd start with the question he hadn't yet asked. "Something about the magic here, it changed Rennear." She met Datha's gaze, a furrow caught between his brows.

"He transformed when he didn't want to. And he ran away before we could find out if he was safe. I-I mean, if he was himself." She'd been careful not to tell Datha how dire things had seemed in the marketplace. Her father was a forgiving, reasonable man, but she doubted that would extend to werewolf-Rennear endangering both Persephonie and Esmeralda even though he'd saved them both too.

Datha took an unsteady breath and stared out after Felix and Velkan. A second lantern shone from just outside the apothecary's cottage. It began to make its slow, meandering way up the hill.

"I'll rouse Stefan and the others," Jezebel announced, the first they'd spoken since they'd made it back to camp.

Down in New Orison, a glowing torch appeared. Two more quickly followed.

Persephonie held in a breath, clutching onto Datha's tunic. *Please let that be all.*

Several more torches, tiny motes in the distance, joined the first three.

Datha murmured a curse under his breath watching the column of flame set out from town. Twin rows of six torches led by one held high—the thirteen flames of Malura. "You were right to warn me, Sephie. Now, take Babu and the elders and hide them in—"

A chilling howl erupted out of the forest, piercing the night with its lone, warbling cry.

Rennear.

Shouts of dismay answered the call across the muster.

"—the woods," Datha added with a sigh, his plan an immediate impossibility. "That is not going to work, is it?"

"It most certainly is not."

Datha jumped at his mother's voice appearing so close behind him. "Mama, I—"

"The signs spoke of the conflict to come." Babu's gaze settled, steady as thunder on Persephonie. "The cost may be substantial. Are you prepared to pay it?"

A second wolf howl sounded beyond the camp with a bugle call of alarm from the border near the forest. The scouts must have spotted Rennear. She had only moments to decide who she would help first.

Persephonie searched the fields for Felix and Velkan, their path leading them nearer to the coming mob rather than away. The apothecary's progress up the hill was unerringly slow—they would need to help her along.

Jezebel's voice rang out, sounding the alarm across the camp, rousing those who could fight.

Rennear's third howl rent the night. The sound tugged against her heart, like he was calling to her.

Babu was watching Persephonie and her son in a way that made Persephonie's stomach churn.

"What cost, Babu?" She tightened her grip on Datha's tunic.

The old woman shook her head. "The one Cassandra demands of you. Whatever it may be."

If she meant Datha, Rennear, her brothers, Velkan, Jezebel—Juliet darted into view and into Persephonie's arms.

Despite the danger marching toward them, Babu smiled at the shivering creature, a curious gleam settling over her eyes. "Costs are not always what they seem," she added.

Persephonie turned to Datha. "I have to help him." The hollows between Rennear's howls were a lead weight in her chest. She couldn't prevent Malura's mob winding their way up the hill, but she could ensure a safe retreat for the elders and the children.

"Go, Sephie," Datha said. He clutched her to his chest one last time before releasing her. "May Cassandra light your steps."

It was the blessing Circe had taught her people after being named the Chosen of Cassandra.

"And may she guide your sight, Datha," Persephonie answered. She set her own sights upon the edge of the forest where a werewolf awaited her.

They mean to kill us. All of us. The words churned over and over in her mind.

There was a precedent for such an attack, one she and all her people knew well. It was the destruction of Orison, during which her people were sacrificed in such numbers, it defied imagining. Thereafter, the saudad had wandered, tossed across the threads of fate. And now . . . Such a sacrifice would forever change the threads, leaving the goddess of misfortune powerful enough to seize the threads of fate for herself.

This was bigger than the wheel which, given the quake and how near it sounded, she was more certain than ever lay at the bottom of the crater. This was about the future, the survival, of the saudad.

A future she would not leave to the priests to write. Jezebel's warning from that afternoon returned to her. The priests of New Orison wanted war. And now they would get it.

She tucked her shawl over her shoulder and darted past the guards on watch.

Rennear's howl sounded, near at hand. He would be able to smell her, to sense her presence.

In the valley below, the torches swayed nearer. She could almost taste the foul smoke of their incense upon the air.

"We will not be the ones to pay the sacrifice," Persephonie promised herself, shutting out Babu's warning. The priests were the ones who had forsaken Cassandra. They would have to be the ones to pay.

CHAPTER 51

BRISERAS

After the shallow rays of the sun had crested over the sky, the cabin Lord Draego had promised beckoned to Briseras out of the fog. Smoke curled out of the stone chimney and dispersed into the scraggly growth of the trees overhead in much the same way as her mother's fire had marked a small place of respite amidst the horrors of Haven.

Light glowed from beneath the rounded wooden door and through mottled panes of glass. Who would keep such a cabin, so far from any of Steymhorod's towns or villages? There wasn't a stable or even a lean-to nearby, nor did she see a garden.

Vera nudged Briseras's leg as she turned back yet again over her shoulder, pushing her back on course toward the cabin. Lord Draego had not balked in the face of the storm creature, yet how would he defeat something so massive and powerful?

Briseras shook her head and returned her attention to Vera beside her. From early in her training, she had learned in situations of heightened stress to focus her immediate attention on what she could influence and control. Her wolf's limp had grown worse in the last few hundred yards, but she could only tend to Vera once they had reached the cabin. "We're nearly there," Briseras murmured, as much to encourage the wolf as herself.

She tightened her hold on the dark gray cloak lined with pale blue silk Lord Draego had wrapped around her shoulders. Her stomach fluttered again at the feel of his finger against her cheek. The forest swallowed the solid *thwap* of her knock—no answer.

After a quick glance down at Vera, she pushed aside the cabin door and raised her hands into fists, preparing to defend herself and her wolf. The cabin door swung open easily, revealing a clean, inviting interior. The stone fireplace glowed against the back wall with a row of cabinets to the left and a wooden-framed bed on the right. Rugs and animal skins warmed the floor, and a velvet sofa rested between her and the hearth. It was similar to the one she'd seen in her dream of Draego's castle—her face warmed— where he'd kissed her, though plush blankets decorated the arms and back of this one.

Beyond her worry for the vampire lord, her body longed for her to rest. She limped from one edge of the cabin to the other, trying to deduce from the empty cabinets and happily roaring fire whose cabin she'd entered, barefoot, and wearing nothing but a cloak.

The most intriguing of the implements inside the cabin was the indoor water spout, a luxury she had heard was part of life in Andel-ce Hevra but which the hunters had never had the time to implement into the collective's lodges.

With little option but to wait—her legs giving out beneath her—Briseras sank onto the sofa.

A few hours or minutes later—she knew not how long—she shot to her feet as the whinny of a horse broke through the stillness of the forest outside. Briseras rushed out into the twilight as fast as her blistered feet and other injuries would allow her.

Lord Draego swung himself down from his enormous horse, his dark gaze never leaving her. She hobble-ran toward him. The corner of his mouth twitched up before he caught her in his arms.

Briseras wrapped her legs around his waist and kissed him before he could say anything. The vampire held her firmly against him, one hand on the small of her back, the other caught against her neck and hair.

He moved his hand to her jaw, pulling himself away slightly to study her face rather than deepening their kiss. "You were worried about me?" The way he asked the question said that he already knew the answer. His smirk returned as he gazed back at her, carrying her into the cabin.

"Yes. That thing—"

Lord Draego shook his head. "They are creatures of the night and of shadows. For one such as you"—he closed his eyes as he rubbed his nose and lips against the column of her neck—"they have their dangers. But they pose little threat to a creature like me."

Any urge to defend herself melted away as he began placing soft kisses against the base of her throat.

Briseras wanted to lose herself in this moment, in his hold. Vera had already returned to the bearskin before the fireplace and laid her head on crossed paws. But she had so many questions. "Is this real?" she whispered.

The vampire stopped his peppering of kisses but kept his face against her skin. "What do you think, Briseras?"

She shivered at the way he said her name, both the extra syllables gifted by his accent and the care with which he pronounced it—care with a hint of . . . possession?

He walked her over to the sofa, sitting down on the edge with her facing him, balanced on his lap.

"It *feels* very real to me." She tore her gaze away from him for a moment and surveyed the cabin around them. Everything here seemed in perfect order—but that was part of what was bothering her. She chewed on her bottom lip and returned her attention to the vampire who had caught the huntress in his snare. "But it also seems too good to be true."

A frown flickered between Draego's brows. "Tell me what you mean."

He traced his fingertip along her hairline as he awaited her response, making it difficult for her to obscure her true thoughts. Eventually she shook her head. "Why would you be here with me?" It all came down to that question in the end. All the possibilities available to a vampire lord, and here he was, in a well-kept yet abandoned cabin in the wilds of his lands, alone with her.

His expression hovered between a question and the smirk she was already becoming transfixed by. "You needed me. And there is nowhere else in all Steymhorod I would rather be than by your side."

His reply did and didn't answer her question. "You've been appearing to me, in my dreams. Is that real?" She forced a slow breath through her nostrils, hoping she hadn't invented those nights, those intimacies.

"It is real to me."

Mostly satisfactory. "What was that thing made of shadows and storm?"

Draego shook his head. "Come, my love. Let us not

waste this first night when we are truly together." He sat up taller and brought his lips to hers. His fingers tangled in the short curls at the back of her neck, and Briseras closed her eyes. She rolled her hips against him, and the vampire's hold tightened, tugging her pelvis flush with his.

A second roll of her hips and Briseras moaned. The way he'd touched her in her dreams had been intoxicating. But this—she wanted so much more.

The vampire lord waited until her breath had quickened, her heart pounded, before easing his lips away. He held the side of her face, holding her gaze. "It is my hope that we have many more such nights to come, but I know as well the wisdom of life—take not for granted the moments that matter. We are not always guaranteed as many as we would like."

And with that he rose and carried Briseras over to the bed. He laid her down gently on top of it, as though she were something precious to be treated with utmost care. "I cannot tell you how long I have been waiting for this moment. For you." He kissed her deeply, his hand tracing up her waist and ribcage. "Do not be in a hurry, Briseras. It is my plan for you to enjoy yourself." He raised an eyebrow and grinned.

◈

THE HEADY MUSK OF THE VAMPIRE'S COLOGNE FILLED Briseras's senses the next morning. For the few hours she had slept, Lord Draego had held her in the hollow of his shoulder. She parted her lips to greet him and then stopped. "I need you to let me call you by your first name."

Draego chuckled. "Good morning to you as well,

dearest one." He rolled over and kissed her, softly at first but quickly building.

She struggled against his distraction but abandoned her efforts. A huntress takes her time. The evening before, his focus had been on pleasuring her. With the dawn, Briseras decided it was her turn.

Straddling his hips, she leaned down and murmured in his ear, "Tell me I can."

The vampire groaned, shaking his head. "I would hope you might be otherwise occupied."

Briseras pressed her lips into the hollow of his throat and reached around behind her hips to show how else she might occupy herself. The groan of frustration morphed into one of bridled desire, and Briseras knew she was close.

Challenge sparked in the vampire's eye, and he flipped her onto her back, his thumb massaging slow circles between her legs as he returned her carefully paced ministrations. "I am relatively certain I showed you last night that it is pointless to resist me." The dark green of his eyes glinted in the pale morning light.

Briseras writhed beneath him, biting her lip in her struggle against this one additional intimacy she insisted upon.

Sensing his nearness to victory, the vampire relented. His lips brushed the edge of her ear. "But I cannot resist you either. Call me Xander, if it will make you happy."

She made fair use of his name as the morning wore on, not parting from his side until the late morning. "You'll find me again soon?" Briseras said in parting.

"In both waking and in dreams," he answered.

She and Vera arrived within the wolves' territory at dusk. Draego had found a shirt and breeches for her within the recesses of the cabin, boots as well, and he'd encouraged her to keep the gray cloak. Its color shifted with the day, paler in the morning than it had been when he found her and growing darker as the afternoon lengthened. As she reached the mountain's foothills, it had turned a deep, gray-blue, the shade of summer twilights in Andel-ce Hevra.

A much brighter blue flashed in the forest before her and Vera. "She's here!" Lavinia cried, raising her voice as she crashed through the undergrowth, jogging to Briseras's side.

To her surprise, Lavinia caught her in a hug and held her close. "We've been so worried about you." She shook her head. "Jorgan told us what happened. He's been absolutely impossible."

Branches swished and shifted behind Lavinia, and Tybalt emerged. He sighed when he saw her. "Arduenne be praised, you weren't sacrificed to the Wolf Mother like we'd started to fear."

Briseras scowled at him. "I have made it clear from the beginning that I could take care of myself. So much doubt—"

"It's nothing you've done wrong save being exactly who you are." Tybalt grinned as he realized that she needed more to take his meaning. "This may come as a shock to you, but for many, preventing a painful, uncontrollable transformation lands higher on their list of priorities than attacking werewolf zombies and, well, devouring them."

She frowned and rubbed her stomach. "Don't remind me of that part."

The elf chuckled. "He's going to be angry he missed your return. I told him not to go far." Tybalt guided them back onto the trail to Wolf's Head Peak, and Lavinia fell into step beside Briseras, returning her mother's necklace and Xander's key. Briseras immediately refastened the two chains around her neck.

"Jorgan told us about the ambush and the undead werewolves. He expanded his scouting this morning despite Solane's warning. He insisted that Nassarq and Kratok were working together and that you and Vera couldn't be left out in the wilds on your own."

Briseras scratched between her wolf's ears. In addition to vomiting up zombie werewolf and her stomach still feeling over-full, she remembered feeling her wolf by her side, hunting together as though they were one, Vera's senses mingling with hers. She shut her eyes, trying to bring back more, gaining only flashes. Vera had tried to steer her away from danger, but Briseras had insisted on going north.

She stopped on the path and knelt before her wolf. "Thank you for staying with me no matter what." Briseras pressed her forehead to Vera's as she had done hundreds of times before. The connection was there still, running just below the surface. She smiled to herself—that wasn't actually different. From the moment they'd met, they belonged together.

She greeted the priestess upon her return and extracted herself from her companions' questions. It was true that she'd been alone all day and missing since two nights before, but even so, she needed more time to think over her night with the vampire lord. The lingering hum in her body told her that what she'd experienced was real, but at the same time, she couldn't help but partially doubt. Draego had never fully answered her question—why her? That he would track her through the wilderness and be aware of giant shadow monsters, she had no doubt of. He'd said she would understand the rest with time.

Jorgan found her as the sun was setting. He jogged along the open wolf's maw and placed his hands on his hips, shaking his head as he stared down at her. "I suppose you have a dramatically self-sufficient story to tell of your exploits?" Though his words were cross, worry creased his brow.

Briseras glanced up at him. The first stars were beginning to appear in the sky behind him while deep reds and oranges painted the opposite horizon. "I do."

The nobleman knelt beside her. He pushed back her hair, checking the sides of her face and neck, the scratched skin of her forearms. Draego had tended to the worst of her injuries with some sort of magical salve that had sped up the healing process, but Jorgan's inspection increased his worry nonetheless.

"Perhaps I wasn't quite so self-sufficient as you would expect."

"Is that so?" He shifted to sit beside her, tossing his feet over the edge of the wolf's jaw. "I'm sure they told you the same for themselves, but I was really worried about you Briseras."

She twisted her feet in a circle before answering, stretching her ankles first one way, then the other. "Why?"

Jorgan leaned forward to peer into her face. "Do you really not know?" He shook his head and settled back, leaning his weight onto his hands behind him. "What was it like, your transformation?"

She could tell him about meeting Draego, but such a revelation would only lead to more questions, and she wasn't ready to share about him, not yet. Briseras rubbed her stomach, her appetite still absent. "Hungry, apparently."

The nobleman threw his head back and laughed. His smile pulled her out of her swirling contemplations, and Briseras grinned.

"It isn't funny," she insisted, but that only made him laugh all the more. She shoved his shoulder to make her point, but his grin remained. "What was *your* transformation like, then? Did you, umm, eat anyone?"

Laughter sputtered in the back of his throat, but this time, Jorgan kept it at bay. "I did not." He described his heightened senses, a feeling of connection to his body and his surroundings that he'd never experienced before. "Maybe that's how you feel all the time already," he added, "but it was really special to me."

He rubbed the back of his neck, suddenly nervous.

Briseras hadn't noticed before, but the ghost was absent from his side. His conversation was focused, so it didn't seem as though the ghost was lodged inside his head either. "Is Teela still angry with you for wanting to be a werewolf?"

Jorgan sighed. "I asked her to keep to the peak while I was looking for you. I was worried and didn't need the distraction. I don't know if she was more upset about me remaining a werewolf, the danger we were in or, well, my insistence on finding you." He shook his head. "She'll come around. Truly, though, Briseras, I want to know. What was yours like? The wild version?" Jorgan's smirk lengthened.

She pressed her lips together. He'd be hurt, later, that she kept her encounter with Draego to herself. Draego had told her that the shadow creatures only transgressed the borders of Steymhorod and that, as lord of the land, he spent quite a bit of his time keeping them at bay. Even his strongest vampire knights struggled to stand against them.

"I don't want you to be frustrated with me, but aside from flashes, it's hard for me to remember. Lots of feeling. Instinct. Bloodlust, perhaps. Or simply no compunction about killing the creatures before me. But losing control like that . . ." Briseras shook her head. "What if I'd hurt you? Or come across an innocent and not realized?"

Jorgan thought for a moment and matched her low tone as he responded. "I think you would have recognized me as a member of your pack. I know it can be scary to think about what might have been or occurred, but the thing is, Briseras, you *didn't* attack me. It's entirely possible that in your frenzy, you protected me."

She smiled at that. Such generosity in her companions still caught her off guard. "Pack recognition is an interesting wrinkle to the transformations I wish I understood better."

"Now that we've done it, maybe Solane can tell us more." He described in greater detail his experience of the fight itself, the transition from wishing he'd kept the Spellbreaker on hand to extending his claws. "I could, well, *smell* you, at first. Despite the river and the blood. That's what kept me going, trying to find you. There were so many of them. And you were fast, almost as though something compelled you away." Jorgan repeated what Lavinia had told her, that in tracking the werewolves, he found tracks of two different packs merging. Their scents mingled those of Kratok and of Nassarq. They were working together.

Briseras swallowed, avoiding his gaze. "I made it to the northern border. It was like I was compelled. There was a shadow creature. Giant. Devouring the forest. Vera and I barely escaped." She gave him more details as he asked but left out the vampire. Lord Draego, she was keeping to herself.

Jorgan fetched berries and wine for the two of them, something light, he said. "Have you given any more thought to my proposition?" He leaned his shoulder against hers. "Do you want to remain a werewolf with me?"

She popped one of the dark berries into her mouth as she looked over at him. "I have thought about it."

He sipped his wine, eyeing her over the rim of the goblet. "And?"

"I'm really glad you've found something that makes you feel connected." She leaned closer, gazing up at her puzzling, newly turned werewolf companion. "For myself, I really like being who and how I am. I trust Vera's senses and instincts to supplement my own." The wine buzzed behind her eyes, and a heaviness seeped into her limbs. She hadn't fully realized just how tired the unaided transformation had made her.

Her shoulder pressed against his, and Jorgan stared down at her, that same frown caught between his brows. "But I am honored that you would want to remain a werewolf at least in part for me. Just so long as you're doing it mostly for you." She gave him a sleepy smile, and Jorgan's gaze intensified. "I was hoping to keep you around regardless."

He took a quick shallow breath. "You were?"

Briseras nodded into Jorgan's shoulder, resting her weight against him. He was warm and solid, and he smelled of damp forest with a hint of sharp spices, some mountain herb she couldn't place. "I am," she whispered.

His arm wrapped around her and tugged her closer.

"Well, good." His lips brushed her hairline, and Briseras closed her eyes. "Because I'm not going anywhere, Briseras. I'll be here, by your side, for as long as you'll have me."

They would need one another, she thought, in the days to come. Through Kratok's return, restoring the Mountain Fane and Arduenne, hunting down Nassarq, and the other adventures they couldn't yet see, hidden beyond the red horizon.

CHAPTER 52

IELLIETH

The wind whistled through Iellieth's hair as she fell, spinning over herself and twisting about as she tried to angle her body toward the seal piece. She hoped she might somehow tug its brilliant emerald light toward herself before it crashed into the abyss.

Screaming was part of falling now, but there was another call upon the air.

The roar of a dragon, swooping once more to her rescue.

And a warrior, silver and shining, balanced upon the dragon's back.

Marcon snatched her out of her freefall, one large hand clamped around her upper arm, the runes along his arm still bright.

His muscles strained, holding her up, her body dangling freely off the side of the dragon—just as it had within another stone chamber. Only this time, the fall wasn't up to her alone.

With a single heave, Marcon tugged her up and into his

chest, rolling them both backward onto the dragon's scaly hide. They slid, flying through the air. The scales tore at the gaps in her armor, but Marcon held her fast, catching the pair of them upon the dragon's scales, using his weight to pin her in place.

"You found me," Iellieth exhaled, tears springing to her eyes.

The champion nodded, tightening his hold around her waist.

Below them, the seal piece glittered as it fell, its light shimmering up to those trying to survive the collapsing temple.

"We can still get the seal piece," Iellieth exclaimed, pointing to the verdant light that grew fainter against the gray stone roots.

Marcon shook his head as a dark shape redoubled back toward them. The lich croaked, his yellow eyes flashing between Iellieth, Marcon, the dragon, and the seal piece's glow. He peeled away, shooting back toward the seal piece of earth. A trail of smoke followed in his wake.

"We can't let him take it," Iellieth insisted.

Marcon's jaw clenched.

Beyond him, from the center of the temple, the yip of a wolf pup called to her.

"Look at me." Marcon's grasp tightened around her.

She did as he asked.

Behind his eyes, determination swirled with pain. "Let it go."

"No!" Iellieth shouted back. Below them, midway between the dragon's wide flight and the base of the pit, Lucien's portal cracked into existence. The green of the seal piece winked as it fell into the swirling void, the lich shooting through just behind.

The champion pulled her head into his chest as the dragon flew them to the center of the fallen temple.

Marcon braced the two of them as the dragon landed heavily, one arm around Iellieth's shoulder and the other clasped against the back of her head. A hard breath burst through his lungs.

The dragon sighed heavily beneath them.

Beyond the tangle of stone roots, across the ancient forest, stillness returned to the trees.

Marcon's hold shifted around her waist. He ran his hand along the back of her hair.

The champion leaned back, staring down at her.

She didn't need him to tell her the conversation he'd had with the dragon, the deliberate choice he'd made about which to save—her or the seal piece. Without hesitation, he had chosen to be bonded as they were over the freedom he would have once the elemental planes were open again.

Iellieth sniffled and blinked her eyes clear. She had failed them both, and yet the way Marcon was looking at her—

"The seal piece fell," Iellieth whispered. "Lucien has it now."

He brushed a strand of hair out of her face and tucked it behind her ear. "Then we will find a way to make one, just as he will have to make five and repair the one he has." His hand was shaking. "You scared me."

"We should be scared. All of that power, the elemental planes . . . We failed, Marcon, we—"

"No." His tone was so certain, his voice resonating in her chest.

She still couldn't catch her breath. "But even if it's

damaged, Lucien has one of the pieces now. He can make a seal of his own."

"Perhaps," Marcon admitted. He curled his finger beneath her chin and angled her face toward his. "You must know by now—I could never lose you." The blue-gray shine of his eyes intensified, a shimmering crystal staring back at her. "Amulet or no amulet, I have sworn to stay by your side." He traced her cheekbone like he had the day they kissed on the ship. Dust and blood smeared beneath the pad of his thumb.

Marcon shook his head as he stared down at her. "You cannot ask me to choose saving a rock, however magical or important, over you."

Beneath them, the dragon sighed, lowering slowly from standing onto the stone dais.

The weight pressed again on her chest.

He leaned closer, holding her gaze. "I cannot lose you." He stopped with a hair's breadth between them. His voice softened further. "Surely you know by now, lady. I would never let you fall."

The elemental planes, the elven council, all of that could wait. Iellieth slid her hands across the hard plane of Marcon's chest. "I won't lose you either." She closed the space between them and pressed her lips to Marcon's.

The champion gave a startled breath, and Iellieth drew back. But Marcon's hold tightened around her once more and pulled her waist against his. His lips were soft at first but hardened in response to her. Their tongues touched.

She relaxed into his embrace, into the rhythm of his kiss. Iellieth wrapped her arms around Marcon's neck. She was a fevered ocean wave and he the shoreline. However close she came it did not feel close enough.

Marcon opened his mouth further. His chest rumbled as their kiss deepened.

She clasped the back of his head, his hair beneath her palms. Marcon's hand danced down the length of her waist, across her low back. Her hips rolled in answer and Marcon groaned.

He broke his lips from hers, his mouth journeying down her neck instead. The entirety of her awareness compressed to where their bodies met, her skin sparkling and alive beneath his kisses. "Lady," Marcon murmured beneath her jaw and against her collarbone.

"More," Iellieth breathed back.

Her champion caught the back of her hair in answer, supporting her head as his lips found hers once more. His hips pressed into her pelvis despite the restraints of their armor. "Lady, I—"

Footsteps thumped closer across grating stone, and Marcon groaned again, irritation rather than pleasure this time.

They both turned as Quindythias cleared his throat from beside the dragon.

"Well, I've been waiting for *that* for ages." The elf's shoulders raised as he sighed and looked about. "Your dragon friend found me in a most indecorous state, I must admit. Now that the two of you have it out of your system, perhaps we might get away from this ravaged temple?" He glanced at the sprawling ruins and shook his head. "Gaia must be so disappointed."

"She is and she is not, Champion of Air." The dragon's voice reverberated on the breeze around them, and Quindythias straightened.

The elf strode forward and reached up for Iellieth who was still dizzy from her kiss. The problem of how to descend from the back of a dragon hadn't yet occurred to her.

"It is best to slide, if you can," the dragon added helpfully. *"Side scales don't scrape like those along the crest. I would have prevented causing you further injury if I could."*

Between the three of them, they found a relatively dignified way to descend. Once Iellieth was settled onto the stone of the temple's tree stump—as she'd begun to think of it—Quindythias reached down, scooped up Daphne around her middle, and bent down again to set her upon Iellieth's lap. "Your wolf became dusty in the tussle. We should give her a bath before we return to what I hope will be a suite in Thyles Thamor as opposed to a ramshackle lodge."

The tip of Daphne's tail flicked back and forth as she looked up at Iellieth, panting happily.

Marcon stared down at the wolf pup. "This one is going to challenge my timing, I can tell." His gaze was warm as he met Iellieth's again.

Iellieth scooped Daphne into her chest and cradled the wolf close. Between Lucien's talons and the dragon's hide, more of her body was bruised and scraped than not. "I think you're up for it." She nodded her chin toward Quindythias. "You manage one with inordinately inconvenient timing already."

"I heard that!" Quindythias stamped. "Can we meet our rescuer and then get back to some semblance of civilization? After we, err, navigate the gap between here and the trees."

Twists of gray roots stretched between the central stump and the forest, with pools of darkness between that led into the abyss below.

"I think I received part of my answer for why you sent

Zelphira to find me," Iellieth thought to the dragon. *"The seal piece showed me. But would you, please, introduce yourself to my friends?"*

To this point the dragon had been inordinately still, in part, Iellieth thought, because she occupied most of the stone stump all by herself.

"I will, returned one."

The dragon swayed back and forth dramatically as she turned about, balancing along the edge of the stump, her tail dragging across the stone roots below.

Daphne wriggled herself into a seated position on Iellieth's lap, one paw upraised, as the dragon turned to face them.

The dragon's scales were a brilliant green, like spring foliage, with an iridescent shimmer like the deep jade of the sea. The dragon's eyes were a brilliant gold, the first sign of life from the creature she'd seen. Around her eyes, small, delicate scales caught against the low, afternoon light. These scales were dark green, the shade of pines in the snow.

The giant green creature tilted her head to the side, studying Iellieth in turn. "She always said she'd come back," the dragon sighed over her and her companions, the breath so powerful it blew back her clothes and hair. It was the first the dragon had spoken aloud, her voice reverberating through Iellieth's chest with the breeze. The dragon bowed her head to them, the long spikes along her scalp bobbling gently.

With that, the dragon rose and adjusted herself to take in her far smaller visitors. Iellieth stifled a gasp. Deep gashes covered the dragon's hide, and half of one of her front legs was missing. How had she failed to notice that when the dragon had held her against her chest? The dragon's uneven stride balanced between the three legs, and she settled onto her haunches on the stump. What sort of creature would be capable—

"Worry not about me, little druid. This occurred a long, long time ago."

Iellieth nodded. She had sensed something beyond the despair in the final vision. Perhaps it was a lingering pain from whatever attack had occurred that the dragon and her soul-predecessor had survived.

"I'm sure you have a great many questions," the dragon said. "It was I who spoke to you upon your arrival here. The task is mine to determine who is worthy to enter my glade."

Some of the pieces were falling into place, but others still eluded Iellieth. "How could you determine whether or not I was worthy?" Wouldn't someone who was worthy have succeeded in their task rather than letting the seal piece fall into the hands of their enemy?

"It was simple." The dragon hummed a sigh, in no hurry to explain herself. Iellieth winced as she shifted her leg, trying to relieve the throbbing ache from Lucien's talon. After seeing Zelphira turned into a giant reptile creature, which she doubted had been Lucien's intent for her, she had no desire to attempt a spell that wasn't absolutely necessary.

"However bleak outward circumstances may appear, the titans' will lives on in this plane. Through those like your friends." The dragon's bright gaze flashed over Marcon and Quindythias. "And in us, their children." At this, the tips of the dragon's wings spread away from her shoulders.

Iellieth held her breath, remembering how spectacularly wide those wings were.

"The titans' children take many forms. For my own hatching, the Lady Gaia intertwined her magic with the goddess Rasvana, the mother of dragons. Her blessing beats on in my chest." The dragon indicated the deep green scale nestled in the center of her chest. Its sheen was softer than her other scales—more like a gemstone than piercing armor. It was the same hue as the seal piece had been. The one she'd lost.

"As one who changes, I recognized another transformed when I sensed *you*. I would have known you anyway, so like the one who entrusted the piece to me in the first place. One whom I held quite dear." The dragon broke her gaze away as she spoke of the past, the change in her expression sending a wave of sadness rushing over Iellieth.

"You've been alone all this time?"

"Hmm." The sad chime of a smile rang within the dragon's voice. "I suppose one might see it that way. Such is the lot of the primordials, little one. But as I said, worry yourself not about me. I have many memories to keep me company. And thanks to you and your companions, the time of my enchantment has ended. A new phase in my story—and your own—must begin."

A breeze twirled through the distant trees and across the expanse, plucking at the loose strands of Iellieth's hair. The primordial lifted her chin and softened her eyelids, letting the breeze whisper through the soft spines along the ridges of her head. For the first time since they'd entered the glade, birdsong flitted through the trees beyond.

"You have restored us and our home," the dragon said, rising to her feet. "A long path stretches ahead, one marked by friend and foe." She bowed her head to Iellieth again, the spines cutting through the air. "May the remaining pieces find you, little one." In benediction, the dragon's eyes glinted in the same shade of green as Daphne's glowing irises and she unfurled her wings. "I will return you to the forest's edge," she said, lowering down on one side to grant them a way of climbing up.

Iellieth held Daphne against her chest as Marcon helped her to her feet. He supported her around the waist with Quindythias holding the wolf pup as they scrambled onto the dragon's back. "Hold fast, small ones," the dragon called back to them.

With a few steady beats of her wings, she leapt off the edge of the stone tree and flew back the way they'd come, the ancient forest spread like a starless green sky below.

Too short a time later, given all that had transpired, the dragon veered toward a gap in the trees small enough for her to land between. Iellieth grimaced, holding her leg as still as she was able while they settled onto the earth.

They disembarked, more gracefully this time than before. Iellieth scooped Daphne up and cradled the wolf against her chest. Unlike the centaurs, the primordial seemed to put Daphne perfectly at ease. The wolf sighed as she curled against Iellieth's chest, her pink tongue darting out as she yawned and closed her eyes. The wolf pup's belly was warm against her hand. "Will I see you again?" she shouted up to the dragon.

"Many and mysterious are the workings of fate, little one. But I shall hope so."

Iellieth smiled to herself at the dragon's parting wish. She would like that too. "Here we go, Daphne," she murmured over the wolf pup's sleeping form.

She wrapped her other arm around Marcon's waist to give extra support to her injured leg. Iellieth glanced over her shoulder before they departed the glade, a holdover from the world her friends had known. The dragon roared her farewell, the sound ricocheting through the dense forest and causing a shiver to rush down Iellieth's spine.

Her thoughts bounced between what the dragon had said outright and what the seal piece had shown her. Who was this third figure Iellieth had seen when returning the seal piece of darkness, the previous iteration of her soul who had befriended a dragon and entrusted the seal piece of earth to the dragon and Gaia's protection?

Iellieth sighed, lowering her head. The dragon had trusted her, as had her previous self. She had failed them all.

CHAPTER 53

GENEVIEVE

Genevieve had held back after her surprise arrival in the Shadowlands, skirting around the dark forest and following at a distance the team of horses that held captive Yvayne, Sariel, and Yvayne's friend with the green fox. It was a relief, in a way, not seeing her allies in pain, not being able to tell whether or not they were scared wherever it was they had been imprisoned within Lucien's fortress. She kept her lips parted as she ran so that Jade might better be able to scent the air.

The entire region smelled of fear—sour and salt—undercut by the crisp pine and sap of the trees.

The forest trailed wide around the mountainside the castle had been half carved into, half built upon. While her friends passed within the castle's gates in a matter of hours, it took Genevieve far longer. A second lavender dawn peeked over the far horizon by the time she'd reached the castle outskirts. She tucked herself away inside the forest, climbing into a tree. Better risk an encounter with shadow panthers or whatever sort of bear undoubtedly called this region home than with Lucien's scouts.

Jade was less enthused at the idea of other alpha predators, preferring only herself and others like her.

Exhaustion took hold of Genevieve, and they retreated from their position near the castle, climbing into another tree. She and Jade woke to a richly purple sky overhead. The forest had faded from silhouettes to shades of teal and deep blue, though the bark was darker than any trees she'd seen in Azuria or her brief time in the Brightlands.

Her stomach twisted at the memory of the daimon pack who had helped her to find herself, her true self with Jade. Without their belief in her, their patience, would she have caved to Athena's wishing she could be simply Genevieve, pushing away the special path she had been called to, that Ophelia and Yvayne had tried to guide her through?

A few months before, in the forest with Mariellen, her magic had often faltered, had been a struggle. She clasped her hand around her conclave's dagger. They were all counting on her now. Trusting her to look after their legacy, ensure their deaths meant something beyond heartache, had some sort of impact at the grand scale.

Somewhat rested, they crept back toward the fortress. Pairs of guards paced the outside of Lucien's castle, others stood watch upon the ramparts. As the sky darkened overhead and the first of the moons appeared, she and Jade had to press themselves against the trunk of their tree, masking their scent with the maple they'd climbed while gray, living wraiths lurched along the forest floor. There were three of them with claws as long as her forearms, scratching and sniping at one another.

She sighed as they passed beneath without noticing her and Jade, too busy squabbling to look up overhead.

If only she could access the castle in a similar way . . .

We are deeply outnumbered, Jade.

Her wolf's pulse thrummed, solid and slow in answer.

She resolved to take her time—her friends were counting on her. Being captured wouldn't help them. But there had to be a way in.

Genevieve squinted up at the mountain that held Lucien's castle, the deep amethyst bulk of it with its sheer cliff faces. Many of the towers had fallen into disrepair. There were several sections along the wall that bore a different architectural style than the rest, blockier and quickly built as opposed to the carefully wrought swirls and arches of the rest of the structure.

The new sections were hundreds of feet long, and the crumbled ruins of those portions' predecessors still lay in heaps at their feet. Genevieve shuddered to think what could cause such wide-scale destruction. Had the creatures and implements responsible belonged to Lucien?

The castle itself didn't suit him, though once on her third day of scouting, she caught a glimpse of the lich perched on one of the iron railings looking out over the cleared fields beyond the castle. Goosebumps raised along her arms and down her spine as the distant fallen guardian, still in his bird-like form, raised his face and screeched at the sky. The wail of mourning in his voice was clear, but why a creature who caused so much misery would have cause himself to mourn she didn't care to know.

With the coming of their sixth twilight within the lands of shadow, Genevieve and Jade's plan took shape. They would travel during the night through the forest and make their way up the mountain as far as they could, avoiding the ground patrols that were more plentiful in number. From this distance, she couldn't tell where the prisons were, though it seemed safe to assume they'd be kept lower in the castle rather than the upper levels. Using the forest as cover, she and Jade had watched for torches in the windows and learned the nighttime patrols' patterns.

The mountain would help them to find their way inside.

⚜

BRUTAL CLIFFS AND PUNISHING CREVASSES HAD stretched between Genevieve and the rear battlements of the castle. Had her original assessment failed her and Lucien had aerial patrols, she would have been spotted on the dark, polished stone of the hillside, so smooth in some places it could have been glass.

The rear battlements had a single point of entry at the foot of a curved wall, more an escape route for someone trapped inside during a siege than a point of entry for an army.

But Lucien's defenses hadn't accounted for an army of two.

She hid behind a collection of boulders and waited for the brilliant moons to paint long shadows across the deep purples and blues around the castle as they did each afternoon, shadows she and Jade could dart between, lost in the cover of dusk for the changing of the guard.

Genevieve placed her conclave's dagger between her teeth and called her inner wolf forward. With a muted scream, they transformed into their hybrid form, mixing together wolf and woman, like the Lycan of old.

They snarled around the dagger hilt in their mouth, lumbering forward onto their sprawled, powerful werewolf arms. They could cover a great distance more quickly on all fours, and they would have only a few moments to slip down the final cliffside and through the reinforced wooden door that led onto the rear of the battlements. Their timing had to be perfect, finding a gap in the surveillance between the ground patrols and those upon the ramparts.

It was the close of her friends' seventh day within Lucien's prisons. Even powerful druids could only withstand darkstones for so long.

As they prepared to make their grand entry to Lucien's castle, the lich's cry reverberated across the fields and against the mountain. It was different from before—almost jubilant rather than a cry of mourning. They caught the silhouette of his dark form against the fading purple of the afternoon sky, soaring away toward the portal.

A Lucien-less castle had to be an easier proposition to invade than one where the lich prowled and lorded over his prisoners, didn't it? Yet Genevieve's resolve faltered as she thought about the fate of her friends, what they might find in the castle. Jade took over for her, taking charge of their shared being. She bounded toward the cliffside and leapt over the edge, landing heavily on the rocky stone below. "Oof," they groaned as they struck the ground, but already Jade was rushing ahead.

A single guard grunted as it appeared from behind the arched doorway, preparing to step out onto the lower ramparts for its shift. Jade snarled, a single swipe severing the gray, wraith-like creature's vocal cords. It gurgled as it fell back, drowning in its own blood.

Genevieve slowed her inner wolf just long enough to ease shut the reinforced door behind them. If all went well, they would escape the same way they'd come in.

As soon as they were able, Genevieve and Jade darted into an interior corridor, skirting around shadowy court-yards and further ruins—the castle's interior was in worse repair than the exterior. Thick cobwebs hung from ceiling corners and piles of debris from rodents had gathered at the edges of hallways. Whenever the option appeared, they wound their way down, Jade's nose as their guide.

The castle depths were even less populated than the ramparts had been. Without hesitation, Jade dispatched a guard who swiped at them as it fell. The wolf only grumbled her displeasure at their way being slowed.

Silver fur and the spice of pine caught in their nose, and they breathed in deeply. *Sariel was near.*

The daimon's scent drifted up and out of a hole in his prison cell, one floor below where Genevieve and Jade had tracked his smell.

"Sariel," Genevieve thought to the daimon. *"Sariel, Jade and I are here."*

It took several calls before the wolf raised his head from atop his crossed paws. Genevieve peered down into the hole, trying to see if there were guards patrolling on the other side. Despite his great size, he looked so tired.

"Genevieve," Sariel thought back to her. *"Is that you?"*

"We're here, yes," Genevieve answered. *"Here to rescue you."*

She couldn't have explained how she had arrived here instead of where she had meant to go to find him if the daimon had asked, and she was too afraid of breaking his already damaged spirit by asking about his pack, if they had been taken too.

Jade growled low from the corner of their mind. *Focus.*

Right. Genevieve nodded. *"We need you to help with the guards—how many are there?"*

"It is dangerous for you to be here, little one."

"You rescued us before. Helped us find our way together. We weren't going to leave you here."

The great wolf sighed and stretched his paws. His claws scraped against the stone of the floor. *"There are two guards. I'll draw them this way."*

"We'll make our way down."

With Sariel in their sights and only two more guards in their way, the separation between Genevieve and Jade faded. Together, they found the winding stair coated in blood. Stepping onto the prison hall where Lucien was keeping Sariel, their breath halted in their chest as though they'd been struck, so strong was the press of the dark-stones around them.

The stones had been a weight on the floor above. Here, without Jade, Genevieve would have barely been able to stand.

But they were two rather than one, and their friend waited on the other side of a darkstone-encrusted cell door.

Sariel had raised his nose and howled, the sound coated in a rasp that hadn't been there before.

"Quiet, you," one of the guards grunted.

Genevieve's nose prickled. Sariel's guards weren't the living wraiths, whatever gray-fleshed, wrinkled beings Lucien had kept on the outer walls.

Sariel's guards were werewolves.

All plans for stealth fadded. The screams of her conclave echoed in Genevieve's ears.

Two hulking werewolves postured before Sariel's cage. They struck the darkstones with a club and growled their threats.

Genevieve and Jade, Lycan-druid reborn, slid forth from the shadow. They held their shoulders back, claws poised and sharp. Green venom dripped from their fangs, not the sort that would infect their victims—the druids of old had been careful. Their venom caused paralysis and, if they wanted, pain.

They were no longer the same druid they had been when the werewolves attacked Genevieve's conclave. After what they'd done, she wanted them to suffer.

Jade snarled, catching the attention of the two guards.

"What the—" the first guard cried out.

His voice faded to a whispered sigh as they latched their jaws upon his throat and tore their teeth free. Blood arced onto the wall opposite Sariel, fresh wet red mingling with the copper stains of whoever Lucien had imprisoned before.

The second werewolf wielded his club, patting its weight into the meat of his paw as he sized up the slighter werewolf-druid before him. His hesitation was his down-fall, though nothing could have saved him from their wrath.

Genevieve extended her paw, remembering Iellieth's spell from the beach. Slithering willow tendrils shot out of her hand, snaking around the werewolf's throat, binding his ankles, his knees, and causing his balance to sway.

She and Jade lunged forward, knocking him onto his back. His breath exploded out of his chest, leaving a dry sigh like a whispering canyon behind.

They balanced their slighter size atop the great beast and dug their claws into his flesh. His head reared back, too weak still to whimper. At Genevieve's will, the willow fronds bound tighter and tighter around his throat. He clawed at his neck, causing blood to pool upon the floor.

They glowered down at the dying werewolf, acidic saliva dripping down onto the werewolf's face from their conclave's dagger, clenched in their mouth. It sizzled where it fell. His movements slowed, and panic replaced the rage that had flared deep within his eyes.

Genevieve and Jade watched until even that faded, his light extinguished, the deadened coal of a darkstone.

Sariel stood opposite them as they raised themselves up from the werewolf's corpse. *"There aren't keys. The fallen one sealed me in himself."*

"We won't need them," they thought back to the daimon wolf. Genevieve and Jade loped over to the darkstone-encrusted doorway. Finally she understood why the city had stolen her conclave's dagger, why her instincts had driven her so firmly to get it back.

They squinted their eyes shut as they balanced themselves against the metal and cursed stone of Sariel's cage. The stones burned their paws where they touched. They tightened their grip on the hilt of the blade and began to saw at the stone-covered crack between the door and the cage wall.

Beneath the revived magic of the repaired blade, the darkstones melted away.

The city had wanted to prevent the conclave from freeing their elders from their prisons. To Genevieve and Jade, Andel-ce Hevra and Lucien had empowered their downfall instead.

They were panting, the hair singed from the side of their furry face by the time they reached the stone floor. Jaw clenched, they tugged at the stone door. It swung open, and Sariel limped out of his cell to stand by their side. He rubbed his head against Genevieve's, healing the burn from the darkstones. The hair would regrow with time.

"*There were two others with me,*" the daimon thought to Genevieve and Jade.

"*We'll find them. And then we'll cut them free.*"

CHAPTER 54

TEODRIC

The clear blue water of the Infinite Ocean crashed against the series of caves on the eastern side of Isla de Hossa. Teodric directed the ship around toward the single bay. Kriega stood at the helm, barking instructions relayed from the trio of lookouts up in the rigging. Athena held the wheel, her brow furrowed as she turned it to Kriega's precise specifications.

The half-orc had grown quiet the last few days as they approached Syleste's stronghold. Maybe Aeogan had been right about her too—was she keeping something vital from him? Obscuring her own desperate plans? Or was she as ready to be rid of Syleste as he was?

They navigated through the narrow channels and shallow shoals that surrounded the pirate queen's island. The mainland was strangely devoid of activity, the usually bustling beachhead deserted. Beams of sunlight broke through gathering clouds overhead, illuminating a curved shape in the shallow waters surrounding the reef. He'd never noticed the creature before. Teodric leaned over the railing—his stomach churned as the sun broke through and revealed what lay below. The skeleton of a great sea dragon lay beneath the water, one similar in kind to what Iellieth had described sinking the *Fairwind*.

Aeogan had mentioned a past connection to Syleste. Was there more the dragonkin was keeping to himself? Had she killed one of his dragon ancestors, igniting a feud between them?

There was so little time, now, just barely enough for regrets and second-guessing.

"I wondered when you would arrive."

Teodric jumped and looked to his side. The admiral's voice had emerged right against his ear, so close he should have felt the breath that carried the words, but there was no one there.

He searched his ship, the docks, and finally spied a figure in a red jacket and crisp, white breeches emerge from the lowered moat in the center of the castle that had been built into the side of the smoking volcano that made up the island's heart. The figure strode forward to the end of the moat. Loose strands of her long, black hair caught on the breeze. She stared directly at the *Amber Queen*.

"I've been waiting for you."

He didn't jump at the voice this time. Teodric recognized it as emerging from within his own mind, not beside him.

On the deck below him, Kriega had fallen silent. A tension hung about her shoulders. Syleste was speaking to her too.

Slowly, Kriega turned to look up at him. She nodded once, confirming his suspicions. They'd worked out a signal for something of this sort, with an additional signal decided upon if Syleste ordered his immediate death outright.

They both knew how unlikely an outcome that was. The admiral would never pass on the opportunity to play with her prey before dispatching them. The more painful, the more pleasurable, the better.

"Come inside, the both of you. We have much to discuss."

"Weigh anchor," Teodric said, his voice too soft. He cleared his throat and shouted the command again. His crew scrambled to do as he'd ordered.

If all went as planned, he'd return, still the captain of this ship, Kriega near at hand beside him, and they'd sail at the behest of Aeogan for the remaining three years of his father's service. Once that was done, they'd strike out into the waters, their aims and journey their own.

❦

SYLESTE'S INSTRUCTIONS HAD BEEN EXPLICIT, AND Teodric passed them along in no uncertain terms to his crew—he and Kriega were to go ashore alone. No one should leave the ship until they gave the signal. If two days passed without word, Ambrose and Athena were to set sail and never return.

He and Kriega did not speak as they rowed to shore. Whatever was going to transpire was unavoidable for them now, and there seemed little need for words to acknowledge what they both already knew.

"It has been an honor to serve with you," Teodric said as they tugged their boat onto the sand.

"And with you, Captain." Kriega bowed her head, the greatest show of deference she'd ever offered him.

The dark-haired figure clad in scarlet and white slid around the side of her island castle, abandoning the stone walls for the natural caverns that had formed with the island's foundation.

Teodric and Kriega followed, picking their way from shoals to slimy rocks and finally into the echoing, brilliant blue shade of the caves.

They wound through the caverns, finding themselves within an underground chamber the size of his room back in Io Keep. Water dripped from a series of stalactites above. The lapping sound of the sea echoed against the back wall of the cave. He skirted around the large hole in the floor of the cavern. It floated above the sea floor, and pale green water rushed in and out a dozen feet beneath the wide hole, several paces across.

"It's good that you've arrived when you did." Syleste's voice emerged first, as it did in his nightmares. She strode out of the shadows from a small cavern off to the side, leaving him and Kriega to turn their backs on the hole behind them in order to face her. Her wide smile gleamed in the flickering light of the cave. "I only need one of you for what comes next."

Before he could react, Kriega shoved Teodric to the side. *Fuom. Fuom. Fuom.*

Teodric caught himself against the slick cavern wall they'd passed to enter the cave, spinning about in time to see the curved, shining tips of sea stars sticking out of Kriega's stomach, chest, and neck.

She stared, open-mouthed, at Syleste and took a stumbling step backward.

Syleste raised her hands to her shoulders—she'd tossed the sea-stars from within her palms, one falling shy of its mark and into the sea foam below. Lightning crackled between Syleste's fingers. Her amber eyes shone so brightly they glazed over, hyper-focused on the fight. "I warned you, Kriega." A mystical enchantment hovered in her voice. "Said you'd have to choose."

"You sent me away," Kriega sputtered. Blood coated the spittle that fell from her mouth. "And he is *my* captain."

With brilliant sparks still shining out from her fingers, Syleste withdrew the long, silver rapier from her side. She stalked across the cavern toward Kriega, who held a shaking hand out toward Teodric, ordering him to stay where he was.

"You still serve me," Syleste snarled. "That was the price." Impossibly quickly, Syleste had crossed the cavern and stood before Kriega, her blade having impaled her lover. Kriega gasped, her body shaking, struggling for breath.

With a flick of her wrist, Syleste tugged the blade free, not breaking her gaze from Kriega's.

Teodric cried out, realized he had been screaming, and rushed forward. Syleste reached out as Kriega had, catching him in a flurry of sparks against his chest, holding him still.

She spun, lithe as a dancer, tugging the lightning up overhead as she twisted away from Kriega, elbowed her in the chest, and knocked her shocked form into the lagoon below. "You will always serve me."

Teodric's body writhed. His tongue fell out of his mouth, numb, as his legs gave way. He collapsed onto the slick cavern floor and Syleste reeled him in toward herself, the lightning fastened as a noose around his waist.

Manipulating the lightning bands as easily as rope, she drew Teodric up, catching his jolting chin upon the tip of her razor-sharp nail, a thin trail of blood falling down her finger where she made contact with his chin. "I could end it all right now, you know." She tilted her head to the side as he continued to quake, considering the possibility.

A cold, sharp talon grazed his temple. "A single prick, maybe two, and it would all be over."

As suddenly as she'd struck him, Syleste released the lightning's hold, grasping his arms in her vice grip and holding him up. Beyond the admiral, Kriega's stilled form began to sink, blades she hadn't had time to draw weighing her down. Spirals of blood darkened the water around her body, scarlet ink within the teal pool.

Syleste clicked her tongue in disapproval. "You'll see her again, Teodric darling." Her long, thin claws slipped from his temple to trace down the nape of his neck. "Just as soon as you hand over that book my former lover gave you. I'm sure he promised it would be innocuous in my hands." Syleste chuckled low in her throat. "I thought he would have learned the dangers of underestimating me before. But no matter. With the book at my command, I'll raise Kriega and all the dead below—a tireless army bent on carrying out my every order."

Syleste pressed the point of her finger into his flesh, breaking the skin. He shouted in pain but then all feeling drifted away. He no longer saw Kriega, the cavern, Syleste. In their place, an entire city, trapped beneath the waters, a broken tower at its center. Broken spires jutted up toward the surface of the sea—towers with gilded arches that must once have played host to the flights of birds that now corroded beneath the waves.

The structures alone were not what Syleste wished him to see. Above all the submerged streets, bodies floated. Bloated corpses with fish-devoured eyes, their clothes billowing and torn all around them. "You can bring her back, Teodric. All of them. Read the spell. Set them free."

He shook his head—what she was saying was impossible, but so was the sight before him. The city seemed at once ancient and recently destroyed, almost as though time had halted only a few days after its passage into the sea. But how could that be?

Syleste answered his thoughts in her way. "We're going to bring down a god, Teodric," she murmured, the music of her voice washing over him, tugging him nearer. Captivating him as she once had, a hold he'd struggled for so long to break. "And I shall become one instead."

She floated beside him—when had they entered the water? Teodric let out his breath with a gust of bubbles, and the figure before him tittered, her laughter a melody he could never tire of hearing.

Instead of the admiral he knew, armed and clad in her trim coat and breeches, a creature of the sea dipped and rose with the rhythm of the ocean before him. The gold of her skin had faded to an intense shade of blue; scales coated the rich curves of her figure, hugging and dipping between the blue of what had once been skin and the midnight shades of the nighttime sky, giving the impression of a clinging evening dress that both concealed and revealed.

Syleste reached out toward him with those same claws that had pierced and threatened. She caressed the side of his neck. Teodric shouted in pain as his skin ripped and then rippled, gills forming where they had not been before.

"You have brought to me the means of my escape and my ascension," she cooed across the waters. "Now you will give life to my army of the dead." The siren's smile spread slow as spilled ink across the scaly contours of her delicately sculpted face. "They will see, the both of them, what it means to entrap a siren queen. Neither Lucien nor the dragon king will be any match for Ruka's army, once raised. And with the trickster god's fall, Alessandra shall have a new hand, a great power upon the sea." The row of her teeth—no, rows, all of them jagged canines—sparkled as she spoke. "And that power, of course, is me."

CHAPTER 55

IELLIETH

The light of Ammon's campfire guided them out of Gaia's Glade and back into the northern mountains between Thyles Thamor and Shade Rest. Beads of sweat formed a crown across Iellieth's brow despite the cool temperature of the forest.

"Lady, are you certain you're alright?" Marcon asked again, his hand hovering at the small of her back.

"Yes, I'm sure it's nothing more than fatigue from the fighting." She pressed her palm against her leg where Lucien's talon had pierced her. The wound was hot to the touch and had continued to bleed, soaking through the bandage Marcon had affixed around her thigh.

Iellieth brushed the sweat away and blinked to clear her eyes. Whatever this was would soon pass. She turned her attention to Ammon instead—the elf had hurried toward them, brow furrowed at finding three rather than the four who had slipped away into the woods.

"You were right," Quindythias said, stomping past Ammon and ignoring the elf's concerned greeting.

"Zelphira betrayed us," Iellieth explained, willing

neither Ammon nor Marcon to read into the quaver in her voice. Her hand shook as she brushed the sweat from the other side of her forehead. She had hoped she and Marcon might be able to discuss what had happened in the forest, but her thoughts kept jumbling together as she replayed the events of Gaia's Glade in her mind.

Ammon's eyes darkened. He muttered a curse in Elvish that made even Quindythias pause in his skulking toward the fire. "You are hurt," Ammon said simply, leaving the longer explanation for a later time.

"Only a little."

A look passed between Marcon and Ammon. "She was cut by a lich's talons. We returned here as quickly as we could—I do not know the extent of the poison or its effects."

The pair of them ushered Iellieth to the fireside. She laid her head on Quindythias's shoulder while they conferred together, muttering over herbs and poultices.

"Mara would have known what to do," Iellieth murmured, as much to herself as to the elf beside her.

Quindythias rested his head against hers. "Perhaps her spirit will guide our friends then."

Iellieth twisted to catch as much of his expression as she could. "That's rather unlike you." Other than his connection to his sister, Quindythias had never been overly sentimental before and while he had never dismissed Iellieth's regret toward what had happened to Mara and the druids, he rarely engaged with that sort of reflection.

"Hmm." She felt as much as heard him smile. "That may be so. Failure puts me in a strange mood."

Iellieth stiffened. Marcon had insisted he wasn't angry

with her, and she believed him. But Quindythias had every right to be.

"I don't blame you, my dear," he added quickly, anticipating her thoughts.

"But—"

"I would have made the same choice, were I in Marcon's position upon the dragon's back. I spoke of myself. Had I been better focused, more alert to the true danger before us . . ." He sighed heavily. "Truth be told, Ellie, I believe I've been to Gaia's Glade before. Or if not there, then very near to it."

"You have? When?"

"*A place out of time*, isn't that what that elf on the council said?" He shook his head, his cheekbone brushing against her hair. "I believe Calixta was guarding the gate you enchanted open the night she was killed. They had sent her to help protect a 'strategically significant' place and wouldn't say more than that. I followed her path when she didn't come back when she should have. The city wouldn't send their own soldiers after her, said they were spread too thin."

His breath was uneven, and his voice grew thicker as he recounted his difficult path through the forest. His parents had begged him not to go, not to jeopardize his studies as he had a qualifying exam to complete his diplomat's training within a few days. Like the city council's aides, his parents had insisted that Calixta would return soon, but Quindythias knew that was not the case.

"Such destruction," he murmured, his voice catching. "The wounds she'd sustained, and those of her companions —it doesn't bear description, but I have never seen its like, and I have seen a great deal." He wrapped an arm around Iellieth, drawing her closer. "Such suffering leaves a mark upon a place. I know you felt it, near the temple. I believe its aura is part of what blinded us to Zelphira's true intentions.

"While we were there, I couldn't focus fully on the task at hand, couldn't prevent my mind from skipping forward, worrying something might happen to you, that I might lose you the way I'd lost her. It prevented me from seeing what was right in front of me. In front of us." He shook his head again. "But we will not allow that to happen a second time this evening, will we?" Quindythias raised his voice as he addressed Marcon and Ammon, who had finished their conferring and had prepared a sour-smelling, bright orange ointment that they'd crushed along a sheaf of bark.

Quindythias tightened his hold around Iellieth, somehow anticipating that she would try to lurch away at the sight of the salve.

"M-Mara made a salve for me." She had to get away from the foul orange substance. Hadn't she thought something similar when Ammon appeared and was ready to help them, that he'd somehow been sent? What if he was a traitor too, all this time? If she fell without the seal piece, Marcon and Quindythias would return to statues. All this would be for naught—

"Marcon," Quindythias growled, a second arm wrapping around Iellieth.

The champion of fire rushed forward and caught her around the shoulders. He was in on Ammon's trickery as well or—Iellieth's heartbeat began to drown out her thoughts—perhaps he was one of Lucien's agents in disguise.

She threw her shoulders, desperate to be free of his grasp.

"Lady," the false Marcon soothed. "Do not do this. The lich's poison has you in its grasp, another of Lucien's tricks. Do not listen to it."

She would not allow Lucien's forces to take her. Wouldn't a false Marcon say precisely this? Had she fallen after all and found herself in a place of torment deep within the Shadowlands, away from Marcon and Quindythias's care—

"Now," Marcon uttered.

Ammon rushed forward then. He flipped the bark onto its edge and pressed the full slab against her leg.

Iellieth screamed at the burning, as the salve bit into her skin. Her shoulders shook, and her head reared back into Marcon's chest. He caught her forehead in his hand and held her in place.

Quindythias grasped her waist as she began to thrash, holding her other leg in place.

"A moment longer," Ammon urged.

Her vision faltered as the burning intensified. Marcon murmured in her ear, trying to calm her.

To her left, there was a rush of small paws, a shifting of leaves and dirt.

Daphne poked her nose into the back of Iellieth's hand, the cold, damp of her nose scraping over Iellieth's skin.

Her mind cleared and Iellieth stilled. The burning continued but less severely. Marcon's grasp no longer felt constricting but intimate.

"There," his gravelly voice sighed above her. "Her fever is breaking."

A blur of white tinged with green burrowed into Iellieth's side opposite Marcon. Daphne smacked her lips as she settled down to sleep on the log beside Iellieth. Slowly, her vision cleared, and three of her four rescuers sighed as one.

Ammon sat back on his heels, allowing Marcon to hold the bark to her leg. "It was an enchanted poison," Ammon explained. "Few possess magic strong enough for such a concoction. Its ingredients are not of this realm but it is possible for it to exist here. Had you been able to see the shadows beneath your eyes, pooling along your skin, you would have known it as surely as we did."

Iellieth relaxed back against Marcon and stroked the soft fur along Daphne's spine. "Thank you." She met each of their gazes in turn. Did they know of the healing magic Daphne had cast, or did they attribute her healing to the salve Marcon and Ammon had made?

The wolf pup's healing powers could wait until the morning. But there was something she had to take care of before she could fall asleep. "There's something I need to tell you all," Iellieth said as she recovered from the effects of Lucien's poison. Exhaustion draped from the posture of all four of them, all the more reason they had to know that a sliver of hope remained.

"Before Zelphira took the necklace, we realized something was wrong with the glade, something broken. When I was in proximity to the piece itself, I found out why. The piece is not only broken—there are two pieces of it missing." She recounted the visions she'd seen, the three figures the seal piece had shown her at first and the fourth it projected when bidden by the amulet.

"I think Gaia was trying to show us that there's still a chance. If we could go somewhere that might have the missing pieces . . . but where to start? The elf I saw, the one that was so upsetting to Lucien"—she glanced at Marcon—"she was wearing the ruby for my amulet." There wasn't time to explain what she'd learned from Idlewylde, what she was certain now was wrong but that, somehow, could lead her on the right path as she came to understand what the soul shards were. Lucien had implied Marcon's connection to Rowan, though it wasn't something he'd ever mentioned to her. Had the vision been from after he was turned into a statue?

"The final elf with the dragon," Iellieth continued, "I think she's the one who hid the seal piece there in the first place. She entrusted it to the dragon, who sensed our proximity and sent Zelphira to find us and lead us to the glade."

"A great help that was." Quindythias scowled. "Were our new friend less large and terrifying, I might have complained more overtly about her trying to fetch us through a traitorous fae who tried to murder me and Marcon. Whatever happened to sending a mechanical owl or charming a squirrel and sending it with a message tied around its foot? Even if the squirrel harbored malicious intent, I should far rather follow it into a dangerous drag-on's lair held out of time."

Iellieth grinned, picturing Quindythias closely questioning the next squirrel to cross their path in case it was enchanted. "That leaves the girl with dark hair, running from something, and the Shadowlands fae who turned into a wolf."

"A werewolf or a wolf?" Marcon asked.

"A wolf."

Ammon frowned at this. "A white-haired fae with amethyst eyes who could turn into a wolf?"

Iellieth assented and answered Ammon's next questions—no, she hadn't noticed any jewelry upon the fae, certainly not an emerald necklace, though both the fae and the horned man she was with were dressed in carefully tailored leathers that looked custom-made for them.

"A Shadowlands fae and a negata, working together." Ammon chuckled to himself. "It could almost be Vengeance and Lilith, one of mine and Sharia's favorite tales from when we were children."

"Wait, I know Lilith." Iellieth's brow furrowed, thinking back to her studies with Katarina and the inspiration for the code name she'd used to correspond with the scholar. "But I thought she was connected to someone else, a brightfae?" It had been several years since her translations with Katarina had focused on ancient folk heroes and faery tales. She shook her head. Perhaps it didn't matter.

"If it were Lilith and this Vengeance person, where would that lead us? Or, more obviously perhaps, where would we find records of a Shadowlands fae who could transform into a wolf?" Iellieth rubbed her hand along the crescent moon affixed to her glove, the one she'd received from Yvayne that allowed her to shift into an animal form, a rare ability even among the druids, the fae had explained. But the fae in her vision hadn't murmured an enchantment or touched a piece of jewelry. She'd simply willed the transformation into being, almost like the Lycan of old.

"You think Gaia is leading us on a trail, lady?" The flickering firelight shaded Marcon's features.

"If either the titan or her dragon guardian had wanted to distract Lucien, they could have done so with a vision of Rowan alone. Why show the others?" The young woman with dark hair and bright eyes Iellieth still couldn't place. The outline of a town lingered behind the girl, but it wasn't a silhouette she'd recognized. Had her elven soul-predecessor—a strange way to think of another being in any case—embedded the visions around the seal piece as a clue to restoring it? She had to believe that was the intention since the guardian had sent for her. The vision couldn't be a trap to keep her out.

"A scavenger hunt through time *does* sound like the sort of trial a titan would devise." Quindythias slumped, glaring at the fire. "Ancient embodied deities with nothing better to do," he grumbled.

Iellieth reached over and squeezed his hand where it gripped tightly to his knee. "What if Gaia is trying to help us instead of trying to lead us toward harm?" After his sister's death, Quindythias didn't trust the titans, even though it was Calixta's death that led to him becoming a Champion of Air.

Ammon took a deep breath and heaved it out. "So what we have so far is a search quest entrusted to us by Gaia where we need to find a fae who can transform who's somehow connected to the seal piece of earth?"

"To its emerald core, yes," Iellieth clarified. "Where would that take us?" It wasn't a lot to go on, and it was admittedly a strange next phase of their mission, but it was a start. There had to be a reason the seal piece had shown her those specific images. "Where would you go if you wanted to find an heirloom gemstone from the court of the Shadowlands?" That would fit both the woman she had seen and the connection Ammon had made to Lilith. "Who would have access to such a piece?"

A slow smile crossed the ranger's face, only the second Iellieth had ever seen. "There is a market between Shade Rest and the kingdom of the dwarves, Hammerfell. Several days' journey underground. It's said to house a portal to the Shadowlands, one of the last ancient Shadowlands portals in existence."

"But there's no telling whether or not we'll find the gem there. And you said there's another shard fragment missing." Quindythias's voice grew higher as his frustration mounted.

"That's true." Iellieth chewed her lower lip.

"It may be a better use of our time to research first, to narrow our potential trails." Ammon turned from one to the next. "The library in Thyles Thamor has an extensive archive of magical artifacts. We could begin there, or divide our efforts between the archives and the jewel market."

Iellieth dropped her gaze, avoiding looking at Marcon or Quindythias. "We have to stay together." Because her plan to save both of her companions and retrieve the seal piece had failed utterly.

"And we'll need to warn our allies," Marcon added, deepening her guilt. "With even a shard of a piece in Alessandra's hands, the elemental planes are vulnerable and, by extension, so is the rest of Azuria."

The four of them agreed—they would make a plan for their next steps at first light and then set out.

She curled up around Daphne on her mat. The centaurs had feared one so small, what she would become. Did they know about her healing magic? The lull of her companions' voices and Daphne's quiet snores sent her to sleep.

LUCIEN

Far away, in the depths of another plane of existence, Lucien landed in his throne room, instantly transforming from winged guardian to the figure of a tall man. The seal piece of earth skidded across the black marble floor, shards of emerald flaking off its sides.

He limped over to the side of the room where velvet curtains blocked off the sight of the Shadowlands beyond. Curse the druid and her fire, using Rowan's magic against him. Her precious amulet wouldn't exist without Lucien's foresight during his extractions. Had Rowan noticed the particular care he always took with the element of earth?

With a yank he tugged a curtain down and dragged it back with him, tossing it over the green-glowing chunk of rock. Striations and scars covered its surface, almost as many as coated his skin.

He had waited for this moment for so long. He would be the one to unlock the piece's magic and present his mistress, the great goddess, with the means to assault the elemental planes. Beyond the portal room, from a distant, dark hall, the screeches of his soldiers reverberated against their holding cells. Lucien smiled to himself. Never before in this age had there been such an army.

The elemental planes didn't stand a chance against his forces. Gaia would be the first to fall.

But that would have to wait until he'd dispatched Ravenna and her darling Yvayne.

Their deaths he would savor, memories to suck the flavor from for years to come. It was Ravenna's memory magic that had severed his bond with Rowan in the first place, allowed her elven and now her half-breed iterations to twist out of the grasp of his command. Taking the last dregs of her magic would sweeten his revenge.

Her daughter was the true prize. Yvayne's druidic magic would be enough to sustain him until he could capture the half-elf. Iellieth fell short of Rowan's true form, but the magical potential lingered nonetheless. Dispatching her champion protectors would be a simple matter after their elemental planes fell.

And then he could take the step he'd intended to all along. With the champions out of the way, he'd remove the half-elf's soul from her body, imbibing her power for himself as he had the druid Fhaona and replacing her soul with the remnants of Rowan's spirit instead. She'd be held in the eternal embrace between life and death as he was.

Unlike the half-elf, Rowan had the wisdom to survive.

He would need a strong queen by his side to conquer his final enemy when the time came. Alessandra. She would pay for the misstep that had taken Rowan from his side, long ages ago. In her place, the worlds and the wheels would be his to command.

❧

IELLIETH

With the golden rays of dawn, Iellieth and her companions' debate about their possible next steps recommenced. To the north lay the chance of finding answers more quickly. To the south, their answers might be more accurate.

The first hours of daylight slipped by as Iellieth and Quindythias went back and forth, Ammon and Marcon chiming in occasionally.

"Wait," the ranger urged, holding up his hand between her and Quindythias.

Rustling emerged from the forest behind their camp—a party of several others approaching from the east, where they'd last heard reports of poachers.

Iellieth slid in front of Daphne, her thoughts racing at the sorts of spells poachers might be able to cast as well as defend against. The face of Ammon's sister flashed across her memory.

And then, strangely enough, the face of Ammon's sister slid into view.

Sharia tilted her head to the side, one half of her face smiling, the other moving only slightly as she climbed around low pine branches and into the remains of their camp. "Something kept nudging at me after the four of you left. I had this unshakeable sense that you might need help." Sharia tapped beneath her missing eye. "Yesterday I caught a glimpse of the trouble and was glad we left when we did."

The four of them stared, speechless, at the elven scholar. Behind her, other branches cracked in the woods. Tanner, Professor Tur, Addah, and a sweating Firan stepped forward.

Sharia sauntered into the center of the camp and draped her arm around Ammon's shoulders. "So the Darkstriders and our resident ranger friend decided, just say the word and we'll follow."

Iellieth glanced between the newcomers, Ammon, Marcon, and a smirking Quindythias. She cocked an eyebrow, mirroring his expression. "To the market *and* the archives?"

The elf raised his fist in the air. "To the market! To the archives!"

EPILOGUE

LUCIEN

Lucien secured the seal piece of earth in the depths of his tower—one held separate from the castle's dungeons so it would be protected where no one beyond himself could reach it. Well, no one beyond himself and the captive druids and fae he'd trapped with it.

He dispatched the first healer who informed him that the wound from the verdant flames could not be healed, then sacrificed two more when he saw how effective the sacrifice of the first healer's blood was in restoring his leg to normal. The half-elf truly was proving more powerful than he'd believed she might be. A promising future for his plans.

But there were other, more immediate concerns bidding for his attention. He leaned upon a darkstone cane as he peered over the scalloped edge of his seeing basin.

The sight before him was curious—Iellieth's would-be lover and his own captive siren queen stood locked together, Syleste's claws jutting into the neck of her young captain, who still breathed. The siren's gaze broke from the figure arched back before her to stare down into a shimmering, teal lagoon where the fronds of anemones rippled beneath a slowly sinking corpse. It was like looking into two seeing pools at once. A curious doubling, too, of what Iellieth must have seen as Zelphira plummeted toward the whirring silver spokes of the wheel waiting beneath Gaia's Glade. He'd so nearly captured Rowan's reincarnation and the seal piece at once but, with one in hand, the other would follow.

The whimpering beside him distracted him from enjoying the victory of these parallel moments. Very soon, the boy would hand over the book to Syleste, the saudad would fall, and his own ascension, following in the very footsteps of Ruka before him, would be complete.

"Her aims are rather like yours, Zelphira," he remarked to the sniveling, crumpled form of his servant, mercifully recovered from the wheel's pull, "though Syleste has the good sense to manipulate events for her own ends rather than trying to free the one she loves." He turned yellow eyes toward the bound, bleeding form of the scale-covered fae on the cold stone beside him. Pale green lights lit his chamber, a soothing effect, and one that showed the weakness of the scales Zelphira hadn't managed to shed, too depleted to complete her transformation. There truly was only one druid capable of such fluid shape-shifting in and out of animal forms, and she had just eluded his grasp once again.

"Perhaps I overestimated you as well. I'm sure the blame shouldn't entirely rest upon your shoulders, though there's little enough you can do to manage what once balanced there." He chuckled to himself though, even for him, the sentiment was cruel. "I've some important matters to attend to while your brethren restore my planar seal." Lucien admired the green glow against his talons. The rippling light made them appear sharp as bone.

The taking of two useful captives was truly a stroke of brilliance, the results of which would allow him to rise in the dark goddess's graces. Kelvren's research into the nature of the soul shards that he'd discovered in the Brightlands had been only the beginning. The senators of Andel-ce Hevra had been easy to manipulate. Once Lucien shared with them the secret to controlling the werewolves, they granted him access to the winding tunnels that ran beneath the city. If only they knew the power that lay hidden inside the ruins of Bastion beneath them.

Syleste had been harder to control, especially after she'd absorbed Aeogan's magic. The dragonkin was nearly as troublesome as his parents had been. But with the undead of Orison awakened and Cassandra and her followers out of the way, he could proceed, unimpeded, in creating an army truly worthy of the dark goddess. And with it, they would make quick work of the elemental planes.

He resisted the urge to look in on the unspooling of Xarmev's long-ranging plan in Steymhorod. The god of undeath had placed too much faith in his vampire servant whose head had been easily turned by the one who walked between life and death. Lucien frowned—how had the one called Briseras come to be? How had she escaped Haven and then the bite of Malthael?

No, no, such questions were a distraction, nothing more. Soon enough, Kelvren's research and the stores of the champions of old would provide the energy needed to reconstitute the threshold seal blocking his access to the elemental planes. The captive fae and his colleagues worked feverishly, believing that so long as they did, Zelphira would remain unharmed.

"It is a burden that comes to us all," he observed to himself, turning his mind to his next steps instead of dwelling on the execution of the pieces already in play. "Depending on others invites weakness, though the risk can be sustained for a time."

Beyond the crumpled fae, his two shadow panthers lounged on either side of his throne. "We've been patient long enough," Lucien called down to them. Lazily, they picked up their heads to follow his gliding path from the chamber. "I think it's time we paid Yvayne's dear mother a visit—see what it will take for the Champion of Fire to remember how spectacularly he failed before."

He clicked his tongue to the panthers and rubbed his fingers together. After an initial wet splat of decay, the remaining flesh he had made a swishing sound, calling for their attention. *Father has a treat for you, my dears.*

Lucien's eyes narrowed as he strode from the chamber, talons sifting through the joined beads of his plan, looking for any weaknesses in the bindings that held the pieces together. Millennia ago, he'd stopped asking himself whether he hated Marcon more for taking Rowan from him or failing to prevent her death. The truth of his resentment was so much worse than that— he'd found a way to free himself of her hold while returning her to life, all thanks to the beneficence of dear, addled Queen Ravenna and one of her memory bargains.

The queen would never renege on a bargain she had made, especially not for the memories that fed her, held her very being together. But he'd finally acquired precisely the leverage he needed to bring the fledgling Soul Shepherds crashing down from within. It had been simple, really, the solution waiting there before him all along.

His captive's lavender eyes glared up at him as Lucien strode into the prison cells. Beside her, the autumn fae trembled, beads of sweat trailing down her brow. If he hadn't been planning on imbibing Zelphira's energy when he returned, he would have saved this one, Vaxis, for himself. But it would be better for Micaela and Madeline to hunt and dine on the fae druid for themselves—important practice should events between the Realms and Brightlands not develop as planned. The fae's fox curled back against her mistress, growling.

"I was just thinking back to another pair I captured, though they at least hadn't been so foolhardy as to invade my domain and believe they could escape again on their own terms. Tut, tut," he scolded Yvayne, "I truly cannot fathom what you were thinking but"—Lucien shrugged—"seeing as you're here . . ." His smile widened. It truly had been a delicious turn of events, finding the druid in the Shadowlands at the mercy of his manipulated portals. "You know I cannot resist pointing out—she warned you never to come back here."

Around the magical silencing gag, Yvayne's jaw tightened.

"But seeing as it's so difficult for you to do as you're told, we simply *must* return you to your mother's side. The moment she sees you, I'm confident she'll agree."

Lucien snapped his fingers and the cage surrounding Yvayne compressed into tight netting. The druid writhed as the darkstone-encrusted rope touched her skin. "Try not to resist, dear Yvayne. I'd hate for Rowan's final sight of you to include you covered in burns."

The lich turned as he crooked a finger, beckoning the

netting to follow, as he walked across the room. The netting lifted the struggling Yvayne from the ground and brought her hovering after him. He could make the journey faster if he chose, but the darkstones would weaken Yvayne over time. It was just what Rowan deserved after what she'd done to him, driving him to his present state of undeath.

There would be no such rescue for Yvayne. When the final living descendant of Verdigris fell, his personal vengeance would be complete, and he would ascend into godhood, first in Alessandra's favor, with an army of undead to command.

"Vaxis, dear one, the moment Yvayne and I depart this room, you'll have an opportunity. Seize it well and make your escape. Trying to come after us to save your friend will spell your doom."

The fae cried out for Yvayne, her shaking hands stretching past the darkstones. He couldn't help but grin at her yelp of pain as the stones singed her skin. A truly remarkable weapon, first devised to combat the Sapphire Circle, and yet how many uses had they found since then?

"It's been an age since I presented myself before a queen," Lucien observed to Yvayne. "The last time I did so in this realm, I was still among the living. Heh, heh. Do you think your mother will recognize me?"

GENEVIEVE

Far above the lich's holding cell, Genevieve hesitated. *"Sariel, what now?"* she thought to the daimon beside her. Jade pressed her fingers into the stone archway, fighting between an urge to leap out of the shadows and remain unseen.

The daimon's upper lip curled. He wanted to attack.

Beyond the chamber at Lucien's back, something stalked nearer. Two somethings, if Jade's nose was correct.

There was every chance this was part of Yvayne's plan, though how, Genevieve couldn't begin to fathom. The fae's friend in the cell below continued to cry out for her, hands pressed against her chest, her green fox crouched and growling in her lap. Whatever was coming her way, she hadn't sensed it.

Jade's paws flexed. Yvayne wouldn't have planned on putting her friend in danger. The time for her mentor's plans had passed—she and her wolf knew what they had to do.

❧

THE DEPTHS OF THE FOREST CALL

An adventure through an underground market. Secrets hidden away within an elven archive.

And a past that won't stay buried.

The race is on for Iellieth and her allies to find the missing fragments of the seal piece of earth and save the elemental planes before Lucien can fashion a planar seal from the piece in his possession.

As Quindythias would say, **may the cleverest and most magical side win.**

The adventure continues in Shadows Beneath.

THE EMERALD HAS A HISTORY ALL ITS OWN

During the harvest festival in the queen's court, a fae bent on revenge collides with a nobleman who places family honor above all else. He notices her because of the necklace she wears.

The emerald choker that once belonged to his family. One he'll stop at nothing to gain back.

But darker forces than Silas's rival placed the necklace upon Natalya's throat—and they don't mean to see her freed from its hold anytime soon.

If Silas wants to claim the emerald necklace from the fae with long, white hair and amethyst-hued eyes, he'll have to place his family at risk.

Especially because Natalya isn't about to let a nobleman get in the way of her revenge.

Adventure and intrigue await in the Heir of Lilith epic romantic fantasy series.

THE PAST BECKONS DEEPER STILL

The white-haired fae isn't the only intriguing entity from the world of Eldura intimately connected to the events unspooling around Iellieth's quest to save her world.

In fact, in an age now passed, a previous iteration of

her soul faced a similar trial—unite the six elements, restore Verdigris, and secure the future of Eldura.

But Rowan has no intention of blindly following the whims of the Pentacle any more than Marcon will settle for being a common foot soldier within the Army of Light.

They have each been asked to relinquish a part of themselves for the greater good. They know how to survive in a world that demands sacrifice without question.

Rowan will have to decide the price she's willing to pay for a magic more powerful than the world has ever seen.

And Marcon's loyalty will be tested beyond breaking point. When faced with losing all he holds dear, one choice remains: Can he rely upon himself to chart a new path forward, or will he have to depend upon those who would see him broken to be made anew?

Find out in the thrillingly dark, first-in-series epic fantasy adventure, Phoenix Rising.

ONE STORY REMAINS
AND LONGS TO BE TOLD...

THE TALE OF A CERTAIN
NOBLEMAN CAUGHT UNAWARES

I could use the phrase "humbling realization" or a similar falsely modest expression to describe my first encounter with Briseras. If I really wanted to, I could lie and pretend that's what I felt in the moment I realized she was hunting me. In reality, it was more akin to being kicked in the groin and punched in the stomach at the same time. Fitting, as I believe that's what Briseras wanted to do to me in any case.

The loss of blood from vampire bites didn't help, and neither did the screeching of my ex-fiancée's ghost.

Even with all those things considered, it's hard for me to envision our meeting going any other way—silver eyes. Dark hair. A flash of steel.

And my world never the same.

***

Lord Adrian Calder Jorgan (or just 'Jorgan' if, like Briseras, you find three names and a title to be excessive) finds his world turned upside down as his common-born fiancée rejects him for another.

This tale follows the usual route: fiancée killed, a monster discovered, a dashing escape plot hatched, all to come crashing down once again at crossbow point, aforementioned crossbow wielded by the devastating, possibly devious Briseras Ravisthinia.

And as Jorgan would tell you himself, that was only the beginning of his troubles.

Join the Circle of Story and get an exclusive copy of Jorgan's short story, "Nocturne," today! Visit bethball books.com/nocturne for your free short story!

ROLL BACK THE
WHEEL OF FATE…

It's easy to get lost in a world of daring heroines, powerful druids, and reawakened ancient warriors. But what about those who came before?

Before Iellieth's mis-transmigration, before Briseras hunted werewolves across the Caldaran continent, an elven diplomat met a captivating human noblewoman, Cassian and Esmeralda sought out Varra Yvayne's wisdom, and an ambitious negata rose through Lucien's ranks.

Visit bethballbooks.com/aurora to join Beth's reading community and receive a free copy of *Aurora*, the prequel novella for the *Age of Azuria* series.

AUTHOR'S NOTE

Thank you so much for returning to Azuria with me! *Wow* was this book a journey! I thought I would be able to jump straight into it after finishing *Amber Queen*, but it turns out, there were things I needed to know that I found in both *Phoenix Rising* and *Phantom* before I could finish *Forest Deep*!

To Jonathan, who supports me day in and day out, who celebrates each day that the word count works itself up and who read through multiple drafts of *Forest Deep* as she was coming into being, thank you for sharing in and co-creating this world with me. I love our people so much.

To Kristen, whose insights helped to hone the story and its execution, thank you for your sharp eye, patience, and thoughtfulness. I really hope we run into Briseras and Quindythias when we meet in Vegas. 😊

To Chris, thank you for your notes on the beta read, for reassuring me, and for nerding out with me about how foul and amazing Lucien is!

And most especially, I would like to extend my thanks to you, wonderful reader! Through the amazing writing days and the difficult ones, I had you in mind with the hope that these characters, this world, and this story would find you when you needed them and that they would mean as much to you as they have meant to me.

If you've been here from the very beginning, thank you for allowing this novel to take the time she needed to come into being! If you're new to Azuria and my books, welcome! I hope you'll join me in the Circle of Story!

Since you've made it this far, I have two requests: In the first, if you could share this series with a friend, that helps so much! (And I'm sure your friend will appreciate learning about a book that they'll love too!) For the second, if you could take a few minutes to leave a review, those are super important for independent authors like myself. I really appreciate your time in doing so!

⁂

CONNECTIONS TO OTHER NOVELS

One of my favorite things about writing in interconnected worlds across interconnected series is embedding hints of those other worlds, characters, and timelines into the novels! *Forest Deep* contains several such connections, and I wanted to share those with you below. How many did you catch as you were reading?!

First, there are major intersections between *Forest Deep* and *Phoenix Rising*, book one in the *Feather & Flame* epic fantasy series set in the world of Eldura during the War of the Champions. In *Phoenix Rising*, you'll find the attack against the druid conclave Marcon hesitantly told Iellieth about. You'll also find a certain witch in Respite undertaking a dangerous research project!

As I hinted at the end of the novel, you can also find out more about an emerald necklace and the fae and negate that Iellieth saw in *Phantom, Heir of Lilith* book one.

Finally, for the saudad's version of Syleste's backstory and the connection between her and Aeogan, check out *Story Magic*!

Beth Ball is a weaver of words and worlds spinning stories of druidic magic and the power of nature that span the epic fantasy realms of Azuria and Eldura. If you enjoy lyrical tales of action and adventure, dragons, werewolves, fae, wily foxes, and more, then grab your enchanted amulet, flaming longsword, poisoned dagger, or other mystical accessory of choice, and let's start our adventure! You can find more of Beth's work and the legends of Azuria and Eldura at bethballbooks.com.

GLOSSARY

The following glossary entries may contain light spoilers for the worldbuilding and characters of Forest Deep. *For a more comprehensive list alongside lore and cross-series interconnections, visit bethballbooks.com/glossary.*

WORLDS & PLANES

Planes of Life, *three interconnected planes,* Azuria, Shadowlands, and Brightlands
Negative Planes, origin planes of the negata, realms of the prime goddess Pandora, location of New Orison
Elemental Planes, one for each element, ruled over by and encompassing the power of each elemental titan
Astralei, spirit plane
Eldura, the name for the world in Azuria's ancient past before the Great Flood

ELEMENTAL TITANS

Ignis, titan of fire
Atamos, titan of air
Ilona, titan of light
Gaia, titan of earth
Thalyssa, titan of water
Nyx, titan of darkness
Verdigris, titan of nature, *destroyed and transformed into the three planes of life*
Izadra, titan of space, *destroyed and transformed into the spirit plane, Astralei*

DEITIES

Alessandra, "the dark goddess," goddess of negation
Cassandra, goddess of fate, patron deity of the saudad
Fenrir, god of wolves, daimon, and Lycan
Malura, shadow of Cassandra, goddess of misfortune
Rasvana, goddess of dragons
Selene, goddess of the greater moon
Xarmev, god of undeath
Llewelyn, prime goddess of the Positive Planes (including the Planes of Life)
Pandora, prime goddess of the Negative Planes

ARCHFAE SISTERS OF STEYMHOROD

Four Archfae who once ruled over distinct regions of Steymhorod; their sacred sites are called fanes

Arduenne, *also known as the Wolf Mother*, Sister of the Mountains
Diannan, Sister of the Forest
Eronia, Sister of the Fields
Lena, Sister of the Rivers

FOLKLORIC HEROES

Hugh & Lilia, a Lycan and a fae, respectively; heroes before the Fall of the First Age who sacrificed their love to save their peoples
Daughters of Verdigris, Evelyn (creator of the lummenfae [Shadowlands fae], mother of Ravenna, and grandmother of Yvayne), Enid (creator of the brightfae [Brightlands fae] and mother of Lilia), and Lyric (creator of druids whose magic transferred to the prime plane)

HISTORICAL EVENTS

War of the Champions, world-defining war between the Cities United and Alessandra, occurs shortly before the Great Flood
Great Flood, rising waters worldwide that brought about the end of Eldura and, in the aftermath, saw the world reborn as Azuria

PEOPLES OF AZURIA

Champions, mortals chosen by the titans and blessed with elemental magic, heroes of the world of Eldura;

deities can also appoint a champion or a Chosen who serves their will upon the Planes of Life

Daimon, great wolves or dire wolves, created by the god Fenrir who also created the Lycan

Druids, mages and those bound to the earth, live in conclaves

Guardians, twelve powerful supernatural entities that protect the peoples of the Planes of Life (includes Apollo and Lucien)

Lorekeepers, ancient order that tracks histories and unearths lost and destroyed records

Lycan, werewolves who were the first humans upon the Planes of Life, the second people of the wolf god Fenrir

Negata, people-group with horns and pointed ears, originating from the Negative Planes

Saudad, storytellers and travelers blessed by the goddess Cassandra

Soul Shepherds, founded after the War of the Champions, those who sought to uncover the hiding places of the Severed elemental champions and restore them to life

THE LEGEND OF THE
DRAGONS' CREATION

FROM THE ARCHIVE OF THE LOREKEEPERS

Long before the First Age and the separation of the planes that followed their creation, the goddess Rasvana looked with envy upon the first creatures of the wolf-god Fenrir—the daimon—wild wolves who traversed the planes of the world, melding leaf, limb, and flower with their fur and living in communion with their creator deity.

Rasvana saw the adoration the daimon bore their creator, and she wished the same adulations for herself. Other deities discouraged her, saying she underestimated the weight of so many dependents, that she should maintain her freedom. But Rasvana was not a goddess to take others' advice.

"Make me a people," she bade the wolf-god. "Give them wings and scales and a living breath. Grant them eyes sharp as daggers and infinite souls in near-infinite bodies. Make them as invincible as I am."

"You are a goddess in your own right," Fenrir replied. "Cast such a people yourself."

Rasvana gnashed her teeth and withdrew to the deepest forests of the world. There she tried, but the creatures who emerged fell short of her visions of what those made to look like herself should be. From these first trials, the drakes, wyverns, and winged serpents emerged, but the goddess wanted something more.

She returned to Fenrir's side. "My efforts have failed. You know already how to craft a people. The daimon look to you to lead them. Teach me your method that I may have the same."

"We must each find our path on our own," the wolf-god answered. "I cannot aid you and preserve my energy for my second people." In this he spoke of the Lycan who were as yet little more than a bright spark in the corner of the wolf-god's eyes.

Curls of smoke slithered from the goddess's nostrils. She trailed a taloned claw around her sister goddess Cassandra's shoulders and tugged her closer. "Let the goddess of fate bear witness to a pact between you and I, then, Fenrir. As you are so confident and wise, you will not mind playing against me in a game of chance. Should you win, you and your wolves will go on as you are. But should you lose, you will serve me a year and a day and teach me to craft a people of my own, those who will fear and adore me in turn."

Fenrir grew tired of the goddess's demands, but he saw the golden glint in her eyes. Rasvana would not allow the matter to rest until she was satisfied. His people would survive his year of captivity, he knew, but the goddess would not count herself so lucky after trying to bridle a wolf, even for so short a time. "Very well, I accept your challenge." The wolf-god bowed his head to Cassandra whose eyes widened, but the goddess of fate held her counsel.

Thrice the deities competed in a game of chance of Cassandra's design. In the first, Fenrir took the match. The second fell to Rasvana. The goddess licked her lips along her jagged rows of teeth for their third match. Fenrir shut his eyes and breathed his prayer into Cassandra's mind.

With a gasp from the goddesses, the pieces fell in Rasvana's favor. Her delight was so great that billows of flame rippled forth from her mouth and rent apart the clouds in the sky. "Victory is mine," she cried.

The daimon howled in despair, believing their lord to have been taken from them against his will. For a year and a day, they stalked the lands, searching for Rasvana's hiding place.

And for a year and a day, Fenrir wove his revenge. He taught the goddess to pour her power into her people, showed her how to weave the fabric of her being into scales and skin. Yet he withheld his own dearly won knowledge of the nature of creation—were the creatures Rasvana designed to be as powerful as the goddess wished, they would each require a spark of godhood itself.

Fenrir taught the goddess to grant each of her creations a gift, divine magic in the form of a changent scale. These would allow them to survive among the fae and later the Lycan for they could hide the secret of their heritage in a changing form. These scales granted them each a unique magical expression—breath that could command shadows, a wind so powerful as to fell even ancient trees. Rasvana poured out her memories, her longing, her greed, making each of her creations more wonderful than the last.

Cassandra watched in silence, held by the pact she and Fenrir had made that day of Rasvana's bargain—*Do not interfere,* the wolf-god had commanded. *Your sister's recklessness yields a price to be paid.*

He was not wrong, the maker of the Lycan. Cassandra knew this in her heart. *I ask but one thing in return,* she answered. *When your lesson is through, entrust my sister's children to me, that I may watch over her soul, the work of her life, until even the worlds yet to come are no more.*

Fenrir knew better than to argue with the goddess of fate—such is the blessing and curse of Cassandra's magic after all. *Let it be as you say.* And the matter was done.

The goddess of fate drew nearer as the days of Fenrir's captivity came to a close. "Is it always so tiring to create?" Cassandra overheard her sister say to Fenrir. The plumes of smoke that had once graced her nostrils were little more than a soft spring breeze.

"Not always," the wolf-god answered, "but in the case of your children, they will be mightier than any other groups of beings could possibly be."

"That is good," Rasvana sighed. "I wish them strength, longevity, and cleverness above all."

The goddess's eyes fluttered shut as she wove the last changent scale into being. Her form rippled and faded into little more than mist and voice.

"What will you call them, my lady?" the wolf-god asked Rasvana's fading form.

"Dragons," she answered, the fire of her gaze finding Fenrir as the last pieces of her essence flitted into the changent scale. "Our battle is not over, Fenrir. For you have tricked me once, but my thousand children will live on through the ages and seek to fool you again and again."

"I would expect nothing less," Fenrir said with a smile. He planted a kiss upon the remnants of Rasvana's brow. "You have done what no other deity had the heart to do," he said in benediction, "and your children will live on, the mightiest in all of creation—"

"Until the very ends of all the world," Cassandra added.

The pair turned from the changent scales and the sleeping, glimmering eggs left in Rasvana's wake. Cassandra smiled sadly as she perceived the lowered head of the wolf-god, the slow thump of his heart as he returned to the daimon, his first people. Such is the love that will make and unmake the worlds again and again, Cassandra thought to herself.

That year and a day left Fenrir forever changed. He has longed for the challenge and presence of the great dragon mother ever since. Neither his daimon nor the Lycan can fill the hole in his heart that she left, for in the final dragon, to protect and seal Rasvana's creation, Fenrir left a part of himself.

And for Rasvana, she who poured her divine essence into each of her thousand offspring who would be born and die across all the ages of the world, she lives on in dwindling number, but her divinity beats still, sparkling in changent scales, each as unique and magical as the goddess who created them.

www.ingramcontent.com/pod-product-compliance
Lightning Source LLC
Chambersburg PA
CBHW061530190726
48289CB00004B/988